MASTER
OF
CHAOS

SHANNON
McKENNA

OLIVERHEBERBOOKS

Cover Design by Wicked Smart Designs

Published by Oliver-Heber Books

0 9 8 7 6 5 4 3 2 1

CHAPTER 1

Cass

I couldn't stop clinging to my little sister Reggie's hand.

I managed to move away from that hospital bed and its beeping machines for long enough for the doctors and nurses to do their thing, but I stayed close by while they did it, ready to pounce as soon as they were done and resume clutching Reggie's limp, clammy hand. I was hanging on to that kid like a screw-on clamp, afraid even to run to the bathroom to pee. I'd drastically reduced my fluid intake to make it less of an issue. There was a solution for everything, right?

Right. Like I could tether Reggie to this earthly plane through sheer force of will. One would think I would have learned how pointless that was two years ago, when Mom died, but I could be selectively stupid AF when I wanted to be. I'd certainly failed at keeping Mom tethered. She'd drifted away while my back was turned.

I wasn't turning my back on Reggie for one second. She was my pal, my companion, my accomplice, in spite of me being sixteen years older than her ten years. It was Reggie and me against the world. Reggie was the whole point to all this nonsense.

Without her, I was nowhere. Nothing. I flinched from the thought of the echoing emptiness that would be my world if she were to slip out of my grasp.

Reggie croaked, and I leaned to put my ear to her lips. "What's that, baby?"

"Mommy," she whispered. "Here."

"No, honey-babe. It's Cass."

She tried to speak and started to cough. I grabbed some tissues, held them up to her mouth. "Spit out the gunk so you don't have to swallow it," I urged. "I know your throat is sore."

Reggie turned her head and weakly spat out a clump of bloody mucous. This was a new and freshly horrible symptom of Varen's Disease. Mom had died of Varen's, but it had carried her away before she got around to this particular symptom.

Shrimpy little Reggie didn't look it, but she'd always been tougher than Mom.

I threw away the tissue, wiped her mouth, and reached for the water, positioning the straw for her. Reggie drank and smiled her thanks, crooking her fingers for me to bend close again. I did so. "What is it, sweetie?"

"I know it's you, not Mommy," she whispered. "I was just saying, Mommy was here before. I saw her."

I jolted up, electrified, and looked around as if I might catch sight of her myself. Unlikely, since she was two years dead. *No, no, no, Mom. Don't come for Reggie. Not yet. Go back to where you came from, alone and unaccompanied. Please.*

"Um... what did she want?" I asked carefully.

"To see us," Reggie said, is if it were obvious.

"Who? Me, too?"

Reggie gave me a 'duh' look, and rolled her eyes.

"Is she here now?" I asked.

Reggie scanned the room and shook her head.

I was desperately relieved. Of course, as far as ghosts went, I was sure that Mom's would be a benevolent one, but I wanted to have a sharp conversation with Ghost Mom about her timing. Namely, that she was here way, way too soon. She could come back for Reggie in, say, ninety-odd years. Not before. Off you go, Mom. Scoot.

But it seemed disrespectful to be such a bitch to someone who had gone to the trouble of visiting from the other side of the veil, so I forced a smile. "That's wild, sweetie," I said. "I wish I could see her, too. Tell her hi for me, if she comes back."

Reggie's giggle turned into another coughing fit. We did the whole tissue-spitting-water routine again, and she smiled at me. "Don't worry," she whispered.

"About what, babe?"

"You think she came to take me with her, right?"

I stared at her, bug-eyed. "Uhhhh..."

"I told her I couldn't go yet," Reggie confided.

"Oh," I said slowly. "So... she wanted to take you away with her?"

"She said I could go if I wanted to," Reggie said. "I told her, not yet." She sucked in a hiccupping breath. "I have to look after you. Keep you out of trouble."

Oh, thank God. My eyes stung and watered. "And she was okay with that?"

"She just kissed me on the forehead," Reggie said. "And then she was gone." Her lower lip trembled. "I wish she could have stayed. I miss her so much."

"Oh, baby. Me, too." I fished out the tissues in time for another coughing fit.

When the spasms eased down, Reggie lay there trembling, breathing as shallowly as she could, to not provoke another one. She reached out a finger, and stroked my wrist, where I had tattooed her name onto myself. It was a fine-line tattoo, in an old-timey, graceful cursive script, and it reached halfway up my inner arm. *Regina.*

"Not fair," she whispered.

"What?" I asked.

"That I can't tattoo 'Cassandra' on my arm, too. Just because I'm only ten."

I laughed soggily. "In a few years you can get your own tattoo, if you still want to. In the meantime, I'm glad you mentioned it, because I have a surprise for you. Things got so crazy when you got sick, I forgot all about them, but check this out."

I dug into my big purse and pulled out an envelope. In it were a handful of long strips of stiff paper, about the size of standard bookmarks. I had asked the artist who did my own tattoo to design a corresponding one for Reggie and print them up as temporary tattoos. "I have ten of them," I told her. "When one wears off, you can just stick on another. Every time you look at it, you'll remember how much I love you."

Reggie's eyes shone. She held out her arm eagerly, and I peeled off the film and pressed the sticky side to her inner arm. I dampened a handful of tissues from her water bottle and smoothed them over her pale arm until the sodden paper clung to her skin.

Then I peeled it off, leaving the delicate tracing of the stenciled 'Cassandra' on her arm. Just like my own tattoo. The same type of lettering. A sister set, but the lettering reached much further up Reggie's skinny little arm. Almost to her elbow.

"This should tide you over until you're old enough to get real ink," I said. "When you finish them up, I'll have more made for you."

I gathered up all the soggy tissues, the wet paper strip, the plastic film, and by the time I had tossed it all into the waste basket, Reggie was sound asleep. That brief interchange had exhausted her.

"Excuse me, Ms. Clarke?"

I turned to see two of Reggie's team of doctors in the room. The tall dark one, Dr. Lukas, and a shorter, chubbier guy with curly brown hair, Dr. Cirillo. "Yes?"

"We need to talk to you about your sister's case," Dr. Lukas said. "Can you come with us for a moment?"

That sounded ominous, but it wasn't the kind of request a person could refuse. I followed them down the hospital corridors until they led me into to a room that had a pale lavender and gray color scheme, muted décor, blandly soothing art, soft chairs.

That, too, struck me as ominous. This was a room designed to soothe frightened, grieving people. I was a lamb being led to the slaughter, and this was going to hurt.

"Is Reggie going to be okay?" I demanded. "Is that what this is about? Do you have any more info for me?"

"Well," Dr. Lukas said reluctantly. "We don't, really. The truth is, there isn't much more we can do for Regina, other than keep her comfortable. There are no treatment options for an acute case of Varen's Disease like your sister's. All we can do is manage her symptoms, as best we can. And... I am really sorry to tell you this, but we estimate, based on how quickly things are deteriorating, that she has one to two weeks. At most."

"You mean until she..." I choked on the unsayable words. "No. That's not possible." I struggled to string words together. "She's only ten! She was fine just a few weeks ago! Aren't there any clinical trials, experimental treatments?"

Lukas exchanged mournful glances with Cirillo. They shook their heads.

"Varen's is extremely rare," Cirillo offered, his voice apologetic. "It occurs in one in two million—"

"I know the stats. My mother died of Varen's two years ago. I'm an old pro."

"Ah. I see. Well, there may be a genetic component to

Varen's Disease, but there hasn't been enough research done on it yet to gather any meaningful statistics. I'm sorry to give you such bad news, Ms. Clarke. But hospice is available to help you deal with the end-of-life choices you need to make for her. I promise, we'll make your sister as comfortable as possible, and there are support groups for—"

"She's only ten! She can't be dying! It's just not possible!"

Cirillo and Lukas droned on, their voices soft with professional sympathy, but I couldn't make out their words over the crackling roar of panic in my head. My sweet, affectionate, goofy little Reggie, who loved Star Wars and science and peanut-butter and jam sandwiches. Reggie, who had been my whole world since Mom checked out.

I got up and ran out. I couldn't understand what they said anyhow. My heart banged against my ribs, and my stomach lurched. I was furiously angry, as if someone had struck a spiteful blow at my baby sister, and I wanted to hit back. And hit hard.

But my anger had nowhere to go, except at myself. Varen's was random, rare. Possibly genetic. It had clobbered me when it took Mom. It was back to finish the job.

I sprinted for the bathroom. Thank God it was unoccupied, because I just barely made it to the toilet as it was, to toss the espresso I had chosen at the bar this morning, based on its high caffeine-to-liquid ratio. It tasted awful coming up, but at least there was no food along with it. There hadn't been for a while. Having Reggie gasping for air in a hospital bed was a real appetite-killer.

Who knew, maybe I'd get Varen's, too. Maybe there was an evil puppeteer up there in the sky, fucking with our lives. Maybe I'd have a whole lot of free time in my future to contemplate big philosophical questions like that. Lonely, pointless, quiet time to rail at God, whoever and whatever God might be. Not my friend right now, that was for damn sure.

I rinsed my mouth out. I didn't have time for freak-outs in the bathroom. I had counted minutes to spend with Reggie. It was all about Reggie now.

I walked out and headed back toward her room, picking up my pace until I was almost running toward my sister, not looking to the right or the left.

"Cassandra." A low, oily baritone voice as I ran by made me freeze in irrational terror, almost pitching forward onto my face. For a second, I couldn't move. The hairs prickled up, on the back of my neck. I got control of my muscles and turned around.

Yes. I was looking at the one person on earth who could inspire knee-quaking, bowel-weakening, blood-pressure-dropping terror in me. He had found me at last, in spite of Mom's and my best efforts. Owen Halliwell, business mogul, billionaire, sociopathic monster, asshole extraordinaire.

And also, incidentally, my biological father.

He held out his arms with a big smile, as if he expected me to run into them.

I stared at him, blank and horrified, my open mouth still bitter from having thrown up. Jangled and confused at the still-unprocessed nightmare; Reggie with two weeks to live, lying in a hospital bed she would probably never leave, plugged full of tubes, gasping for air. Hospice about to call. End-of-life choices.

And then, pow, this guy shows up. The fucking cherry on top of my shit sundae.

My mother and I had dodged this man for eighteen years. He was insane, narcissistic, terrifying, controlling, and he had literally destroyed my mom. She'd done her best, after we got away, to pull herself together and be a parent to me. She'd even bravely tried romance again with Reggie's father, but that had petered out fast.

She had never recovered from her time with Owen Halliwell. And when Varen's Disease came for her, on some level, I sensed that she was glad for an excuse to go, even after eighteen years of detoxing. Halliwell was like a long-acting poison.

"What do you want?" I asked.

His smile froze. "No need to be rude, Cassandra."

I swayed on my feet. He looked just like I remembered, if not quite so gigantically tall and looming. I'd only been eight the last time I saw him in the flesh. He was stringier than I remembered, but he looked good for a guy well over sixty. Tall, fit, wiry, with snow-white hair and a neatly trimmed white beard. Mom had always said that I looked like him, but I disliked hearing it. My curly, dark-red hair and abundant freckles were from Mom, but she said that it was the wide-set green eyes, the sharp cheekbones and the pointy chin that I had gotten from Halliwell. I couldn't see the resemblance myself, which was a good thing, because the sight of him made my stomach flop like a fish out of water, about to suffocate to death.

Not what you want to have happen every time you look in the mirror.

I saw Halliwell's face all over the news. He was one of the three or four richest human beings on the planet, so that self-important smirk was on every magazine cover. He had his fingers in every pie; political, economic, academic, cultural, philanthropic. There was no avoiding Owen Halliwell's mug. His malevolent pale-green eyes twinkled at me from every newsstand and supermarket check-out line.

"I was concerned for my long-lost daughter," he said. "I was devastated to hear of Laurel's passing two years ago. Even more distressed to hear that your little sister has now been stricken with Varen's, too. Terrible luck. My sympathies."

"That's private," I snarled. "You have no right to snoop into my sister's medical records. Only her doctors and I should know the details of her illness!"

He rolled his eyes. "This is no time to be childish."

"You have no idea how childish I can be," I blurted, my voice getting louder. "You're not welcome. You never have been, and nothing has changed. So get lost."

He put on a hurt face. "What did your mother say about me, Cassandra? Because I can assure you, most of it was a lie. Laurel had psychological problems, and she—"

"None of your damn business what she told me. Get out of here."

"Well, that's the thing," he said, almost apologetically. "I'm sorry to distress you, but you really can't throw me out. Essentially, I own this place. I'm on the Board of Directors of this hospital, and I donated a hundred and fifty million dollars for the new children's wing three years ago, specifically so that cures for diseases like Varen's can be researched and defeated. I believe in the triumph of science, the march toward the truth. But it takes time, and unfortunately, poor little Regina is out of time."

"I'm not discussing her with you," I said. "She is none of your damn business. Leave her alone. Forget that she even exists."

"Do you want to spit bile, Cassandra, or do you want a successful treatment for your sister's illness?"

My heart started to thud heavily. "Don't promise what you can't deliver." My voice shook. "I'm not an idiot. They said there was nothing they could do."

Halliwell made an airy flicking gesture with his fingers. "And that is literally true. There is, in fact, nothing *they* can do. But they are not me. I have tricks up my sleeve that they don't have. And contrary to what Laurel told you, I do take pleasure in helping my fellow man. I feel genuinely responsible for making the world a better place with my vast resources. And yes, I can get Regina the treatment that she needs."

"How?" I demanded. "If these doctors have no clue? How

can you know more about a treatment for a rare disease than they do? You're not a doctor."

"No, but I employ armies of them. Cutting-edge pharmaceuticals have always been a big part of Halliwell Enterprises. It's possible. I swear it, on my honor."

That was not reassuring, knowing what I did about his honor, but I pressed onward. "Then let's tell her team," I said. "Let's talk to Cirillo and Lukas, this minute." I pulled out my phone. "We'll see what they say. Has this treatment been tested? Have there been human trials yet?"

He cleared his throat. "Well, how could there be, with a disease so rare? I admit, it's an experimental treatment, but I have seen astonishing results with my own eyes. Bear in mind, Cirillo and Lukas have no idea how the treatment works. They'll be worried, suspicious, they'll drag their feet and cover their asses. They'll slow things down and cost Regina precious time she can't afford to lose. But I have doctors on call who can treat her right now. No delays. No learning curve."

I pulled out my phone. "So? Call these doctors in. Let's get this moving."

His lips curled into a self-satisfied smirk. "It's not so simple. Regina would have to be discharged and admitted to one of my private clinics. You would have to sign waivers, a non-disclosure agreement. The whole thing must be discreet."

"Why? Are you working on a patent?" I demanded. "Jesus, are your hundreds of billions not enough? Would anything ever be enough to satisfy you?"

"Don't be ridiculous," he snapped. "There is zero money to be made from researching Varen's Disease, Cassandra. I pursue it because it's the right thing to do, and no other reason. Projects like that are a stress-reducing side gig for me. Hail Marys, lost causes. They're my guilty pleasure. I find cheating death very stimulating."

"Are you trying to redeem yourself for all the shitty things you've done? You've got your work cut out for you."

He looked pained. "I would never have guessed how judgmental and unpleasant you are up close, Cassandra. You weren't that way the last time I saw you."

True thing. The last time we were together, I was a terrified little kid, and the man I remembered, with his hair-trigger temper and his huge, inflamed ego, would have crushed me like a bug for being so disrespectful.

But he hadn't done that so far. So he must have an agenda.

"What do you want from me?" I demanded.

His eyebrow slanted up, wryly amused. "Filial respect, to start with?"

"Dream on," I retorted.

His nostrils flared. "Fine. Forget that. Baseline common courtesy is mandatory, however. I'll just lay it out for you. I want you to come work for me, Cassandra."

I blinked. "You are the last person on earth I would ever work for," I blurted. "If I were working right now at all, which I'm not. If you haven't noticed, I have more important things to think about at the moment. So that's a hard no."

"You're referring to your sister?" His voice was soft and insinuating. "So am I. She's your top priority, of course. But I need your particular skills. I also need an exclusive licensing deal for Glow-worm."

I gasped, startled. How could he know about Glow-worm? No one knew about it, not even my most trusted employees at Red Queen. It was my private, off-hours home project, and I wasn't even finished with the structural design, let alone all the code. Glow-worm wasn't even meant to be its final name. It was just a working handle.

"Did you hack me?" I demanded. "How did you know about Glow-worm?"

"We'll talk about how I arrived at my intel another time.

Your malware is brilliant, Cassandra. Glow-worm, in particular, is incredibly powerful and innovative. I need it urgently, and I need you along with it. Glow-worm will require its own creator to get it up and running. You're the only one in the world who can do it. That, more than anything, shows that you're my daughter. You make yourself irreplaceable. Which gives you power. Just like me. As if I'd coached you myself. It makes me very proud."

"Don't be," I snapped. "And don't try to butter me up. I legally can't do what you're asking, even if I wanted to, which I don't. I already have a client that I've promised first crack at Glow-worm, so as soon as I—"

"That is a lie," he said calmly. "It's still completely secret. And I know the players who will be jockeying to license Glow-worm when it's finished. You haven't offered it to them yet. But even if you had, I can outbid them all. By a huge margin."

"It's not about money," I said.

He waved that away impatiently. "I've followed your career. You're known all over the world in certain circles, young as you are. You're on the radar of defense contractors, arms dealers, government intelligence agencies, and probably terrorist organizations as well, through no fault of your own, of course. You demand astronomical fees. You get that sense of your professional worth from me. I need that get-it-done energy. It's so hard to recruit that quality. I'll pay top dollar for it."

"No," I said flatly.

"My payment, of course, includes access to my resources to treat Regina."

The implications hit me all at once. "Wait. But... I can pay for Regina's care myself," I said stiffly. "Whatever it costs. I'll cover every penny. I don't bargain with that coin."

"I do," he said coolly. "And I will accept nothing less than your exclusive professional services as payment for Regina's treatment. That's my offer." He started to laugh at the dread in my eyes. "Oh, don't you worry. You'll still get the money you're due for the licensing deal, the whole massive sum. But I get Glow-worm, and I get you. For as long as I need you. That's the deal Cassandra. Take it or leave it."

I felt the walls closing in around me. I thought of my mother, her empty eyes, her broken will. Her horror stories about this man's twisted mind, his grotesquely swollen ego that was never satisfied. How being in his sphere of influence was like a terminal illness. It truly had been for her, in the end.

"I... I can't do it," I whispered.

"Ah." He pulled a sad face. "Well, then. I'll leave you to make those end-of-life arrangements. Will you scatter Regina's ashes in the redwoods with Laurel's? I'm sure she would want to be with her mother in death."

How...? Reggie and I had told no one where Mom's ashes were scattered. "How the fuck did you know that?" My voice was getting shrill. "Are you having us followed? You're black-mailing me with Reggie's illness, you asshole!"

"You won't be permitted to use that kind of language when you are working for me," he lectured. "I find it distasteful."

"I don't give a shit what you find distasteful!"

"You will finish Glow-worm under my watchful eye, and license it to me, for an obscene amount of money," Halliwell went on. "You will work for me for an obscenely large salary while your sister is treated in one of my private facilities. My clinic will treat her with drug compounds no one on earth has ever heard of, and she will get stronger by the day. A fact you will be able to verify with daily video calls. It's a win/win/win, for everyone concerned. See? It's a very lucky day for you and Regina."

I hated the tears that were filling my eyes. I didn't dare to be vulnerable and needy in front of this bastard who had ruined my mother's life and left a smoking hole in my own. But he was dangling hope in front of me. I was helpless not to lunge for it.

"Think about it, Cassandra." His voice was oily and satisfied again, as he felt his absolute power over me, and liked the hell out of it. "Accept my advantageous bargain. Or prepare to scatter your sister's ashes in the redwood grove. The choice is yours."

"You evil, manipulative son of a bitch," I whispered. "I hate your guts."

"I don't mind that," he said. "As long as you work well and give satisfaction."

I could feel the jaws of the trap closing around me, but I was helpless not to take the bait. "So, ah... how long would you need me to work for you?"

His teeth flashed, unnaturally white, as he came in for the kill. "How could I possibly know? Until we're done. My lawyers will get to work this very night on a contract for you, but the job is a good one. Stratospheric pay. Perks of every kind. Luxury accommodations in my headquarters on the Washington coast. A private ocean-view apartment, two minutes from your work-place. Room service at your fingertips when you don't feel like cooking. Every comfort and amenity, day and night."

"I don't give a shit about that," I said. "I need to stay with Reggie. Right at her side. I'll work for you, but only after she's well and strong. That's non-negotiable."

"I'm afraid I can't wait," he said. "You must start tomorrow. Regina will be taken by helicopter to the clinic tonight. You can accompany her there, but you can't stay with her, unfortunately. My own schedule won't allow it. You say your goodbyes, and the helicopter will bring you directly to my Washington coast headquarters. I need you to hit the ground running. Tomorrow morning early."

"Deal's off, then," I said. "I have to stay with Reggie. I can't budge on that point."

His eyes sparkled. "Aww. Look at you, so tough, driving your hard bargain. Like watching a kitten hiss at a German Shepherd. You're just like me, you know? You dictate terms and walk away if they aren't met. But not this time, my dear. The only power you have right now is your willingness to walk away. Are you willing?"

I gulped, willing my burning eyes not to overflow. That bastard.

He saw the answer in my face and nodded. "Good choice, Cassandra."

"I go by Cass," I said. I'd never liked the name Cassandra, not since I read the story in the Greek epic about Cassandra's curse. Doomed to predict the future, but to never be believed. Crazy-making frustration at its worst. "No one calls me Cassandra."

"I do," Halliwell said softly. "And as you will soon realize... I am not no one."

CHAPTER 2
NINE WEEKS LATER…

Shane

"Hey!" I heard a muffled knocking sound. "Shane? Are you awake?"

The low alto voice was caressingly soft, even distorted by the microphone. I was deep in a meditative state. Usually I was able to resist when those assholes tried to break my concentration and command my attention. All of my energy was spent trying to detach myself mentally in every way from this place, this situation, these murderous pricks and what they had done to me. I was pretty good at it by now, all things considered.

But I would come to the surface for Red.

For some reason, I couldn't help but respond to Red's voice. Velvety, sparkly, soft. Feminine. It wasn't good that she had that much power over me. It felt intimate, compromising, risky. I had no idea in what way, but I still sensed the danger.

My eyes opened, wondering what her power over me was. Probably just because she was so fucking pretty, and not an evil, torturing asshole like the others. Banal, but there it was. It was embarrassing, to be so predictable, but fuck yeah, I'd change the frequency of my brain waves and emerge from a meditative state to look at Red. Who could blame me? I'd been locked up for months here, and I'd been in Victor and Nicole's clutches before that, getting all fucked up. After the coma, I'd stopped trying to track the time I spent in here. I had no reference points, so who cared? It felt like eternity in any case.

One thing was for sure. I was never leaving this room. They would keep trying to pry the access to my brother's super-algorithm out of me until I died.

So the hours crawled by, all grim, boring, agonizing sameness... until Red showed up one night. Effectively blowing my sensory-deprived mind.

She stood on the other side of the thick glass wall, gazing at me with those big, worried eyes. She wore jeans and an oversized men's tee-shirt, and a shapeless sweater over that, like she was trying to be sexless. Nice try. Useless effort.

Her curly red hair was twisted into a long, thick braid, and a halo of fuzzy little corkscrews escaped around her face, dangling below her jaw, floating above her head. Her big, wide-set green eyes were luminous in their paleness, like a cat. No makeup. Her lips were naturally pink and luscious. Her eyes looked shadowed. Haunted.

Red had been down to see me six times, if my memory was to be trusted. This was the seventh time. Other women had come down here from time to time to ogle me, some men as well. But none of them had glommed onto my imagination like Red.

Red seemed... angelic.

Confusing, to see an angel down here in the bowels of hell. She was so beautiful. Face, eyes, body, voice. I was starved for it. A beautiful girl, sneaking down to my dungeon to chat with me? It sounded too good to be true. So it definitely was.

My sexy fallen angel was just a sneaky new attack on my defenses. Had to be.

But I was exhausted from keeping my defenses up. Besides, what was I defending? I was all fucked up. My mind was blank. There was nothing for her to find in there. So what harm could she do to me? Why not play along? What could it hurt?

Red's visits had to be scripted, so even pretending to fall for it, just for the entertainment value, might give them an opening into my head somehow. I had no idea how, but in my reduced condition, Halliwell was definitely smarter than me.

Look at me, second-guessing myself, staring, salivating, sweating for her. If they meant to destabilize me, they had succeeded. And I wished she wouldn't keep reminding me of my former name. I was trying really hard to forget it.

I had to forget everything. My family, all the knowledge I had worked to acquire in my life, even my baby girl. It all had to go, into the mist, into the smoke, to keep them safe, shielded. To deny that asshole access to my memories... and SmokeScreen.

Red was no angel, fallen or otherwise. She was just a new attempt to drill into my mind. I had to remember that at all times. Halliwell was like a strip-miner constantly using new angles, new methods for digging for traces of SmokeScreen, leaving a wasteland of poison and slag behind himself.

Yeah, that pretty much summed up my current state of being.

"Sorry to disturb you, but I can't stay much longer, and I was hoping to talk to you," she said.

"I've got nothing to say." My response came out in a croak, thickened from scar tissue and long silence. And the screaming, from back in my time with Vincent and Nicole. I'd damaged something in my throat while they were breaking my bones.

I'd been sitting cross-legged on the cold tile floor for hours. No way to know how many. I couldn't gauge time passing here. There was no natural light, and no regular light-and-dark cycle. The lights were always on. But I could tell from the stiffness in my muscles and the fullness in my bladder that it had been a long time.

I rose to my feet, sucking in a breath while numb muscles remembered that they existed. Blood pumped through the sore parts. Bones that had been broken ached and throbbed. A souvenir from Nicole and Vincent, from before Halliwell had "saved" me.

Halliwell had been at me ever since, but with different methods. He didn't use whips, clubs, or stun rods, the tools that Nicole and Vincent had favored, but he was just as relentless in his own way. He'd tried all the old mind-fucking classics; the heavy-metal music blasting for days at a time, the sleep deprivation. When I was properly softened up, they strapped me onto a cot, hooked me up to a bunch of diagnostic machines, drugged the living shit out of me, and interrogated me for hours, while analyzing my reactions, left, right and sideways.

They measured everything. How fast my pupils dilated, my heart rate fluctuations, my sweat, my rate and depth of breathing. Every fucking physiological response I'd ever imagined, and a lot that I never even thought of.

But Red here... well, wow. She was stimulating a physiological reaction that they had not bothered to measure yet. And my response was off the fucking charts.

I gazed through the six-inch wall of reinforced glass, wondering how this could possibly play out. She was so fucking pretty, she practically hurt my eyes. So tall. Long and willowy and lithe. Haunted eyes ringed with thick sooty lashes. That full, sad, sexy mouth that rarely smiled. That wavy, glossy dark-red hair. Freckles on every part of her that I could see, making me wonder about all the parts that I couldn't.

Just eye contact sent a tingling rush straight to my dick. As if she'd stroked me.

"I can't stay much longer," she said. "I brought you some fruit. I put it in the drawer. If you want it."

Fruit? I went over to the drawer and pushed the button. The mechanism hummed as the shallow steel drawer slid on its rails to the other side of the massive titanium wall.

I slid open the box and gazed down at her offering. A paper bowl of berries, grapes, melon chunks. What were those red things? Currants? All those vitamins and antioxidants and polyphenols were wasted on a guy doomed to die under glass, but hey, it was a sweet thought, even if it was just a sinister plot to peel my brain open like a sardine can. Plus, I admired the way the light behind her lit up her hair, a fuzz of reddish light around her. "Thanks," I croaked. "Looks nice."

"My pleasure. Are you, um... okay?"

I shot her an eloquent look, turned, and went to take a long piss.

I was light years past being embarrassed about her watching me do it. For months, I'd had cameras trained on me while I slept, ate, exercised, showered, screamed obscenities, pounded walls. I didn't concern myself anymore. Let 'em watch, the sick fucks.

And I had a shock collar around my neck. A relic of my time with Vincent. It was one of his hellish designs; capable of zapping me with electricity and also administering any injectable drugs loaded into the chambers. Plus, as a bonus, it featured a strand of strong wire that would tighten on command at the touch of a remote, to the point of slicing my jugular. Should anyone care to do that, at any time.

Back in the day, using the wire on me had gotten Vincent hard. He'd hook the collar to a chain dangling from the ceiling and drag me up off my feet with a pulley. I had to clutch the chain with both hands to keep it from garroting me, and Vincent would stand below, staring up, massaging his crotch as I struggled and swayed, blood pattering down. Fucking pervert. And Nicole had been even more depraved, if possible.

But Halliwell beat them all. He was smarter, more patient,

and much more methodical. I'd been in a coma when he retrieved me from Nicole and Vincent, but Halliwell had kept the collar on, even after I woke up. A constant reminder that I was kept alive only by his sufferance. He got off on that.

No, I was not okay. But hey, it was tricky to think of non-triggering things to say to a half-naked guy in a shock collar rigged with garrote wire, trapped behind six inches of glass. She got points for trying.

The poison gas canister mounted up in the top corner didn't help, either. A tap of a button and my cell would fill with death fog. Halliwell liked to remind me of that fact, when he came down to talk to me. He was just a barrel of laughs, that guy.

Didn't bug me, though. I was ready for the death fog. Bring it the fuck on.

I kept my back to Red as I fastened my pants and washed my hands, trying to think clearly. Okay, so she was a trap. A pretty girl coming to my prison cell, giving me a fresh fruit arrangement. Friendship. Sweet words. Very improbable.

Then again, there was another possibility I had to consider. Maybe she wasn't there at all. Maybe she was a recurring hallucination. Maybe Halliwell's mystery drugs had built up in my system, or I was just having a psychotic break from the strain of solitary confinement, etc., etc. Fortunately, most of my memories were still buried since the coma, and I was careful not to even try to access them. I kept my head as empty as a fucking gourd. I cultivated stupidity the way a gardener cultivated rare plants.

I favored bland, striking images of the natural world to fill my mind, drive out thoughts of the past. Starry skies, ocean waves, jagged snowcapped mountains. A moonscape with shadows as sharp as knives. I had my standbys, always at the ready.

I tried a currant. It was more tart than I expected. Wouldn't a hallucination respect my own expectations? Why would it occur to my subconscious mind to include currants in a fruit bowl? I'd barely known what they were, let alone how they tasted.

Who the fuck knew. I was a soldier, a mechanic, an engineer. I had never studied neuroscience or psychology like my brother Ethan—

No. Even a glancing thought about Ethan was risky. I had to stay in the moment. No past, no memories. As few articulated thoughts as possible. No future, either.

The only big question left for me was when the death fog would flow.

I leaned my forehead on the glass, studying the freckles on her narrow nose. "You're wasting your time," I told her. "I'll never tell Halliwell anything. I'm brain damaged. I can't put out, even if I wanted to. Even if a pretty girl pouts at me."

The soft lips in question tightened. "I'm not pouting. I'm just a human being, interacting with another human being. I'm not trying to trick you, Shane. I swear."

Human, my ass. Not anymore. And hearing her say my name bugged me. It was an outdated name, belonging to a person who was long gone. I was nameless now.

Still and all. I might not be human, but my animal parts were in working order, and they stirred eagerly as I looked her over. My stare brought a blush to her cheeks.

Sweet detail. Maybe Halliwell had hired her for her acting ability. He was definitely convoluted enough to organize a complicated mind-fuck like that, just to amuse himself.

"Please," she whispered into the mic. "I swear. I'm on your side."

I laughed, a painful wheeze of irony that jolted my sore muscles. This girl was not on my side. A person had to be someone, with a name, a life, a personality, an agenda, to have a side. I had let all of that shit go.

That was my only defense. To have no side, no self. I was invulnerable, as long as there was no 'me' to defend. Maybe that was the nature of Halliwell's gambit. A sexy girl, to coax me into having a side again. A self, again. It opened up dangerous doors, and I had to keep all the doors shut up tight. Even to myself.

Some time ago, Halliwell had taunted me with a video of a little girl, blonde, about ten. My daughter, he'd said. If I drove him to it, he'd have to "collect" her, to make me talk. He was just fucking with me, because if he could have gotten his hands on her, he would have done it. Sadistic old fuck.

I knew my daughter existed, but I didn't really remember her. It was more like I remembered remembering her. It was much safer for her if I stayed in the fog. The only way to protect the poor kid was to forget her. Which was fucked up.

The worst thing was, I had pushed the memories away, but I couldn't push away the pain. The ache. It was still there, just not attached to anything tangible.

My brother and sister would keep her safe. That was a comfort, but I was trying to forget them, too. Memories were all strung together, like beads on a string. If I gave them one, they could start yanking them all out. And if I slipped up and somehow gave Owen Halliwell a handle on SmokeScreen, well. It was game over.

That would be an extinction event for humanity.

"Please," she said. "Shane? Talk to me."

"What the fuck do you want me to say, Red?"

"They all tell me about how he wants to get his hands on some super-powerful algorithm, and you're the only one who can get into it. Why does he want it? What does it do? I'm trying to see the bigger picture, so I can figure out what to do next."

"Why should I help you?" I asked, genuinely curious.

"Because we're in the same boat," she told me. "I'm a prisoner, too. He's holding my sister hostage. She needs medical care only he can provide. In return, I license my software to him, and work my ass off in the guts of his machine. He's got me pinned, but I'm not like the others. I am not his bitch. I swear. I want out of here."

Same boat, hah. "No." I pointed at the wire biting into the scar-tissue and scabs over my throat. "You and I are not in the same boat. You aren't wearing a shock collar. You are not in a cage. Your skull was not fractured. You were not tortured. We are not fellow prisoners."

She studied the burn scars on my chest and shoulders, the multitude of scars on my throat. "Did Halliwell do that to you?" Her voice was small.

"Not all of it. Some of it was Nicole and Vincent. His mad dogs."

"Nicole and Vincent are dead, by the way," she said. "Did anyone tell you that?"

Well, fuck a duck. I squinted at her, considering my reply. "I think I'm just going to assume whatever you tell me is a lie, Red. It's safer that way."

"It's not a lie. The others told me what happened. It was before I came here. Those two got into it with your family. They tried to abduct your daughter and your brother's girlfriend. Your sister and brother rescued them. Wiped them and their team out. Very bloody, very public. Halliwell was beside himself. But she's okay. Your little girl, I mean. Your brother and sister, too. So? Score: one for the Masters family, zero for Halliwell. Yay, right?"

I suppressed a shudder of emotion that I did not dare to examine. "Great bedtime story, beautiful. I'll cherish it. Now get lost. I don't want any more news out of you."

"And that shock collar? I hacked into Vincent's files after the first time I saw it, found his specs. He had eight different versions. The one you're wearing was his latest model. He finished it just before your sister shot him to death."

I deliberately ignored the lure she was throwing out about my family, but the collar info was too much to resist. "You have the specs for this fucking thing?" I touched the collar clamped around my neck. It itched and chafed when it wasn't shocking or stinging me or slicing me with the wire. It was a small preview of hell.

"Yes. I've been studying it. If you try to take it off, or move out of range, the system triggers the wire to tighten, and the shock amps up to lethal."

"Sweet." My jolt of laughter made the wire against my throat sting. "Great to know. Thanks for that tidbit. I'll sleep like a baby now."

"I swear to God, I'm not trying to pry that algorithm out of you. I just want to know why he's so obsessed. It's all anyone here has worked on for months. What does he want with it? I need to know, Shane. I don't want blood on my hands."

"I can't comfort you, Red. I can't give you any information. But not because I won't. I literally can't. My head was bashed in. My brain's all fucked up. So if he sent you here to sweet-talk me, you're wasting your breath. End of story."

"No. I'm here on my own. Secretly." She held up a blank silver card with a string of lights on it. "I cloned Halliwell's pass-card a couple weeks ago. So far, no one seems to have noticed the movement in the logs. Fingers crossed. We're alone. For real."

I gestured at the video cameras in the high corners of the room. "There's a recording of every second that passes in this place from five different vantage points."

She looked back over her shoulder, then leaned close enough to the glass that her breath fogged it. "No," she whispered. "I hacked into their security system and embedded a program I wrote. I call it 'Invisibility Cloak.' It swaps in alternate loops of video and audio for whatever camera or mic that I'm walking past, in real time. The signal covers me for twenty meters, coming and going. It's safer at night, because the lighting is more consistent, and the corridors are deserted, and people would notice if people started winking out of existence on the monitors, or if noise suddenly cut out. For the cameras in this room, I have a loop of you meditating, and one of you sleeping. If anyone looked right now, they would see you, sitting cross-legged, in complete silence. So I can visit you secretly. Anytime, in the night. If you want."

I stared at her for a minute. Wow. So my dream girl was a laser-sharp computer whiz, as well as beautiful. Scary, how Halliwell knew just how to yank my chain.

"I don't want," I said flatly. "I'm done with wanting. Don't fuck with my head. The floor show is over for tonight."

"I swear, I'm not—"

"Fuck off, Red. It's past your bedtime."

She straightened up, her mouth pressed tight, and turned. She marched out, head high, her round, gorgeous ass twitching in those worn jeans. Her thick braid swaying.

The dead silence after she left was smothering.

Strange move, on Halliwell's part. A pretty girl offering fellowship, secrecy, confidence, intel. Halliwell must think I was a pathetic slob, to fall for it.

And maybe I was. Damn. I regretted throwing her out. I missed her already.

Whether Red was real or a fantasy, I had a creeping sense that Halliwell was ready to toss me in the shredder. Red might be the last beautiful thing I'd ever see.

If I ever laid eyes her again, I better make it count.

CHAPTER 3

Cass

Jana, one of my Halliwell hell-sisters, was on punishment duty. She was out on the terrace on her hands and knees with a scrub brush, in full view of the rest of us, who were working inside. We were supposed to witness her humiliation as we worked.

It was embarrassing, distracting, perverse, like everything else in this godforsaken place. But nine weeks had gone by, and Reggie was still alive, in his clinic, so I was going nowhere fast.

It was raining heavily outside, and Jana was drenched, her pale hair darkened by water, plastered to her head and face. The terrace was cluttered from the mess from yesterday's base-jumping party. The food, plates, glasses, etc., had gotten blown all over the place by the wind off the ocean. Halliwell had demanded that Jana and I be his smiling hostesses at the party, and I'd done my best to be cute and perky. Jana had done okay for a while. Then something had set her off. She'd started crying uncontrollably.

In the end, I'd escorted her to her apartment, and called the doctor to give her something to calm her down.

Halliwell had been infuriated to have his party marred by her emotional incontinence. So the luckless Jana was out there in the rain with her cart and bucket and mop and scrub brushes, putting on a shame show for the rest of us.

It was a shitty use of resources. The guy had a veritable army of cleaning staff, and Jana was a gifted doctor and scientist with five graduate degrees and three medical specialties. She was a genius in pharmacology, she knew everything there was to know about medicine, and there she was, out there on her knees in the pounding rain, scrubbing. Like fucking Cinderella.

But what skeeved me out even more was that she let him do it. Jana was not free to tell him to shove it and go try her luck elsewhere. Which made no sense to me at all. A woman like her, with everything going for her.

It scared me to death. Since I wasn't free, either. Not with my Reggie under his thumb.

That was the guy's MO. To pin people down with whatever their unique weakness was, and then break them. Slowly. At his leisure. He'd done it to my mom. She'd fought back, run away, saved me, and I would always be grateful for that.

But the darkness had overcome her in the end.

Resisting Halliwell wasn't an option, evidently. At least, not for Jana or any of the other people working here, whom I had learned were my half-brothers and sisters. My Halliwell hell-siblings. That was how I thought of them. Poor, wrecked bastards.

The hell-siblings had been a real jolt. Whoever would have dreamed that creepy guy could manage to persuade that many women to have sex with him? It must be all of his billions. Brrr.

The base-jumping party had made me intensely anxious. I was not a fan of extreme sports to start with, and the whole thing seemed like a gratuitous mind-fuck. Halliwell enjoyed pressuring his business rivals into doing dangerous things.

Base-jumping was basically sky-diving on steroids, this cliff being only five-hundred feet high. There were just a handful of counted seconds for the parachute to open. No margin for error. No second chances.

The air currents could mostly be counted on to waft base-jumpers safely to the sandy beach to the south, but an unlucky jumper could easily land on the jagged rocks slightly to the north, or in the heaving ocean itself. Halliwell feared nothing, even death, but I'd been glad no one had gotten killed yesterday. Things were weird enough around here as it was. Watching someone fall to their death would not have helped my mood.

I rubbed my eyes, which stung and itched unpleasantly. I didn't sleep very well here to begin with, much less when I organized nighttime visits to the mysterious prisoner in the Level Eight dungeon. I had poked around for more information about him, and I now knew that his name was Shane Masters, and that he had been declared missing for over a year by his siblings, Ethan and Freya Masters.

Of course, I was not supposed to know any of this.

After Shane Masters had kicked me out last night, he had proceeded to haunt my dreams. What few dreams I still had time for, in my admittedly short night.

I'd only learned about his existence because one day Haley, another hell-sister, happened to be watching a video of him taking a shower. Probably a compilation video, involving many recorded showers. Six of my hell-sisters and two of my hell-brothers had been crowded around her computer, avidly watching him soap up, rinse off, towel dry. I'd peeked over their shoulder to see what held their attention, and bam, I was hooked. He was so big, so strong. Every muscle defined, gleaming with water. That ass. That face. Grimly, intensely beautiful. Those eyes.

In spite of the hideous electronic shock collar fitted around his neck.

The size of his dick also made them giggle and coo, the silly cat bitches. It seemed sick and dirty, to lust over a man who was locked in a cage.

But I could hardly criticize. I'd fixated on him, too, so how was I any better?

I'd been asking myself that question ever since. And needing to know more like I needed to eat, to breathe. Particularly when they told me that he was the key to that fucking algorithm that Halliwell was so obsessed with. I was getting a clue that working for Halliwell made me complicit in something that was more than just wildly illegal. It was flat-out evil. That miserable guy, locked in a cage. That collar. There was nothing he could have done to deserve that kind of treatment. It was perverse. Wrong.

But in spite of all the abuse, he seemed unbroken. He performed his meditations and his exercise routines with fierce concentration, and somehow, he had resisted all of Halliwell's efforts to interrogate him. I'd unearthed videos of those interrogations, and they chilled my blood. Haley had a vast collection of prisoner-vids. Watching him do his martial arts forms was like watching an incredible dancer, but more lethal.

I was hooked on those visits now. He totally rattled me in person, but even if I weren't rattled by Shane Masters, it was so hard to think a straight thought around here.

I was constantly watched. Not in the shower, like Masters, I hoped, but every word I said was archived, every keystroke logged, every drink I chose from the cafeteria or the beverage machine recorded. My excessive coffee use had been remarked on by the doctor in residence. My insufficient calorie intake as well. Even my menstrual cycle was on their radar. It would have creeped me out completely if I hadn't had much bigger things to worry about. Like Reggie, sick and alone in that clinic.

The suffocating surveillance in this place was what spurred me to write Invisibility Cloak. I'd needed to create a moving pocket of privacy around myself, or my head would explode. I'd coded Invisibility Cloak directly into a phone that I'd sneaked in when I first came here, one of several that I had cleverly secreted in a false bottom in one of my suitcases. I'd created it under the covers, in bed, in complete darkness, to avoid being seen by the cameras mounted in my apartment.

It had been running in their system for a few weeks now, and so far it had not been detected. It was working beautifully. After having sneaked myself a clone of Halliwell's passkey, I'd been moving through the place freely at night. So far.

They would ding me eventually, but I'd push it to the absolute limit until then.

I grimly attempted to concentrate on Glow-worm, my almost-finished malware, and stop thinking about the man I'd visited last night. Up until a couple of weeks ago, his hair had been a thick, snarled mane that hung past his shoulders, and his beard was past his collar bone. But Halliwell had grown sick of the desert-island-castaway look, so they'd switched out the poison gas canister for one loaded with a powerful sedative. They fogged the cell, knocked him out, and sent in a gas-masked team to barber the guy while he was unconscious. All for the sake of Halliwell's esthetic sensibilities.

Haley had a video of the barbering episode, too. I bet she would have come up with a way to tie the poor guy down and fuck him but for the camera surveillance.

Masters was even more starkly beautiful with the excess hair trimmed away. He'd been gorgeous before, but now I could see every detail. His beard was growing out, but every stunning feature was still on display. The chiseled jaw, the cheekbones. The grooves around his flat mouth. That look of grim, sullen endurance in his dark eyes. Brackets in his cheek that could actually be dimples, if he ever had reason to smile.

I'd never seen him smile, but I'd dreamed it. Wild, wishful fantasies.

Just look at me, crushing out on the one person here who was worse off than me, with the possible exception of Jana. But Masters gave me a buzz that was something different than the nervous static of fear, anxiety, uncertainty, anger. I craved it. I'd so much rather think about Masters and clench my toes and shiver in lustful fascination than focus on how messed up this place was.

And ponder the actual depth of the shit I was in.

The overwhelming security layered around Masters suggested that Halliwell was wary of him. That suggested power, danger. If this man were powerless, Halliwell would have flushed him and forgotten him. But he hadn't. He kept trying to grind Masters down. Show him who was boss.

Masters' stubborn 'fuck-you-bitches' attitude made me want to cheer.

A murmur of excitement zinged across the room. I looked up to see Halliwell strolling into "the Bridge," as he called that front room with all of our workstations, the huge picture windows, the French doors to the huge terrace overlooking the ocean. As if it were the helm of a ship. He was our fearless captain, and we were all on a dangerous journey to nowhere good. The way the terrace outside was cantilevered way out over the high cliff, it actually seemed like we were in a steam-punk airship, cleaving our way through the clouds.

"Stand up, you idiot!" my hell-sibling Dean hissed at me, from the next desk. "Do you want us to get slammed for disrespect?"

Disrespect, my ass. I did not spring up like a dog for a door-bell. I deliberately finished the line of code I was working on and switched screens to cover my work. A pointless gesture, since every keystroke on this machine was logged, but it was good form, and I would by God maintain good form, like a normal person. This guy might have me by the throat with Reggie in his clinic, but that was no reason not be dignified.

I spun around in my chair. My hell-siblings were on their feet, like soldiers when a commanding officer entered a room, but they all had that nervous, pinched-but-hopeful look on their faces. Eyes blinking, shifting. Afraid to look at the big man, afraid to look away.

Jesus, what had he done to them? And would it happen to me eventually? I'd rather be dead than like them. Cringing, broken.

Of course, I couldn't die. I had Reggie to think about. But I was sure that the option of my early death was on the table, based on Mom's hair-raising tales. I could easily die in Halliwell's lair. Others had, according to Mom, and their bones had never been found. This place was like Bluebeard's fucking castle.

Halliwell gave me a sardonic smile. "Ever the rebel, Cassandra?"

I looked him in the eye. I had not sworn any oaths to this man. I had not sold my soul. Just my labor and my IP. I did not have to play along with this dysfunctional Big Daddy schtick. "Not at all. Just conducting myself like a normal human being."

"You do have a point." Halliwell gazed around at his other offspring, a faintly bored, critical look in his eyes. "Your siblings should follow your example."

Fucking *yikes*. I saw panicked confusion flash across their faces. Poor bastards. They did as they'd been trained, and he humiliated them for not having the nerve to defy him? That was so unfair. Halliwell must want me dead, or at least, completely isolated. He blatantly favored me, but I would have preferred his abuse to his favor.

With no timeline for Reggie's treatment, I was in a holding pattern with no clue what the future held. Reggie seemed like she was just barely holding on in our video calls. Nine weeks had gone by from the time that Lukas and Cirillo had told me that she only had two weeks left, so clearly, the people in Halliwell's clinic were doing something right, even if they refused to share any of the details with me. She was no longer gasping for breath, coughing, feverish.

But she wasn't rosy and smiling, either. Her eyes looked hollow and sad. She reminded me of Mom, toward the end. Which scared me to death.

That fear kept me stuck here like a bug on a pin. I'd been maneuvered into this position with Reggie's illness, and there was no way out. Maybe that had been Halliwell's plan for me all along.

Scary thought. Like all my thoughts lately.

Halliwell was waiting for a response to that insult to the rest of his spawn, but I had nothing to say to him. Not while he held Reggie's life in his hands.

I kept it bland. "Did you need something from me, Mr. Halliwell?"

"Yes, actually. I'm having a dinner tonight with the Hwang Group and their entourage, to celebrate the new partnership. You will accompany me."

My guts clenched at the prospect, after yesterday's base-jumping debacle and Jana's disgrace. "Someone else should go this time," I said. "I have to implement a new section of Glow-worm tomorrow to stay on track, so tonight is not the best—"

"What on earth made you think that your participation was optional?"

The tension in the room ratcheted up. It scared the shit out of my hell-siblings when I disagreed with Halliwell, or spoke my mind. Not that I could help myself. I was mouthy by nature. "Look, I'm trying to maximize my contribution to—"

"I'll be the judge of where your contribution is most needed. Your dress and shoes have already been delivered to your apartment."

Great. Random people had the access code to my living space and were free to enter at will. It bugged the shit out of me, but at the moment, it was the least of my problems. "I have evening gowns from other events. I don't need another—"

"I didn't like your makeup last time. The freckles are unattractive. I prefer a smooth, monochrome matte finish, no visible blotches or sun damage. We'll have you seen by a dermatologist as soon as possible to see what can be done about that."

I gasped like a beached fish. "Ah... ah—"

"Jana can help you. She's quite competent with makeup. Oh, and blow out your hair. An up-do, I think. The Hwangs are very formal. Most of them are also quite short. If your heels are high and the hair is high... perfect. We'll tower over them."

"I don't want to inconvenience Jana," I said.

"Why not? She's deadweight. She killed the buzz at yesterday's party. She should be eager to make herself useful in whatever small ways she still can."

Oh, ouch. I looked around. The air felt thick with dread. I was surrounded by hostile, dead-eyed, staring ghouls. God, how I missed my sweet Reggie.

Eyes on the prize, girl. Eyes on the prize. Reggie and me, together. Healthy, strong and free, and far away from here. I tried to picture it. Take strength from it.

"Well?" he prompted. "It takes time to blow out your hair. Get Jana. Hop to it."

I went through the glass doors. The rain had eased off, but the wind was still cold and sharp, and the sea crashed wildly on the sharp rocks hundreds of feet below.

Jana was slowly pushing a mop, her movement limp and dispirited.

"Jana!" I called. "Come in here for a sec. Halliwell has a job for you."

Jana's eyes widened in alarm, but I was spared the necessity to coax her inside, because Halliwell followed me out onto the terrace. He looked around, disgusted.

"Good God, Jana. It looks worse than before, if that's possible," he said.

"Sorry," she mumbled, looking everywhere but at him. "I'm going as fast as I can."

"You're stumbling around like a zombie. Sharpen up. Did you at least pack up the unused parachutes? It's been raining all night. I don't want them to mold."

From the corner of my eye, I saw a wet parachute on the slate tiles. A swift shove with my toe slid it behind a potted madrona, out of his line of vision.

Crisis averted. Halliwell mercifully did not notice, his attention focused on the hollow-eyed Jana. "You will do Cassandra's makeup and hair, if you can pull yourself together. Afterward, I've scheduled an appointment for you with Dr. Silvano. It's time."

Jana's eyes froze wide. "Silvano?" she croaked. "Oh, no. No. Sir, please—"

"After you've taken care of that, get your ass back out here and stop dragging your feet. When I start work tomorrow morning, it needs to be immaculate."

He turned and went inside. Jana's haunted eyes flicked to the planter where I'd kicked the parachute.

"I thought he'd scolded you enough," I explained.

"Don't do me any favors," she said. "Favors mean nothing here. You're not my friend, and I'm not yours." She turned away, and shuffled inside.

Well, hell and damn. No good deed went unpunished around here. I took a moment to open up the cabinet that held gardening supplies, and stuffed the parachute inside, just to be thorough. Then I followed her back into the Bridge.

Halliwell had just left. Everyone stared at me as I shut down my workstation. If looks could kill, I would have been flash-incinerated, my ashes floating on the breeze.

Jana and I went to my quarters without a word. Her shoes

squelched with every step. The apartment assigned to me was very beautiful, with picture windows and a big balcony that overlooked the ocean. I let her in and stood there, tense and tongue-tied. It wasn't like I could make conversation with this woman in her current emotional state.

Jana stared out the picture window. I looked at her sodden hair, the bra showing through her soaked shirt. She was shivering. "Ah, do you want a towel?" I asked. "You could use the blow dryer, and I can give you some of my clothes, if you want to—"

"No. I'm fine."

"But aren't you cold? You should—"

"This apartment used to be Nicole's. You never met her. She was Halliwell's favorite, even though she crashed and burned in med school. I graduated top of my class in three different specialties, and he still hated my guts. Go figure."

I didn't know what to do with that. In my mind, being hated by Halliwell would be a shining badge of honor. "This is the Nicole who died a few months ago?"

"Murdered. She was murdered by the brother and sister of the prisoner on the eighth level. The Masters guy. Victor was murdered by them, too. Shot to death."

"Yes. Haley told me about that," I said. "It sounded really terrible."

"Halliwell's still pissed about it," she said. "At least about Nicole. Not so much Victor. Victor was a pretty good engineer, but he was a whiny little shithead, and Halliwell would have flushed him eventually. By the way, the standard story is that they died in a car accident. If anyone asks tonight, that's what you should say."

"Okay. I'm, ah... I'm so sorry for your loss."

"Don't be. It's no loss, to me or anyone. The world's better off without them. Nicole, especially. She was a sadistic, stone-cold, homicidal bitch. That's why he favored her. It was like looking in a mirror for him. He loves that."

The question hung in the air, so I answered it the best I could. "I'm not a sadistic, stone-cold homicidal bitch, Jana. I don't know why he's paying attention to me. I'm not his mirror."

She let out a grunt. "Yeah? Aww. Poor you. Burdened by his favor."

I gritted my teeth. "I mean it. I genuinely don't curry favor with him."

"Dean was next in line for this apartment when Nicole died, did you know that? It's a prime unit. Three times as big as the others, ocean view, big deck, etc. By tradition, it goes to the senior sibling, and he was all set to move. Then you arrived, and Halliwell insisted that you have it. The newest. The youngest. His new favorite."

"Thus ensuring that everybody here hates me," I said. "Including you."

"Not really," Jana said. "I don't care enough to hate you."

I stopped myself from laughing just in time. "That just might be the nicest thing anyone's said to me today," I said wryly.

She leaned closer, and whispered, her lips barely moving, "You should run."

I took a step back. "I would if I could."

"Don't look back," she hissed. "Run. Stay far away. Hide from him. Forever."

"It's not that simple," I explained. "I have my little sis—"

"Don't explain. I don't want to know. They're always listening. It doesn't matter anymore for me. They can take me to the boneyard whenever they want. But you're still in one piece, at least for now. You could make it out there. Not me. I'm done for."

Her words chilled me. "Jana, you can't mean that."

"Wow, you still don't get it. And you're supposed to be so fucking bright." Her face went blank, and the brief moment of emotional aliveness was over. "We should get to work. If you make him wait, he'll rip you to pieces."

So it was out of my clothes and into the shower to shampoo my hair. Jana combed it out as I sat wrapped in a towel, staring in dismay at the outfit I was supposed to wear during the long, tedious process of blowing the frizz out of my long red hair.

The dress was a designer brand that even I recognized, but there was nothing much to it. It was black, and sheer, and no bra could be worn. Some skimpy black lace and beading were stitched over the chest area to hide my nipples but they did a bad job of it. Anyone looking at me would assume that Halliwell was my pimp, not my father.

Jana got to work on my up-do, as mandated, and a long session of twisting and wincing and tugging and scalp-scraping hairpin stabs ensued. The final result was sleek, tight, abstract sculpture on top of my head.

She spread out the makeup kit, and I held up my hand. "Look, Jana, you can go. I'll finish here myself. I can make my freckles go away if I put my mind to it."

She shook her head. "Don't argue. It just makes it harder. First, that tattoo has to go. He'd be so angry if he saw that. As if you were vandalizing his property."

So, I waited, gritting my teeth as she painted over the tattoo on the inside of my forearm. I hated to see my honey-girl's name disappear. I didn't like the metaphorical implications. But Jana was right. I had to be practical.

After the tattoo was hidden, she started in with the freckles on my face. The process was long and ticklish. I flinched back as she came at me with the lipstick.

"Why is it always me who has to go to these things?" I said rebelliously. "I barely know anything about Halliwell Enterprises. I'm not that scintillating, and if it's eye candy he wants, the rest of you are all better looking than me, you included. Why can't we take turns?"

"Aw. Poor you, forced to dress up and get ogled."

I was about say something sharp when my cell phone rang. I picked up, but Halliwell was only drawing my attention to his text.

Enough chatter. Car waiting.

It was uncanny, like he really was listening to every word, in real time.

The driver didn't acknowledge my existence. I wasn't the usually the type that would notice, but after weeks of hostility, I was raw to it. The one person in this place who actually saw me when he looked at me was Shane Masters.

I hung on grimly to the image of Reggie in her hospital bed, full of tubes, to work up the courage to walk into the restaurant. This sexy-hostess bullshit had not been part of our initial deal, but he had all the power. So I put on my best fake attitude and minced into the swank restaurant with my sky-high heels and my terrifying up-do, my slinky dress with the vee plunging practically down to my cooch, just thin beaded straps holding the bodice onto me, my nervous nipples poking the fabric. My girls were relatively small, but I tried to glide so that they wouldn't jiggle.

I needn't have bothered. They all stared at my chest anyway.

The Hwang Group was exclusively men, mostly older men. I was sure they took me for a call girl until Halliwell introduced me as his daughter. Halliwell sensed my discomfort at their surprise and was amused by it. Sleazy old prick.

I was seated next to the youngest guy, Andrew Hwang, the son of the CEO of the Hwang Group. I gritted my teeth, made an effort to be pleasant and talk tech with him. The meal was long and fancy; many courses, tiny portions of meticulously presented food. I was incapable of eating much, or tasting what I ate. Halliwell's hell-bunker killed my appetite. The wine was good, but I didn't dare drink more than a sip. I was scantily clad, and not among friends. The last thing I needed was to be tipsy.

Time crawled by. At a certain point, Andrew refilled my wine glass. "So how is Nicole doing?" he asked. "I expected to see her tonight. Is she out of town?"

My belly clenched. "No. I'm sorry, but Nicole passed away a few months ago."

He looked taken aback. "Oh my God! What happened? Was she ill?"

"It was a car accident," I lied, hoping that Jana had led me true about the official story. "Vincent, one of my half-brothers, died in the same accident."

"That's terrible," Andrew said blankly. "I just can't tell you how sorry I am. I'm surprised we didn't hear about it. We would have sent flowers. I can't believe... I mean, she was so vital. So intense, so charismatic. A truly remarkable woman."

"Yes, it was very sad," I said. "We were, um... all broken up about it."

"Yes." Andrew lay his hand on mine as his gaze slid down the bare skin in the vee of the dress. "It's tragic. But I am glad to have met you tonight. Yet another beautiful, fascinating Halliwell daughter. Who would have thought he had so many?"

Creepy. So I was interchangeable with my dead sister? A consolation prize? I removed my hand from beneath his with a big, empty smile. "I'm actually not a Halliwell," I told him. "I use my mother's name. Clarke."

"So you and Nicole were half-siblings, then? That makes sense. You don't resemble her at all in looks. You must both look like your mothers. Were you two close?"

"Not really," I admitted. "She and Vincent were older than me, and I was raised away from them, with my mom. I came to work with Mr. Halliwell very recently."

"So formal, for an American," Andrew commented. "You don't call him Dad?"

"Yes, it is formal, but calling him Dad seems overly familiar," I said. "I didn't grow up with him, so it just doesn't feel right."

To my relief, Andrew seemed to accept that severely edited explanation. Then Halliwell clinked his glass and started off with long string of self-congratulatory toasts, which touched off still more from the other side. He and Mr. Hwang performed a twenty-minute circle jerk, each lauding the mutual marvelousness of the new partner, their commitment to this shared endeavor, the massive profits sure to follow, blah blah.

I pretended to drink at each toast, smiling until my cheeks ached and burned.

After desserts and liqueurs were served, Andrew Hwang leaned over and murmured into my ear. "Care to go out for a drink after? I found a place down on the beachfront in town that's still open."

I suppressed a shudder. "I wish I could, but I have a really full day tomorrow. I have to be up and functional in less than four hours as it is."

His smile faded a notch. "Ah. Another time, then."

"Certainly," I said, smiling, smiling, smiling. Right. When pigs flew.

After the goodbyes, I walked out of the restaurant and looked around for the SUV that had brought me here. It was nowhere to be seen.

Then a silver Lamborghini pulled up in front of me. Halliwell looked up from the driver's seat. "I sent Ralph home," he said. "I'll drive you back. A chance to talk."

Great. Like I needed to mainline more stress hormones today. Being in close quarters with that man made my liver feel like it had been in the deep freeze for weeks.

I got in, repeating it in my head. *Stay strong. Hang tough. Think of Reggie.*

"I noticed your conversation with Andrew Hwang," Halliwell said, once we were underway. "He seemed quite taken with you. What was he curious about?"

"We discussed systems design, security, penetration testing strategies, malware," I said. "He'd actually heard about Red Queen Consulting. Which was very gratifying to hear."

"Of course he'd heard of it. Everyone in the industry has heard of it. So that's all? I hope you know the futility of lying to me."

I twisted my fingers together, chilled with irrational fear. I had been six people down the table from Halliwell, who had been seated next to Hwang, Sr., the big boss of the Hwang Group. Halliwell had been in constant, animated conversation with Hwang and the other people near him the whole time. How had he overheard my hushed conversation? It was like the guy was telepathic, with a direct line right into my head.

"Come on," he prompted. "Don't be coy. Did he ask you about Nicole?"

I weighed each word. "Um. Yes. He wanted to know why she wasn't there."

"And what did you tell him?"

"I don't know much about Nicole. Her life, or her death. But I was told to say that she and Vincent died in a car accident. I hope it was the right thing to tell him."

Halliwell maneuvered the car onto the road that led up to the clifftop drive, switching back and forth on long loops to gain elevation. "He must have been very disappointed," he said finally. "I'm sure he was hoping to fuck her again."

I flinched away from that. "I wouldn't know. He didn't mention it to me."

"But he propositioned you, of course. You're more beautiful and easier to relate to than Nicole, poor girl, may she rest in peace. Nicole had a savage, feral side that she couldn't hide for long, and it terrified her sex partners, at least post-coitus. You don't have that quality. In fact, you can be quite charming when you make an effort."

"I do not want to talk about this." My voice was strangled.

"I was surprised that you didn't accept Andrew's invitation to get a drink."

I was struck by a horrifying thought. "Wait," I said. "Don't tell me you expected me to sleep with that guy. Did you bring me here to... to *service* him?"

He made an impatient sound. "For God's sake. If I'd wanted you to service someone, I would have sent you to Hwang Sr.'s bed. An evening out with an attractive, wealthy, eligible young man is not a fate worse than death. Lighten up, girl."

Lighten up? That dickwad had the colossal nerve to say that while he was sinking me into cement himself. "So I was supposed to go out for drinks with the guy who sees me as a party favor? Interchangeable with Nicole?"

He waved his hand. "I'm sure he was intrigued with you on your own merits, my dear," he said mildly. "Anyone would be. You're quite lovely."

"Make a note of this." My voice shook. "For future reference. I will never, ever sleep with someone at your direction. Under no circumstances would I do that."

Halliwell sighed. "I miss Nicole's practical mindset," he said, almost wistfully. "She didn't get so wound up about these things."

"Wound up about prostituting herself for you, you mean? How about the others? Do they perform that service? Do you run a whole stable of Halliwell whores?"

"Don't be crass," he snapped. "I only mean that she was well aware of all her assets and gifts, and fully prepared to use them in my service. That's rare and precious."

Sick and twisted, I barely stopped myself from saying. "That's not me," I said.

"I see that. Ironic, though, since you have so much more to lose than Nicole ever did. She had no ailing little sister to fret about. And wouldn't have cared if she had."

My stomach heaved at his casual tone. I decided an abrupt change of subject was called for. "Speaking of my ailing sister. I've been meaning to ask you about Reggie."

He sighed, already annoyed. "Cassandra. Again? Must you?"

"Do you know how Reggie is responding to the treatment?" I persisted. "When I call the clinic, they say they can only talk to you. They won't give me any info."

"Have you not been calling her regularly? Is she not still alive? Talking to you?"

"Yes, of course, but I really need a more in-depth—"

"Do you, Cassandra? Do you have medical training yourself? No. Do you not have enough to keep your mind occupied? Because I can help with that."

My mouth worked helplessly as I realized that this man truly did not understand why I was anxious. He had never worried about anyone's well-being in his entire life.

"Of course, I have plenty to focus on," I began again, doggedly. "But I'd concentrate better if I knew more about my sister's response to treatment. Reggie is—"

"In good hands," he cut in. "If there is any notable change in her condition, they will inform me, and I will pass the information on to you in due time. In the meantime, keep your mind on your work. That's the best thing for you and Regina both."

"But what would it cost you to just let me into the loop? So I won't have to constantly bother you? I could go directly to the source, and—"

"The doctors treating Regina are world renowned experts. They don't have time to hold your hand."

"I have no intention of wasting anyone's time," I said, teeth clenched.

"You're wasting mine right now. And from what I can see, you're not finished with Glow-worm yet. Day follows day, and still you say it's not ready. I'm beginning to wonder if you're having me on, Cassandra. Dragging your feet deliberately."

"I'm doing my best," I said, through my teeth. "It's extremely complex. You knew it wasn't complete when I came to work for you. All I can do is keep at it. It's not done until it's done."

"Well, carry on, but pick up the pace. By the way, you looked lovely tonight. Much better without those unsightly blotches marring your skin. You absolutely have to see someone about treating those. They're unacceptable."

I suppressed a flare of anger. "Mom had freckles, and she looked just fine."

"You don't have to share Laurel's beauty flaws out of misplaced solidarity. Besides, it wasn't a suggestion. You really are a slow learner sometimes."

I bit my lip. Reggie's life was in the balance. I wasn't destabilizing this situation just to defend my freckles. But still. What a colossal dick. Even with the little things.

"You looked very pretty," he offered, as if to placate me. "The dress was inspired. It put all your best attributes on full display."

"I hate being on full display," I blurted.

I cringed silently. There I went again. Cass Clarke, quintessential slow learner.

"Do you think I care if you hate it?" He sounded genuinely curious.

"I am sure you don't," I said. "But why am I on display at all? Why me? I'm the new girl. The youngest. I have no clue, about anything that goes on here. Any of your thirteen other offspring could do a better job in this situation than I could!"

"Actually, no," he said. "They're all just a little bit off. Every last one of them. In different ways, which makes it extremely difficult to pinpoint the origin of the problem. Even Nicole had severe problems with impulse control. They function well up to a certain point, but put them under real pressure, and they fizzle. They're all broken."

Right, you psychotic dickwad. You broke them. You fucking hack. I gulped the words back. "I'm sure they would do just fine at a dinner like this," I said.

"They might pass, but they wouldn't shine. And they should. I chose their mothers very carefully. It does disappoint me. So much time and money invested, and... well, whatever. You win some, you lose some. Jana, for instance. All that training, all those medical degrees, all that pharmaceutical expertise, and look at her. Coming apart like a wet paper bag, right in front of my business associates. Appalling."

That made me shiver. So calculated, doling out his precious seed only to the worthiest of vessels, and then finding his offspring all wanting. He didn't even know that they were people. He only saw them as flawed experiments. He'd broken their hearts, but he had no idea, because he had no heart himself.

"They might surprise you," I said. "People grow." *Except for you, asshole.*

"Nicole and Vincent were actually plotting to kill me when they met their untimely demise, did anyone tell you that?" he said, in a conversational tone.

I gaped at him. "They... but... ah... *what?*"

"They were very piqued that I took Shane Masters away from them. And this after they almost beat him to death, like the undisciplined idiots that they were. So they plotted to kill me, to take control. They thought they could use Ethan Masters, Shane Masters' brother, to get control of the algorithm. They even took Shane Masters' little girl as leverage. It wasn't a bad plot, really. It almost worked. I was always proud of

Nicole's fierce ambition, her ruthlessness. I'm glad to still be alive myself, of course, but I do miss her, vicious, murderous bitch though she was. Vincent was no loss to me, but Nicole was special."

"I, ah…" I groped for words, but what he'd said had wiped my mind blank.

"What she did not understand, however, was that she would never have been able to use that algorithm without me," he mused. "In fact, none of my offspring but you would be able to manage it. Besides which, it requires an unthinkable amount of server capacity for all the computations. Only an entity such as, say, a government intelligence agency, could use it. Or someone like me, with my vast resources and my technical skills. Just imagine, if Nicole had been successful in her plot." He chuckled. "She'd have gone to all the trouble of murdering me for nothing, in the end."

"She actually… she tried to kill you? Really?"

"That's not the relevant part of what I'm trying to tell you," he said impatiently. "Yes, she was a hell-bitch. Yes, she was dangerous and unpredictable. Yes, I still miss her. But now I have you. And between you and me, my dear, you have far more to offer me and my mission than Nicole ever did. Of all my children, you are the only one who can represent me. Nicole was not… well. Properly house-trained, let's just say."

"You mean to tell me that I'm your ambassador to the normal world?" My voice cracked in dismay. "That is a sad state of affairs, Mr. Halliwell. I hate to break it to you, but I am all different kinds of weird."

He gave me his lip-curling smirk. "Perhaps so, but at least you're original."

I just sat there, nerves buzzing with alarm. His approval scared me even more than his anger did.

"By the way, Cassandra," he said, his voice casual. "It has

come to my attention that you are showing a keen interest in our visitor on Level Eight."

I was so startled, my mind just fixated on the euphemism he'd chosen. Visitor? In a cage and a shock collar? That was some sneaky-ass doublespeak if I ever heard any. I stammered a little. "Ah... how did you, ah..."

"Haley informed me that you were enchanted by that naked shower video she compiled. Not that anyone blames you for that. Almost all of my daughters and more than a few of my sons were much struck by his impressive physique. But after, I was told, you dug for more information. Accessed more video. Studied it at great length."

I let out a breath. So Invisibility Cloak was not yet discovered. He hadn't copped to the passkey theft. They'd only seen me perving on the Masters shower vid, mooning at the guy through hacked cameras. The damage was limited. "Yes. I... I did."

"What's the nature of your interest? Beyond the obvious, of course."

"I wouldn't call it interest," I said. "'Curiosity' would be a better word. He's like, I don't know. A tragic romantic character. Like the Count of Monte Cristo."

"As you well know, he's the key to that algorithm that I need," he said. "I expect you know his story?"

I was on very shaky ground here. Tiptoeing. "Ah... ah, I did do some—"

"Of course you did. Forget you ever knew it. I am sure that Shane Masters strikes you as a dashing figure. But his presence here must remain secret. He was never here. Understand?"

"Ah, yes," I said swiftly. "Of course."

"He's the key to the algorithm, but I just can't get it out of him," Halliwell complained. "He did have some legitimate brain damage some months ago, but I strongly suspect that he's just pretending at this point. I'm tempted to cut bait."

I digested that as he slowed to a halt at the big gate, which ground slowly open for him. "What exactly do you mean by that?"

"You're a bright girl," he said, his voice impatient. "Extrapolate."

"I prefer to communicate plainly," I said.

"I don't give a shit about your preferences. But I'd like to attempt one more technique before I'm done with our visitor. A classic, old-fashioned game of good cop, bad cop. I've been the bad cop for months, so he is primed for the good cop. And I have a feeling that you could be very, very good, Cassandra."

I was horrified by the implications of his teasing tone. "Wait. Hold on. By 'cut bait,' do you mean... kill him?"

"Don't be tedious," he snapped. "I need that algorithm. You will be my last-ditch effort to persuade him to be reasonable. Failing that, we move on to harsher modalities. He certainly can't walk out of here free, after what's happened to him. Nicole and Vincent made that impossible. Regrettable, but there it is."

"So I'm his last hurrah before you cut him to pieces?" My voice shook in horror. "Jesus, what am I supposed to do? Tap dance for him, for fuck's sake?"

"Language," he chided. "Talk to him, since you find him so intriguing. Chat with him, flirt with him, charm him. I'll watch, in the monitor."

He pulled into the enormous garage and parked near the northeast stairwell. The stairs that led down, down, down... to Level Eight.

Dear God, he wanted to do this right *now*? I was not ready. I had no plan.

"What's the point?" I tried to mask my desperation. "What am I supposed to ask him? What do you want me to fish for? For God's sake, give me some parameters!"

He unlocked the car with a finger-flick, and walked briskly around, opening my door. "Don't ask me. Improvise. Pull the thorn from his paw. Gain his trust. He's bored, lonely, vulnerable, sex-starved. Use your imagination. I know you have one. Tell me it's useful for something other than sexual fantasies."

"I don't want to mind-fuck him any more than I want to boink Andrew Hwang!"

He let out a theatrical sigh. "Fine. Never mind. I'll just call the interrogation specialists right now. We'll let them get to work, and by tomorrow, it will all be over. And I, for one, will be happy to put the whole thing behind me. It's become tedious."

Interrogation specialists? Oh holy fuck, no. My mind raced. "Wait," I said.

His lip-curl widened to a self-satisfied smile. "Yes?"

"I'll, ah... I'll talk to him. I don't know what point there is, but I'll do it. Just give me the time to run up to my apartment and change out of this—"

"No. Go just as you are. You look very nice."

"But I... but ..."

"You don't have the luxury of arguing with me." His voice snapped like a whip. "If I told you to get down on your knees and fellate him, you would do it. You have no rights here. Not if you want Regina's treatments to continue. Is that absolutely clear?"

I stared at him, appalled. I knew exactly what he was. My mother had told me about him all my life. And even so, this was like a splash of ice-water to the face.

"Oh, stop it," he cajoled. "Don't be all shocked. It hasn't come to that yet. Let's see what results you get by simple flirting, hmm? We'll leave fellatio for a last resort."

Oh God. He thought he was *funny?* I couldn't even unlock my joints.

He took my arm and frog-marched me down the stairs. My ankles wobbled on those ridiculous heels, but Halliwell kept up a brisk clip, steadying me when I stumbled.

At the door to Level Eight, he inserted his passcard. It

buzzed green, and he pushed the door open. "Go on in alone. Seeing me with you would inhibit him."

"I don't know what to say to him!"

"Don't ask me to micro-manage, or we'll never know what you're capable of."

You don't even want to know what I'm capable of, you scheming prick.

No. Think of Reggie. Swallow it down. Like a big, sharp-edged rock.

I picked my way down the corridor. My ankles were rubbery. I was intensely aware of Halliwell, watching. I wasn't doing Shane Masters any favors. This was just a tiny stay of execution. Talking to me was the last thing he would experience before they tortured and murdered him. The responsibility was crushing.

I paced past the seven empty cells. My heels ticked on the tiles. 803... 804... 805... 806... 807... and I gasped to see Shane Masters, standing right in front of the glass wall.

Waiting for me.

CHAPTER 4

Shane

The room was soundproof from my side. They could hear everything I said or did, but unless someone hit the mic on the wall outside, I might as well have been sealed in lead for all I could hear them.

And yet, somehow, I felt Red coming down that hall. It was a tingle in my balls, a prickle on my neck. A soft, caressing contact, humming deep inside my mind.

I'd started having erotic dreams about her, which surprised me. I'd figured that part of me had died. Hope had gone a long while back. Fear, too. Lust was a stubborn bastard, and it had hung on for a long time. Then it had faded away with the rest.

Lately, it had seemed like all that was left was rage. The last holdout.

Then Red popped up, with her big, curious eyes, and whammo, lust sprang up from the tomb and shambled around, as graceless and inconvenient as it had ever been.

Halleluiah. It was a miracle. One I'd have been much better off without.

It took me a second to be sure it was really her, all tarted up in a sexy evening gown with a thigh-high slit and a plunging vee neckline. Long, pale, shapely legs showed through the slit. Her shoulders and arms and chest were bare, to all intents and purposes. And I got a good, long look at the shape of her perfect little tits, nipples poking through the black lace on the sheer fabric. I felt them in my mind, tickling the palms of my hands. It would take barely a twitch to tear that filmy dress right off her.

My dick tented out the limp jersey fabric of my drawstring pants. Not that I gave a shit. Embarrassment had been gone even before hope. Dressed like that, she must be here on purpose to make my dick hard, so I might as well give her the satisfaction of a job well done. Besides, she was probably just a hallucination anyway.

I'd hallucinated plenty of times in here. My little girl had been here to visit me. My parents, too. They had helped me push back against the drug probes, in ways comprehensible only in a dream state. It was nothing I could describe to anyone rationally, but I appreciated the hell out of their moral support.

The fact that Mom and Dad had been dead for over twenty years didn't bother me in the least. I was just grateful for the company.

Strange, that Red switched out her outfit, if she was an apparition. The others never did. Holly always wore the same pink sundress. Mom wore her gardening overalls, and Dad his hiking shorts.

Red had always worn snug, worn jeans and a tee shirt and the sweater. A masculine cut tee, in a dull, drab color. The sweater, too. Shapeless and oversized, chosen to hide the femininity of that willowy body. Utterly failing to do so.

The sexy outfit in itself was weird enough to make me think that she might be real. My subconscious would never have come up with that hairdo, those shoes, that dress. If it was up to my subconscious mind, I would have dreamed her up stark naked and in here, under me, legs wrapped around my hips, while I pounded away.

I stared at her hungrily. Her hands clenched and unclenched, creasing the delicate, sheer fabric of the skirt. Her eyes looked even more big and fearful, all painted up. Heavy black mascara weighing down her long eyelashes.

She'd never looked afraid before. Heavy smudges magnified her pale green eyes. And something else was different... the freckles, spattered with wild abandon all over her face, her arms, her hands. They were gone, at least on her face. It was a smooth matte mask, with just a carefully painted blush at the cheekbones. Like a china doll.

"What happened to your freckles?" I asked.

Her eyes went wide with panic and she lifted her hand briefly up to her ear, beneath one of the artful, dangling ringlets that had been tugged loose to frame her face.

I was puzzled. That urgent, worried look in her eyes did not change. An urgent little shake of her head. Was she trying to tell me that we were being listened to?

For fuck's sake. Duh. When were we not? Was this a new theater piece?

I gave her a what-the-fuck shrug. A frown appeared between her eyebrows, and she gave her head another frantic little shake.

For real? I was fried after months of confinement, torture, interrogation. I was locked in a cage, with an electric shock collar around my neck. The burden of figuring out what she was trying to communicate really should not fall upon me. I wasn't up to interpreting frantic eyelash flutters and finger twitches, goddamn it.

Please. She mouthed it, her eyes staring intently into mine. Begging me to be intelligent about whatever was happening here.

Aw, fuck me. She was just a wishful fantasy anyhow. I might

be having a psychotic break, but at least it involved a beautiful woman. As psychotic breaks went, this one definitely did not suck. I would try to oblige her. It cost me nothing... I hoped.

She didn't want me to mention her vanished freckles... why? Because it would reveal to whoever was listening that she'd been here before? She meant for me to think those visits were genuinely secret and private? Nice fantasy.

But fine. I'd play along. I had nothing better to do. She looked so different from those other dead-eyed zombie pricks that sometimes came down to do Halliwell's bidding. I splayed my hands on the glass and drank her in with my eyes.

"Are you real?" I asked.

She reached up to flick the button that opened the mic. "Yes," she replied.

Well, of course. Any self-respecting hallucination would insist that she was real.

"You're overdressed for this place," I told her.

"Underdressed, more like. I was out to dinner with Halliwell's business partners. He told me to, um... come down here in this outfit. It sure as hell wasn't my idea."

"So now he wants to tickle my dick by dangling a beautiful girl in front of me. Devious old fuck. He can go blow himself."

"Don't." Her voice was hushed, intense. "Just listen to me. Please, listen."

She looked so scared. Maybe Halliwell was punishing her for something. Maybe she was a helpless pawn. Or just an amazingly subtle actress.

Either way, this probably sucked for me. That was the one sure thing.

"Get lost, Red," I said. "Go home. I got nothing for you."

She shook her head. "Please. You have to give him what he wants, or you'll die. He's out of patience. It's now or it's... terrible things for you. Please, give it to him."

Terrible things? I laughed under my breath. "That's okay," I told her. "I'm ready. I've been dead for a while now. My body just hasn't figured it out yet. It's only pain. It'll end at some point. And then I'll be gone. It's okay. Don't sweat it."

That made her lips shake. They were so soft and full, stained red from her worn-off lipstick. "No," she said. "You are not dead. Don't give up. I don't want you to give up."

Wow. Give the girl an Oscar. "I can't give him what he wants," I told her. "Even if I was willing. I have brain damage. I had a fractured skull. I was in a coma. The cupboard is bare. If he wants to cut me to pieces, he can just get on with it."

We locked eyes, and I felt that tickle in my head again, like she was trying to communicate without words. I leaned my forehead against the glass, while feelings I'd forgotten roared through my system. I'd thought I was dead already, but she'd made a liar out of me. This girl could crook her finger, and I'd sit, lie down, roll over and beg.

But she could not pry SmokeScreen out of me. I had buried it so deep, I couldn't access it myself. I didn't know how, but all their drugs and tests had not uncovered it.

Maybe it really was lost. Along with most of the rest of me. The best of me.

My fingers curled like claws, as if they could sink into the glass like it was clay, rip it away, get closer to her. I wanted to touch her skin. Smell her scent. She was a goddamn sorceress.

She was almost as tall as I was, with those towering heels, hair all twirled up into a complicated arrangement on top of her head.

"Take your hair down," I said, because this was just an over-heated fantasy, and I was marked for death anyway. I might as well milk it to the bitter end.

She looked frightened. As if I was in any position to scare someone. "Why?"

"You look like some uptight trophy wife mincing off to have tea with the queen," I said. "I don't like it. Take the hair down."

I didn't really expect her to do it, but she reached up, and started pulling out hairpins. Unwinding glossy red spirals of twisted hair. An erotic spectacle like I'd never imagined. It made me shake. Sweat broke out on my back.

When her hair was unwound, she ran her fingers through it, loosening the curls into a shimmering red cloud. Oh, yeah. That was the siren I was dreaming about. Her makeup was doing a late-night landslide, but on her, it looked sexy, soft, vulnerable.

Halliwell was one smart son-of-a-bitch when it came to mind-fucking. Pinpoint accurate about what I liked. I didn't want that bastard in my head, jerking me around.

"What were your instructions?" I asked. "To make my dick hard?"

"He didn't give me specific instructions," she said. "He just said to talk to you."

I abruptly realized that the loosened hair was a big mistake. My ears were roaring. Lust and rage together were a toxic brew. They were probably logging my physiological responses. For all I knew, they had implanted sensors in my body. That was Halliwell's style, for-fucking-certain.

Fine. I might as well give them a good show.

"You know what would really get me going?" I asked. "Take off your dress."

Her eyes dilated into great big pools of black, ringed with a band of that pale, vivid green. I waited, counting the accelerated heartbeats pounding in my ears, for her to tell me to fuck off. For her to storm away in a huff.

But she just looked hypnotized, reaching up, arms crossed over her chest, to nudge down the glittering black beaded straps that held the dress over her shoulders, letting them slip down and dangle over her arms. Ever so slowly. Eyes dazed, dilated.

Holy shit. She was actually doing it.

The dress just skimmed her body, so without the straps, it fell, snagging for a moment on those tight little nipples… and then slid around her waist, folding down over her hips. Her breasts were small, high and pointed and perfect. Pale, flawless skin. Tight, raspberry red nipples. Goosebumps. Freckles. She was shivering, shoulders back, chin up. Eyes glassy and wide. She looked… aroused.

Or at least, I would have sworn her excitement was genuine. But my judgment was suspect, after being locked in this fucking place for so long. Who knew.

It took me a while to remember how to speak. I coughed a few times, to clear the blockage. "There are three possibilities," I said. "Scenario one, this is some sneaky, next-level technique to get inside my head. It won't work. Scenario two, I'm about to die, and this is the closest you can come to a mercy fuck. If it's that, then why not go all the way? Open the glass. Take off the dress. Turn around. Bend over."

She looked shocked. "But I'm not a—"

"Then there's scenario three. You're a hallucination, so you can walk right through the glass and fuck me senseless. What'll it be, Red? Which scenario?"

Her hands rose up, covering her perfect little tits. "I can't open this glass."

I let out a sigh of regret. So my psychotic break was not destined to play out in the way that I craved. It was too good to be true. No surprise there. "So it's scenario one, then," I said. "Fuck off, Red."

The long, fiery ringlets swayed as she shook her head. "It's none of the above," she whispered. "It's scenario four."

"What's four?"

"We're both prisoners. I didn't choose this dress, this situation, this timing. He's playing with both of us. But I don't want you to die. Or to be hurt. Really. Please."

I pondered that as I stared at the perfect details of her

glowing body. The curve at her hip, the fabric draped around her sinuous curves. She looked as soft as the petals of a white rose. I wanted to tear that filmy fabric away. Feel the warmth of her, the dips and curves and shadowed swells, the hidden female bits. I wondered how her mouth tasted. Her pussy. Probably hot, sweet. "So you're, what? A bird in a gilded cage?"

She let out a sharp laugh. "More like a monkey in a lab. A hamster on a wheel."

"That's real sad, babe, but I hope you're not asking me to feel sorry for you."

"I don't need your fucking sympathy! I'm just telling you the truth!"

"You're flaunting your tits," I said. "So either you're fucking with my head or your boss is. We're done, Red. Put your dress on and go."

Red was just opening her painted lips to speak when an incredible thing

happened. The glass block started to hum and grind. The glass shifted under my splayed hands as the heavy transparent slab began retracting into the wall.

At the same time, the lock of the outside door at the far end of the corridor, the one through which she had come, snapped shut with a loud *click.*

Locking her in here... with me.

Red's eyes were wide with shock. The wall slid fast on its well-oiled tracks. In less than five seconds, it had completely retracted, and we stood there, inches apart.

I could smell her. Her hair, her skin. Her soap and shampoo. Warm and sweet and flowery. Intensely female. Everything I'd imagined... times infinity.

I got slammed by all that sensory input right when the realization hit me. This wasn't scenario three. If Red were a hallucination, she wouldn't look so terrified.

If this were my fantasy, she'd smile seductively and advance on me. She'd knock me down onto the cot and swing one of her long, gorgeous legs over me. She'd be naked under the dress, ready to sink right down right onto my stiff, aching cock, take me inside in one seamless thrust, and ride me hard into mindless oblivion, those sweet, tight-tipped perfect breasts shaking, every stroke a wet, tight, suckling caress on my dick. She'd stop only to let me reposition her, to see every inch, try every angle. Top, bottom, from behind, on the side, against the wall. All her secret places, slick and hot and flushed. Spread open, laid bare, plundered, pleasured.

But no. She looked fucking petrified.

Which negated also scenario two, the mercy fuck. If this was her devious plan, why so shocked? She was trembling. Her lips colorless under the stain of makeup.

"Are you out of favor with him?" I asked her. "Is he punishing you for something? Throwing you in here like a live mouse into a snake's cage?"

"Maybe." She backed away, giving the nearest camera a panicked glance. "Except that I'm, uh, not a mouse."

I shrugged. "I'm definitely the snake in this scenario, beautiful."

That made her flinch. "This is not fair," she said, addressing the camera. "This was not what you said! Get me the fuck out of here, goddamn it!"

I took a step toward her. She scrambled back. "Is this some twisted test of your loyalty?" I asked. "Or is he just a dirty old man, and he wants to watch me fuck you?"

"No!" She turned and hurried down the corridor to the exit door. She rattled the handle in vain. Locked. She banged on it, ineffectually.

Well, I'd be goddamned. So Halliwell wanted to watch me ravish the redhead. It struck me as weird, that he'd rather watch me have her than have her himself. Hard to fathom it, but hey. People were all different flavors of fucked up. Him more than most.

I saw myself reflected in the shiny metal of the door, and I really did look scary as shit. Feral, beard-stubbled, skinny, half-naked, wild-eyed. No wonder she was terrified. But I didn't care. I needed to get another big sniff of that sweet, hot scent of hers, more than I needed oxygen. When I got to the door, I planted my hands on either side of her, caging her in, like the wild, ravenous animal I now was.

"Jesus, Red, stop cowering," I said roughly. "You said you weren't a mouse, right? If you're supposed fuck info out of me, this is a piss-poor way to do it."

"I was told to talk to you! Not to... to... fuck you!"

Her awkward hesitation made me smile. I tilted her face up. Pretty as a fucking angel. "The joke's on you," I said. "Welcome to Halliwell's Hell, beautiful."

My mouth was inches from hers. Maybe it was scenario two after all. The mercy fuck before my gruesome demise. But if so, it was Halliwell's mercy, not hers.

Red had not signed up for this. I was being used to punish her.

And even that unsavory realization could not stop me. I wound my fingers into the silky floss of her long hair, pulled her closer... and kissed her like I wanted to eat her alive.

The shock of contact made us gasp. She let out a startled whimper.

We broke apart for a second, panting. Staring into each other's eyes, astonished.

Then we came together again and kissed again... but this time, she kissed me back. Tentatively, awkwardly, but there was no mistaking her enthusiasm. She wound her shaking arms around my shoulders, digging in with her nails. Her bare breasts pressed my chest. I held her head with one hand, ran my other hand down her body as I plundered her sweet mouth, cupping her rounded ass, feeling her smooth, warm belly.

I hoisted her up against the door so that she straddled me, my erection pressing against the heat between her legs as my tongue plunged, twined with hers, her skirt straining, twined around her thighs. She writhed against me, her legs winding around mine, moving helplessly against the pulsing bulge of my cock, until... oh, God.

She went rigid, gasping... and came, intensely. She didn't cry out, just a choked, shuddering gasp, but I felt those quick, strong pulses of her climax, vibrating through her mound, throbbing against my desperate, aching dick. So sweet. So incredibly hot.

I slid my hand under her skirt, between her legs. Found sheer panties, hot and damp. Slid my fingers under the fabric, and caressed her clit, which was taut and slick. Sopping wet. She squirmed and clenched around me. Absolutely ready for it.

"I want to feel you come like that with my cock inside of you," I told her.

She licked her lips, shook her head slightly. "But... he's watching."

"Too bad." I shifted away from her, twisting to look up at the nearest camera. Took my hand away from the slick, hot heaven of her pussy... and flipped him off.

A brutal jolt of electricity zapped me. The wire across my throat tightened, cutting into me. The shock collar sent waves of white-hot agony through my body.

The floor swung up, smacking me out into an endless black nothingness.

CHAPTER 5

Cass

My back hit the wall. I shrieked in horror as Shane writhed on the ground, jerking and seizing as electricity pulsed through him. He clutched at the collar, choking. His throat bled from that wire. Any deeper, and it would slice his jugular.

"Stop!" I shrieked. "Stop it! Fucking stop it! Right now! You asshole!"

Then the bright white lights on the collar went green. The thin buzzing sound ceased. Shane lay still, shuddering. I saw his chest moving.

He was still alive. Oh, thank God.

I braced myself against the wall, dragging in choked, gasping whimpers, but my lungs wouldn't open up for air. The door lock to the corridor clicked, the door opened, and Halliwell strode in, and stood over the unconscious man, nudging him with his foot.

"Well, well," he said, his voice light. "That was entertaining. Did you come on to him like that just to shock me? I'm not so easily shocked, you know."

"Y-y-you fucking m-m-monster!"

"Ah, ah, ah! Language. Come on, girl, help me get him back over to his side of the glass. We certainly can't leave him out here."

"I will not help you, you sick son-of-a-bitch!"

"You're very agitated, Cassandra," he said a soothing tone. "Calm down. Breathe deeply. And, ah... if you would make yourself decent? Please? It's a bit much for my delicate sensibilities." He gestured at my naked torso, his face faintly pained.

Oh, God. I'd actually forgotten. I tugged the dress straps back up over my shoulders with fingers that shook.

Halliwell crouched to grab Shane's ankles, and dragged him briskly back into the part of the cell delineated by the tracks for the sliding glass wall, leaving a long red smear of blood from his lacerated throat.

Shane's head bumped heavily over the tracks, making me wince. "He needs medical attention! Antibiotics, bandages! You should send someone down to—"

"You just don't get it yet, do you?" He dropped Shane's bare feet to the floor. "This man's need for medical attention is directly proportionate to how useful he is to me. Which at the moment is, not at all. Except for entertainment value, of course. These last few minutes... my goodness. My poor heart. Who knew? Naughty minx."

"You are a goddamn pervert," I said. "Who are you spanking? Me, or him?"

He straightened up, rolling his shoulders. "I don't see why you're so distraught," he said coolly. "I didn't give you any electric shocks. Are you just angry because I stopped him before he was able to complete the sex act with you? You oversexed vixen."

"You are disgusting," I told him. "Don't make light of this. It's horrific."

"Possibly, but think of your sister, all alone in the Cascade

Clinic, fighting for her life. You are in no position to scold me, girl."

I let out a shuddering breath, my hand pressed so hard against the rough textured wall, I scraped off my own skin. Reggie. Oh, God, I was in such deep shit.

Halliwell tugged his suit jacket into place and adjusted his tie. "He can look after himself. If he has a stroke, or his heart stops, or that wound goes septic, or whatever else, it's just destiny, looking after itself. Don't concern yourself." He keyed in a sequence on his phone, and a mechanism began to hum. The thick glass slab once again emerged from the groove in the wall and ground across it, sliding deep into the recessed opening on the other side. "In any case, you'll be glad to know that I've decided he has nothing left in his head worth prying out. And as a special favor to you, I've decided to eliminate him humanely. No interrogation experts. You'll come down with me tomorrow and witness his termination."

"No!" I yelled. "You can't do that to him!"

"I can do anything I want, Cassandra. It's time. He's a dangerous distraction for you. You cannot fixate on anything other than your job right now. I need Glow-worm finished, and here you are, spending all your time mooning over this fellow. Watching shower videos, for God's sake. It's ridiculous. Tomorrow, you cut that bond. Snip-snip, and on you go, marching toward your ultimate destiny. No more frivolous diversions."

"I will not witness that! I cannot watch you murder him!"

"So you won't offer the poor man a single kindly face to gaze on as he breathes his last?" His eyes were wide with fake compassion. "You'd deny him that?"

"But I... but he—"

"You need a sharp lesson about choices and consequences. It's always a problem with extremely gifted young people like you. They aren't used to things not going their way. It's such a rude surprise to them. Often, they behave badly." He held up his passcard. It flashed green. The door clicked open. He offered me his arm.

I shrank away. He rolled his eyes impatiently. "For God's sake, Cassandra," he grumbled, as I lurched out the door after him. "You're being such a child."

The door shut. The lock clicked shut. We walked in silence to the elevator bank.

He hit the button for Level Three, where the apartments were located. I winced away from my own reflection in the gleaming metal wall. My hair was a wild hag's mane, my dress was crooked, my boobs were clearly visible through the dress... Jesus, had they been that visible at the restaurant? No wonder Andrew had sussed me out for sex. No wonder Shane concluded that I was his farewell pity fuck. I was dressed for sex, and I looked like I'd had a rough night of it already. Face hot red, makeup smeared, lipstick worn down, lips puffy and swollen. Red scrapes from Shane's beard stubble. Eyes bright with terror, and other complicated emotions.

Shane was lying there, injured and untreated, on the floor. And tomorrow, he would die... right in front of me.

The elevator pinged, the door opened. Halliwell held it open for me.

"Sleep well, Cassandra," he said briskly. "I need you in top form tomorrow. You'll be my hostess for another business dinner tomorrow night, after we deal with the prisoner's disposal. I'm holding this party right here, at headquarters. The OlgarCorp team responds well to eye candy. Another dress will be delivered tomorrow. That one you're wearing appears to be... well, not salvageable, after tonight's adventures."

"I am not eye candy," I snapped.

"You are whatever I need you to be, girl, so shut up and behave."

I backed away from him, as the door closed on his low, mocking laughter.

I had a hard time keying in the code that opened my apartment, my eyes were so full of furious tears. It seemed silly that there was a code at all. Everyone in this place seemed to have access to it. Hell, why have a door at all?

I was not a weepy type. Mom had always called me a stoic. But whatever my natural emotional blocks, they had all been pulverized tonight.

Tomorrow was unthinkable. But I'd better start thinking, and fast. The parameters of how bad things could get in this place was expanding every minute that passed. Halliwell could demand anything he wanted in exchange for Reggie's life. And he clearly liked doing it. He got off on making me feel vulnerable. Exercising his power. He was going to kill that man in front of me just to show me who was boss.

Eventually he might use Reggie the same way. That would be the end of me.

I tore off the dress and shoved it into the garbage chute. The shoes followed, and the underwear. My hands shook. Halliwell had made it look as if I were his accomplice. Like I had deliberately lured Shane into that sick ambush by kissing him. And Halliwell had opened the glass wall just to scare me. A threat of second-hand rape.

I bet the twisted old bastard hadn't expected me to like it.

It had surprised me, too. I'd never been all that interested in sex. I was too stuck in my head to let go and enjoy it. After trying it a few times, I had basically concluded that it wasn't worth the mess. That my hormones were permanently stuck at the "take it or leave it" setting.

So I'd left it. I'd been busy with a sick mom at the time, anyway, and then with an orphaned sister. I simply could not be bothered.

Well, I sure was bothered now. And Halliwell had seen exactly how much that man moved me. How deep those feelings went. I sobbed it out in the shower, then toweled off, trying not to think about the cameras probably hidden all over the apartment. Wondering if people were always watching me in my most private moments.

Get real, Cass. Of course they fucking are.

My phone rang as I was swabbing inky black smudges from beneath my eyes. At four AM? Reggie. I wrapped myself in a robe and lunged for the phone. Reggie's thin, hollowed face appeared on the screen, lit with eerie blue light from her tablet.

"Babe, what are you doing awake?" I asked. "It's almost four AM!"

"You're always working in the daytime. And I can't sleep anyhow. Whenever I try, I have nightmares. So I mostly just doze. Sorry if I woke you up."

"No, I was in the shower, see my towel? I'm glad you called. I miss you like crazy."

Reggie's face crumpled. "I miss you too."

The next several minutes were spent soothing her, trying to figure out the problem, which unfortunately was not one I could solve. She wasn't being overtly abused or maltreated, just ignored. Bland, unappetizing meals arrived three times a day, delivered by an orderly who wouldn't speak to her. A team of doctors examined her every day without talking to her or acknowledging her when she spoke. The nurse took blood and tissue scrapings from her throat every day, but not one of them had a fucking kind word for a lonely little girl locked in a windowless room. She might as well be in a cage in a kennel. Worse, even. At least the dogs could bark at each other for company.

"You can always call me," I said. "Whenever I'm not at work."

She snorted. "When is that? Only late at night."

This was sadly true. I clocked twenty-hour days on a regular basis trying to finish Glow-worm. "I'm sorry about that, honey. Did you read the books I sent to your tablet? And the films?"

"Yeah, they were great," she said listlessly. "Could you send me some more?"

"Sure, sweetheart. I'll find something really special for you."

She stared at me through the screen with sad brown eyes. Her hair was as red as mine but in this light it looked black. "Am I going to die, Cass? I ask the doctors, and the nurse, but they don't hear me. I feel like a ghost. Like maybe I'm dead already."

Those fucking *assholes.* "Of course you're not going to die," I assured her. "Halliwell said he had a cure. You're better than before, right? No more of those rashes, or the fevers and nosebleeds or coughing or snot, right? All that stuff has stopped."

"Yeah," Reggie said. "But there's not much point being alive here. They never let me go out. There isn't even a window. Just cinderblocks. And I'm locked in."

Those sick fuckers were being cruel just for the sake of being cruel. It drove me mad with fury and frustration. "Then I'll be your window," I told her, walking out onto the deck. I flipped the screen so that I could pan the phone around, showing her the white surf surging up on the wide, dark beach below, the sharp crags of rock, the morning star hanging heavy and bright over the dry hills. "This place is messed up, but at least the Pacific Ocean is beautiful to look at."

"I can't stand it, Cass," Reggie said, her voice thick with tears. "I'm sorry. I know you're working really hard for me. But I can't keep doing this. I'd rather just be with you now, and whatever happens, happens, you know? At least we could say goodbye, right? I don't want to die here alone with people who don't even see me."

"You won't," I promised rashly. "I'll find a solution. Hang on, okay? Please, babe. For me. Try to get some sleep. Think of the ocean waves I just showed you."

"Okay," Reggie said faintly. "I'll try. I love you."

"I love you, too, angel. Remember that. Think of the stars,

the waves. That waterfall we went to, that one time, remember it? The forest, with the long hanging moss? As soon as I spring you out of there, we'll go back to all our favorite places."

"Promise?"

"Pinky swear. Cross my heart."

"Let's not hope to die, though. And never mind the thousand needles." Reggie gave me a fleeting ghost of a smile. "I do a thousand needles every day as it is."

"No needles. Just freedom. The wind in your hair, the sun through the leaves. Lazy afternoons by a stream with a good book. You and me."

"Okay," Reggie said. "I'll let you sleep. Bye, then. I love you."

"I love you, too, sweetheart."

She gave me that shaky, brave smile that broke my heart. After we closed the

call, I started crying again. It was so confusing. I had to be strong for Reggie, but paradoxically, I had to be soft for her, too, because everything around her was so fucking hard.

I'd done some hard things in my twenty-six years. Been proud of them, too. But being strong and soft at the same time was the trickiest thing I'd ever attempted.

And by far the most important.

CHAPTER 6

Cass

There was no way to sleep after Reggie's call, so I pulled on my drabbest clothes, got my work laptop, and headed to my workstation, down on the bridge of the benighted airship on its cursed voyage to nowhere. I'd just settled in and taken a bracing swig of my black coffee when I felt a rush of cold air from outside. Someone was coming in from the terrace, pushing a big, rattling cleaning cart.

Jana. At four-thirty AM, Jana was still doing janitorial work, all alone in the dark. She'd been working alone, in the cold, all night long.

She'd said earlier tonight that she didn't care enough to hate me. Which I supposed meant that she was as close a thing to a friend as I had in this place.

I felt a rush of protective anger for her. She was being bullied and abused, and it was just fucking wrong, on every level. This shit simply could not continue.

Jana looked terrible. Her eyes were red, her face shiny and flushed, as if she had a fever. She stumbled, clutching the cart for balance, eyes straight ahead.

"Jana?" I said.

She jumped, letting out a shriek.

"Sorry," I offered. "Didn't mean to scare you. Just wondering what you're doing up at the ass-crack of dawn. You don't look so good. Are you getting sick?"

She rubbed her cheek, which looked weirdly swollen. Jana would have been a beautiful woman, but for her clammy, colorless skin, the grayish lips, the puffy eyes. Even her thick, wavy blond hair looked limp and defeated right now.

"Just trying to get this terrace done." Her voice sounded slurred.

"Here, let me push the cart for you," I offered. "You look whipped."

"No! You're supposed to be working on Glow-worm, and he'll be furious if he sees you doing my scut work! Don't even think about it!"

Invisibility Cloak flashed through my mind. I was almost tempted to tell her about it. I knew it would be dumb, but I wanted so badly to help her in some way.

"If I help, we'll get it done fast, and we can go grab coffee and a pastry from the breakfast bar before anyone else is up," I suggested. "Nobody could fault us for getting coffee and a Danish. I doubt anyone's watching right now. And I'll take the heat, if we get caught."

"You still don't get it, do you?" she asked.

"Get what?"

"He watches all the time." Jana's voice was low and strangled. "The cameras are always running. He watches it all, processes it all, at super-high velocity, and he doesn't miss a fucking beat. Not a single goddamn eyelash flicker. Not ever."

"How? How does he do that?" I asked. "He did that to me last night at dinner! He was talking to the guy next to him the whole time and he still somehow overheard a whispered conversation I was having, six people down the table. It's scary."

Jana wheezed with laughter, and her face twisted in pain. "I don't know how he does it. I don't think he knows, either, because God knows, he's tried to teach all of us the trick, with biofeedback, hypnosis, implants, brain surgery, you name it. But we all suck at it, to his enduring disappointment. Don't you dare touch that garbage bag!"

I stepped back reluctantly. "I don't see why helping would be so terrible."

"Go ahead, if you really want to watch me get punished. Again."

I gazed at her reddened, blurred looking jaw. "What happened to your face?" I asked. "It looks like someone punched you. Did he... Jesus, Jana, did he *hit* you?"

Another smothered, manic burst of laughter. "Hell, no," she muttered. "As if he'd lower himself to actually touch me. I disgust him. If I needed to get hit, he would outsource the job." She touched her jaw with gingerly fingertips, wincing. "I got my tooth last night, after you went out. This is what I get, for being a worthless piece of shit. It's your future, too, so take a long look at what's in store for you."

"Tooth? What are you talking about?" I asked, bewildered. "What tooth?"

"It's a special ritual for the unluckiest and the least worthy of the Halliwell offspring," she said. "It binds me to him forever. Silvano, his sadistic pet dentist, pulls out a molar. Then he implants a fake tooth, right into your raw, bleeding jawbone. No anesthesia. If you're lucky, you don't die of shock. Some have. Not that he cared."

"No anesthetic?" I gaped at her, horrified. "But what was wrong with your tooth?"

"Nothing. But the new one has a poison gas capsule inside it, a tiny charge of explosives, and a miniature receiver. If Halliwell's vitals stop, a signal gets sent out to all the teeth. They explode... and then we die."

"But that's... that's nuts!"

"Don't think you're immune just because you're the flavor of the week," Jana warned. "He'll get mad at you eventually. That's when you get your tooth."

"I would never let him do that to me!"

Jana's face twisted. "Oh please. Don't make me laugh. It hurts too much. You think you'll have a choice? That'll change, Cass. That's what he always does. He keeps you whole for a while. Lets you think you can survive this, maybe even eventually escape. And bit by bit, he grinds you down until you don't even remember who you were before. And then it's too late. It was too late for me even before the tooth, but now..." She shook her head.

"But I'm just here for a little while," I said. "I'm just doing this in exchange for medical treatment for my little sister. She has a rare disease, and she needs this experimental treatment only he can get for her. So I'm stuck here for the duration. At least while she's being treated."

"Oh, yes." Jana's voice sank to a hollow whisper. "Of course. The little sister. That's an old classic. Come here." She grabbed my shoulder and led me outside the Bridge to the alcove of the nearest snack bar. "We're just barely out of camera or mic range right here, if you don't move and you keep your voice way down," she murmured. "So, about your sister. Don't tell me, let me guess. DeLuca's Syndrome? Tamiko's? Varen's Disease? Which one is it? Those are his favorites. The big trifecta."

Something inside me went silent and ice cold. The *hell?* Even some seasoned medical specialists had never heard of Varen's Disease, it was so rare.

"Varen's," I admitted, reluctantly. "Really quick onset. Just a couple months ago. Halliwell heard about it. He told me he had a treatment, so he made a deal with me. Glow-worm, and my labor, in exchange for the cure. How did you know it was Varen's?"

"It's not," Jana said.

"Of course it is! My mom had the same symptoms. Mom died of Varen's two years ago. They say there could be a genetic predisposition. Maybe I'll get it, too."

"Shhh. It's not Varen's," Jana whispered. "He told you he had experimental medical treatment that would save her, right? Tamiko's, DeLuca's Disease, Varen's. He has a few others in his arsenal, but those are his favorites. They're the most reliable, the most controllable. He creates dummy diseases. Then he infects people with them, and hey, presto, only he has the cure. Or the antidote, rather. And then he owns you."

"No," I said. "That's not possible."

"I wish it weren't," she said. "But the real Varen's, Tamiko's and DeLuca's have no treatment options. No cure. You get them, and you die. So if she's still alive... then it's not Varen's."

"No." My voice was muffled by my hand, pressed to my mouth. "Not possible."

"He made your sister sick," Jana said. "And he could make her well, too, if he wanted to. But he'll never give you the cure, because you have that big, souped-up brain, just like his, and he wants it. He thinks you're the mini-me he's been waiting for. He'll never let you go. So he'll never let her go, either. Sorry, but it's the truth."

I couldn't stop shaking my head. "Not possible." My voice shook. "It has to be Varen's. My mother died of it, too, so how could it—"

"No, she didn't. Halliwell murdered her. He murdered my mother, too. It was Tamiko's, for my mom. I was fourteen. It took me another fourteen years to figure it out. I learned the truth when I was at the Coatesworth Facility, where all the pharmaceutical research is done. I was rising in the ranks, and I got a higher clearance, and I started poking around, and I found this file. It had all the details. How he developed this technique, using fake diseases to control people. How he killed my mother. He killed your mother, too. He'll eventually kill your sister. He always does."

"You're lying," I said, but the words were hollow. Her voice was flat, hushed, but it had the ring of truth. And it fit with everything I knew about Halliwell. Everything Mom had told me.

"He makes people sick, dangles the cure, and makes a devil's bargain," Jana whispered. "He gets complete control of people that way. He got my mother to sell me to him for the medicine. Then he let her die, so that I would be more 'focused on my training.' He'll do that to you. He'll decide your sister is a distraction, and bye-bye." She winced and touched her face. "Oh, God, that hurts."

"You need antibiotics," I said.

She snorted. "Antibiotics are for pussies. Besides, he's sick of me. He'd love it if my tooth went septic. He'd be happy for an excuse to let me die."

I stared into her hollow eyes, and awareness sliced through me like a bolt of lightning. For that stinging instant, I saw right through the comforting bullshit I had been trying to feed myself. The fantasy that that there was a civilized, acceptable way out of this hellhole, with a healthy, rosy-cheeked Reggie at the end of it.

There wasn't, and I knew it, with every cell of my body. I had been scammed. It was up to me to fix it now, and there was no time to waste.

"He made Reggie sick," I said slowly, still trying to make room in my mind for the unthinkable. "Mom, too. And he had the cure all along."

"Shhh. He's done that to most of us," Jana said. "I know you're this hot-shit hacker, but don't even think you'll be able to find it. He will never give you the cure. Never. The only thing that could possibly penetrate deep enough into his files to find the cure would be that algorithm. The one they're trying to torture out of that poor guy."

That startled me. "Really? I could dig out Reggie's cure with SmokeScreen? That's what you're saying?"

"Shhh! The mic will pick you up if you yell! I don't envy you. Everyone I ever cared about is dead now, so all I have left to do is work up the nerve to go out there and jump." She gestured toward the terrace outside.

"Don't say that," I said. "Please. You're not done yet. Don't give up hope."

She rubbed her jaw and gave me an eloquent look. "It's a little late for hope, Cass."

"Halliwell's executing the prisoner tomorrow," I told her. "He just told me."

Jana's eyes slid away. "Oh," she said softly. "Well, then. That's it for your sister. My condolences."

Data crunched in my mind at high speed. SmokeScreen was the key. Halliwell, with the cure. Shane Masters, dying tomorrow. That could not happen. No, no, and no.

I pulled out my phone, and tapped the code that activated Invisibility Cloak, and jerked my chin to Jana. "Come with me." I let my whisper vibrate with urgency.

She looked puzzled, but she shuffled along after me into the corridor. I stopped. "They can't hear us or see us now," I told her.

She frowned, glancing up at the cameras all around us. "But—"

"I wrote a program. Invisibility Cloak. It works. If you stay with me, or right near my phone, rather, you're invisible. And inaudible."

Her eyes were big with wonder. "Wow. If I had something like that, I'd..."

"What?" I asked.

She shrugged. "Something loud and destructive. Vindictive.

And explosive. Bombs, probably. I'd blow this fucking place sky high. What a rush."

"Best thing that could happen to it," I told her. "Hey, tell me something. Do you really think I could get Halliwell's cure for Reggie if I had SmokeScreen to work with?"

"You have the skills," Jana said. "So yeah. Maybe. If anyone could do it, it would be you. But their encryption is watertight. You could only open SmokeScreen if one of the Masters family personally, voluntarily helped you."

"So let's leave," I said. "And we'll take the Masters guy with us."

Jana frowned. "Halliwell would never let him out of here alive."

"So we take him out dead," I said. "Apparently dead, I mean."

Jana's eyes flashed with wary interest. "You mean, fake his death? Change the gas canister? Huh. Problematic. Interesting idea, though."

"Could we switch out the gas?" I asked.

"If you're invisible, you could. I could load a canister with the downer we used for his haircut and shave. But it would have to be a monster dose to depress his respiration enough to make him look convincingly dead. Which means that the attempt could actually kill him. There's always that risk."

I thought about it. "He's going to die tomorrow anyway," I said. "This way, he has a fighting chance. He'd go for it if I asked him. I'd bet my life on that."

"You will be," she said wryly.

"No, Jana. *We* will be," I pointed out. "You're coming with me, remember?"

"Oh, no. I'm not going anywhere. I've been taken apart way too much to be put back together again. Once I pronounce him dead and take him to the morgue, you have to attack me with a needle. You have to take me down. To make it look good."

"You should run away with me. Halliwell will still suspect you."

"That's all right," she said. "Maybe he'll finally kill me. It'll save me the trouble of doing it myself. Which requires more energy than you might think."

Her flat tone chilled me. "Please, come with me," I implored her. "We'll run together. I could handle him better with help. You can help me save Reggie, and I'll do anything in the world that I can do to help you."

Jana gave me a smile that was almost sweet. "No, Cass. You're on your own."

I had no intention of accepting that, but I just nodded. "So? This place is about to wake up. I need to switch out the gas, and get a needle from the morgue. What else?"

Jana's face had changed. Even sallow and peaky, with those bruised shadows under her eyes, I got a glimpse of the woman she should have been before Halliwell crushed her almost out of existence. Vital, purposeful, switched on.

"So you're doing this?" Jana's voice vibrated with suppressed excitement. "For real?"

"Hell, yes. If you're telling me the truth, then this is my only hope to save Reggie. But that's a big 'if.'"

"I wouldn't lie about that," Jana said. "In honor of my mother's memory, I would never, ever lie about that."

I stared into her eyes, gauging her sincerity. She'd been so completely deconstructed by Halliwell. It was dangerous to bet on someone so compromised.

But Jana looked back at me, unflinching. Her love for her lost mother was pure and whole. I could trust a promise based on that. I hoped so, anyhow. For Reggie's sake, I couldn't let myself be silly, naïve, overly trusting.

Not that I had any other option. In this case, it was trust Jana, or die.

"So?" I urged. "You'll help me?"

She rubbed her swollen jaw, and nodded. "Come with me. And hurry."

We ran through the halls toward the infirmary. Jana had shaken off her shuffling zombie gait. It wasn't dawn yet, but Halliwell's spawn weren't the types to linger in bed. They were robot drones on the one hand, and pathetically eager to prove themselves on the other. And as always, once the corridors were populated, Invisibility Cloak was useless.

I used Halliwell's passcard to access the infirmary, and Jana led me into the huge supply closet at the back end of the examining rooms, which was more like a warehouse than a closet. Jana was the pharmaceutical expert, and this place was her kingdom. Or had been, before she'd been demoted to scullery maid.

She unlocked a cabinet, and took down a canister like the one I'd seen loaded into the frame above Shane's cell. "The red is for the lethal gas," she told me. "The blue is the sedative. But I'll put the sedative into the red one, and you can switch it with the one mounted outside the cell right now."

"Got it," I said.

She opened another locked cabinet, pulled out a drawer that was full of glass vials. She selected two, unscrewed a chamber on the top of the red gas canister, and snapped open the vial, pouring it all in. Then she hesitated, frowning as she did mental calculations, and opened another vial, counting out fifteen more drops.

"It's a huge dose," she told me. "But he's a big guy. Very strong. It has to depress his respiration and slow his heartbeat so that he looks really dead. Which could kill him for real, particularly considering that you won't have the opportunity to revive him for a while. You'll be driving, and you have to get the hell away from here and find a place to hide before you can wake him up. It's a very long shot."

"If you came with me, I could drive while you gave him the—"

"I have the tooth now," she broke in, her voice harder. "Which means that scenario is not possible. If I went with you, the minute Halliwell figured out what happened, he would detonate it remotely. If I'm in an enclosed place, like a car or a van, the explosion or the gas would kill not just me, but anyone who's with me. I'm a walking bomb now, Cass. Let it go."

I hated the idea of leaving her behind undefended, to pay for my sins. "But I can't just go without you," I protested. "I can't just leave you. If he finds out—"

"If he finds out, tough shit. Get as far away as you can with Masters before you stick him with this." She pulled out a hypodermic with a yellow plastic ring on the bottom. "This is a powerful stimulant. If he lives, and if it works, he'll be confused, disoriented, violent. Possibly psychotic."

Her eyes asked me if I had the nerve. I reached for it. "If this is my one shot, I'm taking it," I told her.

"Good." She passed me three more syringes, these ones with black plastic rings. "Knockout needles," she said, in response to my questioning gaze. "One for me, when you attack me in the morgue. He won't buy it, but we should at least try. The others are for whoever else you might run into. You still have to steal a catering van, or something like that. On the fly. It's too late to put together anything clever now."

"Um. Yeah." I was reeling at the thought of all the desperate things I had to do, each building on the success of the last, each more improbable than the one that came before.

"Don't mix those needles up," she reminded me. "You'll kill me if you do. Probably him, too."

A horrible thought occurred to me suddenly. "Oh, shit," I said blankly. "When can I even try to do this? The timing is all off! I'm supposed to work one of Halliwell's bullshit kiss-ass parties tomorrow after the execution. Another fucking evening dress."

Her eyes narrowed. "Maybe. Maybe not."

"Yeah? Can you see a way out of it? Because I can't."

"You have to get yourself banished," she said. "I do it all the time, but I do it involuntarily. Like my crying jag the other day, remember? You have to do it on purpose, at just exactly the right time."

"I'm not following you," I said impatiently. "What are you talking about?"

"Come on, Cass. You're supposed to be smart, right? Disgust him, embarrass him, gross him out. He'll shoo you away. It's an automatic reflex for him. Wait. I have an idea." She opened another drawer of vials, and rummaged until she found whatever she was looking for, a small, squat glass jar. She pulled a gelatin capsule from a bag, inserted a few grains of yellowish powder into it, closed it and handed it to me. "That's your get-out-of-jail-free card."

I looked at it in blank incomprehension. "What is this?"

"You're allergic to shellfish, right? I read that in your file."

Whoa. I had not told anyone about that. "Uh, yeah, actually, I am. And?"

"This is a histamine, mimicking the shellfish. It'll make you break out in hives and swell up like a balloon. It works very fast. You can't work the party if you look like shit. That totally horrifies him. He'll send you to your room and call for one of the other girls to be the Halliwell Whore. It's the one brief moment when he might not be paying attention to you."

I stared down at the capsule. Fucking *yikes*. "How sick will I be?"

She shrugged. "I doubt you'll die. The important thing is that you look terrible." She rummaged again, and handed me a small epinephrine autoinjector. "Stick yourself with this if you start to choke. Try and do it before your throat closes up. Or you'll pass out."

"Gee," I said faintly. "Thanks. Great. That's, ah... a brilliant plan."

"Your sister's in one of his bogus clinics? It's really just a prison, you know."

It made me sick to think of it. "I took her to the Cascade Clinic about two months ago, right before I came here," I said. "In his goddamn helicopter."

"She won't have much time," she warned. "He'll come down on her like a hammer the minute he figures out what happened, so you have to get her out fast. That's a very tall order. You're a three-hour drive from the Cascade Clinic, at least."

My belly clenched. "One thing at a time," I muttered. This was my one chance to save my sister. I couldn't stall out now just because it was hard.

I stared down at the pill, my stomach clenching. "Are you sure that I—"

"I'm not fucking sure of anything, Cass. Look me in the eye. Do I look like someone who knows anything for sure? Don't be a baby. You're probably going to die. Probably both of us will. But if you live, maybe you'll save your sister. Maybe. There's a slim chance. Take it if you want it. If not, then get the hell away from me, because you're wasting my time and putting me in a bad spot for nothing."

"I'm taking it," I said rapidly. "I'm in."

Jana grabbed a white plastic bag for the stuff she'd given me, and tossed a bunch of tampons and pads on top of them. "There's your flimsy excuse for being in the infirmary," she said. "I have to get back to my punishment shift before this place wakes up. Go switch out that canister, or you'll miss your chance. You better hurry."

"I have to walk you back to the blind spot outside the Bridge with Invisibility Cloak," I told her. "Or it'll look weird on the monitors."

Running would have looked suspicious, but walking at a normal pace almost killed me. We reached the spot where I could finally leave her, and she grabbed my arm. "Hey," she whispered.

"What is it?"

"I know I'm going to die for this." She sounded slightly puzzled. "But it feels kind of good. So, uh... thanks for that."

"You're welcome. You can't even imagine how much. And I hope you don't die. Later, Jana."

"One more thing." Her fingers tightened on my arm. "That shock collar. You have to deactivate it, or Halliwell will just cut Masters' throat remotely. Or fry him with electricity. You'll also have to think about any possible GPS tag of the car you steal. Think ahead, Cass. Lots of moving parts, here."

I winced. Still more impossible tasks. "Fuck me."

"Don't whine," Jana said. "You're supposed to be way smarter and more outside-the-fucking-box than all the rest of us clapped-out boneheads, right? So pick up the pace, cupcake. Impress me."

That got me going. I gave in to the impulse to sprint for the stairway down to Level Eight. Halliwell's passcard got me into the stairwell. I hurtled down four stairs at a time and let myself in. The long smear of blood from Shane's collar wound was drying now, dark and ugly against the light floor tiles.

I ran down to the last cell. Shane lay just as we had left him, sprawled on the floor. Unconscious, maybe dead. I had no idea how to get that glass wall open, nor would I have dared to open it if knew. I needed to have the upper hand before I tried to bargain with Shane Masters. Even Halliwell was extremely careful with this guy.

They kept a throne-like wooden chair down here so Halliwell could sit in state and observe while they worked on the prisoner. I dragged it over to the glass wall, situating it under the mechanism that held the red canister, climbed up and unscrewed the one mounted in the mechanism. I replaced it with the doctored one, climbed down, dragged the chair back to where it had been. Then I hit the mic.

"Shane?" I called. "Shane, are you awake?"

He didn't move. I leaned against the glass, biting my lip. "I'm so sorry," I said shakily, hoping he could hear my voice on some level of his consciousness. "I am so sorry that he did that to you. I did not set you up for that, I swear to God."

No reaction. He was motionless, and I couldn't get near him to help. I shoved the old canister of lethal gas into the plastic bag, burying it under the pile of tampons and pads, and headed straight for the Bridge at a purposeful trot.

No more sprinting. My chances of being seen were rising every second that passed. I had made a two-minute loop of myself, hunched over my computer. I assumed that position again, and disabled Invisibility Cloak with a swipe of my finger.

Jana was nowhere to be seen, but the cleaning cart was gone. Halliwell was supposed to be able to see all things at all times, but I could only hope that he'd miss this morning's anomalies.

People were starting to trickle in. I grabbed some more coffee, took my plastic bag, and retreated to my apartment. I didn't dare activate another loop once I got there, though I desperately wanted to. Too many anomalies in the system already. More people awake to notice them.

I went into the bathroom, shoved the syringes into a pink silk makeup bag, thinking of how Jana's eyes had brightened as she measured out drugs. How that dead tone in her voice came to life as she used her skills and powers to help me, selflessly, and to her own personal danger and detriment.

God, how I wanted to make her come with me. To force her

to believe that she had a future, away from this place. Away from Halliwell.

But I couldn't make her do it. And that tooth was a hell of an impediment. I did not know how to solve that problem, but I still wanted to give her something.

I got into the closet, dug into the false bottom of the suitcase, and got out one of my contraband smartphones. All activated, charged, ready to use.

I went out onto the balcony to one of my deck chairs, held the phone down between my legs, and downloaded Invisibility Cloak onto it. Then I sent a text to the number.

> u have the power now. do as u like with this. use it, toss it in the ocean. your choice. thx forever.

She was going to do my hair and makeup later. I could discreetly slip it to her then. But that video would be heavily scrutinized, analyzed, after the fact. Too risky.

I pocketed her new phone and wandered out into the corridors to the best blind spot on this floor, and activated Invisibility Cloak again. Then I made my way swiftly to Jana's apartment, which was at the far end of the residential hall from my own.

Halliwell's passcard let me in. Invisibility Cloak had no loop for this place, so I had to be quick. It was completely different from my luxurious apartment, just a plain, cramped one-bedroom with a small window that looked out on an inner courtyard. Like a hotel room, but more drab. The walls were plain and bare, like a nun's cell.

I went to her featureless bedroom and slid the smartphone under her pillow.

That was all I could do for her. I hoped she'd appreciate the gesture, and not feel oppressed by it. The woman had enough problems already.

Afterward, I steeled myself to go back to the Bridge and work on Glow-worm. Cool, calm and collected. As if I didn't have this whacked out, deadly adventure planned for later in the day.

I still couldn't believe I was doing this. Breaking Shane Masters out of jail— and persuading him to help me save Reggie. If he survived the escape at all.

He couldn't possibly object to me breaking him out. It was that or certain death, right? So I hoped that having freed him would make him kindly disposed toward me. That he would be willing to help. If the drugs didn't make him, well... psychotic.

So many unknowns. But this was Reggie's only chance, and there was no looking back. After all, there was nothing to look at back there anyhow.

Just scorched earth on every side.

CHAPTER 7

Shane

I dragged my miserable, raggedy ass back to consciousness with great reluctance. I hurt too much to be awake and aware. My head pounded, my neck burned where I'd been shocked, the scabby, bloody mess of my throat stung, and every other fucking part of me ached and throbbed. My neck was swollen up, that fucking wire digging deep into raw, puffy flesh. My body was sticky with blood, old sweat.

I dragged myself slowly up into a sitting position as recent events reassembled themselves in my head. It seemed more like a dream, not a logical sequence. It still made no sense. The redheaded siren in the sexy evening gown. Taking down her hair. Dropping her dress. The glass wall, grinding miraculously open. The siren, in my arms. That kiss, that climax.

Then zap, the collar, burning and cutting me full force. Fucking *wow.*

What was the point of all that drama? Beat me all to hell.

It took a long time and grim concentration to steady my legs enough to walk on them. I staggered over to the food drawer. A meal had been left in it. A paper-wrapped sandwich, a bottle of water, an apple. I took out the water, but didn't bother with the food. After a bout with the strangle-wire, I could barely get water down.

I usually passed my long, empty hours meditating, focusing on moonscapes, star fields, ocean waves, migrating birds. Not today. I just dragged my body over to the cot and sprawled on it. At some point, I heard another meal being automatically delivered through the mechanical drawer in the wall. I didn't even roll over.

I wished the sick bastard would just kill me. The difficulty of breathing through my inflamed throat made sleep impossible. I just lay there, and fought for every breath of air I took, while pain hammered at my brain with every stubborn heartbeat.

Time crawled by. I slipped in and out of consciousness. I kept seeing my redheaded siren seductively unbraiding her hair for me. Showing me her tits. Then I heard the microphone buzz. The line was open.

"Mr. Masters? Are you awake?"

Halliwell's voice. *Fuck.* My gorge rose. The cat was back to play with its prey.

"Mr. Masters, I am sorry to inform you that you've reached the end of the road with us today. Your time as our guest has come to an end."

Huh. So I was going to die today. Funny, how that pissed me off so much. Just when I'd been devoutly wishing for it just moments before. Something about the tone in that prick's voice as he informed me. So condescending and self-important.

"Mr. Masters!" Halliwell's voice took on a wheedling tone, like he was trying to get a toddler to eat his vegetables. "The young lady who visited you last night has also come to say goodbye. If that information might induce you to sit up and face us."

Well, that sneaky son-of-a-bitch. He'd found the perfect

way to jerk me around. I hated him for it, but my eyes snapped open involuntarily.

I couldn't pass up a chance to lay eyes on Red again. My pride was gone, along with fear, and all the rest of it.

If I was going to die, I wanted to look at something beautiful one last time.

I dragged in a breath, braced for pain and wrenched myself up, swinging my legs down off the cot for ballast until I was sitting. *Fuck*, that hurt. Fresh blood ran hotly down my neck. It tickled.

Several people were out there. It was quite a crowd today. Halliwell in the center, as usual, enthroned in his big wooden chair, legs crossed, a shit-eating grin on his face. He wore a tux, and was surrounded by young women, but I only saw Red.

She stood beside him, wearing a fucking ball gown, of all things. It was a luminous green, like her eyes, and it caught the light. Taffeta, maybe. A big, puffy, Disney-princess kind of skirt, a strapless corset top. Her perfect little freckled tits popped cheerfully out the top, just her raspberry pink nipples hidden. Her hair was wound up into another towering hairdo featuring a crown of braids. My hot, dangerous, sexy czarina, on her way to the ball to make trouble.

Her face was pale, her eyes big and scared looking. She wore a full mask of fancy makeup, just like yesterday. And once our eyes locked, I couldn't look away.

Out of the corner of my eye, I saw familiar faces. Six or seven of them. Many of these women had come down to lick their lips and ogle me in the past several months. I always ignored them. They were fine-looking females, every last one, but they were cold. Dead-eyed. When they looked at me, all they saw was a piece of meat to whack off to. They chilled me to the bone.

Then Red showed up, and somehow, she saw all that I was. Even the parts I was trying desperately to forget.

"What do you want from me?" I asked him.

Halliwell shrugged vaguely. "You know what I want," he said. "But you won't give it to me. Today is actually more about what I thought you might want. As a final request. After yesterday's steamy spectacle, I thought perhaps you'd appreciate a final look at your new little friend. A chance to say goodbye. Just a sentimental notion."

"So I make my grand exit today? What'll it be? The Iron Maiden? The rack?"

"Nothing so barbaric," Halliwell's voice was almost jolly. "Just lethal gas, as we've discussed before. It's a gentle death, I promise. You fall asleep and drift away. But all these young ladies wanted to take one last look at you, since you're so popular. The ritual became a rather bigger deal than I first anticipated. I hope you're gratified."

I ignored him, and stared at Red. Trying to send her a telepathic message. *Get away from here. Run, before it's too late, or you'll end up just like me.*

"So," Halliwell said. "It's time. Last words?"

I cleared my throat, which hurt like a bastard, and staggered over to the glass wall, right in front of Red. "Not for that guy," I said to her, gesturing at Halliwell without looking at him. "I kept my eyes locked onto hers. "Just for you."

She took a step toward me. "Yes?"

"You can do better than these blood-sucking ghouls," I said. "You don't belong here. Get away, Red. First chance you get. Run like hell. Please."

She nodded, her eyes somber and clear.

Halliwell's smile faded. "Needlessly rude, as always," he said peevishly. "Goodbye, Mr. Masters." He pushed the button on the remote with a flourish.

Gas hissed out of the canister. My cage started to fill with a fine mist.

So this was it. I let go, and finally let myself think about

Holly, about my brother and sister, with a pang of intense sadness and longing. Red had moved over to the wall, putting her hands up. I put mine against hers. I couldn't feel her body heat, not with six inches of glass between us, but I could imagine it. My knees were starting to give. I leaned against the glass, and hung onto Red with my eyes.

I would keep hanging on until the death fog dragged me down into the dark.

CHAPTER 8

Cass

I was crying for real. Loud, over-the-top ugly-crying. Hiccup-sobbing, my hands pressed against that wall of glass, snorting back tears while Shane's eyes locked with mine like I was his last lifeline. Which I was, for all he knew.

I am trying to save you, I wanted to scream. *I have a plan. It's a weak, shitty, dangerous last-minute plan but it's all I've got, so don't break my heart like this.*

Here I was again, like with Reggie. Needing to be strong when I was falling apart. Needing to be soft at the most dangerous moment, while Halliwell stared at me, his eyes cold and speculative. Judging and assessing me, while this man who might or might not be dying reached out to me for comfort in his final moments.

My misbegotten, robotic hell-sisters rolled their eyes at each other, snickering. Fuck those icy-hearted bitches. So much for my careful mask of cosmetics. Jana had deliberately used non-waterproof mascara, to increase the shock value of my hideous jump-scare face when I finally sprang it on them. I had been so immersed in Shane's eyes, I had actually forgotten the pill tucked between my forefinger and middle fingers.

Luckily, the gel capsule had stuck fast to the stress sweat between my fingers.

Shane's eyes were losing their laser-focus. He gasped for air as the fog grew thicker. It was hell on earth, watching his eyelids flutter. He sagged against the glass.

He toppled over, and I sank down to my knees to follow him, skirt billowing like a parachute. In the silence, I heard a keening noise. I realized, startled, that it was me.

I was out of control, emotionally raw from watching Shane be put to death. God, he really did look dead. Who knows, maybe I'd I fucked up. Put in the wrong canister. Maybe Jana had played me, and put a lethal dose of gas into the canister.

It's done, no matter what. Move on. Take the pill. Now.

I clapped my hand over my tear-soaked, grimacing, sobbing mouth, and sought the gel capsule with my tongue. Found it... swallowed it. There was enough tear-goop in my throat to choke the capsule down, but I still coughed and gagged.

I slumped my shoulders and kept my hands over my face, taking care to smear the mascara and the lipstick around as much as possible, to intensify the oomph of my big scary reveal.

Hello... there it was... yikes, a nasty sensation. That threatening flush of heat in my face, the itchy tingling, the cold chills. My face started to sting. My immune system was freaking out, right on cue. Now I had to play for time, until the reaction had made me look as grotesque as possible.

"For God's sake, Cassandra," Halliwell's voice was cool. "You're carrying on like a spoiled child. Get a hold of yourself."

I thought of ten different rude things I would have loved to say in response as my eyes puffed almost shut, my lips swelled and distorted, my chin, my cheeks. I felt a clutch of pressure in my throat. Cold chills, as my blood pressure dropped. I had a narrow window before I needed the epinephrine, or I was going down.

I swung around, showing my face.

Their reaction was spectacular. Halliwell gasped and jerked back. At least four of my sisters-in-hell screamed. I struggled to my feet and lurched toward them, lumbering like Franken-stein's monster. They scurried back to put distance between us.

"What in the hell is wrong with you?" Halliwell yelled.

I staggered toward him, as if I was about to fall into his arms, suppressing a manic urge to laugh. "I'm so sorry." My voice burbled with snot. "I'm just having a stress reaction. From seeing him murdered. It's, you know. Upsetting."

"Get away from me!" He shrank back in disgust.

"It's not contagious." I slurred my words, but it was no act, because my tongue was swelling up. "It happens when I get upset. The last time was when I heard Mom had Varen's disease. It'll pass. I'll be able to do the party—"

"No! Nobody can see you like that!" Halliwell snapped. "Go to your quarters! Make sure none of our guests see you. You'd scare them to death. Stop by the infirmary on your way and get yourself a pill, for God's sake."

He turned to the others, looking them over. "Haley," he said. "Get dressed and made-up, top speed. You'll be my hostess today."

Haley gave me a triumphant smirk. "Yes, sir! Right away, sir."

"Jana, get him loaded into the incinerator. I want him gone."

"Yes, sir." Jana spoke with her usual lifeless tone, but her eyes caught mine for a glancing moment, and I thought I caught a fleeting gleam of amusement.

Halliwell stalked out. The sisters-in-hell filed out after him like a flock of ducklings. Silence settled after their voices and footsteps faded.

Jana stared at me, stiff and unfriendly and wary of the cameras. This video had to be convincing. It could be the only thing that saved her. If Halliwell bought it.

"Stop sniveling," she said, in her flattest, deadest voice. "I have to get the cadaver loaded up. You don't have a gas mask, and there's a massive lethal dose in there, so if you don't want to die along with him, you should fuck off right now." She fitted her gas mask over her face, glaring at me. "God. You look like ten different kinds of shit. Eeuww. Get lost."

I caught a glimpse of myself in the glass, and almost yelped. No wonder I'd scared them. I looked like a swollen-up, spray-painted goblin in a ball gown. I sagged against the glass, staring down at Shane's crumpled body. Shit. My blood pressure was plummeting. I could fuck everything up by fainting. Wake up in a hospital, my last chance gone, Shane Masters cremated alive. Reggie next on the list.

No, no, no. Not gonna happen. Stay strong. Hang tough.

I caught sight of the remote Halliwell had used for the gas lying on the arm of the chair. It was similar to the one that was used for the prisoner's collar. I grabbed it and staggered down the corridor to the bathroom. Once inside, I dropped the remote into the bag fastened around my hips under my skirt, and scrabbled frantically until I found the pen-shaped autoinjector.

I stuck it into my arm, felt the sting. Shoved the thing into the garbage. Then I splashed my face with cold water, dabbed it with paper towels, which came away smeared with makeup, and focused on breathing as I waited, ear to the door. The allergic reaction subsided, and my throat opened up. Thank God.

Then I heard it. The *squeak-creak* of the gurney wheels going by. The door of the Level Eight elevator bank opening.

I scrabbled under my skirt again for the syringes and fished out one of the ones that were banded with black plastic. When

I came out the door, the elevator was gone. She'd gone up to Level Six, where the incinerator was located.

I ran as fast as I could in kitten heels toward the stairwell. Pounded up to Level Six. The door was locked, but Halliwell's passcard got me in.

The place was dark. I hoped that would help, if anyone was watching. I wanted them to see the footage of this attack on Jana, but well after the fact. Not in real time.

The elevator dinged, opened. Jana shoved the gurney out with a grunt of effort, turning the lumbering thing away from me and down the hall, toward the open door at the end of the corridor. Light shone out of the door. The only light in the place.

I sneaked up behind her, and stabbed the needle into her neck.

Jana yelped, and crumpled to her knees. "You stupid... bitch," she croaked.

"I'm so sorry. I'm so sorry. I'm so sorry," I babbled. It would be better for the story if I sounded meaner, more pitiless, but fuck it. That was beyond me.

I got behind the gurney with its motionless cargo, and shoved it back toward the elevator, picking up dangerous speed in my panic. When I stopped, our momentum practically made Shane's body bag slide off the gurney. I grabbed his still, limp form just in time and steadied him.

I grabbed the phone and activated Invisibility Cloak. There would be an ugly, anomalous bobble in the footage, but I was hoping that everyone would be distracted enough today with the execution and the big party not to notice. I shoved the gurney into the elevator and pushed the button for Level Three, where the garage for the service crew and outsiders was located. Not Halliwell's private garage with his own fleet of vehicles on Level Two.

Jana's voice echoed in my head. *The shock collar. You have to*

do something about it, or Halliwell will just cut Masters' throat
remotely. Or fry him with electricity.

I had to disable the fucking thing right now. I'd already
memorized the master codes and specs that I'd dug up from
Vincent's files, so I unzipped the bag, entered the codes to deactivate the thing, the codes to unlock the hinge. It was lucky I
memorized things involuntarily, even when stressed. A weird,
freaky quirk of mine. Sometimes it was useful, sometimes it
was a torment. It could be really fucking hard to forget things
that I wanted to forget. But this time around, I was desperately
grateful for it.

I felt the lock snap open. All that was left now was to physi-
cally open the hinge.

Later for that. After he'd agreed to help Reggie. Then I'd be
his benevolent savior. It was evil and manipulative, but a girl
had to do what a girl had to do.

I left Shane on the gurney in the elevator bank, and peeked
out the door into the garage. Here it was, the blank spot in my
improvised escape plan. Could I break into a car and hot-wire it
with only my pocket-knife? Could I find someone to carjack, in
my ball gown and spike heels? Stellar planning, Cass. Just
lovely.

As I looked around, I saw a van driving in. Maybe caterers. I
checked myself in the metal door knob. I looked bad, with
reddened, goopy eyes and smeared makeup, but at least I
looked human. The van was pulling into a parking space. It was
show time.

I clutched the two syringes, and caught up with the driver
as he got out of the van. A tall black guy with a short beard, in a
blue windbreaker. I moved toward him rapidly. "Um, excuse
me?" My voice sounded high pitched, breathless, quavering,
and I didn't even have to fake it. "I was wondering if you could
help me out."

The guy looked me over as I approached, his eyes widening with alarm. Maybe I looked weirder than I thought. "Are you okay, miss?" he asked.

"Not really," I admitted, lunging down to stab the needle into his thigh.

He let out sharp grunt, staring at me as he tried to speak... and failed.

He sagged to his knees. I guided him down as best I could, trying to keep his head from bumping on anything, until he was lying safely on his side.

I straightened up and called out to the guy who had just gotten out of the passenger's side. "Hey! Excuse me? I think your friend is sick! He's down here on the ground, passed out! I don't know what's wrong with him! Could you come over here?"

The other guy, younger, also wearing a blue windbreaker with the same lettering, hustled around the back of the van, alarmed. "What the hell? Galen? What's the matter?" He crouched down over his colleague, shaking him, patting his face.

I stabbed the third needle into the younger guy's shoulder, and let him fall, right on top of Galen. "Gentlemen, I am so sorry," I murmured to them. "I really hope someday I can find you and make it up to you." I crouched down and tugged the windbreaker, with no small difficulty, off the younger guy who lay face down over his friend. It would be huge on me, but a lot less noticeable than a strapless ball-gown.

I tugged the two unconscious men out of the way of the van's tires. Then I opened up the back, and was confronted with a huge ice sculpture, breathing out a fog of awful cold. Oh, God. I was going to have to put that poor guy into a literal ice-box.

I ran for the gurney, shoved it through the garage to the van at a dangerously high speed, rattling and bumping. I got the gurney up right at the edge of the van and climbed inside, kitten heels and all. I grabbed the top of the body bag, and slid Shane inside. I almost didn't manage it. He was so freaking heavy. Six foot two or three, at least, and all solid muscle and sinew. It felt like he was made out of cast iron.

I unzipped the body bag over his face and neck, to make sure he had air. His face looked terrifyingly still and gray. And now I had to worry about hypothermia, too.

Shane's life depended on me getting somewhere fast enough to revive him, before he slipped away, from drugs, from depressed respiration, from the cold. The growing weight of responsibility was driving me wild.

I put my finger to his neck and had a little scare before I felt it... very slow, very faint. *Go-go-go, Cass. Like a bat out of hell. Or he'll drift away, and Reggie's last chance along with him.*

I shrugged on the windbreaker and suddenly thought of what Jana had said about the GPS. I didn't see anything on the dash, but I ran my hand under the frame of the van, all the way around just in case... and oh *fuck,* yes. I got lucky. The magnetic casing of the GPS trace under the car frame was over the back left tire.

I pried it out, and left the thing on the pavement next to the two guys. Then I dug the car keys out of Galen's pants pockets, got into the van, and backed away, leaving those two slumped bodies, one on top of the other, behind me. Hoping desperately that I had not hurt them. Or Jana. Or Shane. Oh, please. I did not want to be responsible for hurting anyone.

Keep moving. When they stop you, they stop you.

There was a pair of cheap sunglasses in the beverage holder between the seats, big goggle-style ones. I put them on. They were huge on me, but they did a good job of covering my smeared makeup. My feet felt unsteady on the pedals. I'd never driven in shoes this ridiculous before. I sped toward the gate, pulled to a halt, and held up the security pass lanyard that dangled from the mirror to show to the guy at the gate.

He leaned over, peered inside. "Wait. Didn't I just let you guys in?"

"Me and my boss, Galen," I said. "He's sending me back to pick up the other ice sculpture. I should be back in about twenty minutes. Thirty, max."

I hunched down, smiling, holding the windbreaker closed. Hoping he hadn't registered the face of the guy in the passenger's seat. Hoping he wouldn't lean close enough to see the big, puffy skirt. That would definitely sound WTF alarm bells.

The guy beckoned me impatiently out. I took the briefest second to feel bad for the fact that he was about to lose his job, and then I swiftly rethought it. He'd be much better off finding a job somewhere other than this scorpion's nest, for fuck's sake.

The gate crawled open, while I jittered in the driver's seat like a pan of popcorn. Tires squealed as I pulled out onto the road. Ouch. Smooth, Cass. Real unobtrusive.

And then I was out on the open road, in a ball gown, in a stolen van, a trail of drugged bodies scattered behind me and an escaped prisoner in the back. I was having a hell of a time easing off the gas pedal. A couple of hairpin turns where I started to spin into the guardrail forced me to slow down. It would be tragically stupid to pitch off a mountainside now and fall to a screaming death.

I knew the countryside, theoretically. I'd spent several sleepless nights at Halliwell's headquarters, studying satellite maps, memorizing every road, every stream or gully or forest. Just in case I found it necessary to run away.

I racked my brains for the first safe, secluded place I might be able to stop to give Shane his wake-up shot. I couldn't wait until I got to my mouse-hole.

I called my hideouts mouse-holes because that was what Mom had called them. She'd always been waiting for the cat to pounce. She'd spent a lot of money outfitting our mouse-holes with stored food, clothes, documents. We had never been forced to use them, but it was a habit that was hard to break, expensive though it was. After she died, I saw no reason to stop the practice. I was careful to contact real estate agents anonymously, to use shell companies and fake names to ship supplies and equipment.

The mouse-hole I'd outfitted near here was a humble cabin in the hills. The agent had followed all my instructions, and when I'd checked it out, everything I needed had been there waiting. An old but functional Jeep was parked outside under a tarp, with a full tank of gas. It had everything I might need to hole up for a little while.

But Shane couldn't wait, or I'd open up the back door to find a corpse.

I came up on an old logging road that led down into a thick stand of fir trees near a dry river-bed. I dug once more into the bag, and pulled out the yellow banded syringe, my hand shaking.

I got out of the van, tottered on my kitten heels on the rocks around to the back. Threw the door open, and climbed in. Jesus, it was so cold. The poor guy was probably getting frostbite. I realized that the ice sculpture was a 3-D rendering of Halliwell Enterprises' corporate logo, a huge stylized HE.

I zipped the body bag down, uncovering the scrapes and bumps and burns and blood smears on the poor guy. I wished I could get that collar off him while he was still unconscious. If he convulsed, he could hurt himself still further with that wire. He might even fatally slice his own throat, like he almost had last night.

But I didn't dare. I had to have some leverage. At least, the remote I had was a dummy prop. That made me feel slightly less cruel and evil. But only slightly.

He had a pulse, barely. So far, so good. I plunged the air out of the syringe Jana gave me to wake him, and injected him before I could psych myself out of it.

Then I waited for all hell to break loose. One second... two... three... four...

I'd just gotten to ten when he yelled, exploding into frantic movement.

CHAPTER 9

Shane

I was in Mom's garden. Dad was there, too. I ran toward them through the sunflowers, the hollyhocks, the tall corn.

"Mom! Dad!" I sprinted, heedless of pea-vines, beans, raspberry canes.

"Stop!" Mom held up her hand.

"Why? Why stop?" I reeled back, heart pumping. Bewildered.

"You can't be here," she said. "Baby, I'm sorry. But no."

I was gripped by a terrible grief and betrayal. "Why not? You don't want me?"

"Always," she said. "But you're not done. You can't stay."

I was frozen in disbelief. Not done? Where to even begin with that?

"Mom," I said. "Get real. No one, in the history of being done, has ever been more done than me."

She shook her head. "No, you're not. Go back. You have to finish this, baby."

I heard a whirring, the grinding, and suddenly the thick slab of glass was between us. I was trapped behind it again. I pounded on it, yelling. I couldn't hear her through the glass, but I saw her reach out *to touch the glass, like Red had done. Her eyes looked so sad. Her lips were moving. I love you, baby, she was saying. Sorry.*

Then she transformed into Red in her pale green ball-gown, mouthing 'I am so sorry, I am so sorry,' as stark agony stung me in the throat, a thousand bees all stinging, inside, outside. Every part of me in burning, writhing pain...

I was screaming. Struggling to breathe, gasping, choking, fighting. Light blazed into my eyes. My arms and tried to flail, but couldn't. I was bound in a straightjacket.

The convulsions slowly eased. I panted for breath. I was so cold. I shivered violently, as if I were naked in the snow. So much light. My eyes stung. The air smelled so different. I was swaddled in... what the hell? A sleeping bag? No. Colder. Tighter.

Red was huddled in against the wall of tiny room that I slowly realized was the back of a van. I saw daylight through the windows on the sides. She was still in her ball-gown, the skirt all puffed out in a circle around her. Her hair had come down.

What the fuck is this? I tried to say it, but I couldn't make my mouth work. I tried again. "Red?" I coughed out.

She was crying, her face wildly smeared with makeup. She wore a shiny blue wrap around her shoulders. "I am so sorry," she said. "But you have to help me now."

Help her? She wanted *me* to help her? That was so messed up, I started to laugh, always a mistake. It made the wire across my throat saw savagely at my raw and swollen flesh. "For real? Have you seen me, Red? You're hallucinating."

"No. I'm not hallucinating, and neither are you," she said. "I found out Halliwell was going to have you gassed to death, so I switched out the gas canisters. I loaded it with a sedative. They thought you were dead."

"So... I'm free? That's what you're telling me?" I could hear the skepticism in my own voice.

"Almost." She reached behind herself, and turned the door handle, pushing open the back door.

The rush almost knocked me out. Blazing outdoor light, the intensely perfumed, hyper-oxygenated outside air. The smell of earth, trees, stone, plants. The rustle of wind in the trees. I sat up, struggling to move in what I abruptly realized was a body bag.

Red pulled the van's back door shut. The wind stopped, the light diminished. The cold made my teeth clack in my mouth.

I struggled to unzip the body bag and peel it off. "What does 'almost' mean?"

"You have to help me out with something first. And then you'll be free."

I puzzled over that for a second, then realized that she was trembling. Her lips were blue. Like she was afraid of me... or of what she had to do. What the fuck?

"Red," I said. "I'm in no condition to help anyone. My resources are all tapped out. So open up that door and get the hell out of my way."

"You have to help me," she said, desperately. "My little sister is trapped in one of his clinics. He said he'd cure her, but I just found out that he was the one who made her sick in the first place. The son of a bitch. He scammed me."

I waited for more. "And? So?"

"I have to save her!" she wailed. "As soon as he knows I busted you out, he's going to punish me by hurting her!"

I shook my head. "How am I supposed to help you? Lady. I'm barefoot, half naked, drugged out of my gourd, fucked up in every possible way. I barely remember my own name. What the fuck do you want from me?"

"Anything! Anything you can do! You owe me!"

"I do?"

"Yes! I broke you out of that place! At great risk to myself! You have to help me now! You're a Masters. You guys are massively rich. Influential. You know all kinds of people from the security company you ran before, right? You could call people. You guys could stage a rescue for Reggie really fast, with the Masters security apparatus."

I shook my head. "I never made any deal with you."

She waved her hand impatiently. "If I had come to you and said, 'will you help me save my sister if I break you out of here,' would you have accepted?"

I snorted. "I would have said you were full of shit."

"Well, as you clearly see, I'm not. So? You owe me. This what I need in return."

I felt a bizarre urge to smile at her wacky reasoning. "Doesn't work that way, beautiful. You never offered me a bargain. I never accepted one. I am not bound by your convoluted reasoning, or a deal that you dreamed up in your head."

"Goddamn it, Masters." Her shaking voice was low, furious. "You fucking owe me this, at the very least. You could get me the help I need. We both know it."

"Why should I put my people in harm's way? It could be a trap."

"What would be the point?" she yelled. "All Halliwell wants is SmokeScreen. Your team wouldn't have that to give him. It would be stupid to set a trap like that. He's not stupid."

I shook my head. "I won't be your tool, Red. I'm very sorry for your problems, and I've got nothing against your little sister. But no. Fuck, no."

She shook her head, eyes streaming with tears. Her mouth shook as she reached into a bag under her skirt... and pulled out a white plastic remote control.

My head buzzed, my belly flopped, my whole body tightened in anticipatory agony. "So," I ground out. "It's like that, huh?"

"It... it doesn't have to be." Her hand, holding the remote, shook as hard as her mouth. "Don't make me do this. Please.

This isn't who I am. I'm not like him. I don't enjoy hurting people. I don't get off on control."

"No?"

"No, I fucking do not! I just want to save Reggie! My innocent little ten-year-old sister! I have money, Masters. As soon as I get access to it, when this is over, I'll give you whatever you want. Hell, I'll give you everything I have. I truly do not give a fuck about any of it. All I care about is Reggie. And I need your help to save her! Please!"

I studied her mascara-smeared face as I pondered my next words. "Pro tip, Red," I told her. "Don't cry and plead when you're holding a mortal weapon on someone. It confuses the living shit out of the person you're trying to compel."

"Oh, fuck you," she snarled. "I'm just asking you to help me save a sweet, awesome little girl. She's a great kid, and she's all I have in the world, and I would do anything to save her. Absolutely anything, okay? Including hurting you. If I have to."

I studied her for a moment, the snarled hair, the heaving bosom, the wild, wet eyes, the red-stained lips. She was a chaotic bundle of emotions. She was not in control.

"No," I said.

Her lips tightened in fierce resolve. "I swear, I will use this on you, Shane. I don't want to, but I will."

"Go ahead," I said. "Do your worst. I'm done being jerked around. I was ready to die back in my cell. I'm still ready. So go ahead. Really."

She just blinked at me, mouth hanging open.

"What's your preference? To fry me with the electricity? Or to garrote me with the wire? There's a lot of water in here, so consider the dangers of conductivity before you pick the electrical option. But the wire, oh man. That'll make a big fucking mess, so brace yourself for it. It'll look like a slaughterhouse. Five quarts of blood in a human body, but it looks like a lot more when it comes shooting out under pressure."

Her face crumpled, and she wiped her eyes angrily with the backs of her hands. "Goddamn you to hell, Masters."

"I'm all ready for hell. My papers are in order. Do it. I'm sick of waiting."

She stared at the remote that was clutched in her hand for a long moment.

Her fingers went limp. The remote thudded down onto the floor of the van.

I let out a slow, even breath, and put my hand up onto the collar. "Can you get this thing off me?"

"Yes," she said.

"I thought it would kill me if I left that place. Isn't that what you told me?"

"It would have, but I entered Vincent's deactivation codes before we left."

I puzzled out the ramifications of that with some difficulty, as fogged with pain and drugs as I was. "So you were bluffing all along?"

She nodded, her mouth tight.

"The remote wouldn't have sent a signal? The collar doesn't work?"

"It's not even the right remote," she admitted. "This was the remote he used to activate the gas in your cell. I swiped it before I left."

"To use as a prop," I said. "To jerk me around."

"That's right," she said stiffly.

"Can you get it off?"

"Take it off yourself. I unlocked the mechanism before we left Halliwell's complex. Pull the sides apart from the back. The hinge in front will open now."

I reached back, my battered, sore shoulders screaming in pain as I felt for that seam with my fingertips. I'd tried to open it before, of course, way back in the day. Many, many times. But it had always held as firm as a rigid, solid ring of steel.

This time, it opened easily, with a gentle, barely audible *click*.

I lifted the thing carefully off myself, hissing with pain as the scabbed skin that had adhered to the metal pulled, tore, stung. *Fuck*, that hurt.

I looked at the hideous thing in my hands, disoriented at how small it felt. My neck felt cold and naked without it. My raw skin burned in the open air.

I looked up at the huge mass of ice beside me. "What the fuck is this?"

"Ice sculpture," she said. "A decoration, for one of his parties. I was all dressed up for it." She plucked at the skirt of her ball gown. "It's the Halliwell Enterprises corporate logo, carved into a ton of ice. What a perfect medium for it."

"How did you get me out of there?"

"I stole the gurney with your body, after your fake execution. Right outside the incinerator room. You were already in a body bag. I brought a stimulant to throw off the effects of the sedative once we were away from the place. Sorry about that. The drugs, the shock. I know it must have felt awful. And probably still does."

"Better than the alternative," I mused. "Which I assume was death."

"Yeah, that was my line of reasoning, too. This van belonged to the ice sculpture guys. I knocked them out. I really hope I didn't hurt them. There was a GPS trace stuck with a magnet under the van, which I pulled out. I hope that was the only one. Not that it matters. If I can't help Reggie, it's all for nothing. Who gives a fuck about any of it."

I tried to picture it all, but it wouldn't come together. This fragile looking creature had mounted a prison break for me, by herself, while I lay unconscious. In the thin hope that I would help save her sister when I woke up. That was true desperation.

I suddenly saw Holly in my head, in her pink sundress,

laughing. Her blond hair wind-tossed. I felt it, right down to my core. What I'd do to protect her.

Which was to say, any fucking thing I could think of. I would do anything, try anything, risk anything. And this girl had given it her all. I saw it in her eyes.

I couldn't throw that back in her face. That wasn't me. That was Red's unique, particular magic. She reminded me of who I was, even when I preferred to forget.

"Do you have a functioning phone?" I asked.

She pulled up her skirt giving me a tantalizing glimpse of her slender, shapely legs, digging into a bag she had rigged to hang beneath it. She pulled out a smartphone, and tossed it at me.

I caught it, and there I was, holding a live telephone in my hand. Smooth, heavy, full of power and potential. It was a heady feeling, after being locked out of time and space for so long. Red sagged against the door, looking tragic.

I pulled up the keypad, and for the first time in I had no idea how long, I deliberately tried to remember something. Ethan's phone number.

My brain didn't have a fucking clue, but fortunately, my fingers did. They plugged in the numbers. The phone rang... and rang... and rang.

Click. The line opened. "Who's this?" Ethan's voice was brusque, suspicious.

Tears sprang in my eyes. I tried to speak, but a dry croak was all that came out of my ruined throat. I coughed and tried again, "Ethan."

Ethan was silent for a moment. "Who is this?"

"It's me," I said.

"Shane?"

"Yes." My voice broke. My throat was shaking now. Too hard to speak.

"Really? Your voice sounds different." His voice was low, tight. Suspicious.

"Yeah, it got pretty fucked up. From Vincent's collar."

"Yeah, I got a taste of that thing. Tell me, Shane. What's Mom's favorite poem?"

"Nature's first green is gold," I said.

"Okay. How about Dad's?"

I hesitated, thinking about it. "Dad didn't like poetry," I said. "He liked westerns and mysteries. And the blues. Old, classic stuff, from the twenties and thirties, like Mississippi John Hurt. He liked 'The Candy Man Blues.' 'You and your Candy Man are getting mighty thick, you must be stuck on your Candy Man's stick.' Remember?"

"Oh, fuck, Shane." Ethan's voice shook. "Where are you?"

"I'll tell you in a minute but first, I need a favor," I said.

"The fuck? What kind of favor?"

"There's this girl," I said. "She busted me out of that place just now, on the condition that I help save her little sister. The kid's stuck in one of Halliwell's clinics."

"So it was Halliwell who had you all along? That fucking lying bastard."

"Yeah, it was him. The kid is Holly's age. And this girl risked a lot to get me out of there. But I don't want to put you guys in danger."

"Fuck danger," Ethan said. "Tell me what you need."

Red stared at me, mouth open, eyes wide and shining with terrified hope.

"I'll put her on the phone," I said. "She can tell you what she knows. It's time-sensitive. He'll punish her for breaking me out by hurting the little sister."

"Like I needed another reason to hate that prick. Pass her over."

I handed the phone to Red, who started talking a mile a minute to my brother, too fast for me to follow. I'd been shaking before, from cold, stress, and whatever mix of drugs were in my system. Now I felt the whole earth shaking. For so long, I had not permitted myself to feel those feelings, or remember my people. I had closed the door on all of it. Hope, love, family, the future. I'd let it all go.

Red had blown all of that up. In just a few seconds, I was rubble.

She was still chattering. I tried to focus in on the words. "... the Cascade Clinic, outside Issaquah. Regina Clarke is her name. She's only ten. I think she's being held in a sub-basement room. She told me she smelled humidity, mold. And she saw big, fiberglass wrapped pipes in the ceiling of the corridor outside when the doctors come in and out. She's never seen another patient there... yeah, I took her there. She said they haven't moved her, unless it was while she was unconscious... I have no idea. I saw what I thought were doctors, nurses, orderlies, admin types. The place looked totally legit, but when I tried hacking into their inpatient database, I couldn't find one... did the building blueprint come through? Yeah, exactly. She'll need a supply of whatever meds they're using, too. Okay. Yeah. I know. I understand. Thanks for giving it a shot. I appreciate it immensely." She leaned to pass the phone to me. "He wants you again."

I took the phone. I craved the sound of Ethan's voice, but the intensity of my feelings were literally painful. I cleared my throat. It was stiff, tight with emotions I had forgotten how to name, let alone negotiate. "I'm here," I croaked.

"You aren't under duress? She's not holding a gun on you?"

I felt my chest shake with dry, rusty laugh. "Nah. She doesn't have the stomach for it."

"That girl is a piece of work," Ethan said. "So. You want us to go save this kid?"

I hesitated. "She busted me out, Ethan," I said. "He was

going to put me down today. With poison gas. She got me out just in time, on her own. It's quite a feat."

"I want to get you first," Ethan said. "Then we get the little girl."

"It'll be too late for the kid if you do," I said. "It might already be too late."

"Okay, we send a helicopter to Issaquah. We hit the clinic with some shock and awe, we get the little girl, and with the other chopper, we come get you. Where are you?"

"No fucking clue." I turned to Red. "Where are we?"

"Washington coast," she said. "About fifteen miles north of Cray's Cove and ten miles inland. No place for a helicopter to land around here. Maybe up on the plateau, near the cabin. I'll send coordinates once we're up there."

I relayed that to Ethan. "Can you do this for her?" I asked. "Are you sure?"

"For you," he said. "I'll do it for you, Shane. If you want me to."

"Okay," I said. "Do it for me. I owe this girl."

"Fine, but I can't believe this. I keep thinking I'm being pranked."

"Me too," I said. "I gotta go. Tell us what happens with the kid."

"Will do. Get me those coordinates. The first second that you can."

"Yeah. Uh... thanks for picking up the phone."

He let out a sharp laugh. "Thanks for still being alive," he said. "Now stay that way, goddammit. Or else."

"I'll do my best. Later, Ethan." I closed the call. My hand shook as I held the phone out to her. "There you go," I said. "I kept my side of your imaginary bargain."

Red's eyes glittered with tears. "You called them," she whispered brokenly. "You didn't have to. Thank you. Thank you."

"Don't thank me," I said. "Thank them, after it's done. I'm

not the one putting my life and my freedom on the line by attacking Halliwell's people. You had better not be fucking with me, Red. Because if my brother or sister or any of my friends get hurt because of this, we are going to have a serious problem."

"I understand, but thank you anyway," she said stubbornly.

"When it's done," I insisted grimly. "It's bad luck before."

Silence fell. Birds sang outside, and the sound that pierced my ears was high and thin and pure, and intensely sweet warble. I focused on her outrageous dress. The big skirt. It was heavily spattered with blood, I realized.

"Are you hurt?" I demanded. "There's blood on your dress."

"Not mine," she said. "It's yours. Your throat, when you were flailing around. After I injected you with the stimulant."

I looked down. Sure enough, my chest was covered with sticky blood. So what else was new. "Bummer about the dress," I told her. "I liked that dress."

She let out a soggy little laugh. "Yeah, this is my life now. On the run in a strapless ball gown." She plucked at the skirt. "This thing was Halliwell's choice."

"He has good taste in ball gowns," I said. "And that is the first, last, and only good thing I will ever say about that perverted, conniving piece of shit."

"No arguments from me," she said swiftly.

"So are you winging this? Or have you got a plan?"

"I don't know if you could call it a plan, but I have a mouse-hole," she said.

I squinted at her, bemused. "A what?"

She looked embarrassed. "Sorry. That's what my mom and I called them. A safe house. She had good reasons to be paranoid, and she liked organizing off-the-grid places we could retreat to. Kind of like mice skittering into a hole in the wall. She went to great lengths so that the paperwork never had her name on it."

"Did you ever use them?"

"No, but they made her sleep better. After she died, I kept them stocked and ready. When Halliwell blackmailed me into this, I organized one nearby. Just in case."

"How far?"

"About ten more miles on the highway, then eight more on a rough mountain road. It's way up in the hills."

"What's there?" I demanded.

"Well, fresh clothes." She looked up and down my bloodied, half-naked body. "At least for me. Cash. An alternate ID, with credit cards and a driver's license. A vehicle with a full tank of gas. And a gun."

That made me sit up and take notice. "A gun? Just one? With ammo?"

"Of course there's ammo. Yes, just one. A Glock 19. Better than nothing."

"Could we get trapped up there? Is there more than one way out?"

"There is a back way. I picked the place out on purpose for that. We could follow a rough dirt road across the plateau, and hook up with a road that goes down into the next valley over."

Huh. It did sound like she'd thought it through, and the prospect of a loaded gun was fucking irresistible to me. "Okay, then. Let's go."

Easier said than done. She tried to help me out of the back, but my legs gave out when I tried to stand, and I almost knocked her down. We steadied each other, leaning against the van. She felt strong, lithe, vibrant. Those long, tangled red curls blowing across her face. So pretty. Those incredible bright green eyes.

"You're freezing, from lying next to that stupid ice sculpture. Hold on." She shrugged off the blue windbreaker that hung around her slim shoulders, and started wrestling it onto me. I tried not to stare at her freckled little tits, dangerously close to popping out of the corset top. "What's the story with this jacket?" I asked. "Where did you get it?"

"Swiped it off one of the ice sculpture guys. Come on, let's get it onto you."

I felt so thick, clumsy. I hadn't worn anything on my upper body since the Vincent and Nicole days, and even then it had been a bloody, sweat-stained tee-shirt. The thing was too small. It twisted and pulled.

"Get into the van," she urged. "Hurry."

She nudged me toward the passenger side door. I was having trouble breathing. The sky was fucking huge. Too much light, too much oxygen. The colors, the smells, the moving air. It was going to my head. Making me dizzy, queasy.

She pulled open the passenger side door, pushed me until I climbed in. Even just sitting in a car seat felt... fuck. So normal. Like a real, regular person.

Red got into the driver's seat, put the van in gear, and we bounced and jounced on the dirt road, climbing until we met a narrow highway. Picking up speed.

I might have signed my own death warrant, believing this girl. Falling for her pleading wiles. But I'd be dead without her for sure. So fuck it.

Watching a gorgeous redhead in a strapless ball gown speeding down the highway like a post-apocalyptic road warrior... damn.

If these moments were to be my final moments, at least they'd be badass.

CHAPTER 10

Cass

I was tongue-tied and shy as I drove. Overwhelmed with emotion. He'd actually taken pity on me and Reggie, after the hell he'd been through. And after I'd just done my absolute best to bully and coerce him, just like Halliwell and his spawn had done.

Admittedly, I hadn't been all that convincing, but still.

Shane Masters was impossible to bully, but I could probably inspire pity in a stone, in my current wretched state. Fine and good. My ego would have preferred to inspire fear and awe, but results were what mattered. And I was disadvantaged in every possible way. For fuck's sake, I was deliberately costumed as a damsel in distress.

Reggie's fate was in someone else's hands now. They would either act on my rushed, spotty, incomplete info, or they would not. And there was nothing I could do about it. I'd played every card, exhausted every idea. I was in no condition to mount an attack on the Cascade Clinic myself, unarmed, dressed in a blood-spattered ball gown and kitten heels. Besides, the place was hours away from me by car.

Halliwell had to know we were gone by now. The anxiety was driving me wild.

I sneaked a glance at him. Shane looked strange, with the blue windbreaker I'd swiped from the ice sculpture guy straining over his broad shoulders. His blood-stiffened hair stuck out every which way, his lacerated neck looked awful. He needed disinfectant ointment, bandages, clothing, shoes, antibiotics, fluids, a decent meal. There was no end to what he needed. And yet, he sat there, calmly taking it all in. Tough as nails.

He shot me a frowning glance. "Eyes on the road, Red."

"My name is Cass, by the way." I told him. "Cass Clarke."

"Okay. Good to know."

We were in the woods now. The road was very rough. The van with its massive load of a ton of ice and the heavy melt mechanism and tank beneath it lurched and wallowed in the muddy road, which was wet from the recent heavy rain. "It's not far," I told him. "Just a few miles."

"You really think we're better off stopping rather than moving," he said.

"I do, actually," I said. "We look like a circus act. Anyone who sees us would remember us. And we're driving a stolen vehicle. I want to ditch this van."

"Yeah, that would be smart."

"I have an old Jeep up at the cabin. Registered to one of my alternate identities."

"Alternate identities, plural? You have more than one? What are you, a spy?"

"I lead a complicated life," I said. "The Jeep looks like hell, but it goes."

"I feel his breath on the back of my neck," he said.

"Yeah, me too, but we won't stay long. Just to wash off the blood, change, grab my go-bag, switch out vehicles. We can get

ID, credit cards, gas, cash, shoes I can actually walk in..." I cut myself off, shooting a guilty glance at his feet.

A faint smile curved his mouth. "Don't have my size, huh?"

"I have stuff to fit me and Reggie," I admitted. "That's all."

"I'll manage," he said. "My people will get to us soon."

I abandoned my attempts at conversation to concentrate on the road, which climbed steeply, switching back often. I had to slow way down on the broken, narrow sections, many of which were washed out. I hoped that the heavily-laden van would make it up that steep final grade to the cabin. I supposed we could stop and dump the ice sculpture, but time was tight, and I didn't want to lose a second.

We reached the approach to the cabin, which was in a pine grove near the top of a bluff. The last stretch of road rose steeply, at what felt like a forty-five-degree angle.

I muttered encouragement and random profanity to the van, insulting and encouraging it in equal measure it as it spun out in the mud, struggled, lurched... and finally gained traction, lumbering up and over the muddy, stony ground. Thank God.

Near the cabin, the tree branches of several pines had grown down into a shaggy canopy over the road. The van crashed through them, crunching, scratching, swishing over the vehicle. We were temporarily blind, and then suddenly we emerged into a gloomy, green-tinted enclosure. The cabin was hidden inside of it. A tree cave.

That green canopy was what had sold me on the place when I was looking for a mouse-hole near Halliwell's lair. I loved that tree cover. I felt like I could go to ground, like a fox. Maybe even be hidden from the possible drones above me.

The road leveled out at the top. I braked near the funky little cabin, almost hidden by overgrown foliage. It looked just as it had when I had left it several weeks ago, when I'd sneaked out to check that the place was properly stocked.

I let the phone take note of the longitude and latitude,

pulled the number Shane had called up. I texted the coordinates, and then a message.

> We'll be here briefly, then we'll head due north on the dirt road that cuts across Burnt Prairie.

"Who are you texting?"

"Your brother," I said. "He wanted coordinates."

He nodded his agreement, and we got out. It was so quiet here, hushed under the shelter of the trees. He strode out into the middle of the clearing and looked up, staring at the sun filtering through the trees, head flung back. Chest heaving.

It must be an incredible feeling for him. The sky, the trees, the air. The world.

I picked my way with some difficulty to the tree I had chosen, the hidden notch in the branches where I had left the keys. Almost broke a leg tottering back over the rocky ground. I made it to the front door and up the weather-beaten steps to the porch.

It was pitch dark inside. I'd left the shutters closed. I made my way around the main room and opened them, which helped, but it was still dim because of all the tree cover. I switched on the light, kicked off my hellfire-and-brimstone kitten heels, and gave myself a brisk shake. I needed a plan. Sensible, methodical. I looked out the door, and saw Shane, still motionless, staring up at the trees. Overcome by it all.

I got it. I'd do the same in his shoes... or lack of them. But we had no time to bask in the glory of nature, no matter how much he needed it.

"Shane," I said. "This is a quick in-and-out, okay?"

He looked at me. "Yeah," he said hoarsely. He cleared his throat. "Fine."

He looked so overwhelmed. His eyes burned with emotion. It made me want to cry, and I didn't have time for empathy. I was asking so much of the poor guy. He'd been viciously mistreated, and I didn't even have time to be nice to him right now.

Aw, screw it. He might as well stare up into the trees while that bathroom was being used. That gave him a few minutes of grace. "Could you stay out there and keep watch for couple of minutes while I change?" I asked.

His eyes sharpened. "Sure. Where's that gun you mentioned?"

Whoa. So much for letting him emote and commune with the trees. "It's inside, in the safe," I told him.

He sharpened right up at the prospect of a firearm. I opened the small wall safe behind a cheesy wall-hanging, and handed the Glock 19 to him. His face got sharply focused as soon as he had a gun in his hands. He slid in the full magazine into it with a soft click, and glanced at me with a frown. "Do your thing, Red. I'll be outside."

Well, well. Look who just put himself in charge like he was born to it. But it seemed ungracious to complain, considering, so I snapped right to it.

I opened up the box of clothes I'd left on the bedroom floor. One had summer clothing, another had winter stuff. I pulled out a few items that looked just right. Dark colored, comfortable, durable, oh God, yes. I brought the clothes into the bathroom, and took a few moments to swab off the raccoon mask with makeup wipes, a truly magnificent invention. I was one of those lazy bitches who took off makeup with a pack of wipes while lying in bed. If I took it off at all.

My hair was a snarled mess, but no time to fuss with it. I twisted it up into a knot and showered just long enough to rinse away the sticky smears of Shane's blood.

I tossed the ball gown and underwear into the corner, pulled on my fresh clothes. Ahhhh. When I was dressed, I looked out the front door. He stood there like a sentinel. Prehistoric man, listening with all his keen senses for some approaching predator.

"Shane?"

He jerked his head around, eyes questioning.

"Want some bathroom time? I have antibiotic soap in the first aid box. You should wash those wounds on your neck in the shower, and I'll put some disinfectant on them. I think I have some bandages in there, too."

"You'll keep watch?" he asked.

I nodded, and he handed me the gun. I'd learned to use it, at my mother's insistence, but I'd never enjoyed it. Still, I was grateful we had it now.

We? I was thinking 'we.' That was very dangerous. It would be better to think of him, and me. Absolutely separate. I had to keep that very clear in my head. Shane was an unknown quality, with an unknown agenda. In spite of that phone call, and, well... everything.

Until I saw Reggie safe and well, the vote wasn't in on Shane Masters.

I'm sure he expected me to stand outside scowling at the world with the gun clutched in both hands, but we didn't have time. I checked the go-bag for my essentials. Thirty thousand in small bills, a car title for the Jeep registered to Layla Stearns. Layla also had a credit card, a driver's license and a voter's registration card. I hadn't bothered to stock the pantry, but there was a box on the kitchen counter. I tore into it and pulled out wrapped items with more or less nutritional value. Candy, nuts, protein bars, and the like. I tossed a handful of them into the go bag.

That was the extent of my culinary talents, as Reggie could attest. I was the queen of takeout, in normal times. Reggie was a good sport about it, thank God.

"Why aren't you outside keeping watch?"

I jumped at his disapproving tone, and then gasped.

It never ceased to amaze me. Freshly showered, still toweling off, wearing only the blood-spotted jersey sweat pants. Naked chest, cut, lean, powerful. His oh-my-freaking-God stunning good looks on full display again. His eyes looked laser sharp.

But oh God, his neck. It looked like raw meat. That must hurt so freaking much.

I focused on that, to keep myself honest. "Ah... your neck. Let's work on it."

"That soap stung like a motherfucker. I might have screamed a little bit."

"I didn't hear you, so it doesn't count," I told him. "Let me put some stuff on it."

"Later for that. We're in a rush."

"No," I said. "You can't leave that wound exposed. It needs disinfectant, a bandage, and a doctor, in that order. Let me medicate your neck. This fucking instant."

He gave me a brief, amused smile. "Fine, if you insist. But be quick."

I followed him with the first aid box into the bathroom, and he sat down on the closed toilet to let me do as I pleased. It was disconcerting, being so close to him. He winced as I smeared the ointment over those raw sores. It was worse on the front of his neck, from all the wire cuts, but it was red and angry and inflamed all the way around.

I wound some gauze bandages gently around it, and tied it off. "There. That'll have to do until you get to a doctor."

He stood up, and looked at himself in the bathroom mirror. "Very stylish," he said. "I should tie a silk scarf around it."

His skin was goose-bumped from the chill, and his lips were pale and bluish. He needed to warm up, and that windbreaker just wasn't going to cut it.

I had a sudden idea. "Come into the bedroom," I said. "I

have a long sweater. It might look a little weird on you, but
you'd be warmer, and it's just until we get someplace safe."

I rummaged through the winter box, and pulled out a beige
and cream striped cashmere thing with a big, wide boat neck.
On me, it hung down to the middle of my thighs. He pulled it
on, and made a doubtful sound in his throat as he looked at
himself in the mirror. He tugged one side of the boat neck
down over one shoulder.

"I look adorable," he remarked.

I giggled helplessly. "Don't make me laugh, or I'll cry. And if
I start to cry... well, you don't want to deal with that, trust me.
We're on the clock here."

He struck a fey pose and batted his eyes girlishly, and
suddenly I was snorting and giggling like an idiot. "Fuck you,
Masters. Not fair. Don't. No time."

"Sorry," he murmured. "Oops. My bad."

My phone rang, and we both practically levitated off the
ground. "Oh, God," I muttered, racing to the bed where I had
left it. I grabbed it, hit 'talk.' "Hello?"

"Is this Cass?" It was a woman's voice, low and purposeful.

"Yes, that's me."

"My name's Kat. I work with Ethan. Talk to your sister. She's
confused and upset." An instant's pause, then, "Cass?" Reggie's
voice, high and thin and wobbling.

Tears filled my eyes. "Yes, baby, it's me. Are you okay?"

"Um. Yeah. Just... I didn't know what to think! These people
just exploded into my room. This lady with them asked if I was
Regina Clarke, and she said they were your friends, and to
come with them. But I didn't know! So they just grabbed me
and took me out of there with them, but I didn't know who they
were!"

"Of course you didn't, and I'm so sorry. It all happened too
fast to warn you. They are my friends, baby, they truly are.
They're helping me. I needed to get you out of there fast. I saw

my chance, and I took it. I'm so sorry I didn't give you a heads-up."

"Okay," Reggie quavered. "Where are you? Why aren't you here?"

"I'm on my way, sweetheart. Go with them, okay? They're on our side."

"Okay. Cass, when will you—"

"That's all we have time for." The woman's voice again. "I'm hanging up now so that Ethan can call you for the rendezvous."

In seconds, the phone rang again. I silently handed it to Shane.

He locked eyes with me as he opened the line. "Yeah?... yeah. We're about to take off. Too dangerous to stay. We'll go north, off-road. Burnt Prairie... yeah. I'll call you... yeah. Later, bro." He hung up, and smiled at me. "Mission accomplished."

I wiped away astonished tears. "It all happened so fast."

"My brother is one laser-focused sonofabitch."

So are you, I wanted to say, but I could barely get the words out.

"Cass. Don't cry. I like it better when you laugh." His arms encircled me.

And it hit me again, that blinding rush of emotion that just picked me up and carried me away, just as it had on Level Eight, with that prick Halliwell watching us like a big spider. But Halliwell wasn't here now. It was just me and Shane, all alone.

He was so strong. So solid and powerful, vibrating with energy. My face was pressed against the beige striped sweater, my lips touching his hot skin. His collarbone right at eye level. His chest hair rasped against my cheek. I grabbed that sweater. Lifted it up over his head. Flung it away.

I wrapped my arms around his shoulders, and it was like it had been ordained since time began to grab him, to kiss him, to wind around him, frantically drinking him in like someone was trying to snatch him away from me.

CHAPTER 11

Shane

I didn't have a hope in hell of controlling this. I was gutted inside, so when something powerful swept through me, it found no resistance. And I felt none from her, either. Just hunger, eager and sweet and seductive.

Maybe this was a thank-you fuck for brokering her sister's rescue. I didn't know, and I didn't care. I gave in to the clawing need. My hands were all over her slim, sinuous body. I cupped those high, tight little tits against my hands as I wrenched off the stretchy gray sweatshirt, tossing it off to the floor. Her hair rose up, electrified, clinging to her face and to mine, to my hands, buzzing with static, silky soft. Her lips were so fucking sweet, so tender. Opening to me in soft, dreamy surrender.

She let out little choked gasps of delight as I touched those sweet tits, those tight little dark pink nipples. I bent to taste them, suckling them, swirling my tongue around, around. Her hot velvety skin was so smooth, so exquisitely perfect.

She sobbed, dragging my head to her chest as I suckled and licked her breasts. Her legs wound around me. She was pulsing her pussy against my thigh.

I jerked the pants and the panties down, and she was naked, shivering in the cold air. Pressed up against the cheap pine-paneled wall, her eyes dilated with excitement. She let out a cry, writhing against my hand as I slid my fingers up and down her pussy slit. God, she was so hot and wet, so slick and silken and perfect. I caressed her hot, tight little hole with slow, thrusting caresses of my fingers while I sought out her clit with my thumb. I let her body guide me. She was circling her hips, squeezing her pussy desperately around my fingers, working herself eager, making those awesome pleading sounds.

Almost there... and oh... *yes.* God, yes.

She let out a wrenching cry as the orgasm throbbed through her. Her face was cherry red, and so was my dick, when I pulled it out, prodding her eagerly as I cupped her ass and lifted her up to just the right height. Her legs draped over my arms, legs spread out wide. I pressed my aching cockhead between her slick, tender pussy lips, pressing against the resistance. She licked her lips. "Shane," she whispered.

"You want it?" That was the most eloquent thing I could manage.

She gave me a nod, thank God, and I pushed forward. We both made noise as I forced my cock slowly inside her hot, clinging depths. I loved her whimpering moan of pleasure as I eased back out. Fucking incredible.

I surged forward again, deeper. Each stroke left me shiny, gleaming with her balm. Long, slow, gliding strokes, at least for the first few minutes. We wound together, her legs twined around my thighs, bracing herself. Lifting herself. Thrusting, sighing.

Then the pace picked up, and her nails dug in, and I was driving deeper, harder, jolting her against the wall with each stroke. She was so damn beautiful, her soft open mouth panting for air, her hypnotically gorgeous eyes gazing into mine, dazed with astonishment. Her beautiful, flushed, heaving tits. Her fingernails, clamped into my shoulders. Her beautiful pussy lips, hot pink and shining, yielding to me. Each thrust was a wet, eager, suckling caress, on the in-stroke, on the out-stroke, and oh wow... she was working up to another big one. And now I was, too. Couldn't stop it, or slow it.

There were a million good reasons why this was a terrible idea. The time, ticking away. The danger, circling in. But nothing seemed as important as fucking this woman just like she needed me to fuck her, until the tension shattered, and pleasure surged through her body, massaging my dick like squeezing fingers, milking me... pulling me.

I exploded, and gave her all that I was in that crashing release.

I was squishing her slender body against the wall, I realized. I leaned back, looking into her face. "You okay?" I ground out.

She nodded. "Great," she whispered.

I forced myself to drag my reluctant dick out of her, realizing all at once that I had come inside her. Without a single thought. I'd never done that before. I was always careful. I always used latex. But with Red, I had forgotten that latex existed.

I set her on her feet, and without a word, she gathered up her clothes and fled with them into the bathroom.

I pulled my pants back up and put the tight, girly sweater back on. Water began to run. I went out, amazed that I had left the door unlocked and the gun unattended.

Halliwell's goons could have just walked in here, completely unchallenged.

I went out the back door, and peered down into the narrow space between the trees where I could glimpse the road far below ... and saw a flash of movement.

My heart thudded. I saw another. Big black SUV's. Shiny as black widows.

I barged into the bedroom. "Red!" I yelled. "We've got company!"

Cass

I rinsed off the evidence of my complete and total lapse in judgement, which was currently trickling down the inside of my legs. God, I could barely stand, or hold the detachable shower nozzle in my shaking hand. My legs shook.

I had not known that an orgasm could be... well, on that scale. It was too much. Overwhelming. Like being disassembled, down to my smallest parts. Everything I thought I was, everything I thought I knew, zeroed out, gone. No certainties, no self, no clue, until my brain floated back and resumed doing its job.

And my brain took its own sweet time about that.

How he could drive me to that place when we were under such pressure, I would never know. He must be some kind of sex god, because I was a tough nut to crack. It was difficult to make me come. Hell, I had a hard time doing the job all by my own lonesome self. Let alone when I let someone else try to do it.

But one touch from that man, and I melted down into a writhing, whimpering mess. I did not even know that wild, desperate woman.

Probably it was the rush of energy that the good news about Reggie's rescue had given me. It had shocked my glands into freak-out mode. Temporary insanity, brought on by a shock of unexpected joy and relief.

I dried off with my sodden towel, and was yanking my pants up over my shaking legs when a sharp knocking on the bathroom door made me jump and squeak.

"Hey! Red!" Shane called, his voice urgent. "We've got company!"

That killed my buzz in a hurry. I vaulted out the door and pulled on my shoes with feverish haste. "Where? Who?"

"On the road. On the switchbacks down below. We don't have much time."

I tied laces with icy, shaking fingers, messed them up, tried again. "Couldn't it just be some random car using the road?"

"Two identical black late model SUVs, one right after the other? I doubt it. Is this your only gun?"

"Yes. It never occurred to me that I'd need more than one," I said.

He was already in the kitchen, rummaging through kitchen drawers and pulling out random items. A corkscrew, a bunch of old, battered kitchen knives. He picked out a couple of the knives. "There's probably at least four, maybe five guys in each vehicle," he said. "I'll take the gun. Which means that you can't help me except by disappearing. The cabin is a death trap. Run into the woods, and do not come back unless I call you."

"No! I can't just leave you to—"

"You can't help, Red. You'd just fuck my focus."

"But I—"

"Give me the car keys."

"You mean, the Jeep? You want to try to outrun them?"

"No, the one we came in," he said.

I grabbed the van's key fob off the kitchen counter and offered it to him. He seized the back of my shirt, and frog-marched me out onto the porch. "Run. Go. Now."

"But you can't go anywhere with that van! It can't handle the bluff road up over the ridge! I told you! Particularly not with that huge block of ice in the back!"

"I have a plan. No time to explain." He shoved me out the door. "Run!"

I just stood there, utterly dismayed, as he loped toward the van. I darted back inside, and rummaged through the same drawer that Shane had looked through. He'd taken the likely looking knives. The rest looked barely capable of buttering bread.

There was a big rolling pin, so I grabbed that. Better than nothing.

When I got back out, Shane had backed the van down to the steep incline, and the edge of the tree canopy that hid the cabin. He came around to the back, and opened both of the van's back doors. Then he looked over at me, his dark brows knit up with fierce disapproval. "I told you to run," he said, eyeing the rolling pin I was clutching.

"You did," I said.

"You don't follow orders very well, do you, Red?"

"Nope. And I told you. My name is Cass."

"Let's make a deal," he said. "I promise to use your real name if you run like hell. When the time comes, I'll call out and say, hey Cass! All clear! Come out, Cass! Okay? Do we have a deal?"

"No," I said. "I started this thing, and I am not running from it."

"Fuck," he muttered. "You are a pain in my ass, Red."

"So they all tell me," I said, following him through the big, draping boughs thick with tufts of pine needles, to a spot where we could peer through the waving foliage and see a piece of the road below.

The first vehicle passed, not more than a couple hundred yards down the hill from us. Then the second one stopped, and two men got out. They were dressed in forest camo, and heavily armed.

"Friendly neighbors, hmm? Rando cars?" he murmured.

"Shut up, Shane," I snapped. "It was a perfectly reasonable question."

"You can ask reasonable questions in a reasonable world,"

he said. "Ours isn't. I bet those motherfuckers are armored. I bet they're counting on me being all fucked up, and you being a clueless bimbo who won't run and hide. Easy pickings."

I just stared at him, not taking the bait.

He made an impatient sound. "You stay put right there, and watch the road," he said. "As soon as they pass that bent-over tree next to the big bare rock tower, with the monolith bit up on top? Give me a signal. Can you do that for me?"

I nodded. Shane moved, swiftly and soundlessly on his bare feet over the rocky mountainside. He got into the van, his eyes fixed on me, waiting for my signal.

I peered through the branches, my heart in my mouth, watching those vehicles, their occupants hidden behind the dark tinted glass as they crawled up the steep hill, getting closer and closer. They passed the bent-over tree. I gave Shane a thumbs-up.

He jumped out, ran around to the front of the van, and pushed it hard downhill, stumbling down to his hands and knees as it took off, rolling backward faster and faster.

It exploded out of the canopy of branches with a loud crunching and snapping sound. The SUVs braked. The doors of the vehicles flew open as the van hurtled down the bumpy road toward them, but they didn't react fast enough, and *crash*, the van plowed into the front SUV, crumpling it and crushing the men trying to get out.

The huge HE ice sculpture inside flew out of the back, soaring as if from a catapult, tumbling, turning...

Crunch, it landed on the second SUV, caving in the driver's side.

Holy *shit*. I stared down at the carnage, mouth agape. I felt a hand on my shoulder, and almost yelped. I turned to find Shane with his finger on my lips, his eyes intense. He was shaking his head. He held up four fingers. Pointed down.

Four of those guys, still on the loose out there.

He gestured at a grove of sapling fir trees that was the closest cover we could see, his eyes fierce. Then he melted into the trees, to do God knows what. The guy was half naked, barefoot, alone, and he was already kicking their asses. Wow.

I crept through the pine boughs, getting cobwebs, pine needles and pitch in my mouth, trying to see what Shane was doing down there, but he was a ghost. At one point, I saw some small trees shaking violently, and then an angry shout. Not Shane's voice. Shortly after, I heard gunfire... then three shots of return fire.

Shit. Now what? I couldn't run away now. Shots had been fired. What if Shane was lying down there, shot? Bleeding out?

There were two levels to my thinking. One was just thinking Reggie, Reggie, Reggie. I could not face these people and say, 'so sorry, but I couldn't keep him alive long enough to make the trade for my sister.' That would go over like a lead balloon.

Chances were, these people weren't monsters. Shane wasn't. Only sociopathic freaks like Halliwell would hurt a little girl for revenge, or for fun. But still.

The other part of me was just screaming Shane's name. *Come out, damn it. Show me you're okay. Please. I'm dying up here.*

I sneaked down the hill, keeping myself low, mostly crawling on my belly or sliding on my ass, depending on the incline. I slithered down low, between the biggest rocks or tufts I could find for cover. Finally, I heard sounds of combat, feet hitting flesh, grunts, pants, thuds. I was close to the vehicles now. The closest one, the one wrapped around the ice sculpture van, was a blood drenched, gory mess, and I looked away quickly. No one had escaped that impact. I kept going, finding big chunks of broken ice scattered here and there. An almost complete H, missing half of one of its legs. I crab-walked around a big rock, and found myself alongside a sprawled man in forest camo with a cheap kitchen knife sticking out of his eye.

His remaining brown eye looked blank and surprised.

I hurried away, and crawled alongside the second vehicle. I spotted the Glock 19 lying on the grass, and was just starting to go for it when a man flew past my face and hit the ground, with a sharp, huffing grunt.

I felt a hot liquid against my face. Blood spatter. The guy was blinking at me, as blood sprayed out from his neck. His throat had been slashed.

I peered around the car. Shane was fighting with another guy, ducking back, evading a booted foot that whooshed past his nose, dancing to evade a knee to the balls, but with every move the guy drove him back, toward the steep, rocky slope behind him.

Shane danced back to avoid a face kick, but leaned too far, sliding and scrambling down the hill as he tried to find purchase.

The guy dove for the Glock, and scooped it up with a bark of laughter. "I'll shoot you in the face with your own fucking gun, you piece of shit!" he howled.

His gun arm rose, and I darted out from behind the SUV and swung hard with the rolling pin. It hit the back of the man's head. *Crack.*

He made a surprised sound, wobbled... and fell forward.

I stood there, swaying on my feet. The wind whipped my tangled, blood-spattered hair into my mouth. I tasted salty blood. Couldn't even remember whose.

"Sh-sh-shane? Are you there? Are you shot? Are you okay?" My voice sounded small and insignificant. Like the wind was whipping it away from my mouth.

Shane's face appeared as he clambered up over the rocks below, scratched and bloodied, but alive. He stopped when he saw me, and analyzed the scene in one sharp glance. He nodded in approval. "I'm good," he said. "Thanks to you."

"Me? Hah! You just took out nine commandos, barefoot, with one handgun!"

"Eight. And they were hesitating to shoot me. That's the only reason I'm still on my feet. Their orders must have been to take us alive. Me having a gun surprised the living shit out of them. That last guy probably just lost his temper. But you were the game-changer, Red. You saved my ass."

"You are so full of shit," I quavered. "You crazy bastard. My name is Cass."

"Let's argue about that later." He crouched beside the guy I had bashed with the rolling pin. None of these guys were in my hell-sibling group, and I was very grateful for that. The hell-siblings may have been hostile and petty and contorted, but I had felt sorry for every last one of them. I did not want to see them meet an ugly death.

"This one's still alive," Shane said. "And two of the others are still breathing. They won't be chasing us, but it looks like Halliwell knows exactly where we are. Which means we should get the hell out of here right now."

"Fine by me," I said, and then I noticed the blood on the rocks where his feet had stepped. "My God, Shane! Your feet! They're all torn up! We have to—"

"Later. Let's get the Jeep keys and your phone, and scram."

He set the pace himself, messed up feet and all. We hurried up the hill, past the wrecked vehicles. I saw a body twitching. Still alive, but he wasn't getting any first aid from me. "Can't you get a pair of boots from one of them?" I asked. "Or another gun?"

"I'm tempted," he said. "But I'm too worried about GPS traces, and he already tracked us once. Probably the van. Halliwell is a devious bastard. It's his defining characteristic. Better not to give him any openings."

"I wish I hadn't," I admitted. "But he creates his own openings. Like when he made my little sister sick on purpose to manipulate me."

"Well, she's safe now," Shane said.

I didn't reply. Partly because I couldn't breathe, partly because I knew that she wasn't safe at all. I didn't know how Halliwell had made Reggie sick, or know how to fix it. Maybe the Masters team had snatched her before Halliwell could make an example of her, but if she got sick again now, I was right back to square one. I would have my sister, but no cure. Which amounted to a handful of dust and ashes.

Later for that. I ran inside for the go bag. My alt identity was fried now that Halliwell had found this place. So much for the very expensive Layla Stearns and all her credit and gear and well-establish background. But the phone, the protein bars, the clean underwear and the cash, those might come in handy.

I yanked the tarp off the Jeep, and we got in. It smelled damp and stale in there, and I was pretty sure I heard the skittering of tiny frightened feet. Some rodent or other had nested in there. I just hoped to God that they hadn't chewed through any cables or belts, or gobbled up brake fluid, or whatever hungry forest rodents liked to gnaw.

I got the thing in gear, and the engine gave me a reassuring roar. I tossed my bag onto his lap. "Phone's in there. You do communications."

"You have a route planned out?"

"Yes. There's a sort of a road up to the top of the bluff, and then a track that leads all the way across the plateau," I said. "We'll just get up to the top and drive right across Burnt Prairie until we hit the road for Dalton Mills. It's rough, but doable."

"Prairie? Sounds flat."

I tried to retrieve the images from the satellite photos that were in my head. "Yeah, more or less," I said. "It gets flatter a few miles northeast."

He made a phone call to his brother, and I concentrated on

keeping the Jeep moving. It wallowed and jounced in the long grass, banging and scraping over rocks. I couldn't concentrate on what he was saying, but his tone was brusque and practical as he recounted what happened in a few terse words, and shared where we were heading.

He was in studly-hero mode. What he had accomplished was incredible. On the fly, with every possible disadvantage. Nothing but his wits and what he scrounged up from a cheap vacation rental kitchen. Barefoot, bleeding, toxic from being jerked around by drugs and put on ice in a body bag. And all that after suffering months of imprisonment, interrogation and torture.

Images of the bodies scattered on the hillside kept flashing through my mind. Strange details, the blood spray across the angle of the E of the ice sculpture. A symbol of Halliwell's influence, carved into a ton of ice. How fucking appropriate was that.

Well, suck it, Halliwell. Suck it like a big old blood-spattered popsicle.

That silly thought made me almost laugh, but I quelled the impulse. Just like crying, it could push me over the edge, and I would end up gibbering and useless.

Shane was looking at me, with a worried frown. "You good?"

That almost made me laugh, too. What about any of this could be called good?

Come to think of it, being pinned against the bedroom wall by a big, hot, sexy guy while he furiously fucked me into mindless oblivion... that had been very good. "I'm fine," I said shakily. "What's your brother have to say?"

"They're on their way to Burnt Prairie with a helicopter. Let's hope Halliwell doesn't send a helicopter after us. He's closer than my brother."

This thing kept getting bigger in scale. Like a world war. "God," I muttered.

"Sorry. Never mind what I just said. Just drive. Chances are, he won't want that kind of exposure. Someone could see."

We jolted and bounced over the rough track in the grass. The trees had thinned out, and we were finally at the top of the plateau. I could see the ocean from up here, beyond the clefts of the lower hills. The sun was low. The sky was turning a bloody color, like that blood-splotched rolling pin. I kept hearing the blow as it connected with the man's skull. The contact, vibrating through my body.

The guy with the knife sticking out of his eye. The spatter of blood from the slashed throat. The huge crash of the van hitting the SUV, all the crumpled, fragmented bodies. The ice sculpture, flying, turning... landing. *Crunch.*

"Whoa! Slow down" Shane touched my arm. "You'll break the axel!"

"Sorry," I whispered.

"Want me to drive?"

I looked down at his bare, bloodied feet. "I can do it."

"Okay, but simmer down, okay?"

"Fine," I said, and very suddenly thought of the perfect way to distract myself. "Um. I have a quick question for you. If we're going to see your family soon."

"Yeah? Let's hear it."

"Do you have a wife? Girlfriend? Your daughter's mom? Is she in the picture?"

He shot me an incredulous look. "Really? We're having that conversation now?"

"Well, you just fucked me now, so yeah. I'd like a chance to brace myself for... whatever. It's not too much to ask. To avoid, you know. Weirdness."

He was silent for a moment. "Holly's mother is dead."

I negotiated swiftly around a series of Jeep-swallowing-sized holes in the road. "I'm, ah, sorry to hear it."

"It was a car accident," he said. "Holly was two. We'd had a huge fight, and Trish took the car to pick up Holly at the baby-sitter. At ninety miles an hour. She was a rage-driver. Very hot-headed kind of woman. She ran a light, and a truck plowed into her. Spun her around, flipped her car. She wasn't wearing a seat belt."

"God," I whispered.

"Holly wasn't in the car. But she very easily could have been."

"That's so awful," I said. "I'm glad your daughter was okay."

"My parents died that same way, oddly enough," he said. "It really laid me out for a while. Lucky for Holly, my brother and sister were both there to help."

"Ah. I see. Yeah. That was... lucky."

"I was a mess. For a long time after. We were already in trouble as a couple when it happened. At that point, I was sick to death of her tantrums and about ready to throw in the towel. But after the accident, I was so angry at her for depriving Holly of a mother. And at myself for handling things badly. Getting her all wound up. The whole thing was a total shitshow."

"I can imagine," I said carefully.

"It put me off relationships for years. I haven't had what you would call a serious girlfriend since then. Sex, yeah. Plenty of sex. But no strings."

"Is that what we just had? No-strings sex?"

"I don't know what we just had. It just happened. Just drive, okay?"

I did so, as the light started to fade. The clouds faded to a darker pink, then a sullen purplish gray like a bruise, and then, it was fading twilight, with fog gathering all around. A cloud was sitting on the top of this mountain, and we were about to plunge into it.

He put his hand on my arm. "Slow down. Let's wait for Ethan here. If we go any further, we'll get lost in that fog. I don't think you could even see the road."

My instinct was to keep moving at all costs, but Shane was on the phone with his brother again, so clearly, they had a plan, along with my baby sister.

I jerked to an abrupt stop, and the long grass stopped swishing loudly against the undercarriage.

"They're coming," he assured me. "Any time now."

Sure enough, in barely over a minute, a helicopter took form out of the darkness, like a wraith in the clouds. It got bigger, louder. It hovered over the Jeep, insanely loud, then moved over to the open ground. It hovered there until we got out of the Jeep.

I grabbed my bag, and we started making our careful way over the rocky ground. Slow going for Shane, with those tormented feet. The helicopter touched down.

The door opened, and two men jumped out and ran toward us.

Shane stopped as they came closer. The look on his face took my breath.

I recognized the man running toward him. The paparazzi followed him everywhere. Ethan Masters, tech-bro billionaire, ladies' man, too handsome for his own good. He used to be America's favorite dreamy bachelor, until he fell for a mysterious blonde who didn't give interviews. He subsequently retreated mostly out of sight with his beautiful lady friend, breaking all the ladies' hearts in one fell blow.

But even if I hadn't seen him in magazines and online, I could have guessed that they were brothers. Ethan was also incredibly handsome. The amazing cheekbones, the piercing eyes. It was a family trait, evidently.

Ethan grabbed his brother's arms. "We have to hurry," he said roughly. "We saw them from the air. Four more SUVs on their way. Probably armored. They'll be here in minutes. Can you guys run?"

"Sure," Shane said.

"His feet are all bloody and messed up," I called out. "You should help him."

Without another word, they flanked Shane, their shoulders sliding under his armpits. They lifted him up off his feet and ran toward the helicopter.

I followed as fast as I could. For a while, I could hear Shane bitching about how they could put him down, he was fine to walk, etc., the stubborn bonehead, but thank God, they ignored him. Soon the helicopter's roar got too loud to hear him at all.

My hair whipped and snapped in the rotor's wind. They passed Shane up to someone. Arms reached down, pulling me up into the helicopter.

We rose up before they even closed the door. Someone I couldn't see in the darkness strapped me into a seat, and wrapped a shiny thermal blanket around me. That person turned, and wrapped one around Shane.

Ethan poured something from a thermal carafe into the cup, offering it to Shane and then pouring another one for me. It proved to be tea, hot, with lots of sugar and lemon. It warmed and steadied me. In the darkness, images kept flashing through my mind in gruesome detail. The slashed throat, the blood-stained glass from the crushed SUV, the knife sticking out of that guy's eye socket. When my eyes closed that was what I saw. Not the wishful, improbable vision of a helicopter taking form in the fog, sweeping us away from all the badness... toward Reggie. My happy dream.

Shane's brother touched my arm, and pointed toward the window. For just a moment, before the helicopter entered the raggedy mist, I saw the line of black off-road vehicles, speeding up the road. They were traveling much faster than my aged, struggling Jeep ever could have. Four SUVs, probably packed to the gills with armed operatives. They would have been on us in minutes. They would have flattened us.

I grabbed Ethan's arm, and leaned toward him, mouthing the words. *My sister?*

He gave me a thumbs-up. *Home*, he mouthed, patting my knee. *Safe.*

That was heartening. But things had been so shitty for so long, I wasn't sure it could be real. *Reggie. Home. Safe.* A grouping of words I hadn't dared to hope for.

I would believe it when I saw it.

CHAPTER 12

Shane

Red glowed like a bioluminescent creature in her seat, the silver thermal blanket draped around her shoulders like a shining stole, her eyes huge and shocked looking. It occurred to me that today was probably her very first taste of deadly violence, up close.

I had forgotten how startling that was to a newbie.

I couldn't talk to Ethan or the others, in the dark and the noise, and that was a good thing, because I had fuck-all to say. I was frozen, fried. I felt numb and stupid, and not really here at all. I looked at my own brother as if he were a hologram.

Or maybe I was the hologram. I had made myself into one on purpose to keep Halliwell out of my head, and I didn't know the way back. I hadn't left any trail of bread crumbs for myself. I hadn't allowed myself to hope for anything but death since before I had passed from Vincent's and Nicole's hands into Halliwell's.

I'd gutted my own emotional wiring. Now I was looking at my brother as if I had never met him before. I knew I shared memories with him. I felt the space they took up inside my brain. But my access to them was cut off. I just couldn't feel anything.

You sure felt plenty when you had Red gasping up against the bedroom wall.

That dry observation from my own mind just confused me even more.

Then again, a dick had an agenda all its own. Particularly a starved, neglected, long-suffering dick like mine, left to languish without even help from a friendly hand from time to time. Being constantly watched by the camera really squashed that impulse.

I didn't know how to think about what happened with Red today, so I did what I'd been training my mind for months to do, and thought of nothing.

Ethan sat next to me. I peered through the gloom at the others. Remy Drake had helped carry me to the helicopter. Trey was in there, grinning at me. Shelby was piloting the helicopter, with a huge smile on his face. All of them were old friends from our Army Rangers days. I'd worked with them for years. They were part of that tight group of brothers in arms that we'd coined 'the Unredeemables.' Most of them worked for Ethan, on his security force, or as bodyguards. Some of them had worked in my own security company, Ready Line. I'd trusted them all with my life many times.

The Unredeemables had saved my sorry ass yet again.

Ethan had mobilized two helicopters, one to snatch Red's little sister, and another to come to our rescue. He'd been poised to jump in any direction to help me, on a dime. After all this time.

For that kind of love and dedication, Ethan deserved a brother who wasn't a hologram. A hollow man.

I thought about asking Ethan who the woman was who had called Red to talk to her sister, but didn't have the strength. I'd find out soon enough.

We circled around the rocky hill where the complex we called the Mountain House was built, right on the crest of the hilltop like a medieval fortress. The top floor was lit up like a Christmas tree. The building itself looked excited for our arrival.

We touched down on the helipad my brother had insisted on building, even after Frey and I gave him no end of shit about it. We'd teased him about being a pampered, capricious billionaire with a golden bathtub, the fleet of Ferraris, a yacht the size of the Titanic, a rocket ship to Mars. All that was missing was a fluffy white Persian cat for him to stroke while he plotted his next moves.

Ethan had calmly ignored our ribbing and done whatever the fuck he pleased. Which, as memory flooded back, was pretty much how he had been his whole life. Stubborn bastard. Fucking genius. Sheltering hero. Bossy, pain-in-the-ass big brother. The memories sparked an intense rush of emotion—and something inside me slammed a boot down on it, killing it dead before I could even figure out what it was.

As if the feeling itself was dangerous. As if it were safer to be numb.

Damn. My new emotional wiring was going to be problematic. I had wired myself up to survive hell on earth. Not... home.

My brother and Amos gripped my arms again and lifted me down, setting me reluctantly onto my fucked up feet.

They reached up for Red, but she'd already jumped out of her own accord.

"Where's Reggie?" she yelled, her hair whipping wildly.

Ethan pointed down the stairs to the breezeway.

But we didn't get that far. As soon as we came down the stairs, a tall blond woman came out onto the breezeway, holding a little girl's hand. The girl had curly red hair, and a thin, pale face with big, shadowed eyes. She wore a pink sweatsuit that was too big for her, and a pair of knitted alligator slippers that came partway up her legs. She'd probably come here barefoot, too. It did something to a person, having no shoes.

"Cass!" the girl yelled, pulling away from the blond woman.

"Oh, my God, Reggie. Baby."

The two ran to each other, colliding. Red dropped to her knees, and they were sobbing, murmuring incoherently, rocking together. An undifferentiated mass of wild red hair. No emotional blocks there. Lucky them.

Remy turned to me with a quick, satisfied smile. "Some days, I love my job."

Angela, our longtime friend/housekeeper/butler/general keeper hurried toward me and skidded to a stop, dismay on her round, rosy face. "Good Lord, Shane. What did they do to you? Can I hug you? Would I hurt you?"

I cleared my throat. "No," I rasped. "Only if you didn't."

Angela grabbed me and hugged me carefully, as if I were made of blown glass. "You're so thin," she said, her voice tear-thickened. "It's like you're made of steel cables wrapped around bent rebar. You need some feeding up, young man!"

"Sounds good to me." I hugged her back.

I saw Ethan's face over Angela's shoulder, and realized that I had not hugged him yet. Like I was afraid of the emotional charge. I'd been shocked too many times.

Speaking of emotional charges. I looked around. "Where's Holly? And Frey? Aren't they here?"

"They're still in Spain, with Jed," Angela said. "But they're in the airport already. The second they heard about this, they came running. They couldn't believe it was true. None of us could. After all this time, having to swallow the idea that maybe we would never know what happened... oh God, it's been hard on everybody. We missed you so much." Her voice shook.

I patted her shaking back, my mind automatically seizing on a random piece of information that did not fit. "Jed? What the hell are they doing in Spain with Jed?"

Ethan let out a laugh. "You missed a few notable events, bro. Jed is Frey's husband now. He's our brother-in-law."

My jaw sagged. "Her... he's... the *fuck?*"

"Yup," Ethan said. "They fell in love. Frey was sneaking around doing something she shouldn't have been doing, trying to find you. He kept her from getting killed. A few different times. She returned the favor, and in the meantime, they fell in love. So they're married now. Go figure. But they seem really happy. So it's all good."

My mind had gone blank at that news. "How in the hell—"

"How about you boys save the catching up for after you've washed off the blood and gotten all stitched up and bandaged?" It was the blonde bombshell, striding briskly toward them. "Dr. Demiguel just arrived."

"Who are you?" I asked.

She gave me a smile. "I'm Kat." She gestured at my brother. "I saved his bacon, more than once. After that, he sort of grew on me. So I stuck around."

"Huh? So you're—"

"My fiancée," Ethan said. "She saved Holly's bacon, too, by the way. She was the one who took down Nicole."

"Give credit where credit is due," Kat said. "Freya helped, and so did you. And so did Holly, for that matter. Team effort. But dudes, please. Later for that. First, the doctor. I mean, look at the poor guy."

I felt intensely self-conscious. "I know I look like shit, but I'm fine."

"Oh, fuck off," Ethan snarled. "Like hell you're fine. I can barely tell it's you." He seized my arm. "Amos, let's get this guy to the—"

"Do not push me or drag me," I said, wrenching my arm away. "Ever."

Silence fell. The violent edge in my voice had startled them, as if they didn't know me anymore. Which was literally true. Fuck, I didn't even know myself.

"Ah, okay," Ethan said carefully. "Shane? Hello. It's me. Not Halliwell."

"I know. Sorry. But nobody tells me where to go or what to do. Ever again."

Ethan cleared his throat. "I didn't mean to push you around. It's just a big brother thing. The bandages on your neck... was that from Vincent's collar?"

"I wore the fucking thing the whole time they had me," I said. "However long it's been. I have no way of knowing."

Ethan winced. "You will be glad to know that sick fuck is now safely dead. Frey did the honors personally. She shot him right through the heart."

I blinked. "Frey? Really? She shoots now?"

"She's a crack shot now. Jed taught her. So, will you formally give your official consent to accept Remy's and my help down the breezeway, so we don't have to clean up your bloody footprints after? Please?"

I forced out a shuddering breath, which swiftly devolved into a cough. "Fine," I said. "But check out Red, too. She's been through some wild stuff today."

"First, you," Red said sternly, looking at me over her little sister's shoulder.

"We'll cover everyone, in due time," Angela fussed. "Come on inside, everyone. There's dinner waiting. How long has it been since you all had a decent meal?"

I smiled at her, a sensation that almost cracked my jaw. "Since I saw you last."

"Aww, you flatterer. We'll get you fed up. Come on, honey. Everyone inside, where it's warm. Look at you, no coat. I'm surprised you're not dead from pneumonia."

We made our way to Ethan's apartment on the top floor. The two floors below, equally large and deluxe apartments, were mine, and my sister's. We all had other residences, but this place had always been a favorite. A retreat where we all felt safe.

I should be feeling safe right now, but I realized suddenly that feeling safe was an internal thing. An inside job. If your brain didn't consent to it, you were screwed.

There was no refuge. Danger was all around. All the time.

There was a confusing few minutes while we figured out what to do first, which culminated in my brother and Remy gingerly herding me, without ever seeming to push, into a bathroom to shower off the blood and dirt before being seen by the doctor.

The hot water stung. I'd gotten slashes, bruises, a graze from a stray bullet, and plenty of contusions from being knocked around on that rocky hillside. No big deal, except for my feet, which had gotten torn up from frantic sprinting over sharp rocks. They'd been very soft, from a year of feeling nothing but the smooth tile floor of my prison for months. The soap and water hurt like a motherfucker. I was standing in a swirling pink puddle for the entire time I was in the shower.

Angela brought up some of my own clothes from my apartment. I barely recognized them, or remembered the man who wore them. Athletic pants, a soft, comfortable sweatshirt. Everything felt loose on me. I looked taut and stringy when I caught a glimpse of myself in the mirror. Like I'd been boiled down.

Dr. Josef Demiguel, an old friend of Ethan's, was waiting for me in the bedroom when I shuffled out of the bathroom.

I submitted to a doctor's examination, teeth clenched. Demiguel was a short, chubby guy, usually cheerful, but very serious looking tonight. He was as gentle as possible, but having my feet worked on was an ordeal, even with the anesthetic spray. He tweezed out embedded grit, smearing the wounds with salve, put stitches into the slash on my arm. Shone a light into my eyes.

Then, he unwound the bandages that Red had put onto my throat and let out a sharp gasp. "What is this? Did someone try to garrote you? Fifty different times?"

"More or less," I said, wincing as he explored it with latex-gloved fingers.

"From the sound of it, you have some vocal damage," he said, his voice worried. "You'll have to be seen by a voice specialist. Among other things."

More smearing of antibiotic salves followed. I had to endure an injection of some broad-spectrum antibiotic or other that the doctor insisted on, to ward off all the possible infections. I steeled myself for the blood-drawing for various lab tests. But I drew the line at getting an IV bag of electrolytes. No fucking way was I lying here on my back with a drip in my arm.

Demiguel closed up his bag, his eyes worried. "You should be admitted to the hospital immediately," he said. "After an ordeal like yours, there's only so much I can do for you here at the house. We need to run tests. X-rays, ultrasounds—"

"Later," I said. "Not now."

"I strongly advise you to do it now," he said. "You should come with—"

"Later." My voice slashed down, silencing him.

Demiguel's mouth tightened. He grabbed bag of blood samples. "I'll go take a look at the young lady and the little girl, then," he said stiffly. "And be on my way."

"Won't you stay for dinner, Josef?" Ethan urged.

"No. I'm sure you all have a lot of catching up to do." He shot me a nervous glance. "And it's late. Just please. Consider going to the hospital. As soon as you can."

I nodded. Sure, fine, but I was locked in mortal combat with a blood-drinking monster at the moment. The check-ups and the spa treatments could wait.

Ethan waited until the door closed behind the guy, and then stared at me with cool eyes, arms crossed over his barrel chest. "This experience hasn't done much for your manners," he said.

"It sure fucking hasn't," I agreed readily.

As we locked eyes, I felt it. The pull inside me, toward something that I just could not reach. Like I was trapped behind a six-inch wall of fortified glass, screaming, pounding on it to get his attention. But he couldn't hear me through the barrier.

"What happened, Shane?" he asked.

I shook my head. "It's just like I told you. I was taken, chained up, fucked up. Vincent and Nicole worked me over. Then Halliwell took his turn. I had some brain damage after Vincent and Nicole bashed my head in. That was lucky. It was the only thing that kept me from spilling what I knew about SmokeScreen. Somehow, Red got me out. I'm not even quite sure how. I'm still alive. That's all I can say. And I don't really want to dwell on it right now."

"You can't just grit your teeth and pretend it never happened."

"Watch me," I said.

His jaw tightened. "Shane. For fuck's sake—"

"We are not having this conversation. Not tonight. Maybe not ever."

Ethan let out a sigh. "Fine. But I killed some of the people who took you, by the way. So did Freya, and Jed, and Kat, and the Drakes. Even Holly got in a couple of good licks. We'd do anything to help you. So try to keep track of who you're really pissed at. We don't deserve it. I'm sorry we didn't rescue you. I'm jealous of this girl for doing all the heavy lifting. Grateful as hell, yes. But I still wish it had been me."

I nodded. "I'm not pissed. I'm just... like this, now. I don't want to be, but I am. Don't know how to be any other way. At least not yet. I'm just... you know."

Locked behind a wall of glass.

"Yeah," he said slowly. "I mean, of course, I can't really know. But I can imagine."

"No," I said. "You can't. Be glad that you can't."

He nodded. "If you say so."

"Look, Ethan," I blurted. "I'm sorry. Truth is, I'm still not even sure this is real. I'm not convinced you're here at all. I've hallucinated you before, more than once. Maybe I'm dying, and this is some wishful end-of-life fantasy. Maybe I'm just having a psychotic break. I just can't relax into it. I just don't dare. So don't take it personally."

"Gotcha," he said. "Maybe when Halliwell is finally dead, you can relax into this dimension of reality. It's a good dimension. You're going to like it. Eventually."

I flexed my hands, trying to breathe out the tension in my chest. "I hope so," I said. "I don't want Holly to see me like this."

"You can't put that off," Ethan warned. "She's on her way here, right now, and she's wild to see her daddy. So whatever complicated stuff that you're feeling or not feeling right now, you have to pull your shit together and put on a good show for her. The rest of us can be patient and understanding. Not her."

"Understood."

"And think about what Demiguel said," Ethan scolded. "Going to the hospital to get checked out by the doctors is pretty damn basic, Shane. You know it's the smart thing to do."

"Give me a minute, okay?" I said. "Give me some time to be here. I'll be fine. I'm not shot or stabbed or bleeding out. My bones have healed. I know who you all are. The big stuff is still intact. Let's think about keeping Halliwell off our throats before I let down my guard in a public hospital setting. Because I just fucking can't right now."

Ethan made a frustrated sound. "We'll get right on this. The Drakes are all over it, and Jed and Freya will be too, when they get here tomorrow. Say. About that redhead. What's the deal with her? Are you, ah… you know?"

I was so started by the gossipy frivolity of that question, I actually laughed, rusty and stiff as that sensation was. "What the hell does that mean?"

"Well? What is her deal? You made this fraught bargain with her, you got us to save the cute little sister, she busted you out of that hellhole all by herself. She's brave, she's tough, she's smart. And, ah…"

"She's also smoking hot? Drop dead gorgeous? A walking wet dream? Were those the phrases you were looking for?"

Ethan's lip twitched. "You said it, not me. But I'm only flesh and blood, so yeah, I couldn't help but notice. So? What's up with that?"

I rubbed my face, feeling the weird, aching strain of rusty smile muscles unused to doing their thing. "I don't know what to think," I admitted. "She blows my mind, definitely. Can't deny that. No one could blame me for it. But I'm fucked if I know."

Ethan's eyes narrowed. "Meaning?"

I was reluctant to voice the thought, which felt ungrateful and unworthy. "She just came to me, out of the blue," I said. "I'm not sure if she's real, either. I mean, what are the odds? I was buried in that place. There was no way I was getting out. It was like being locked in a bank vault. And then, abracadabra, a shining princess in a fucking ball gown spirits me out single-handedly."

Ethan looked puzzled. "Ball gown?"

"Literally. I swear to God. She was wearing a ball gown to my execution. With a corset top and a big, puffy skirt. Like a cartoon princess, except sexy. She said she switched out the lethal gas for a sedative, and then stole my apparently dead body. I woke up in a body bag in the back of a van. I take no credit for any part of it. And she was still in the ball gown at that point. It was surreal."

"Sounds like you got busy later, when those goons came at you at the cabin," Ethan said. "Based on what you told me before we picked you up. You can definitely take credit for that fight. That was some quick thinking. Using the van against them."

I shrugged. "Yeah, I guess. But that was later."

"So," Ethan said. "You're wondering if she's too good to be true."

I shrugged. "But I'm out of there, right? It's true. I'm home. If this is real, and not a dream or a hallucination, then she has to be real, too. Right?"

Ethan looked troubled. "Right. And I saw how she was with her sister. That was pretty goddamn convincing. But I have a hard time believing my luck, too. It happened so fast. I haven't adjusted yet." He placed a hand on my shoulder. "But you're real. I'm real. And whatever this girl is doing, or why she's doing it, I'm grateful."

I lifted up my scraped, scabby hand, and laid it carefully over his.

We stayed there, stuck in that stiff, awkward pose. Afraid to break the tenuous contact.

A knock on the door made me jump, and the moment was gone, like a soap bubble bursting.

"Are you decent?" Angela sang out.

"Come on in," Ethan called.

The door opened, and Angela leaned in, beaming. "Just so you know. Dr. Demiguel examined Reggie and Cass, and says they seem fine, as far as he can tell. I'm getting dinner on the table now." She looked at me. "You'll sleep in here tonight, okay? There's no time to get your apartment opened up tonight, and I think you should all stay close together. At least until you have a clean bill of health."

"Agreed," Ethan said. "We'll get your apartment ready later."

"I put Cass and Reggie in the corner bedroom. There's a nice big king-sized bed, so they have plenty of room in there. I've left towels and night stuff and toothbrushes."

Ethan's eyes flicked over to mine, too fast to catch, but I knew that he was hiding a smile. "Thanks, Angela," he said. "You're the best."

"Don't you forget it, hon. So come eat! The enchiladas are about to come out of the oven. There's chili, fresh cornbread, green salads and savory salads."

"Sounds awesome," Ethan said. "We'll be right in."

He squeezed my shoulder. "Can you deal with a family dinner? You could eat in here and just power down. You must be exhausted. Everyone would understand."

I thought about it. It was tempting, but it would be a dick move, to ruin the triumphant hero's return by cowering in my room. "I'm good for the family dinner."

"Okay. Put your arm over my shoulder so I can take the weight off your feet."

"I can walk," I said. "I'm good."

"Would you just please fucking give me this, Shane?" His voice had an edge. "I know it was way worse for you, but we had a year of hell too. Just this. It's all I ask."

"It won't be just this," I told him. "There will be more. Lots more. I know you."

He snorted. "Well, good. That's an encouraging sign."

He had a point. Fuck it. I was being stupid and stubborn. I lifted my arm, draped it around his shoulder, and almost howled when I put my weight on my freshly bandaged feet. The adrenaline had worn off. So had Demiguel's anesthetic spray.

I leaned on my brother as I hobbled to the dining room. The physical contact felt both familiar and alien. So did this place that I knew so well, where I had spent years with family and friends.

We got to the dining room. Everyone stopped talking. The Drake brothers were there, all three of them, plus the blonde that I had met in the breezeway. Kat, she had called herself. Amos and Darius both looked me over and gave me a careful embrace and a gentle pat on the back, as if I might fall apart on them if they squeezed too hard.

The table was loaded with food. I was used to the small plastic trays of dry, bland, tasteless food that appeared in the metal drawer at intervals, like mediocre magic.

The colors and aromas of Angela's feast made me dizzy.

"You sit next to your rescuer, of course," Angela directed, herding me over to the chair next to Red. Or Cass, she'd said. That was her real name, but I couldn't think of her as anything but Red. I'd make that adjustment later. One thing at a time.

Her gorgeous hair was freshly washed, and a cloud of warm, perfumed air hung about it. She wore a thick, fuzzy green sweater that clung to her slim body.

Reggie leaned forward to study me with intense curiosity. "Are you the guy who told them to come and rescue me?"

"Yeah, that's me," I confessed.

"Thank you," she said solemnly. "I was dying in there, locked in that room."

"Yeah," I said, with feeling. "Same. Your sister made it happen, though."

Reggie's face shone as she looked up at her big sister. Red seized her in a rocking side hug. When they came apart, their eyes were freshly wet.

"I'm so glad you got me out," Reggie said. "Even if I die of Varen's now, that's okay. I'd rather die when I'm with you than stay in that awful room one more second."

That was followed by horrified silence.

"You most certainly will not die!" Angela sounded insulted by the very idea.

"Sure I could," Reggie said matter-of-factly. "People die all the time. Mom died. I know it can happen. Fast, too. Boom, and off you go."

"We'll see about that," Ethan said. "We've got a supply of your medicine from the fridge in your room. We're going to get all the smartest people we know to examine those medicines to see if those clinic types were being straight with you. Considering how crappy that place was, I wouldn't trust anything they told you."

"Absolutely," Reggie agreed. "If I could live, it would be great. I actually want to, now. This place is really nice."

Ethan turned to Kat. "Did you call Rose?"

"First thing," she replied. "She'll be here tomorrow morning." Kat turned to us with a reassuring smile. "Rose is a friend of ours. She's a brilliant pharmacologist. She'll check out that medicine we got from the clinic. We'll know more soon."

"Thank you," Red said gratefully. She turned to me. "Your family is awesome."

"Glad you like them," I murmured.

"I like them, too!" Reggie announced. "They're nice!"

"The feeling's mutual, sweetheart," Amos told her with a grin.

Angela bustled in with yet another steaming oven dish loaded with something that smelled amazingly good. I was overloading with all the sensory input. Even the fabulous food felt like an assault on my brain. But I'd be damned if I was going to run away from these people, or from Angela and her food, which was her primary love language. Or my family, who had just dragged my sorry ass out of the shit.

No fainting, no seizures, no running for the bathroom allowed. Just... breathe.

"You okay?" Red reached under the table and grabbed my

hand, which made my dick perk right up and take notice. Which, under the circumstances, was a welcome distraction. "You're looking a little green. Overload?"

I shot her a grateful glance. "Little bit."

Her fingers tightened. Her hand was strong. Reggie leaned forward on the other side of her and smiled, and I saw the resemblance, beyond just their complexions. The smile that lit up her little face. Cute kid. I liked her on sight.

"You'll meet my daughter Holly tomorrow," I told Reggie. "She's about your age."

"Kat told me," Reggie said. "She sounds great. She likes the same kind of books as me. I looked through her bookcase. Fantasy adventure. Those are the best."

I felt my face ache again at the unfamiliar smile. Then Angela leaned over my shoulder. "You've hardly eaten anything, honey. Can I get you something else?"

"No, I'm fine," I assured her. "I'm just not used to this much food anymore. My stomach is confused."

"Well, it's just going to have to get used to proper eating, that's all I have to say about it." There was a catch in Angela's voice as she leaned down and pressed a kiss onto the top of my head. She patted Red's shoulder. "Thanks for bringing him back to us, honey. We were lost without him."

Red's smile was luminous. "We rescued each other," she said. "And you guys got Reggie for me. So I think I'm actually a little behind, in the ledger sheet of favors."

"Nonsense," Angela said.

"It's really romantic," Reggie observed.

There was a sudden silence, broken by Remy's chuckle. "That's for sure."

Then Angela's caramelized bread pudding came out, goopy and tender and amazing. I hadn't tasted anything sweet since my world exploded. It jarred my brain with its intensity. I could only manage a couple of bites.

Reggie was yawning and nodding, eyes half closed. "Think it's time for you to hit the hay, honey girl," Red told her.

"Will you come, too?" the little girl asked sleepily.

"I'll tuck you in, and then I'll come back out here for a little while, to finish dinner and talk for a bit. But I'll be back really soon," Red promised.

"Okay." Reggie got up, swaying. "G'night," she said, waving at the room at large.

"The bathroom's all stocked," Angela reminded them. "Use anything you need. I laid out pajamas on the bed for you. Holly's stuff is a little big for her, but it'll do."

"Thanks," Red said gratefully.

I watched, feeling weirdly abandoned, as the two redheads filed out of the room, leaving me staring at my brother, his fiancée, and the Drakes.

Angela brought out a carafe of coffee, and set it in the middle of the table. Cups were poured all around. They stared at me expectantly.

"So," Remy said. "How did that tiny girl pull off a rescue op on her own?"

"I think she's some kind of tech genius," I said. "Ethan and Frey will have to investigate those details. It's way over my head. Truth is, she hasn't told me much. We never had time. She found out that Halliwell was having me gassed to death. She switched out the canister with a sedative. Stole my body on the way to the incinerator. She stole a van with an ice sculpture in it. Halliwell's corporate logo, carved into a half a ton of ice. She booked out of there at high speed, and then brought me back with some ass-kicking upper that made me wake up kicking and screaming."

"Far-fucking-out," Darius murmured. "So you were out the whole time? Until the van?"

"Right," I said.

"And all this in a ball-gown and heels," Ethan said.

"It was a sight to behold," I agreed. "And that shit she shot me up with in the van was scary stuff. I went totally nuts. I could have killed her in that state."

"Yeah, it all sounds extremely dangerous," Remy said.

"She was hyper-focused on getting her little sister out of Halliwell's clutches," I said. "I can relate to that."

"That looks super-legit," Amos commented. "The little sister. Cute as a button. Looks just like her. The red hair, the same smile, the tearful reunion. Hard to fake."

"You're still wondering if she's on the level?" Kat asked. "I believe every word of it. I saw the room they kept that poor kid in. A blind basement room, no ventilation."

"Yeah," Amos agreed. "The air was bad, the light was bad, the sheets were dirty, the mattress hard, it smelled like mildew. She was in a prison cell, not a clinic. You should have seen her face when we came in."

"I had to press the doctor hard to get info about the medicine," Kat said. "If he's really a doctor, which I doubt. Scared the guy to death. He said that box in her room was all the medicine they had on hand. That a fresh supply was delivered weekly. And I put the fear of God into that guy. I don't think he was lying."

"Dear God," Angela whispered. "That poor little sweetheart. So brave."

"I'm grateful the redhead decided to partner with you to rescue the sister," Ethan said. "I just feel like there are a blind spots in this story. Blind spots make me nervous. Anything can jump out of them. I'm happy, but I'm twitchy as hell."

"Before he had me gassed, Halliwell sent Red down to ask me about SmokeScreen," I said. "In the spirit of full disclosure. He's still hot for it. And I think that Red is hoping that if things go sideways for the sister, that we could use it to dig into Halliwell's databanks for the cure."

Ethan's jaw tightened. "I see."

The silence that followed was heavy with words that didn't need to be said. We knew all too well what happened the last time SmokeScreen had been used... by me. Everyone's lives had been blown up. Men had died. All because I was a fucking idiot who thought that I could wield lightning without getting fried.

Well, I was humbled now.

"Hey." Red's melodious alto voice from the dining room entryway. "Any more of that yummy dessert?"

"You better believe it." Angela bounced up, grabbing a dessert plate from the pile. She served up a generous plateful without missing a beat. "Here you go. So what's your story, honey? What do you do?"

"Well, before I got stuck working at Halliwell's outfit, I had my own consultancy," she said, licking sweet, goopy sauce off her fingertip. "Red Queen Consulting."

Amos whistled. "Wait. Red Queen Consulting? The top shelf malware outfit?"

"Yeah, that's me. You've heard of it?"

"Of course we've heard of it," Darius said. "You've consulted for all the big defense contractors and all the big intelligence agencies. You're famous."

She snorted. "Oh, come on. Hardly."

I was taken aback. "Malware? No shit. How did you get into that?"

"My mom's computer got infected when I was a kid, not much older than Reggie," she said. "I set myself to figure out how to beat it, and started geeking out on it. I get hyper-focused on things. One thing led to another, and a few years ago, Red Queen Consulting was born. Don't worry, I stay on the side of truth and righteousness, when I can figure out where that line is. It tends to move around pretty freely."

"Red Queen Consulting," I repeated. "Is that a reference to your hair?"

She smiled sheepishly. "It's more about Reggie's hair. When

I started consulting, Reggie and I were watching the Alice in Wonderland movie on repeat. She got a big kick out of the Red Queen, and Regina means queen. And Mom, Reggie and I were all redheads. So Red Queen Consulting was born. Off with their heads! I loved that she was such an unapologetic bitch. It's a kind of superpower."

Kat nodded in perfect understanding. "Agreed. From one unapologetic bitch to another. Angela, too. She's as bad-ass as they come. Long may we reign."

The women exchanged grins. The men, including me, stayed strategically silent.

"My corporate logo is a drawing that Reggie did for me," she said. "Reggie's an incredible artist. It was the perfect image. I love it."

I pulled out the phone she had given me and pulled up Red Queen Consulting to check out the logo.

It was, in fact, a cute drawing. Catchy and memorable. A simple cartoon face, with Red's pointed chin and big, tilted green eyes, a crown, and wild, Medusa-style locks of red hair waving around her crown. "Talented kid," I said. "She really caught you with that sketch."

"How did Halliwell get his hooks into you?" Kat asked.

Red's mouth tightened. "Reggie got sick," she said. "The doctors told me it was Varen's, the same thing that killed our mom two years ago. They said there was no cure, no treatment, and that she'd be dead in two weeks. Then Halliwell pops up and tells me he has a treatment for it... but only if I license my new software exclusively to him, and come to work for him." She shrugged. "I figured, I had to try it, right? So I went. But that place was a horror show, and it wasn't going so well with Reggie, either. Her symptoms improved, but they wouldn't talk to me about her treatment. It was driving me mad. She was fading day by day in our video calls."

"But Halliwell's treatment worked?" Ethan asked.

"Well, she didn't die, if that's the only metric we're talking about," Red said. "The fevers and rashes stopped. But she was peaky and miserable, and she was locked in a windowless room. A woman I met in Halliwell's headquarters told me that's a thing Halliwell does. He makes people sick with manufactured diseases that mimic real diseases, and then he dangles his ready-made cure. He did it to her mother. And killed her mother with it, in the end. That was when I realized I had to make a move, fast."

"Dear God," Angela murmured.

"I am so glad you guys grabbed Reggie before he punished me through her," Red said. "Now I just have to figure out how to keep her alive."

After a moment, Kat broke the silence. "Well, Rose will be here tomorrow," she said. "We'll get to work. Start gathering info. Considering our options."

"Thank you," Red said again.

"You don't have to thank us," Ethan said forcefully. "We owe you. Forever."

"That means a lot to me," she said, smiling around the table. "Look, people, I'm wiped out. I'm going to join Reggie and get some sleep. I'm so glad to be here. Thanks for your help. And for being so welcoming."

"Our pleasure," Ethan said.

"I'll say," Angela added heartily. "Until the end of time."

A chorus of good-nights followed her out the door, followed by silence. It went on so long, the air began to feel charged. Everyone was looking at me, or else deliberately trying not to. Which amounted to the same thing.

"Wow," Amos said. "That is some epic badassery, in a small, intense package."

"You don't need to tell me," I said. "I tried to make her run away when they came at me at the cabin. She was having none of it. She followed me down the hill. Got one of them in the back of the head with the rolling pin. Saved my ass."

"Sweet," Kat said approvingly. "Good material there. Very tough."

"All I'm thinking is..." Remy's voice trailed off.

"What?" I demanded.

Remy sighed. "I'm just thinking, fuck. You've been through hell. I just really hope that this girl is all that she claims to be. That it went down exactly like she said it did. Being as how you weren't conscious to corroborate her story."

"You think it's an elaborate set-up? Those nine guys I killed, the sick little sister locked in the basement? Those are some heavy-duty set pieces to put in place."

Remy raised his hands, fending me off. "I'm just saying that if the redhead's not being absolutely straight with you, then that prick Halliwell will have found a way to make this thing suck even harder for you. That filthy sadist lives for that shit. So just be ready to jump. That's all I'm trying to say."

I grunted under my breath. "I'll be ready to jump until the day I die," I said.

The worry in their eyes made me miserable. I stood up, grimly not permitting myself to gasp at the pain in my throbbing feet. "I'm going to crash," I said. "We'll see more clearly in the morning. Thanks for coming for me. And for saving Reggie. I'm glad to be home." I knew it was true, even though I couldn't feel it.

Ethan sprang up. "I'll help you."

"No, no, no." I shuffled to the door, waving him down. "I'm fine. A hot meal makes all the difference."

"Wait until you see breakfast," Angela warned. "Be afraid. Be very afraid."

I made that weird, rusty coughing sound as I went out the door, realizing belatedly that it was laughter.

I kept my gait steady, not allowing myself to limp until I was inside the bedroom door. Even there, I felt watched. Of course I did, after months of having cameras pointed at me. The air went out of my lungs as I sank down on trembling legs, my heart pumping agony into the soles of my feet. Thud, thud, like hammer blows.

Remy was right. If the Red story was a fiendish scheme of Halliwell's designed to fuck me up still worse, well... it would work. No question. It would fuck me up.

I just had to make sure that my family and the rest of the world didn't get fucked up along with me.

CHAPTER 13

Cass

I lay there cuddling Reggie's wiry little body, my mind buzzing with leftover adrenaline even though my body was utterly exhausted.

I still couldn't believe my luck. I had gotten my precious Reggie back. She was right here, in my arms, her hair tickling my nose and mouth. I'd been horrified when I helped her into her pajamas and saw all the needle marks and bruises on her pale arms. Furious at those cruel, clumsy hacks. Guilty that I hadn't protected her better.

Now, I cuddled closer, intensely conscious of each slow breath. Grateful for it. Every breath was beautiful, precious. A treasure. A small victory to celebrate.

Please, God. Give her a long, happy lifetime of them.

Shane had looked starkly miserable at dinner. His face was like a marble mask. And I was not the only person who noticed. Of course, he'd been through hell, but I could sense, from the way he tensed when Holly's arrival was mentioned, that he was deathly afraid to see his little girl tomorrow.

He was afraid of disappointing her. Of not having whatever

he thought that she needed from him, after being altered for the worse by his ordeal.

Halliwell's cruelty was a gift that kept on giving. Shane was free, but he was tense, joyless. He couldn't rejoice at being home. That was tragic. And unacceptable.

I was in the same boat, of course. Scared shitless of how vulnerable and exposed Reggie's illness made me. But Shane had it worse.

That bastard was not going to drive a wedge between Shane and his little girl if I had anything to say about it. Shane could not possibly disappoint his kid. He was like a demigod. What he'd endured, what he'd survived. She might be shy with him, wary of what the experience had done to him, but once everyone relaxed and adjusted, his daughter was going to be so proud of her dad. I was sure of it.

I eased my arm from beneath Reggie's arm, inching away until I could climb out of the bed. She was in the deep sleep of total exhaustion. My sweet, brave honey.

I got up and made my way slowly down the hall on tiptoes, to the room where they had put Shane. I put my hand on the knob... and hesitated.

I knocked, very softly. If he was sleeping, I didn't want to wake him.

"Yeah?" I barely heard the low rasp of his voice through the door.

I pushed the door open. He sat up in his bed.

"It's me," I whispered.

"Come on in."

I closed the door. The only light was the outdoor lighting that came through the picture windows. Just enough to show the shape of the room, the outlines of his dark form.

"I couldn't sleep," I said.

"Me neither," he said. "Maybe I never will. Or maybe it's just the wake-up drug you gave me. I hope so. That means it'll wear off eventually. Time will tell."

"I couldn't say what that stuff was," I said. "Jana gave me that dose already loaded into the syringe."

"Who's Jana?"

I hesitated for a moment. "A woman I met there," I said. "The one I told you guys about, whose mother was killed by one of the fake diseases. She helped me. I had to steal your body from her. At least that was how we played it. She gave me a knock-out syringe for her, and a wake-up syringe for you."

"A woman helped you?" he said slowly. "Why did she help you?"

"Like I said. Halliwell played the same dirty game with her that he's playing with me. He sickened and then killed her mom with one of his fake diseases."

I regretted opening up this avenue of questioning. I certainly didn't want to mention being half-siblings with that crowd. Revealing that I was Halliwell's daughter would compromise any alliance I might form with these people. I didn't dare to do that.

Reggie came first.

"So she helped you for her dead mother's sake?" He sounded doubtful.

"That was the sense I got," I said cautiously. "I tried to get her to come with us, but she refused. She gave me the syringes. Told me to knock her out before I took the gurney, to make it look good."

"He must suspect her, then. Because nothing looks good in this mess."

I swallowed. "I don't think she really cares anymore," I said. "I think she's at the end of her rope. She's a good person stuck in a poisonous place. I felt really bad for using her, in the shape she was in, but I was desperate. And we got this far, right?"

"We sure did," he said.

His tone, and the silence that followed struck me as odd and suspicious. "What? What's on your mind? Talk to me."

"There's a lot you didn't tell me, Red."

My jaw sagged. "For real? Think back over the past eight hours! Was there a good moment for a blow-by-blow debrief?"

"It just seems improbable. That this woman turned her colors on the spot. Convenient for you, right?"

I thought about Jana's haunted eyes, her swollen jaw. The grief in her reddened eyes and gaunt face. "It wasn't on the spot. It was a long time coming. You're not the only one Halliwell has hurt, Shane. He has a long history of destroying people. Lots of people hate him independently of you. You have to take a number and get in line."

He grunted. "Fine. But as soon as you've gotten a good night's sleep, I'd like a... how did you put it? A blow-by-blow debrief. Every piece of information you can give us might help, once we go on the offensive."

That made my body clench in alarm. "I despise the man with every cell in my body, but I don't want to go to war with him. I just want to save my little sister."

"You won't have a choice. Not if he goes to war with you."

God, how exhausting this was. My mother had told me all my life, and I still hadn't understood how destructive being near Halliwell would be. But this was no time for a pity party. "I'll do whatever I have to do," I said grimly.

He let out a harsh laugh. "Yay for you. That's the spirit."

"You think this is funny?"

"Gallows humor," he said.

"You're not on the gallows." My voice was intense. "You're home, Shane. Surrounded by smart, strong, powerful people who love you. Your circumstances have changed. You should let them in. Let it all in. You can afford to."

He was silent for a moment. "I wish I could feel it," he said. "But I can't."

"You've only been here for a couple of hours. Give it time."

"We don't have time. It's all happening right now."

I reached out, placing my hand on top of his. "I know how you feel. I can't believe that this is happening, either. It seems like a dream. Having Reggie here, asleep on a soft bed with clean sheets and fleece pajamas. Safe, well fed, happy. With me."

He nodded, staring down at my hand. I turned it, palm up. His fingers closed around mine, and a shudder of excitement stole my breath.

"One thing feels extremely real, though," I said softly.

He didn't need me to name it. He just nodded. "Yes," he said. "Same."

His laconic words set off fireworks deep inside my body. "So?" I prompted.

"Is that why you came in here?" he asked. "So I could make you feel real?"

His words stung, like he was accusing me of using him. I pulled back at my hand. "Not if you're not into it," I said. "Don't do me any favors."

"I'm always into it, if it's you," he said. "Don't get mad. You want real, you get real. I'm not tiptoeing around anybody's tender feelings right now. I couldn't if I wanted to. And with you, the truth just falls out of me."

I nodded. I wished I could tell him all of my truths. It felt wrong to hold anything back.

"Hey," he said. "Speaking of truth falling out. This afternoon, at the cabin. I came inside of you. We didn't talk about it at the time. Is it a problem?"

"No," I assured him. "A couple years ago, I got an implant. It was for a brief thing that went nowhere, because right about then Mom started getting sick. So I basically forgot about the guy. And the implant, too, for that matter."

"Ah. Okay." I sensed his relief, and the anticipation that suddenly buzzed the air.

He still wouldn't let go of my hand. "Tell me exactly what you want from me, Red," he said. "I don't trust myself to read nonverbal cues right now."

My hand tightened around his. "Let me make you feel real."

His breathing quickened. The air felt hot, charged. "Reggie's sleeping soundly?"

"Like a rock," I told him.

He slid off the bed and headed for the door.

"Hey! Your feet!" I protested.

He flicked the door lock closed. "They're fine. Truth-telling with you turns me on. My endorphins just shot through the roof. I'm feeling no pain." He whipped off his sweatshirt as he walked toward the bed. Dropped the pajama pants.

He was naked beneath them. His long, thick cock stood up, magnificently erect. He stood there waiting, gripping his cock, stroking it. "Your move, Red," he said.

I slid off the bed, tossed off the soft nightgown that Angela had left, and dropped my underwear. I was stark naked, in a locked room with my fantasy man, all hot, bothered and breathless, having made vague, extravagant promises about sexual pleasure that I didn't necessarily know how to fulfill. That was Cass Clarke for you. Always stumbling around, way outside her comfort zone.

But that was just fine. It wasn't comfort that I wanted tonight.

My move, he'd said. Well, then. I put my hands on his chest, stroking him. What was it Angela said? Steel cables wrapped around bent rebar. But something more. My fingers dug in, stroking, exploring his heat and power and vitality. He pulsed with it.

His hands covered mine, and moved them down, over his belly, lower. He wrapped my hands around his thick, hot cock, clasping over mine. Squeezing, moving on his stiff shaft. My thighs squeezed and trembled. I was already wet. Hot. Breathless.

The impulse just came over me. I sank down onto the discarded nightgown, gripping his cock in both hands, and took him into my mouth.

I was too excited to worry about my lack of technique. I was so turned on as I played with his gorgeous cock, and it made all the difference in how much fun it was. I felt hot and sinuous and uninhibited, licking him, swirling my tongue around his cockhead, memorizing every different surface and texture. Smooth and taut, velvety, suede, throbbing, hot, salty, musky, yearning.

I pumped my hands up and down his shaft, licking the pre-come that gleamed on the tip. Slippery, salt-sweet perfection. The sounds he made were encouraging. Breathless, gasping moans, choked off to not make too much noise. His hands, winding into my hair, guiding me. He was shaking with eagerness.

I took his cock even deeper into my mouth than I ever knew I could. Clutching his rock-hard ass cheeks as he thrust deep, stroking him with my lips and tongue.

He let me set the pace and the depth, fucking my mouth in a slow, pumping, sensual rhythm, his hands tightening... and he stopped, pulling away.

I murmured in protest, but he held me still, his body rigid, his gleaming cock pulsing in my clutching hands.

I leaned back, wiping my mouth, gasping for breath. "What's wrong?"

"Nothing." He grabbed me under my arms, lifting me effortlessly to my feet, and tumbling me onto my back on the bed. "I just want to fuck you. Right now."

And suddenly, he was on top of me. He was so big and hot, and I ached with need, splayed out beneath him onto the bed. I shivered at the slow touch of his fingers over my mound, teasing my pussy slit, and he murmured in approval at what he found there. Slick and wet and gasping at every caress.

"Wow," he murmured.

"Yeah," I said. "I know. You drive me nuts."

He settled on his knees between my splayed legs, bracing my feet against his broad, hard chest, and set himself to pet and explore, stroking my tits, my belly, then my pussy, with a rasping groan of appreciation. "Damn," he said. "So beautiful." He gripped his cock and stroked me with the tip, sliding it over all the slick, tender bits, concentrating on my clit, around and around... and it felt so good. I lifted myself against him helplessly. "Please," I gasped out.

"You want more?"

"Yes. Yes. Please."

But instead of pushing inside me, he slid down my body and put his head between my legs. I jerked up onto my elbows, startled. "Hey!"

"I want to taste you," he said, between skillful circling swirls of his tongue and his caressing finger. "You have to come before I fuck you."

"I have to? You have strict rules for this kind of thing, then?"

"Special rules. Just for you. I'm making them up as I go along."

It felt so shockingly good. It terrified me, to feel it all like that. Everything so sharp and distinct and urgent. Shane's clever, lashing tongue thrust and swirled, flicking and circling... then a slow, seductive, suckling pull... and the wave broke over me.

It crashed around me, through me, a chaotic, pulsing churn of utter bliss.

When I opened my eyes, I was shivering. Still damp with sweat, still panting. Shane had repositioned himself, and was nudging his cockhead between my pussy lips, pressing delicately. Rocking against the opening, without pushing inside.

"Ready now?" he asked.

I licked my lips, pulled in air, but couldn't speak, so I just grabbed his shoulders. Squeezed. Tightened my legs around him, trying to pull him into me.

That was enough. He surged forward, driving inside, and I cried out, arching, opening, moving with him, craving his heat and strength, this slick, hard, rhythmic fucking. His big body blocked out all the light, his big cock filled me, each heavy stroke working all my sweet spots. Lit up, with heat, emotion. Legs winding, arms clinging, whimpering with each pounding stroke. Torn between giving in to that desperate urgency, wanting all the pleasure now, now, now, and wanting it to last forfuckingever.

But it wasn't up to me. I was caught in a torrent much stronger than me, and it was launching me out into that wild, mindless nowhere of delight.

After, I floated back, feeling soft and renewed. As fresh as the dawn.

I held him tight, as if clinging arms could keep anyone close. I knew that it was way more mysterious and complicated than that. But something about touching this man transformed me. I felt powerful, charged with energy and magic, like someone to be reckoned with. I couldn't resist that feeling. I craved it.

And that made me feel so vulnerable and exposed.

Shane

The tight, fluttering pussy clenches around my cock were amazing. I never wanted them to end. So sweet. So hot.

She hugged me, arms and legs squeezing me tight while the aftershocks faded. Her pussy was still clutching my dick, delicately clinging to me. Her nails dug in, keeping me close. I was collapsed over her body. Gasping for breath.

It hit me all at once, the shit trouble I was in. I'd opened all those doors in my mind for her. Blasting them off their hinges with no regard for all the bad shit that was behind them. And now it was flying out into my face. And oh, *fuck*. It was bad.

I pulled out of her, flopping over onto my back. She cuddled up next to me. Now was the part where I should pull her into my arms, cuddle her, nuzzle the top of her head. Lazy kisses, murmured conversation. Secrets, confidences, sweet nothings.

And I wanted to. I wanted it bad, but there was a vortex in my guts, and it was dragging me down. It was all I could do to just not get sucked straight down into hell.

I had nothing left for pillow talk.

She sat up, putting her hand on my chest. "Shane? Are you okay?"

I wanted to lie, but couldn't. "No."

She placed a hand on my chest. She didn't start in with the clumsy platitudes, or demand reassurance. She just waited quietly while I struggled.

"I should have known," I ground out.

"Known what?" she asked gently.

I didn't know how to say it. "I turned off my feelings, in Halliwell's jail," I said. "With you, they turn back on all at once. Like a landslide. And I'm fucked."

"I'm here." Her hand pressed down on me, fingers tightening.

I stared up at the ceiling. My gut was clenching, my breath shortening. It was getting worse, not better. Like a screaming hurricane inside me. A sense of deadly urgency, like I could snap. I had no idea who I was, in that state. What I was capable of.

"You should go," I told her harshly.

"But I don't want to leave you when—"

"It's not safe to be with me right now. Go, Red. Right now." I lifted her hand off my chest and shoved it away. "Go!" The ugly energy into my voice rocked her back. "Get the fuck out of here. Now."

She slid off the bed, picked up her nightgown, tossed it on. Then she stalked out the door without saying another word, chin up, back straight. Regal as a goddess.

Who would have thought I could feel even shittier. But that was one thing that Halliwell had taught me. There was no end to how bad things could get. No bottom.

You could just keep going straight down forever.

CHAPTER 14

Cass

I went back and forth from uneasy dozing to tossing wakefulness, but luckily the bed was huge. I could flop around without disturbing Reggie, who slept very soundly.

These emotional extremes were exhausting. Euphoria, after escaping and getting Reggie back, terror that Halliwell could still hurt her. Passionate gratitude to Shane and his family. Violent lust. Hurt pride. Crushing humiliation after being thoroughly dicked down and then dismissed, like a silly little bitch who had fulfilled her purpose.

What did I expect? I'd acted like such a good little concubine. Bouncing in, flinging off my clothes, falling to my knees to suck his dick. Begging him to fuck me.

And after I'd put out, after his orgasm, it was 'get the fuck out of here.'

Harsh. Embarrassing. But I had been through worse. I was being threatened by much worse. My hurt pride would heal. Eventually. Time and distance would do the job. I had to focus on Reggie's health. Not my own shitty impulse control.

I needed these people. Their immense resources. Two helicopters, for fuck's sake? An army of smart people who knew useful things? Yes, please. They snapped their fingers, and medical and pharmaceutical experts appeared. And the place was a fortress, beyond being beautiful and luxurious. It was the best place that Reggie and I could possibly have landed.

Which was so damn lucky, I couldn't help bracing for the other shoe to drop.

Reggie's lashes quivered. She yawned and opened her eyes. The smile of delight on her face made my eyes fill up instantly.

"I didn't want to wake up," she said, reaching out to touch my arm. "I was sure it would just be a dream. But it's not. It's real."

"It sure is, babe." My voice cracked, and I covered by scooting over to grab her and hug her. She felt so thin and small. Much thinner than I remembered. Like she'd blow away in a high wind.

We smiled at each other. "I'm going to find a way to make you better," I said, hoping desperately that it was true. "There has to be a way, and I'm going to find it."

She patted my arm. "It's okay, even if you don't," she said earnestly. "I'm so glad you got me out. That clinic, it was like... I don't know, being in hell, or something. I just want to be with you now. Whatever happens, happens. And it's all okay. Really."

My heart felt squeezed, as if by a clenching fist, at the other-worldly calmness in Reggie's words, like she had one foot in that other world already. It broke my heart, and it scared me to death. Whatever mellow zen calm she had achieved, I did not share it.

I wanted her to pull that foot right back here and stay in this world. With me.

"Well, I'm going to fight like a freaking demon," I told her. "So watch out."

"I know," she said, smiling. "You're the Red Queen. Off with their heads!"

"Right." I kissed her forehead and hugged her until she started to laugh.

"You're squeezing me like a python!" she protested.

A knock on the door cut off our giggles, and we both jolted straight up, jangled by stress hormones. "Yes?" I called out.

"It's Angela. Good morning!" she called out from behind the door. "Just letting you know that the breakfast buffet is piping hot and ready right now, and the coffee is nice and fresh. Does Reggie like pancakes or waffles?"

Reggie looked at me, eyes blank. "Ah... I'm not really all that hungry."

"You have to try, babe," I said softly. "Please, try. Waffles!" I called out.

"With strawberries? Cream?"

"Both!" Reggie called, always a good sport.

"A girl after my own heart," Angela said. "One waffle, coming right up!"

We briskly got ourselves up, washed, brushed, dressed. I dreaded seeing Shane after last night's debacle, but I couldn't afford to be a whiny baby about it. I would just interact with him as seldom as possible. I just had to keep Reggie safe and well. My sex life, or lack of one, was of absolutely no importance in the grand scheme of things.

The rules were simple from now on. Head up. Chin out. Legs closed.

We followed the sounds and scents of breakfast, which were actually waking up my appetite from its long sleep. Coffee, pastry, toast, fried potatoes, yum. We heard voices murmuring, cutlery clinking. Reggie's hand stole into mine as we stood in the doorway. I squeezed it gratefully.

"There they are at last!" Angela sang out, as she emerged from the kitchen with a waffle on a plate, topped with a heap of quivering crème Chantilly and juicy, dark red strawberries. "The heroines of the moment! Sit down and have some of this!" She beamed at me. "One for you, too?"

"I'll stick to eggs and toast myself, thank you," I told her.

"Anything you like. Help yourself. Plates and cups over there, hon."

The room was full, which did not surprise me, considering the delicious breakfast buffet. Shane was sitting with Ethan and the other guys I met last night, the Drakes. They were conversing in low voices. I had no way of knowing if he looked at me, because our gazes were never, ever going to cross again in this lifetime.

I got Reggie set up with silverware and a glass of milk, and dished up some food, which made my stomach rumble. There was a delicious looking ham and veggie omelet, some sliced fruit, fresh toasted bread, fresh squeezed orange juice. I got a cup of coffee, and I sat with Reggie, who was nibbling her waffle with grim resolve.

I had seated us as far away from Shane as it was possible to sit. Which would be my strategy from now until the sun expanded and consumed the entire solar system.

Kat poured herself a fresh cup of coffee and ambled over to sit with us after a few minutes. "Did you guys sleep well?"

"Great," Reggie announced. "No bad dreams! And I woke up and Cass was there. Best night ever."

Kat reached out to ruffle her hair. I sensed a hint of sadness in her smile. "Glad to hear it, honey. Look at you go. That waffle is history. Where did you even put it?"

"Well, I only ate half the waffle, but I ate all the berries and cream," she said.

"If you went to the kitchen and asked Angela to pile on more berries and cream, I bet she'd do it."

"You think?"

"I'm sure of it," Kat assured her. "Angela has a weakness for cute little girls. She's like putty in their hands. Go on, try it."

Reggie jumped up and took her plate. She scampered toward the kitchen.

Slick move, on Kat's part. I could just tell that she was gearing up to have some kind of 'talk' with me. I hid in my coffee cup and avoided eye contact.

Kat was undaunted. "Um. I couldn't help but notice a certain chill in the air."

"Not from me," I said crisply. "Far as I'm concerned, there is absolutely nothing in the air."

"Yikes," she murmured. "Interesting night, huh?"

"Not the word I'd choose."

She opened her mouth, then shut it, frowning for a few minutes. "Trauma is tricky," she said. "It shuts you down at the worst possible times. Always when it's positioned to do the absolute maximum damage. Make the biggest, ugliest mess."

I set down my coffee and met her eyes. "We're not having this conversation."

"Don't tell me, let me guess. It was all totally awesome, until *bam*, his trauma popped up and kicked you both right in the teeth. Am I right?"

I stared at her, unnerved. "Ahhh…"

"Been there, done that, don't love the memory. But we got through it."

I tried to resist, tried really hard, but my curiosity got the better of me. "Whose trauma?" I demanded. "His? Or yours?"

"Mine. My sisters were shot to death in front of me when I was fourteen."

I gazed at her, mouth agape. "I… ah…"

"I spent the next fourteen years on the run from the guy who did it."

"Oh, my God," I murmured. "So, um… where is he now?"

She smiled. "Ethan took care of him for me. Very poetically,

I might add. I'll tell you the story sometime. I would have handled it myself, but Ethan just had to be the big hero. These Masters dudes are super macho. As you will come to know."

"I've noticed already," I said.

"It's hard to miss. They need a very strong hand." She gave me a thoughtful onceover. "Which you clearly possess."

"My strong hand isn't going to do him much good, the way he's acting."

"Please," she said gently. "Give it time. Don't come to any conclusions yet."

I snorted. "Conclusions, my ass."

"Conclusions about what?" It was Reggie, back with a waffle that was hidden under a teetering heap of berries and cream. "What about your ass?"

"Nothing, sweetie," I said. "My ass is fine."

"I'm not a baby anymore, you know," she told me solemnly. "Particularly not after the clinic. You can tell me stuff. I won't break."

Not this stuff, babydoll. "Sure, honey. I know. That looks amazing."

"It is, but I'm stuffed. Already. Here." She slid the plate my way and smiled at Kat. "Want a bite?"

"Already had mine," Kat said. "But thanks."

I took a bite and let out an involuntary moan of pleasure. Dessert for breakfast.

There was a brief commotion on the other side of the room as five guys simultaneously got an alert on their phones and leaped up, at the ready. They checked the camera feeds on their devices, and all of them visibly relaxed.

"It's just Rose," Ethan told us. "Not to worry."

"Oh, good." Kat sounded relieved. "We can start getting some answers."

I was hopping with eagerness to get right to it, but I had to wait through all the rituals and pleasantries. Rose was a beautiful young woman, about my age, with strawberry blond hair. She was luscious and curvy and eye-catching, and she seemed very bright and focused. But of course, Angela had to fuss over her, feed her breakfast, catch up on every detail of her life, yada yada.

Thirty nail-chewing, knuckle-grinding minutes later, we were finally ensconced on the generous square of big couches in the big living room of Ethan's house, armed with fresh coffee and staring down at the little box of vials and IV bags that had been in the fridge in Reggie's clinic room. The object upon which all our hopes were pinned.

Reggie herself came in and sat down on the edge of the couch next to me with a businesslike air, folding her hands, eyes expectant. Everyone looked at her, and then looked at me. Amos coughed. "Ah... are we sure we want to talk about all this, ah..."

"With me here?" Reggie asked. "Of course. This is all mostly about me, right? Who knows more than me about what happened in that place?"

"She's not wrong," Remy observed wryly.

Everyone exchanged eyebrow twitches, but they talked to Reggie with careful respect as we hashed through it all, again and again. Reggie was patient about repeating herself. "I knew they were dirty somehow pretty early on," she told us. "As soon as I started feeling better. I saw how the nurses and doctors treated Mom when she had Varen's Disease. These people didn't treat me that way at all. They were really mean. They all ignored me when I tried to talk to them."

"I was struck by the way the staff behaved when we stormed into the place," Kat said. "They didn't act like busy professionals who resented being interrupted from the important job they were doing. They acted like assholes who'd gotten caught doing something nasty. They scattered like rats. I had to chase down one of the doctors to question him, if he was a doctor at all. Probably just a shill."

"Well, the people there were definitely assholes," Reggie said solemnly.

The rest of them chuckled, but I couldn't afford to, being the only quasi-authority figure in Reggie's life. "Hey," I said. "Watch that language, babe."

She gave me a look. "Really, Cass? From you? With your mouth?"

I had to laugh, along with the others, but it made me sad, that my sweet little sister seemed more like a jaded adult than the cheerful little girl she had been.

"I sent people over there this morning," Ethan said. "The place is deserted. Doors unlocked. Papers scattered everywhere. Property records show it's rented by ABC Properties, a shell company located in Delaware which no longer exists as of today. These people know how to cover their tracks."

I stared down at the medicine, my stomach clenching around the food I had eaten. "So if they weren't doctors, what is this stuff?" I gestured at the box.

"It seems like it hadn't hurt her yet," Ethan offered. "Maybe the drug is for real, even if the clinic isn't. We don't know."

Rose angled herself toward me and Reggie. "Tell me about the symptoms," she urged.

I racked my brains to remember. "It was about three and a half months ago that it started," I said. "Maybe a little more. It came on slow. Fatigue, a nose bleed, another nose bleed, a rash, then a fever. All this over about twenty days or so. Oh, except for that episode about a week before it started. You fainted on the steps leading down to the track field, remember?"

"I told you," Reggie said impatiently. "I didn't faint. I was pushed. Probably the mean girls from my class."

I turned back to Rose. "The school told me she was found at

the bottom of the steps, out cold, and with a bump on her head."

"The mean girls pushed me," Reggie repeated stubbornly. "Probably Kylie."

I shrugged. "Maybe so. Anyway. If fainting could be thought of as a first symptom, it came on about a week before the fatigue, the nosebleeds, etc."

"How soon did the symptoms improve once you were at the clinic?" Rose asked.

Reggie frowned thoughtfully. "Maybe four, five days? It got better right away, but it was about five days later that I felt well enough to get up and see what was outside the door. That was when I found out I was locked in."

Kat winced. "Bastards," she murmured. "I'm glad I put the fear of God into at least one of those pieces of sh... ah. Sorry." She coughed. "Garbage, I mean."

"What did the garbage tell you?" Rose asked.

"He said that her medicine was in the fridge in her room. One injection, morning and evening, and the IV bags had vitamins, minerals and various other supplements."

"Which I don't want to do anymore." Reggie held out her arm, and everyone in the room flinched at her pale, scrawny arm, the bluish color of skim milk, completely covered with needle scars and hematomas of every color.

Rose made a horrified sound. "God! Whoever did that was a total hack!"

"Yep," Reggie said solemnly. "Not gonna argue with that."

"I'm going to take one of each to test," Rose told me. "One vial, one IV bag. Until we know what's in it, my instinct would be not to give her any more of it."

"Good," Reggie said, with quiet satisfaction. "I hate those damn needles."

It made sense, weighing dangers against possible advantages, but it ratcheted up my tension still more, reminding me how naked in the dark I was, with such a limited ability to help and protect my sister. Nothing but questions, uncertainties, doubts. Fears.

"I'll get back to my lab right away and get to work on this," Rose assured me.

Rose was invited to lunch, but she insisted that she needed to get to work, a sentiment I appreciated with my whole heart. I gave her a grateful hug before she even got her coat on. "Thanks for caring," I whispered.

"Oh, God, yes." She hugged me back hard. "I'll get back to you as soon as I can, I promise. This will be my number one priority. Actually, my only priority."

The phones began to ding-ding-ding again. Everyone grabbed them and checked.

Ethan looked up at Shane. "They're here," he said quietly. "Jed, Freya and Holly are back from the airport. Get ready, bro. You're on."

CHAPTER 15

Shane

Get ready, my ass. There was no prepping for something like this.

I'd faced death more times than I could count, but I had never been so fucking scared as I was at this moment. I also hated myself for feeling afraid, not happy. And I was ashamed of being such a fucking coward. This was my baby girl, for God's sake.

I was a tangled knot of pure, unfiltered suck right now.

But it was all happening, here and now, so I followed everyone out into the chilly mountain air. I caught a quick, furtive look from Red, but her curious gaze whipped away as soon as my own crossed with it. I pushed that mess to another part of my mind. Locked the door on it. One snake's nest of overwhelming feelings at a time.

Holly was the first one down the steps. She moved slowly, as if she were afraid it was a trap. She looked different. Taller, thinner, her hair had grown longer. Darker than I remembered. Her eyes sought out my face as I walked toward her.

Instinctively, everyone else held back. I caught Frey's eyes as she did the same. She stopped short, holding Jed's hand, and letting Holly come on alone.

Just me, and my little girl, everyone watching, pacing toward each other like two gunslingers at high noon. Staring at each other's faces. Trying to recognize each other.

She stopped a few feet from me, her lip starting to shake. "Daddy?" she asked.

The word, the tone, took me down like a landslide. I lunged forward and dropped to my knees. "Baby," I rasped.

Suddenly she was in my arms, sobbing. She smelled just like I remembered. Her hair was warm and silky against my nose.

"It's really you?" she asked.

I let out a short laugh, the one that sounded like a rusty cough. "More or less. Such as I am. You're as beautiful as ever, sweetheart. You got so big. Look at you."

"Yeah. I'm growing like a weed, Auntie Frey says." She hid her face against my shoulder, then lifted her gaze to the bandages around my neck. She brushed her fingertips over them. "Was this from that awful collar?"

I was startled. "What do you know about the collar?"

"I know a lot," she said, but her voice wobbled. Now clearly wasn't the time to talk about the bad stuff.

I grabbed her again, holding her small, shaking body as tightly as I dared.

We swayed there together for some time, and after a while, the others started to converge around us, talking softly. I looked up, my eyes blurred and hot. Frey stood there waiting her turn, eyes wet, clutching Jed's hand.

I rose to my feet, never relinquishing my hold on Holly, and held out an arm to her. Frey wrapped herself around us both, and then I was holding two sobbing females.

It took a while to get the nerve to lift my head, but I finally looked up at Jed, who also looked glassy-eyed and tight-lipped.

I narrowed my eyes at him. "What the hell is this I hear about you hooking up with my little sister?" I said. "The hell, dude? Who told you that was okay?"

He grinned. "Nobody. I saw my chance, and I took it. Can you blame me?"

"Maybe later," I said, and held my arm out to him, too. Now Holly was trapped between all three of us. She started to squawk and wiggle in protest.

Somehow, it went on from there. Holly began to talk a mile a minute, and all my energy and attention was spent on trying to follow what she said. I'd gotten through the wall. I hadn't crushed anybody's heart by not being enough. Not feeling enough.

Damn. I'd felt plenty. I was still feeling it.

I walked along awkwardly, Holly clutching my waist, Frey's arm above hers, hugging them both and trying to match steps to both of them, which was impossible. We shuffled and lurched down the breezeway, through the crowd. Holly stopped when she saw Red, who stood there holding Reggie's hand, wiping tears from her own eyes and trying not to show it. Holly and Reggie exchanged swift, curious glances and smiles, and then Holly looked up at Red.

"Are you the one who helped my daddy get away?" she asked.

Red gave Holly a misty smile. "It was a mutual thing. We helped each other. I wouldn't have made it here without him."

Holly let go of me and lunged for her, hugging her fiercely. "Thank you."

"Oh, honey." Red's arms circled her shoulders. "My pleasure."

"I second that," Freya said. Then she descended upon Red as well, and Holly was once again squeezed into a sandwich until she started giggling.

Eventually we made it inside. The period that followed was

a blur, Holly on my lap, Freya next to me, telling me incoherent, outrageous stories about hers and Jed's and Holly and Kat and Ethan's wild, dangerous adventures in their attempts to find me.

God. It was a miracle that any of them were alive to tell the tale.

At some point, Angela came in and told Holly and Reggie that she needed them both to help her make dessert. Holly looked at me and gave me another fierce hug.

"Don't disappear," she said sternly. "Don't you dare. Ever again."

"I won't," I promised.

And all at once, her eyes were swimming again. I pulled her into another hug, feeling my own eyes tingle and burn. Murmuring senseless promises about how I wasn't ever leaving her again. Wild horses couldn't drag me away.

Finally, she let out a soggy giggle at my nonsense, sniffed loudly and accepted a tissue from Angela to blow her nose before heading to the kitchen with Angela and Reggie.

When the girls were gone, Ethan closed the door. "So how much downtime do you need before we start working on taking that sonofabitch down?" he asked.

"None," I said. "I can save the downtime for later."

"Keep in mind that we can proceed with the full support of the law, guys," Freya reminded us sternly. "We don't have to do anything illegal or dangerous. We have Shane's testimony, and Cass's. Halliwell tortured him and tried to murder him. Shane can accuse him, and Cass can bear witness, so what's stopping us? We can certainly afford an army of lawyers as big as any he could bring."

"Yes, I saw it," Cass said, her voice vibrating with tension. "And yes, I will testify. I'll do anything you want. But please. First let me figure out what he's holding over my little sister, and if there's a way to undo it before you come down on him. I need data, options, leverage. The minute you guys move against him, I lose them all."

We pondered that stark truth for a moment. Sneaky bastard that he was, Halliwell had managed to jerk us around even here. Inside my family stronghold.

Kat drummed her fingers on the table by the couch. "The fake doctor said that the medicines were compounded in the Coatesworth Facility weekly and delivered to the clinic every Monday. We need to know who compounds it. What's in it."

"But we shut the clinic down already and scattered his shills," Ethan said.

Cass lifted her hand. "The woman who helped me mentioned the Coatesworth," she said. "She used to work there. That's where his pharmaceutical research is done."

"Yeah. The Coatesworth is a big deal. Halliwell Enterprises makes billions from pharmaceuticals."

Angela walked in. "People, I'm serving an early dinner, since brunch was so late. The gingerbread pudding is in the oven, what small part of it isn't smeared all over the kitchen. Dinner will be served in ten."

"Thanks, Angela. It smells great," Freya said.

"The girls seem to have bonded," Angela said, her voice tender. "They went to Holly's room, and they're in there on the bed, talking books and science. It's adorable."

A smile flashed across Red's face. "That's great," she said.

"Need help setting the table?" Kat asked.

"I had the girls do it. I just need someone to pick out some wine. We're having steak and a potato, artichoke and cheese bake, so choose accordingly."

"I'm on it," I said, rashly. As if I remembered anything like what wines tasted like, if I ever knew. Everyone else scattered to go and do whatever could be done in the ten minutes allotted before dinner. Red stalked past me without acknowledging my existence. Freya hugged and kissed me before she left. Jed slapped me on the back. Everyone passed with the usual worried looks, like they were poised to catch me at any time if I started falling to pieces.

I took my chance to retreat to the dim privacy of Ethan's wine cellar, where I proceeded to just put my head down between my legs and try to fucking breathe.

CHAPTER 16

Cass

"You're kidding," I said to Jed, incredulous. "You broke out of prison just in time to save her from a band of killers?"

"In a snowstorm, no less," Freya said.

Jed nodded solemnly. "The prison break had been programmed already," he said. "It's not like I could break out of a max security prison on the fly. But saving her from Wes Boer and Nicole's goons was off the cuff. The woman keeps me on my toes."

"Oh, stop it," Freya scoffed. "I saved your fine butt too, several times, so don't you act all long-suffering and put upon."

He leaned over to give her a swift but very passionate kiss. "All my suffering is worth it."

They gazed into each other's eyes. A glimpse of total intimacy and trust, marbled with scorching lust. It made my heart squeeze with longing.

Which made me angry at myself, for craving something so silly and unreasonable. I was asking a wounded, damaged, traumatized guy to be whole, and to fulfil all my stupid girlish fantasies. It wasn't fair. It wasn't Shane's fault that he didn't have what I needed. That was Halliwell's fault. And fate's. Tough shit for me.

After all the intense events of the day, last night's ice-cold dismissal still hurt. But I didn't have time for this bullshit. I should be grateful for the help. I should be cool and focused and businesslike, scheming for Reggie's well-being.

Not sulky and sad because Shane wasn't fulfilling my maidenly longings for romance. Longings I never knew I had until now.

Let it go, damn it. Let him go. He can't be what you want.

I savored another bite of dessert. Today's offering was a tender gingerbread with a whisky-tinged cream sauce. Holly and Reggie had their heads together and were cheerfully arguing about which of the Harry Potter books were the best ones. I loved to see it. Reggie had never had much social interaction with peers, which was partly Mom's and my fault. Mom was introverted and often depressed. She'd made very little effort socially. On top of that, Reggie was at least four grade levels ahead in terms of her cognitive development, which had always made friend groups problematic for her.

And it made social isolation and being bullied at school practically a given.

Holly was perfect for her. Smart, cheerful, bubbly, kind. Drawing her out.

Reggie looked over at me, her face bright with enjoyment. "Can I sleep in Holly's room on her pull-out bed?" she asked.

"It'll be like a slumber party," Holly said with obvious satisfaction. "I haven't been able to have a slumber party since before that thing happened to Daddy. But that's over, right? You can tell the police to arrest that guy and put him in jail now, right?"

"That's the general idea," Ethan said. "But it's more complicated than that."

Holly sighed. "It always is," she complained. "Well, whatever. I want that guy in jail. But Reggie and I can start making up for lost time already. We'll have a slumber party every night."

"Until you start up school again," Ethan warned.

"Oh, school, schmool," Holly said airily. She glanced over at Reggie. "School's pretty boring. For you, too?"

"God, yeah," Reggie said, with feeling. "Do you sneak books in?"

"Yes, or else I'd totally die. Let's go get into our pajamas now."

Reggie looked over at me. "Can I?"

I felt a little bereft, letting go of her already. I could have used a few more days of sleeping with Reggie clutched jealously in my arms like a teddy bear. But this, her bright, happy eyes, the color in her cheeks, was a beautiful thing to behold.

"Of course," I said heartily. "Let's go get you ready."

A chorus of good-nights followed us out the dining room door. I was careful as always not to look at Shane. Reggie chattered in our room about everything that was cool and awesome about Holly as we got her into her pajamas.

"You know, she's different from other kids," Reggie said thoughtfully.

"Different how?"

Reggie paused, thinking it over. "It's hard to explain," she said. "She's had bad things happen. She knows how bad things can get. Most kids have no clue. Remember when Mom died, and all the kids at school were afraid to talk to me? They were embarrassed. Scared by it. Holly's not embarrassed or scared."

My heart clutched. "Yeah, I understand."

"She had her dad taken, and then Nicole kidnapped her and Kat. She's been locked in a room, too. Not for as long as me or Shane. But still. She knows."

"Babe, I'm so sorry that you have to know," I said. "It's not right."

"Well, it's too late to fuss about it now," Reggie said sagely. "Once you know, you can't ever un-know it. No matter what your age."

"I get it," I said.

"I know you do," Reggie said. "I love being with you, after missing you for so long. But this is the thing. We don't know how many more chances I'll have to do stuff like this. Like, a slumber party with a friend. I should grab it while I can, right?"

"You'll have as many as you want," I said fiercely. "You'll have a whole long lifetime of it. We're beating this thing, Reggie."

Reggie's smile was sad. "You're super tough and badass, but you can't make me better by being badass. You're super sweet for wanting to, though."

Maybe not. But I could hold a knife to that bastard's throat and demand the cure. Hardly sweet, but whatever. I swallowed that back. "We'll see," I said. "You just go on and have your slumber party. The first of many slumber parties yet to come."

She got into fuzzy flannel jammies, with a pattern of pteranodons flying over a blue sky, and I walked her down the hall to Holly's room.

I saw Freya as I was going in the door, and realized, too late to retreat, that Shane was sitting on Holly's bed. Holly was on his lap.

I kept my eyes on the girls. Holly greeted Reggie with a burst of excited chatter, which I only pretended to follow. I couldn't hear it anyway, not though the roaring and pounding in my head, the nervous thudding of my heart. *Breathe, Cass. Breathe.*

Of course he was here. It was right, it was obvious, it was inevitable that he be here. In what universe would a loving father separated from his kid for over a year not give her a goodnight kiss the first night they were together? How did I not think this through? There was Cass Clarke for you. Selectively stupid AF, that was me.

I kept a big smile stamped on my face as I watched Holly and Reggie talking and giggling. I spouted some silly, predictable, teasing bullshit about being good, not staying up all night giggling like ninnies. It made them eye each other and snort with laughter. So far, so good. Then I kissed them goodnight, waved at everyone and backed on out of there. Smiling, smiling, smiling. Everything was just great, folks. See yah!

I heard Freya calling as I hustled toward the refuge of my bedroom. Oh, *crap.*

I wiped tears away as her quick footsteps approached, and re-established the smile as I turned around. She was hurrying to catch up. "Cass? Hey. Hold on."

I ramped up the smile. "Hey, there. Looks like loads of fun is about to be had."

Freya glanced back over her shoulder as a burst of laughter came out the door of Holly's room. Her smile was tender. "Holly's so excited to have a friend here," she said. "Her life has been so restricted since Shane got taken. Even before, it wasn't easy for her to find kids with her interests. She's so far ahead, and this year just made that gap even bigger. But Reggie is amazing. And wise beyond her years."

"Too wise," I blurted out, louder than I meant to. "She shouldn't have to know how shitty things can get. Not yet. She's too goddamn young. It's too soon. Those fucking bastards. I want to kill them all." To my horror, my face started to shake.

Freya gave me an impulsive hug. "I get you. I feel the same way about Holly."

She squeezed me close, which made it even harder to fight the tears. I did not want to subject the poor jet-lagged woman to one of my crying jags, so I swayed back, sniffing aggressively. "Sorry," I mumbled. "Didn't mean to leak on you."

"Don't apologize," Freya said fiercely. "Cry on me all you want. You deserve it, a million times over. You switched out that canister of poison gas for Shane and hauled him out of that place. Which makes you my hero until the end of time."

"Aw. Thanks. But really. It was a transactional thing, not a heroic act, so—"

"Don't even try. I know perfectly well that he was unconscious at the time. You said so yourself, and so did he. So that's actually a big fat lie. Just give it up, Cass. What you did was brave, amazing, and heroic. Accept it. Own it. End of story."

I laughed, but I still felt self-conscious and a little guilty. It seemed to me that what I had done for Shane had been far too self-interested to merit all this gratitude.

They had snatched back my precious girl for me. So we were oh, so square.

But being appreciated did not suck. Particularly since Shane had seemed quite underwhelmed by me. Not thrilled enough to keep me in his bed all night, that was for sure. But there was no point in thinking about that.

I hugged Freya again and exchanged good nights, and headed back to my room thinking about how much I liked her, Kat, Rose, Angela, Ethan. The Drakes, too, come to think of it. I wanted them for myself, goddamn it. I wanted this tight, safe, intimate family vibe they had going. What a fantasy. To have people I trusted, respected and admired, all around me. This place was like a shimmering oasis in the desert.

But the hard truth was, they belonged to Shane. And if Shane didn't want me, it was back out into the flinty desert once again. Alas, poor me. Cue the fucking violins.

My pity party ended now. I had my sister. I was away from Halliwell. Thanks to these people, my lot was the best I could hope for. No more wallowing allowed.

I took a shower to get the rest of the tear gunk rinsed out of my face and dressed for bed. I wrapped a fleecy robe around myself and settled into the big, soft couch that faced the window, leaving the light off. I stared out into dark, letting my brain sift and sort the events of the past few days. Trying to see it through different lenses. None of them yielded great insights. None of the viewpoints looked good for Reggie.

If Halliwell could hurt me through her, he would. He had us stalemated.

No. I had to face reality. Halliwell had *me* stalemated. I could not count on these people to back me up, in spite of their friendliness and their warm welcome.

I was so anxious for Rose to get us more info about the medicines Kat had retrieved from the fake clinic. What it was, if it worked, if more could be made. If I had a working solution for Reggie's problem, I'd fear absolutely nothing. I'd spit in Halliwell's eye without a care.

A knock sounded on the door, making me start. I stared at it for a moment.

"Yes?" I called.

"It's me." It was Shane's voice.

Oh, God. A new tangle of conflicting emotions to jerk me around and tear me apart. Fear and hope, anger at myself for being so damned vulnerable.

"It's late, Shane." I kept my voice crisp. "Get some sleep. See you tomorrow."

"Can I talk to you? Please?"

I let out a sigh. No way could I resist that deep, scratchy voice. "Just for a minute," I warned. "I'm very tired."

He opened the door and stood staring into the dark room, trying to find me in it. His tall, lean body was silhouetted in the light from the corridor.

"Sitting in the dark?" he asked.

"Seemed appropriate for my mood."

He came in, shut the door, and flicked the lock shut. Hmm.

That was bold, but I didn't feel articulate enough to call him on it. This was hard enough as it was.

He stood there, letting his eyes adjust. I was grateful for the darkness. The less he saw of my face, the better.

He moved toward me like a shadow and sat on the far end of the couch.

"Holly loves having your sister here," he said, like an offering.

"I'm so glad for them both," I said. "It was the best possible thing that could have happened for Reggie. Besides a cure for her mystery illness, of course. Holly is a blessing for her, too, after being so lonely for so long in that hellish place."

"Like you were for me," he said. "In Halliwell's dungeon."

Anger kindled inside me. "No way, Shane," I said, my voice vibrating with emotion. "Don't do that. Don't you dare. No way can you come in here and whisper sweet nothings at me after last night."

"I'm sorry about last night," he said. "I can't tell you how much."

"Sorry's not good enough." I kept my voice clipped. "Go back to your own room. Get some sleep. We'll keep up the cordial strangers routine until we can get out of each other's faces."

"I love having you in my face. I've never seen anything so fucking beautiful."

I pressed my hands over my shaking face. Goddamn him all to hell.

"Shane," I said, through my teeth. "You're killing me. I seem to remember you throwing me out of your bed. I seem to recall words like 'get the fuck out of here.' It didn't feel good, and I'm not doing that to myself again. So get your ass up off that couch, and get out. Good night."

"Last night was amazing. And then I had... a bad moment."

"Bad moment?" I repeated slowly. "Really. Which made you

feel justified in dismissing me, like some insignificant fuck-bunny you were finished with?"

"It wasn't like that," he said quietly. "I don't know how to explain it. But if you were with someone you cared about, like Reggie, and the earth suddenly opened up and there was a pool of boiling lava at your feet, you'd try to get Reggie away from it as fast as you could, right? It felt... kind of like that."

I tried to make out his features in the dark. "Ah. So you were protecting me? By being rude and horrible? Please, Shane. Don't do me any more goddamn favors. If you want to fuck with my head, you're going to have to up your game. I am no dummy."

"I know you're not. You're brilliant. And I love that about you. It turns me on."

I got up from the couch. "I can't deal with this," I said. "It's all compliments and kisses, but who knows when the earth will open up? Is it just random for you, when the lava starts pumping? Can you see it coming? Do you want me to lower my guard just so that you can fuck me again? Not in this lifetime, buddy."

He reached for my hand, but I swayed back, evading him. "Red," he said softly. "Please. You didn't deserve that. It was awful. I got slammed, and I couldn't handle the feelings. I couldn't stand falling to pieces in front of you."

My eyes were leaking again, to my dismay. Goddamn that man. "News flash, Shane. I can't handle it, either. Get lost, so I can fall to pieces in peace."

"No." He leaned over and grabbed both my hands. He bent over to kiss them.

I didn't know what kind of sneaky sex god sorcery he was doing on me, but the soft warmth of his lips on my knuckles made everything go soft and hot and shivery inside me. Some dark, potent magic that effortlessly melted down my anger, my flinty resolve, my treacherous heart, and turned it all into desperate longing. Like there was a direct line from his soft, hot, pleading kisses against my knuckles, right to my heart.

He slid off the couch and kneeled in front of me, redoubling those hand kisses. The gesture was so seductive. It promised infinite patience. It implied that he'd be happy to just stay there all night, kissing the joints of my fingers. Slowly, softly, every point of contact deliberate, thorough, worshipful.

Until I was betrayed by that hot ache in my heart. Practically screaming for it.

I was infatuated. It was so stupid. Such a bad time. But I just stood there, my face wet, my mouth shaking, letting him worship my hands. Helpless to stop him.

And he felt me softening, the slick, sneaky bastard. He maneuvered me expertly so I was over the couch again, and tumbled me backwards, then kneeled in front of me, parting my legs. Pushing the nightdress up over my knees.

I was naked beneath it. He let out low rumble of delighted approval as his hands stroked up my thighs, pressing them wider, petting my mound, tracing my slick pussy lips with teasing fingertips. Opening me.

"Can I taste you?" he said.

"Oh." I laughed shakily under my breath. "So now the nice manners come out, huh? Beg me, dude."

He vibrated with silent laughter. "I don't mind begging," he said. "I beg for forgiveness. I beg for another chance. I beg for the privilege of making you come. I'm already on my knees." He cupped my ass, tugging it to the edge of the couch cushions. "Let me lick you until you scream," he murmured. "Pretty please."

"No screaming," I said primly. "My innocent little sister is right down the hall. Sleeping right next to your innocent little daughter."

"It's on you not to scream, Red." There was dark laughter in his deep, scratchy voice. "Good luck with that. I'm not holding back."

And he went at me. Tenderly, hungrily, the same worshipful kisses against my pussy lips that he'd done to my hands, but more, deeper, wilder. Opening me with slow, teasing swipes of his tongue. His plunging, caressing fingers were made slick with my juice. Licking and swirling, tongue lashing, fingers delving. Suckling on my clit oh, so delicately. Working me into a helpless froth of pure, shaking need.

I bucked against his face, clutching at his hair, whimpering and gasping as the first orgasm wrenched through me. Obliterating me.

He waited afterward, kissing my thigh, petting my mound as if it were a purring kitten. As soon as I was close to normal consciousness again, he started again.

His instincts were spot on. He knew just when to push and when to wait, and when to speed up and go for it, insisting. I abandoned all control and let myself be carried away on that voluptuous ride. The pleasure built and crested, again and again, until I was limp and soft, thighs slick, every cell of my body humming with pleasure.

He finally leaned back, got to his feet, and pulled me up, pushing the robe off my shoulders, letting it tumble onto the couch. He pulled the nightgown off me, tossing it away. I couldn't see his eyes, in the dimness, but he knew he could have anything he wanted of me in this condition. I was unraveled, undone. Lost to all reason.

He took my hand, wrapping my fingers around his thick erection. I stroked it appreciatively, remembering how it felt inside me. Aching to have him there again.

"What do you want from me, Shane?" I couldn't control my shaky tone. I didn't want to sound this vulnerable, but it wasn't up to me.

He pulled me up onto my feet and turned me around, pushing me toward the couch. "This."

I tumbled against the couch, my knees on the cushions, face pressed against the back positioned me right how he wanted me, thighs wide, ass out. But his hands slid up my inner thighs and boldly stroked my pussy again. I pushed myself against him as I felt his thick cockhead prodding me, sliding into the slick, sensitive opening of my pussy, pressing forward against the resistance, pulsing against it, teasing, taunting.

Staying there. Stroking the opening, swiveling, caressing my pussy lips. Making me wild for him to thrust his cock into me.

"Goddamn it, what are you waiting for?" I demanded.

"To be sure it's what you want," he murmured.

"You're the one who was supposed to beg," I said tartly. "Not me."

He vibrated with silent laughter, and thrust deep.

After all my fine words about not screaming, I had to press my face against the couch to muffle the gasping moans that jerked out of me at each slick stroke. He gripped my hips and pumped hard, fucking me expertly into a blinding explosion.

This time, as I drifted back, the sweat on my naked body made me shiver as I braced myself for a repeat performance of last night. The post-coital lava pit.

He was collapsed over me, panting. If he was cold and rejecting to me now, I'd be destroyed. I would also have to go through the whole emotional routine again. Feeling stupid for letting my gullible, wretched, silly-ass self be seduced into this vulnerable position once again, when I already knew better.

Cass Clarke, the eternal slow learner.

But he didn't pull away. He just stroked me, hip, waist, ribs, cupping my breast, teasing my nipple as he squeezed the side of my neck. So far, so good.

He withdrew from my body with a low, grinding sigh. "So

do you want first crack at the bathroom?" he asked. "Or shall I go first?"

Huh. Maybe he wanted to sneak off while I wasn't looking. Well, let him. That might be the easiest thing. Slightly less humiliation involved. But only slightly.

"Sure." I stumbled for the bathroom and shut myself safely inside before I dared to turn on the light.

I was shocked at the look on my face. Good thing it was dark in the bedroom. I didn't want to show my eyes to anyone. It was written all over me, how scared I felt, how uncertain I was. How needy.

I washed up hastily with the shower nozzle, wishing I'd had the wits and foresight to bring the nightgown into the bathroom. Just to feel more protected when I walked out. But there was no effective protection, not after being pounded into sobbing, wailing oblivion by the man of my dreams. As it was, in that shaky state, I had to strut out there, stark naked, like the queen of the world. The Red Queen. Hah.

I switched off the light before putting my hand on the knob, and tightened every muscle in my body to get ready for... whatever was on the other side.

Which was to say, probably an empty room.

I opened the door and found him standing right there. I jerked back. "Whoa!" I said. "You scared me!"

"Sorry," he said. "My turn?"

"Sure," I said, bemused. "Ah... go for it."

So. He hadn't left. Now I had to deal with him. Was that good, bad? Who knew.

At least it was interesting. It wasn't sad and flat and stupid, like an empty room would have been. So I was going with... good. Very good.

Yes. I would dare to think that this was a promising development.

I put my nightgown back on and paced. Restless, nervous

and excited. After a few minutes, the door opened and the light was still on, spilling out, blinding me. He sauntered out, magnificently naked. So freaking gorgeous, it was just too much for my poor, overloaded sensibilities. It shouldn't be allowed.

"Could you turn that light off?" I asked him. "It makes my eyes hurt."

He flicked it off obligingly. "But I want to see you. Can we turn on the bedside—"

"No."

"Okay," he soothed. "Whatever you want. So, ah..." His voice petered out.

"So what?" I asked.

"I was just wondering if you'd like to get into that bed," he said. "With me."

"You want sex again? Already?"

He let out a short laugh. "Full disclosure? I want sex with you all the time. That's just a given. But I was thinking right now I could just, ah. You know. Hold you."

"Hold..." I stopped, speechless. "You want to *cuddle?*"

"Is that so outrageous?" he asked, defensive. "I'll always be up for sex, believe me. Say the word, and I stand ready. But we don't have to. We can just..."

"Cuddle," I said again, still unbelieving.

"Yeah," he said. "It would be nice."

Nice. The word made me want to break out into hysterical laughter. Cuddling. Nice. Those words didn't belong in the apocalyptic shitshow that was my current life.

"It's okay, if you don't want to," he said carefully.

"It's not that." My voice came out shakier than I wanted it to. "I'm just wondering. Can you guarantee that whatever fiery pit opened up inside you last night won't come back and slam me in mid-cuddle? Because that would really suck for me."

He was silent for a long moment. "It comes when it comes," he said cautiously.

"Ah. So I won't ever know when you might morph into an instant asshole. At least you wouldn't be able to throw me out of this room. You'd have to get up and leave yourself. Slightly less horrible, but still a thing to be avoided."

"I can't swear it won't happen again," he said, his voice low and careful. "But I'll try not to push you away if it does. It's just that, ah... it won't be pretty. So just... you know. Be ready."

I was taken aback at the stark vulnerability in his voice. It moved me. Then again, maybe I was just being managed. The guy had some very smooth moves.

"I'm not that pretty inside right now myself," I told him. "You be ready, too."

"You seem great to me," he said. "So? May I get into your bed?"

I couldn't keep back a bark of laughter. "Wow, Shane, you weren't so delicate and polite about it when you were putting your dick into me."

He crossed his arms over his chest. "If I did anything you didn't like—"

"Oh, no! No worries on that score," I assured him. "If you did anything I didn't like, you would by God hear about it. I'm not the type to suffer in silence, believe me."

"I do," he said. "Believe you, I mean."

That bewildered me. "You do? About what? What are we talking about exactly?"

He waved his hand. "You," he said. "You still seem too good to be true. You're too gorgeous, too brave, too smart. You're just... too much to be real. But you are real."

I pondered that for a moment, bewildered. "Ah, gosh. I'm not sure if it's necessarily a compliment to have one's existence on this mortal plane duly acknowledged, but whatever. Thanks. What was it that persuaded you?"

"Mostly, the way you are with your little sister," he said. "You can't fake that."

"That's true." My voice caught.

"It went all right today," he said. "Reuniting with Holly, I mean. I was shit-scared of that. But I didn't smash or break anything. It was okay. Better than okay."

"It certainly was," I said. "You were fine with Holly. Great, even."

"I'm grateful. And that gave me the nerve to try this again. Being a real person, I mean. Doing risky things like reaching out to an amazing woman. Touching her. Wooing her. Begging for her to forgive me for being such a fucking coward last night."

"Ah," I said, cautiously. "I see. Well, um. Consider yourself... forgiven. I guess."

"Thank you," he said. "So? May I get into your bed?"

I crossed my arms over my chest. "You should think about it long and hard. The Red Queen's bed is a dangerous place. Are you sure you have the nerve?"

He was grinning. I saw his teeth flash in the dimness. "Will you chop off my head if I disappoint you?"

"You'll never disappoint me in bed," I told him. "It's after that's risky."

"I won't do that to you again," he said. "If the lava pits open up, I'll just try not to freak out on you. I'll do everything I can. I'm so afraid of fucking this up."

I harrumphed. "Well. That would imply there was a thing between us to fuck up. We've never discussed it, ever. And just sex, no matter how scorching hot it might be, does not count as 'a thing.'"

"We could discuss it in bed," he suggested.

I laughed at him. "Nice one, Masters. You already had your wicked way with me tonight. It's a bad precedent. Make you think everything is yours for the taking."

"I'll take nothing for granted, I promise. And yes, there is something between us, apart from the spectacular sex. There has been since you sneaked down into my dungeon to see me."

"You think so?"

"I know so," he said. "I was ready to die, Red. I was actually looking forward to it. Then you came tiptoeing in, and you fucked that all up. And suddenly, I didn't want to die anymore. Which was kind of a huge fucking problem for me."

"Aw," I said, shakily. "That's sweet."

"Please, don't jerk me around. I'm trying really hard. I'm sorry about last night. And I'm sorry if I was too aggressive with the sex. It just... comes over me."

"You weren't," I said. "I liked it. Besides, I'm pretty aggressive myself."

I thought I saw a brief smile flash over his face in the dimness. "Off with their heads," he murmured.

"Exactly," I said. "So. You solemnly promise to be good?"

"Good as gold," he said.

"Well, then. In that case, you may get into my bed," I said primly.

It felt comically awkward and shy, after all his hot moves on the couch. We went to opposite sides of the bed in silence, lifted the covers, and got in, like a couple of virginal noobs. Then we scooted closer, and closer still, until we met in the middle of the huge king-sized bed. And ahhhh. Yes.

As always, touching his hard, hot, naked body was a fresh, delicious shock to my senses. He was so dense and solid. A sweet rush of emotion and sensation flashed through me. He slid his arm under my neck, gathering me into his warmth. It was a wonderful and terrifying sensation. No one had ever done that for me. I'd cuddled my darling Reggie, of course, but she was my precious little honey to curl around and protect from the big bad world. Not that I'd had so much luck with that.

SHANNON MCKENNA

Touching Shane... that was a new type of cuddling. A very different vibe.

"So," I said. "You said before that you had decided that I was for real."

"Yeah." He sounded like he was wary of a trap. "And? So?"

"This implies that there was a time in which you were wondering if I wasn't."

He grunted. "I wasn't even sure if you were a hallucination, Red. But my family all sees you, too. And they're all grateful. So I'm pretty sure you're flesh and blood. If this is a dream, I don't want to wake up. If it's a drug trip, I don't want to come down."

"But why would you think I wasn't real?"

He laughed at me. "Oh, come on, Red. Beauty, brains, and nerves of steel? You seem like a fantasy. My hot, sexy, indomitable red queen."

His. Wow. Bold words, but this guy was fresh out of a long imprisonment in a uniquely horrible prison. Nothing he said could be held against him, or considered binding in any way. I had to remember that. Remind myself of it constantly.

And even so, I liked it. I liked it so much, it scared me.

"Holly really gets along with your little sister," he said.

"Reggie is soaking it all up," I said. "Tonight, she told me she doesn't know how long she has in this world, so she's going to make the most of every moment."

I felt him tense. "Jesus. She said that? She's so sure she'll get sick again?"

I nodded. "She saw our mother die of Varen's. She almost died herself, before she went to that clinic. If he actually did infect her somehow..." My voice trailed off.

"You're still doubting it?"

"I doubt everything these days," I said. "But Jana was very convincing. Her own mother died of Tamiko's. But Jana discovered later that Halliwell has this collection of fake diseases to play God with. Tamiko's is one of them. Varen's is another."

"Rose will be here tomorrow. She'll tell us more. We'll find a solution."

"Thank you for saying that, but some problems have no solutions," I said. "You just have to swallow the pill. Reggie told me that this evening. More or less."

"We'll see," he said stubbornly. "I won't accept that."

I hesitated for a moment. "If we could use SmokeScreen, I could hack deep enough into the Coatesworth to find whatever compound they were sending to that clinic. Or at least find out how he's making her sick."

Shane was silent for an agonizingly long minute. "It's not up to me, Red," he said finally. "When I told Halliwell I didn't have access to the code, I wasn't lying. The access codes were bashed right out of my head, or else I would have given them to Vincent and Nicole when they were torturing me. Or to Halliwell, later on. The only way to resist torture is to just fucking not have the information to give."

"I understand," I said quietly.

"SmokeScreen is Ethan's baby," Shane said. "And he regrets creating it. He was going to destroy it, but I convinced him to let me use it, just once, and then never again. And I fucked all of our lives sideways. He won't make that mistake again."

Not even to keep Reggie alive. That was the subtext. A wave of sadness came over me. I hid my face against his chest.

"Red—"

"Please, just stop talking," I whispered. "It won't help."

"I'll help you find a solution. I swear it."

Yeah, he'd help look for a solution. Just not that one. The best one. And if the truth were acknowledged, probably the only one. I gritted my teeth and just didn't say it. It wasn't fair to him. But he heard it in the air.

"We'll see what Rose and Demiguel tell us." He rolled me up onto his body, straddling him.

I crossed my arms on his chest and rested my chin on them. "Hey, you."

"I keep thinking about that kiss," he said.

"Which one?" I asked. "All of them have been memorable."

"The first one," he said. "The first time I touched you. When the glass wall magically disappeared. I was so shocked by actually touching you, I forgot that bastard was watching us. I couldn't see anything but you. And you know what?"

"What?" I demanded.

"I still can't," he said.

That sound in his voice just reached deep inside me and squeezed. He could play me like a fiddle. I pushed up, hands against his chest, straddling him, and leaned down to kiss him. A demanding Red Queen kiss. It caught fire right away.

Neither of us was in control, not me, not him. The kiss had its own agenda, its own ruthless demands. He tasted so good, his hard body, his thick, steely cock that I gripped and stroked. I shook with an irresistible clutch of hunger.

I lifted my head for air, my breath rasping heavily. His chest heaved beneath me.

"Jesus, Red," he muttered.

I had settled myself over him so that my naked pussy was right over his cock, which now lay stiff and hard and hopeful against his belly. It could have been the worst idea in the world, stupid, wrong, even lethal, but my body insisted. I ground against him, sighing and whimpering, sliding my slick, aroused pussy lips up and down the length of his cock. Bathing him, anointing him. Teasing him.

It made me feel wild and powerful. The Red Queen, bestowing her favors on her chosen lover. He shuddered with every slow, undulating stroke, his hands clenched in the sheets. "Red," he rasped. "For fuck's sake. Have mercy."

Mercy. Something that was in my power to give. I rose up, seizing his cock, nudging it between my slick pussy lips.

Swirling it around and around my clit. Petting myself with his blunt, smooth cockhead, panting in anticipation.

Shane groaned, his body rigid, arched beneath mine. He was so strong, but right now, I had the power, and I liked it. He grabbed my nightgown, tugging it down until the loose gathered neckline revealed my breasts. Cupping and caressing them.

He seized my hips, holding me steady, and drove upward. I cried out as he filled me, surging, and I threw my head back and gasped for air as we rocked and heaved toward that promise of pleasure that kept swelling, lifting me higher, and higher...

It crested, broke, and I was borne under by wild, thundering bliss.

I came to and found Shane embracing me after, his cock still inside me. Then, he rolled me over, rocking and grinding deep inside me.

"You didn't come yet?" I asked, shakily.

"Not yet," he said. "I couldn't let it end yet. You ready for another go?"

I wanted to laugh but had no breath. This position made me feel pinned, wide open, utterly vulnerable, but it felt good to be vulnerable. I craved it. And I wanted to feel him come inside me. I nodded, jerking my hips up to meet him.

He covered my mouth and tongue-kissed me as he fucked me. We moved frantically, wild and sinuous, bucking and twining together. I was mewling beneath his mouth as wild sensation overtook me again. This time, he followed me over the edge, pumping hard, hiding his face against my shoulder as pleasure exploded through him.

He rolled off, but pulled me very close, keeping my leg flung over his. His cock was still inside, still half hard. I felt his heart thud in time with my own. In sync.

As soon as I had the necessary motor skills, I reached out

and switched on the nightlight by the bedside. I rolled back and looked searchingly into his eyes.

"What?" he asked. "What did I do? Are you okay?"

"I'm great," I said. "I'm just wondering if that massive orgasm knocked open Pandora's box for you. I'm just checking for, you know. Gaping chasms. Lava pools."

He gave me a lazy grin. "I think that when you leave Pandora's box wide open, it's okay. It's when you nail it closed that things get weird. I'm okay. I'm great, even."

"Oh. Well, good." We smiled at each other.

It was scary, how happy his answer made me. Like this could go somewhere. Like there could be hope for some kind of future.

But I didn't dare to hope for that, on top of everything else. That was too much.

Love, with this gorgeous, powerful, mysterious, unstoppable, indomitable being that I had found in chains? Really?

That would be pushing my luck to the breaking point.

CHAPTER 17

Shane

O nce again, I didn't sleep. Though this time, it was less from adrenaline and more just a giddy feeling of astonishment that wouldn't let my eyes close.

I still couldn't believe it was real. I was home, more or less whole, with my sister and brother and daughter and friends. It was a fucking miracle.

And so was Red. Curled up in my arms, fast asleep. Those gorgeous freckles everywhere, that wild mane of fuzzy, curly dark hair exploding out of the covers.

She was miraculous. I memorized every detail of her face as dawn revealed them to me. Finally, her eyes opened, and blinked, startled.

"Oh," she whispered. "Wow. You."

"None other. I'm the one you went to bed with last night. In case you forgot."

She snorted. "Hah. One does not just forget the golden dick of the great Shane Masters. It leaves a legend in its wake."

Now it was my turn to snort. "Give me a break."

"Never," she said. "I can't do that. I just don't know how. It's my worst personality trait. Maybe you've noticed."

"Sounds like a warning. Should I be scared?"

"I just don't know how much nerve you have, that's all," she said.

"A fuck-ton," I told her. "Enough to handle you."

That was a risk, but it seemed to pay off. Her shapely dark eyebrows climbed. "Brave words," she murmured. "I suppose it's promising, that you're still here, at dawn. You didn't chicken out on me."

"Nope. I just watched you sleep. All night. Peak moment for me."

We smiled at each other. Ridiculously, unreasonably happy.

"I could just lie here with you all day," I told her. "I would, if you let me. But I don't know how you feel about Reggie running in and finding me here."

"I doubt she'd be surprised, sharp as she is," Red said. "But even so. She has enough stuff to process right now. And I definitely want your clothes to be on, whenever the door is unlocked. That'll be the rule, going forward. Okay?"

"Fine," I said. I liked the implications. 'Going forward' implied there was a future unfolding for us. Possible rules, expectations, habits to establish. It had been so long since I made a plan or entertained a hope, I'd forgotten how it felt. It made me want to grab her and make love to her again. But that would be greedy.

I detached myself with difficulty, pulling away from her low murmur of protest. I slid out of bed and pulled my pants on.

Red sat up, smiling from beneath that wild mop of tousled, fiery hair. She stretched seductively, letting the cover fall to her waist and leave her slim torso bare. Those high, gorgeous little pink-tipped tits made my mouth water.

"Don't tease me like that," I pleaded. "I'm trying to be good."

"I appreciate that," she said, her voice a seductive drawl.

"But it's a point of pride. I don't want it to be easy for you to walk out my door. I want it to be hard."

"No problem there." I glanced down at the hard-on tenting out the loose pants. "It's very hard."

"Terrible pun," she said, giggling. "Off with your head."

She flung a pillow, which hit me in the ass as I went out the door. I picked it up and hurled it back, smiling. I closed the door, careful to make no sound. I pulled my shirt over my face as I turned, and stopped short as my head emerged, startled.

Ethan was watching me from the end of the hall. His eyes were somber.

I felt brought up short. Like I'd been caught doing something I shouldn't. "Hi," I said carefully. "You're up early."

"Couldn't sleep," Ethan said. "Too much to think about."

"Same," I said.

He gestured toward the kitchen. "I made coffee. Come have some."

I followed him into the kitchen, poured out some hot coffee, which was wickedly strong, since Ethan had made it. Angela had a lighter hand with the beans.

I saw the cake stand, lifted the lid, and sliced a piece of last night's gingerbread. Damned if I hadn't worked up an appetite.

"Ahhh," Ethan said quietly. "Finally."

I couldn't say much with all that cake in my mouth. I washed it down with a gulp of the coffee. "Finally what?"

"You're starting to act like this place is your home," Ethan said. "You've been acting like a nervous guest. Unsure of your welcome."

I swallowed the cake with difficulty. "It takes time to let it all in."

"Yeah? How about with the hot redhead? Seems like you let her in, from the looks of it. Or she let you in. Looks very playful. I actually saw you smile when you walked out of the room. It vanished the minute you saw me, but still. Baby steps."

I chose not to acknowledge that small dig. "Yeah, she took me by surprise," I said. "The girl is incredible. Brave, smart, gorgeous. And she saved my ass."

"Weird time to initiate a hot love affair," Ethan said.

"I know that," I said sharply.

"Not criticizing. Just observing."

"We know that it's risky," I said. "But it was inevitable. It started back when I was in the dungeon. She sneaked down to visit me. Reminded me that I was alive."

"You don't have to be defensive. I don't blame you. I actually had my own smoking hot babe rescue me from a horrible fate just a few months ago. That kind of maneuver really gets your attention. Believe me. I get it."

"Did you think that Kat was too good to be true, back then?"

"God, yes. I couldn't believe my luck for the longest damn time, I thought she had to be the hottest honeypot anyone ever saw on this earth. But I kept her close to me until we had time to calm down, get the facts straight. And I also managed to resolve some of her long-standing problems. That's key, for making a hot mysterious babe relax joyfully into your arms. I highly recommend it as a tactic."

"Uh... about that," I said slowly. "Her long-standing problem is the little sister's health issues. She's hoping we'll use SmokeScreen to penetrate Halliwell's security. That's one solution."

Ethan's jaw tightened. "Fuck me," he muttered.

I nodded. "I know. I know."

"You know what happened last time. The only reason I haven't erased it is because I was using it to look for you. I should have set it to self-destruct the minute I had you in that helicopter. I knew that thing would bite my ass. One last time."

"I'm sorry about that," I said. "I was stupid."

"Me, too. We both paid for it. But you paid more. I'm sorry, Shane. But I can't."

"I understand," I said grimly. "So we try everything else. We see what Rose comes up with. I already told Red that Smoke-Screen wasn't mine to give."

"Fuck, Shane," Ethan said, his voice tormented. "She gave you back to us. She deserves the best we have. But I don't think anything on earth is worth that risk."

I nodded. "Don't get all wound up yet. So far, the kid seems fine. Maybe she'll stay fine."

Ethan just looked at me. "You really think Halliwell will let Cass off that easily?"

I shook my head. "Nope," I said, staring down into opaque black depths of my coffee. I looked up at Ethan. "Fuel up," I suggested. "The gingerbread is great with coffee." I cut him a slice and held it out.

Ethan stared at the cake in his hand, and took a bite, savoring it. "Damn," he said.

"Yeah," I agreed, lifting my cup. "Here's to small pleasures."

And large ones, I added in my mind as our mugs clinked together. That night with Red was no small pleasure. It was vast, all-encompassing.

Worth fighting for.

CHAPTER 18

Cass

I f I kept eating like this, I was going to be in trouble, I thought, nibbling my fresh-baked cinnamon roll. Then again, I'd been unable to eat at Halliwell's lair, so I had a lot to compensate for, and Angela was in wild celebration mode. She had to calm down at some point, and in the meantime, I might as well take advantage of the yum.

So, excess was the way to go. Maybe I'd have some coffee cake, too. What the hell.

I sipped coffee, watching Holly and Reggie giggling over a word game that they had found in one of Holly's magazines. It soothed my heart to see her laugh, though she, unlike me, had eaten hardly anything. She'd nibbled toast, drunk a little juice. Her small square of egg casserole looked untouched.

And she looked... not great. Strangely, she'd looked better yesterday. Her eyes looked sunken and bruised, and she had lost the color that she had yesterday. Today, her face had a dull, grayish tone.

Maybe it was just in contrast to Holly, who was rosy and blooming, all pink lips and cheeks and bright sparkling eyes. I was being paranoid. I should give the poor kid a few days to recover from months of solitary confinement before I started to panic.

But panic swiftly overtook me anyway. "Hey, Reggie," I said, interrupting their whispered conversation. "Can't you eat a little more of your eggs?"

Reggie looked down at it and back up at me, her eyes apologetic. "It makes my stomach hurt," she admitted. "I ate some of the toast. And I had a cup of hot chocolate."

"Okay," I said. "But try to eat, babe. Please."

"We're going to watch the latest episode of Relic Hunter now," Reggie said. "It's this adventure show that Holly showed me. It's the best."

"That's wonderful, sweetie. Go have fun."

Shane stood in the doorway, smiling at me, and them. He ruffled each little girl's hair as she passed, and then sat down next to me. "Reggie looks pale."

"Yeah, I noticed," I said.

"Demiguel is coming up the driveway," he said. "Maybe he has some news for us. Come on up to the meeting room?"

"Yes!" I leaped up and refilled my coffee before following him.

The whole extended family was there when we came in. I saw various surreptitious looks, smirks and grins. So it was no secret, where Shane had spent the night.

So much for discretion. Shane had sat down, so I marched over to him, trailing my hand intimately over his shoulder for everyone to see, and sat down next to him.

No kisses though, because that shit was private, thank you very much.

My performance touched off another couple of minutes of intense non-verbal communication, which at last was blessedly interrupted by the arrival of Dr. Demiguel, accompanied by Trey, one of the security guys.

We leaned forward eagerly as he spread out the array of blood test results, but his expression was worried and apologetic. "I wish I had something more conclusive for you," he said to Shane. "Your bloodwork seems normal, considering your ordeal. You're low in a few key nutrients, but that could just be stress. I've made up a list of supplements you should take, to shore up minerals and B-vitamins and suchlike, but that's easily handled. We didn't find drugs in your blood, but hair and saliva is still being processed."

Shane waved his hand. "I'm fine. Never mind me. Tell us about Reggie."

Demiguel's eyes flicked down to the second file that was fanned out in front of him. "Well," he said. "She was definitely malnourished—"

"Motherfuckers," Amos snarled under his breath. "Starving a little kid, all alone in a basement closet? They need to die screaming. All of them. In a fire."

"It's against my Hippocratic oath, but in this case, I have to agree," Demiguel said grimly. "I read up on Varen's, and I consulted with my colleagues. The blood test results are consistent with Varen's, but they could also indicate many other things. I would never have thought of Varen's on my own if you hadn't mentioned it to me."

"I don't think it's genuinely Varen's," I told them. "I was told by a person at Halliwell's complex that Halliwell create fake illnesses that mimic real diseases. They have specific antidotes that only he has access to. So if that is true, then essentially, Reggie was poisoned, and the results mimic Varen's Disease."

"And you trust the person who gave you that information?" Demiguel asked.

I thought of Jana's haunted, tormented eyes. "Yes, I do," I said. "And I can't think of any reason why it would have been in her best interests to lie."

"Well, I suppose it could have been some drug she was

given," Demiguel said slowly. "But it's hard to tell. We'll keep working on it."

I braced myself. "So I take it you don't have any treatment options to suggest?"

He shook his head. "Sorry. Not until we know more. I'm hoping that Rose will have some more information."

"She's coming here today," Shane said.

"Good," the doctor said, looking relieved. "In the meantime, as I said last night, I strongly recommend that you admit Regina to the hospital."

"She doesn't want to go to any hospital after what she's been through," I said firmly. "Unless the circumstances are dire, I don't want to insist on it."

Demiguel let out a sharp, frustrated sigh. "Then I just don't know what to say." He shoved the files of bloodwork to the middle of the table. "I'll leave these with you. Look them over at your leisure. Let me know if you change your mind, and I'll expedite everything for you. Please. Consider it."

He stalked out, his mouth tight, and shut the door smartly behind himself, right in the face of Trey, the security guy who had gotten up to escort him.

Trey opened the door and followed the doctor without comment.

I let out a slow breath. "Shit," I whispered.

"Why do you say that?" Freya asked. "She's stable, right? So it's a no-news-is-good-news situation."

I shook my head. "Halliwell's not done fucking with me yet. I'd like to just kill him now, but I can't until I know how he made Reggie sick. And how he makes it stop."

Shane's hands clenched and flexed. "Ethan?" His quiet voice asked the question he didn't have to put into words. It was hanging in the air all around us.

"It's too dangerous," Ethan said grimly. "He could be luring us into a trap. If he gets his hands on SmokeScreen, he's one of the few people in the world with the resources to actually use it. And he would have absolute power. All the money, all the information, all the access, all the time."

"It's hard for me to care, if Reggie is the sacrifice I have to make to prevent it." I got up, shoving my chair back.

Shane put his hand on mine. "Red—"

"Don't." I shook his hand off. "I'm sorry. I know I'm being bitchy and unreasonable, but I'm just scared. I feel helpless, and I need a minute. So if you'll all excuse me. I'll let you all talk this through without me."

"Wait," Ethan said. "Just wait, Cass. Please."

I let out a shaky breath, and waited.

"We are on your side," he said. "We will help Reggie in every way we can. We'll find out everything there is to find about the Coatesworth Facility. We have skills, and we are going to exercise the shit out of them for Reggie. We won't let you down. I swear. Please, trust us."

"Okay," I said, in a small voice.

We got down to business after that, and several hours of hard, focused research followed. I had never worked on any project with people who were as skilled, or perhaps even more skilled, than I was. I'd pretty much concluded that I was a top-shelf, shit-hot hacker, but Ethan and Freya Masters were neck and neck with me, keeping pace. Plus, they were accustomed to the way each other's minds worked, and brainstormed ideas and solutions with blinding speed. Shane wasn't shabby either, and the Drakes also had their moments. It was a formidable group.

After a while, Kat got up, shaking her head. "My eyes are crossing," she said. "Call me when there's some ass to kick. I'm going to go check on the girls."

The day flew by. Coffee and sandwiches appeared, at one point. Eventually, the personnel winnowed itself down to Ethan, Freya, Shane, and me, deep in the weeds of the

Coatesworth Facility databanks. But Halliwell's cybersecurity was of the highest order, as I well knew. I'd done some penetration testing on his security myself when I was testing Glow-worm.

The day began to dim. Angela gave us a heads-up about dinner, which would be served in about twenty minutes, and I was a little horrified to realize that I'd spent all those hours in hyper-concentration mode and had not checked on Reggie once.

"Where are the kids?" I asked.

"Last I saw, they'd gone to the gym with Kat, who was going to teach them a martial arts kata," Angela said. "They were making Bruce Lee battle yips, and karate-chopping at each other, having a grand old time. Don't worry about Reggie."

"Where's the gym?" I persisted. "Just tell me where. I'll find it myself."

"I'll take you," Shane said swiftly. "Follow me."

He led me across the inner courtyard, which was enormous, with gorgeously landscaped gardens. I'd been so busy and distracted, the luxurious details of the place had not registered in my mind at all.

He led me across the huge inner courtyard garden and past a swimming pool to a building on the other side of the quadrant. Inside, in a huge practice room, Kat was slowly demonstrating a graceful crouching move in a karate form.

The two little girls tried to imitate her, Holly with more success than Reggie, who was weaker and frailer after her illness and captivity. Then the girls caught sight of us and came running full tilt. Holly barreled into Shane and Reggie into me, both of them chattering about their ninja training.

"We can do somersaults, Daddy!" Holly said proudly. "Kat's been teaching me, and I love it, but it's going to be a lot more fun to have someone to spar with. Want to see my somersaults?"

"Love to." The words were barely out of his mouth before Holly took off sprinting across the tatami with an ear-splitting yell, and launched herself, tucking and rolling admirably and bounding back up onto her feet. She'd been well taught.

Reggie took off after her, slower, but game, as always. She pitched herself forward more awkwardly, and didn't roll up onto her feet, but flopped sideways onto her butt. She stayed there, face buried in her hands, shoulders hunched. Motionless.

"Reggie?" I called out, sprinting toward her. "What is it? Are you okay?"

I dropped to my knees in front of her and tried to lift her head. She looked up, her nose streaming with blood. It ran down over her mouth and chin and all down her lap, dripping all over the tatami. Her eyes were terrified.

It took everything I had to keep my shit together and not make this scarier for Reggie. I had to project the idea that it was no big deal, nothing to worry about. My voice had to stay cheerful and reassuring. She'd just bumped her nose. Dry winter weather. No biggie, no emergency, nothing to see here. La-di-dah. Big whoop.

But my guts felt like an anvil. This was how it had started with Mom, and this had been how it had started with Reggie, too, the first time around. First, generic aches and pains and fatigue, clammy hands, pallor, that bruised look around the eyes. Then the nosebleeds. Then the fever, and the rashes. The gastro stuff. The mucus.

Of course, it could just be nothing. A stupid flu. A banal, run-of-the-mill normal nosebleed. Everyone got nosebleeds.

We waited for the bleeding to stop, which took a while, and I finally managed to get the softly sobbing Reggie into our bedroom, where we washed off all the blood. When we came out, we found a fresh set of comfortable athletic clothing on the bed.

I got Reggie dressed in the soft, fleecy outfit, and hugged her until she stopped shivering. She looked up at me. "It's starting up again," she said flatly.

"I'm reserving judgment for now," I told her. "Let's not psych ourselves out, okay? Sometimes a nosebleed is just a nosebleed."

Reggie gave me an ironic look. "Come on, Cass. I told you. I'm not a baby."

"Maybe not, but I sure am," I told her. "Let's spare my tender little feelings, okay? And this might be a setback, but I still think that our luck has changed."

There was a knock on the door. Holly poked her head in. "You guys okay?"

"Fine," I assured her.

"Angela sent me to say that you and I could watch a movie and eat on the coffee table in the TV room if we want. I almost never get to do that. It's really fun."

"I'm not hungry," Reggie said.

"She has some chicken soup for you," Holly said in a coaxing voice. "If you don't feel up to lasagna. Her chicken soup is really good."

"Maybe a little," Reggie conceded.

I got her established in front of the TV, where a lively debate ensued about the relative merits of comfort movie franchises, the two in question being Lord of the Rings or Harry Potter. I left them to it, smiling in spite of myself, and followed the aroma of lasagna. But when I got to the dining room, I saw Rose, her coat and hat still on, the cold still clinging to it. Her eyes met mine, and her lips smiled, but her eyes did not.

Not good news, then. Neutral at best. I had been hoping for a quick solution to my worries. I might have known. So much for my appetite. It hid under its rock in a flash. It was belly clenching, chest-constricting anxiety time now.

Angela fussed, taking her coat and hat away and making

polite noises about dinner, and why not stay and eat, yada, yada. But Rose's eyes held mine, and once her coat was off, she grabbed my hand.

"About that medicine," she said.

My fingers tightened around hers. "What about it? What's in it?"

"Nothing," Rose said.

Shane leaned forward, startled. "What do you mean?"

"I mean, literally, there's nothing to it," Rose said. "I tested the hell out of it. It's just sodium chloride and water. There's nothing else, in either the vials or the IV bags."

"But... but how did they treat her, then?" I asked, bewildered. "What did they give her that made the symptoms stop?"

"That son-of-a-bitch fake doctor at the fake clinic was lying," Kat said, through her teeth. "Shithead. I should have liquefied his balls when I had the chance."

"So what, then?" I said. "What now? I'm nowhere! No way to copy the cure, no way to pinpoint the pathogen or the poison. What the fuck am I supposed to do now?"

Rose looked miserable. "I'm so sorry I don't have better news," she said. "Do you want me to test the rest of the vials and IV bags as well? Just to be sure?"

"Sure, but I can't imagine that they would be any different," I said.

"You're probably right, but I want to leave no stone unturned," Rose said.

They were careful not to look at me when she said that, since it wasn't true.

There was one huge, fat fucking stone that they were not turning... because they didn't dare to turn it.

And there wasn't a damn thing I could do about it.

CHAPTER 19

Shane

From that point on, the day went even more steeply downhill. Red was white-face, tight-lipped, unreachable. Rose stayed for dinner, which was a subdued meal, forks clinking in the gloom, hushed conversations, no laughter. Everyone was trying to be positive, to think proactively, but there was a feeling of dread in the air. The square of Angela's fabulous lasagna sat on Red's plate, untouched.

Freya and Rose were looking over the list of medical specialists they were considering. They tried to involve Red in the conversation, but they had to keep calling her over and over before she heard them. She was locked inside a nightmare in her head.

I could relate.

We helped Angela clear off the dinner dishes, and then she brought out some hot Dutch apple pie and a tub of ice cream.

"Honey?" Angela called out to Red, holding out a loaded dessert plate. "Want some dessert? Sweetheart? Cass?"

"Hmm?" Red saw the pie and shrank back. "Thanks, but I'm full."

Angela's eyes darted to her untouched place. "Hmm. All right. I'll dish some of this up for the girls, and we can... oh! There you are, sweetheart. Speak of the devil. You two ready for some pie?"

We turned and saw Holly standing in the dining room entryway. She looked frightened.

"What happened?" Red leaped up, her chair scraping. "Is Reggie okay?"

"She fell asleep during the movie," Holly said. "And when she woke up, she seemed confused. She was calling for her mom. Isn't her mom, um..."

"Dead. Yes." Red hurried around the table. "Two years now. She's delirious."

"She does feel really hot," Holly offered, as Cass hurried past her.

We trailed after her, crowding into the TV room. Cass was crouched in front of her sister, talking softly. I kneeled down next to her.

"Baby?" she repeated. "Hey. Talk to me. What's going on?"

"Mommy?" Reggie's voice sounded weak, higher and younger than before, like a five-year-old. "Is that you?"

"No, it's Cass, sweetie-pie. I'm right here."

"Is Mommy coming?"

"I'm here, baby." Red pressed her hand to her sister's face and shone her cell phone's flashlight into the neckline of Reggie's sweatshirt. "She's hot, and she's starting to get that rash again. Do you guys have a thermometer?"

"Right away. And I'll bring the Tylenol drops." Angela scurried away.

"Tylenol's not going to do it." Red's voice was bleak. "It didn't help her the last time. And saline solution certainly won't. I've got squat to help her."

"I'll call Demiguel." Ethan pulled out his phone, backing out of the room.

I stood there, outside the bubble of Red's great storm of trouble, watching her hunched over her sister, her back shaking as she stroked Reggie's hair. Angela bustled in with the thermometer and the Tylenol drops. Ethan was talking in low, urgent tones in the corridor, and I was helpless and inert, watching from behind six inches of glass.

Ethan closed his call and met my eyes. I walked out and beckoned for him to follow me. We went to the sunroom, which was chilly and dark and private.

"You know where this goes," I said to him. "You know exactly what happens to that kid if we don't stop it."

"You know what else?" Ethan said savagely. "I know that bastard Halliwell knows we're having this conversation, and he's rubbing his hands together, chortling."

"He taunted me about Holly," I said. "He'd show me videos that his people had filmed of her. He'd tell me he was going to 'collect' her, to motivate my memory."

"He's fucking with you, Shane. Can't you feel the strings jerking?"

"I see a little girl dying," I said. "One who doesn't have to die."

"Shane—"

"The reason we got shafted the last time was because Wes Boer was dirty," I said. "My bad. I was the fool who hired the guy. That's on me. But there's no Wes Boer here. It's just our inner circle. If we use it to find Reggie's cure, who's going to know?"

"Look, brother. I know you're in love with Cass, and I swear, I don't blame you. But I wouldn't call her inner circle. We've known her for, what, twenty-four hours?"

"What she did for us gives her a free pass," I said. "Straight into the circle."

We shut up as Red knocked and peeked in the door.

"Excuse me," she said. "But did the doctor say when he would get here?"

"He's on his way," Ethan told her.

"Her temperature is almost 104," she said, her haunted eyes meeting mine. "It's happening so fast. The last time, it came on slower."

"We'll do everything we can," Ethan assured her.

She nodded silently and turned to go.

"Does she look unconvincing to you?" I asked, a few seconds after she'd left.

"Goddamn it, Shane," he growled.

"It could have been Holly," I said. "Just shuffle those cards a little and it could have been Holly, turned into a weapon to beat us with."

"We'd be exposing Holly to danger too, if we used Smoke-Screen, particularly to penetrate Halliwell's security," Ethan said. "We'd be exposing the whole fucking world. You know how badly he wants it. And you know what that guy is capable of."

I nodded, lifting my hands. "Yes, I do," I said. "He's rotten to the core. And it's your call. It always was. You wrote it. You decide. But if you value what Red did for us, that's the fee she's asking for. Decide for yourself if you feel like paying it."

"Fuck you, Shane," he snarled.

I turned around without replying and headed back toward the TV room. If I couldn't save Red's sister, I could at least stand with her while she faced her own worst-case scenario. I would be completely useless, but I'd be there for her. I wouldn't run and hide.

"Yes," Ethan said quietly, from behind me.

I froze for a long moment, then turned to look at him. "Yes what?"

"Yes, I'll use it. We'll cut through the Coatesworth security with it. And as soon as I am done, I will wipe that motherfucker off the face of the earth."

"Which one?" I asked. "SmokeScreen? Or Halliwell?"

"Both," he said, his voice low and savage. "And then it will be over."

"Thank you," I said. "I'll tell Red."

"I'm doing the search myself, though," he said sharply. "Cass doesn't touch the algorithm. I don't even want her in the room."

I thought about Red, huddled anxiously over her sister. "That's fine," I said. "She's busy now anyway."

"Good. Tell Jed and Freya and the Drakes to join me in the war room. We'll get to work. You just focus on keeping your girlfriend from falling to pieces."

"She's not my..." I cut off the words. Damn. I was still afraid to tempt the gods.

Ethan gave me a wry look. "You were saying?"

"Yes," I said, with grim determination. "I'll concentrate on helping my girlfriend."

I ran back into the TV room. Reggie was tossing restlessly on the couch.

"Let me take her to the bedroom," I said. "She'll be more comfortable in bed."

Red nodded, wiping her eyes and sniffling. I scooped up the little girl, who weighed practically nothing. She was limp and shivering. Red scrambled ahead of me, opening doors for me, opening the bedclothes so that I could lay her down.

Red peeled off Reggie's goofy, alligator-swallowing-foot slippers, and tucked the blankets around the shivering child. Then she sat down cross-legged next to Reggie on the bed and grabbed her sister's hand.

"Mommy?" Reggie murmured.

"It's Cass, sweetie pie."

I sat down on the foot of the bed and just blurted it out.

"Ethan's going to hack into the Coatesworth database with SmokeScreen," I said. "He's getting started right now."

Her eyes widened. "Oh God," she whispered. Her mouth began to shake. "Thank you."

Her dazed reaction made me nervous. "Don't pin too much hope on it yet," I warned. "We don't know if he'll find anything. Or if what we find will be useful, or accurate. It's just…"

"It's the last stone to turn," she said quietly. "Thank you. For turning it."

"Save it for when it actually helps," I said.

"It helps me right now, whether you like it or not," she told me.

I scooted closer to her, hesitated, then scooted closer still, wrapping my legs and arms around her so she had something to lean on while we waited for the doctor.

CHAPTER 20

Cass

"I want her at the hospital," Demiguel repeated stubbornly. "And yes, I know that Ethan could outfit a clinic for her at the Mountain House, but not fast enough to help her now. We need to run tests now, and I have four different specialists on their way here to examine her. We save time if she's at the hospital. We don't have time to waste."

My body was as tight as piano wire at the thought of leaving this small paradise of safety and going back to the wide-open setting of a public hospital. Not that the last one had actually been a hospital at all, but still. Trauma never listened to logic.

In any case, in Reggie's condition, she wouldn't know the difference.

"I have to stay with her," I told Demiguel. "That was my mistake the last time. I got bullied and strong-armed into leaving her there. That won't happen again."

"Stay if you want," Ethan said. "She'll have a private room. And a two-man guard detail outside, at all times. Darius and Amos volunteered to go watch her."

Things moved fast after that. Angela and Kat packed for me

and Reggie, which was great, because Reggie and I had no possessions or toiletries of our own to pack. Holly gathered up books, which I hoped that Reggie would soon be well enough to read. Then Shane wrapped Reggie up in a blanket and soon we were rocking and swaying in the back of an ambulance.

If there was paperwork needed to admit her, someone else dealt with it, thank God, because I was useless. All I could do was hang over my sister, who was unresponsive to any attempt to talk. I tried to brace myself, but I just couldn't do it. I'd gone through this with Mom, and that had been horrible, but this time, it was uniquely horrible in fresh new ways.

I sat there near her hospital bed, doing my best to stay out of the way of the hospital staff, as they drew blood, gave her oxygen, set up an IV. Watching that made every muscle in my body contract. Reggie's poor little arms and wrists and hands hadn't even had a chance to heal from the last attack of needle-wielding hacks. But so far she hadn't woken up to protest, and hopefully these nurses weren't hacks.

Shane was squeezing my shoulder. "Earth to Red? You there?"

"Sorry. What?"

"I'm going back up to the Mountain House to work with Ethan while he digs for that cure," he said. "Freya, Jed and Remy will be up there with me. Rose is coming over to join us. Darius and Amos are right outside your door, and Kat and Holly will be here first thing in the morning. Will you be okay if I go back to work with Ethan?"

No, no, no. don't leave me please. I swallowed the words back and stared into his beautiful, worried dark eyes. "I'll be fine. Thank you. I'm very grateful that you're working on this for us. Will you call me if you find anything?"

"Right away," he assured me. "And call me if anything happens with Reggie."

"Sure thing," I said.

And so it was that I found myself alone in the dim lit room, my chair scooted up to the bed, clutching Reggie's clammy hand. I'd gone from heaven to hell, in the space of just a few hours.

It seemed that heaven and hell weren't all that far from each other after all. All it took was one hard shove, and there you were. Dodging the pitchforks and the flames.

CHAPTER 21

Shane

The sky was getting light and Ethan was still staring into that screen, scrolling and sifting data while we watched. I personally had only used SmokeScreen that one disastrous time a year ago, the one that ended with me being abducted and six of my colleagues murdered. Not being a gearhead like Ethan and Freya, I didn't really know the intricacies of how it worked. I just hoped that it would.

My ignorance had served me well in Halliwell's dungeon. All I had was vague sense about vastly accelerated dynamic machine learning. The algo wrote new mini-algorithms for itself instantly whenever it encountered an obstacle, and if the computer had enough juice to make the vast number of computations, SmokeScreen would find a way to gently, unobtrusively, secretly ooze around any obstacle, like... well... smoke.

Or so it had been described to me, back in the day.

Rose, Jed, Remy and I all sat there guzzling coffee, nerves thrumming, while Frey and Ethan conversed in a code only a fellow super-nerd could understand.

We jolted up six feet into the air when the door opened, but it was just Kat, poking her head in. "Trey is taking me and Holly down to the hospital," she said. "Angela said to tell you there are breakfast sandwiches ready. And three-berry muffins. We're taking a box of them down to the hospital. Get 'em while they're hot."

"Okay," Jed said. "Thanks."

Ethan smiled at her. The energy that buzzed between them gave me a stab of jealousy. Lucky bastard. He'd passed all the trials on his quest to save the fair lady. He'd come through with flying colors. So far, I hadn't won any battles for mine. The only thing she cared about was helping Reggie. If I failed at that…

I turned my mind away by force. That train of thought led to nowhere good.

Kat left, and the rest of us paced around, waiting for something to happen. Finally, Angela came in with a platter of food, muttering in disapproval about the importance of a good breakfast. Her usually beaming face looked pale and drawn.

An hour or so later, Frey and Ethan crowed loudly in triumph. "Yes!" Ethan and Freya high-fived with a resounding smack, and then hugged each other hard.

"What?" I demanded. "What did you do? Did you find something?"

"We got around another important wall," Freya said. "With no apparent detection so far."

"Well, that's excellent, but now what? Have you gotten into their files?"

"Working on it," Ethan said. "These things take time."

That was a brief bright point that preceded another long, deep valley of boredom. I began to regret my decision to be up here to witness the search, rather than staying down at the hospital to support Red. That had been stupid. I was about to announce my decision to drive down to town when Frey and Ethan erupted again.

"Whoo-hoo!" Freya yelled. "Yes!"

"There's a file here named R. Clarke, with an extensive document list," Ethan told me, grinning. "At least a hundred items. All of them are dated within the past three months. There's also a record of drugs being sent to the Cascade Clinic, on a weekly basis." He looked over at us with a frown, his smile fading. "That seems strange, considering what Rose found in the medicine."

"Maybe the stuff in the fridge was a decoy," Freya said.

"But what about the compound itself?" I insisted.

"Working on it... hang on." Ethan's eyes were fixed on the screen. "Here's a document with a long list of chemicals. Rose, you're up. Come take a look."

Ethan rolled his chair away. Freya leaped up to fling herself at Jed for a celebratory kiss passionate enough to freak me out. I had not processed my baby sister being married to my old Ranger buddy and long-time colleague Jed yet, but I was too distracted right now to be too uptight about it. Rose leaned toward the screen, studying the recipe for Reggie's medicine. Damn. It was actually happening. It had worked.

Ethan looked over at me and grinned, holding up a warning hand. "Don't you dare," he said. "I've been up all night and my defenses are way down. If you get sloppy and emotional on me, I'll fall apart all over you."

"Fuck you, man. Don't you dare try to shut me down." I grabbed him and hung on. Ethan hugged me back, then pulled away, grinning.

"Let me call Kat," he said. "I promised I'd keep her up to date."

"Yeah, I said the same to Red."

We turned away from each other, each pulling out our phones. Red picked right up. "Did you find something?"

"We found a file, with Reggie's name, and lots of documents. Records of shipments of medicine to the Cascade Clinic—"

"And the medicine? Is there a file with the compound itself?"

"Rose is studying it now," I said.

"My God, Shane." Her voice wobbled.

"I know," I said. "I feel the same way. Maybe we lucked out. Maybe we got this licked. If we can get Reggie off the firing range, we can take this fucker down. And after that..." My voice trailed off.

"Yes? And after that?" she prompted.

I felt a pang of nervous doubt. "We shouldn't tempt the gods," I said. "I guess afterward will take care of itself. As long as my afterward has you in it. And I mean, forever. Until the sun supernovas. If you're willing, of course."

She let out a joyful sniffle. "Count me in," she said. "Willing doesn't even begin to describe it."

I walked over to the window, trying to get out of earshot of the rest of the room's occupants. "Red," I said, my voice low. "I've never said this to anyone, in my life, except for my family, but I—"

"Don't feel like you have to say it just because I broke you out of that place," she said. "That was pure self-interest on my part. I needed help for Reggie."

"I'll be grateful if I damn well please. And I'll fall in love with you for whatever damn reason I want. You can't dictate that, Red."

"Um. Okay." There was a whisper of laughter in her soft voice. "If you say so. Look, we'll have to argue about why we're in love some other time, because—"

"So you're in love with me, too?" I blurted. "Damn, that's a relief."

She laughed under her breath. "I can't think of any other explanation for this incredible feeling," she said. "But we can analyze our tender emotions later, because one of Reggie's doctors is signaling that he needs to talk to me, okay?"

"Call me back after?" I asked. "I want to continue this conversation. It was going to really interesting places."

"Sure thing," she said. "I love hearing your voice. I want to go those places, too. And I want to hear all about everything that Rose finds. Talk to you in a few."

We closed the call, and I turned to see the hidden smiles, the twinkling gazes that flicked away.

"What?" I demanded. "What's all the smirking about?"

"I could have told you she was in love with you," Frey said. "If you'd asked me. Might have saved you a little suspense. But it's good to keep a man on his toes."

"Is that a fact?" Jed complained. "Always the toes. My poor, aching toes."

At that moment that I registered the tone of Rose's voice. No longer happy and excited. It sounded confused. Apprehensive.

"... strangest ingredients," she was saying to Ethan. "This can't be right."

"What can't be right?" he asked.

Everyone had tuned in at this point. We clustered around the computer to hear better.

"The ingredients. They make no sense," she said, frowning. "It's pharmaceutical gobbledygook. Formulas of common over-the-counter drugs, painkillers, constipation relievers, blood thinners, beta-blockers, antacids and anti-inflammatories, all tossed together. Plus random stuff like baking soda and rubbing alcohol. It's a big, poisonous nothing-burger. As if someone were pranking you."

"Oh shit," Freya whispered.

"Only one reason anyone would do that," Ethan said. "Move over, Rose."

She slid swiftly away. As Ethan rolled into place in front of the screen, it turned a luminous green color, and files began to scroll all their own, faster and faster.

My gut flash-froze. Oh fuck. Oh no, no, no.

"Fuck me." Ethan muttered, as his fingers pounded at the keyboard. "I can't get in. But SmokeScreen never sensed any malware! It didn't show up on any of the scans!"

The scrolling turned so fast, it became a dizzying blur followed by a brief, blinding flash of light... and the screen went black.

In the horrified silence that followed, we watched as a pinpoint of light appeared in the center of the screen, growing like the light of an oncoming train. It got bigger, until I recognized it. It was an image, one that I'd seen just the day before.

It was the logo for Red Queen Consulting, the one that Reggie had drawn, and that Red had been so proud of. That cat-like cartoon face, with the big, tilted light green eyes, halo of curly red Medusa-like locks, waving wildly out from her golden crown, but this image had been animated. The Medusa hairs wiggled like real snakes, the laughing mouth was continually blowing a kiss, one of the green eyes kept winking.

And a rainbow-tinted, glowing worm wiggled in an endless circle around her.

Beneath her, a short piece of script began to cycle. *Red Queen Consulting – Off With Their Heads! – Red Queen Consulting – Off With Their Heads!*

"Cass's outfit," Remy's voice was heavy.

"It's one of her worms," Ethan said, his voice expressionless. "It swallowed SmokeScreen, and everything else with it. And we are fucked."

I pulled out my phone and dialed Red's number again.

It rang, and rang, and rang.

CHAPTER 22

Cass

I was floating on air as I closed the call with Shane. Darius and Amos high-fived each other, grinning ear to ear. Holly and Kat were hugging, too. Kat slid her phone into her pocket and came over to give me a tight hug. "Ethan came through," she said proudly. "That guy is magic. It gets me every time."

"Runs in the family," I said.

She laughed. "That it does," she said. "All those Masters. Genius, guts, and an incredible talent for getting themselves sunk knee-deep in shit. It's spectacular to watch, if a little nerve-wracking. But we both have nerve. So it's okay, I think."

"I think so, too," I told her.

"Excuse me, Ms. Clarke?"

I turned, and remembered the doctor who had been gesturing for my attention the whole time that I was talking to Shane. "Oh. Sorry. I got distracted. Yes?"

"Congratulations, by the way!" he said, grinning. "I'm so pleased for you!"

I focused on the young guy, mousy-blond and balding. His name tag said Dr. J. Avery. I didn't recognize him, but God knows, I hadn't been paying much attention lately. "You already heard?" I asked.

"Dr. Demiguel told us! Our pharmacy people are already working on it. We just want to expedite things, so I have a couple of quick questions for you about Regina's medical history, if you wouldn't mind coming with me for a moment. Just down the hall a bit. It won't take long. To speed things up for Regina. We want to work fast."

"Sure, of course," I said, waving at Kat. "I'll be right back!"

I followed Dr. Avery down the hall, around the nurses' station. The man was tall and walked quickly. I had to scurry to keep up, but I was thrilled to hurry, if a cure for Reggie was in the offing. "Are they already compounding the drug?" I asked. "What kind of medicine is it, anyway? How does it work?"

"I'm sorry, but it's not my specialty, so I can't really say," he said, his voice apologetic "Dr. Demiguel and the others will be able to tell you more. Come right on in... here." He opened a door, standing aside and beckoning me in, all gallantry.

I hurried in, my mouth already forming questions, and stopped short, sucking in a horrified gasp.

Halliwell stood in front of me, hands in his suit pockets. Smiling.

The door swung shut behind me. I inhaled to scream, but he held up his hand. "Not a sound, if you don't want Reggie to die right now," he warned.

"But what... how..."

He held up a white remote control. "This controls how sick she gets." His voice had the tone of someone explaining a simple lesson to a slow-witted child. "Remember last night, when she took a sharp turn for the worse around dinnertime? That was me, moving this dial from ten to twenty-five. It goes up to a hundred, though I suspect that little Regina would be long gone before I got up to sixty or seventy. But we can't know unless we experiment. Shall we see how she does at, say, thirty-five?"

"No! Don't!"

"Well, then." He slapped the remote into his opposite hand. "I will need you to follow my instructions carefully."

"What do you want?"

"Many, many things," he said, smirking. "Some of them, you have already delivered, with spectacular success. Which puts me in a benevolent mood, in spite of your bad attitude. Very lucky for you. And for little Regina, incidentally."

"Spit it out, Halliwell."

"We start by walking out this door together... smiling. There are security cameras in the corridors. One across from this door. We walk together, with my arm around your shoulders. We smile up at the camera. Then we go out into the parking lot, get into the car, and go. Simple, no?"

"So you want... you want them to think..." My voice trailed off, appalled.

"That you were working for me all along, yes, Cassandra. Because in a way, you were. But I can explain that later. We have no time to waste. If you don't smile at the camera and chat with me politely as we walk, I will dial up Reggie's illness right now. Off you go, my dear. Left foot, right foot."

I just stared at him, horrified.

"And as a very special treat, I will turn Reggie's dial from 25 down to 15 once we are in the car," he added. "That will make her fever break, at least, and will probably make the rash recede. The coughing will ease off, as well."

I looked at the remote in his hand, and he chuckled under his breath, and wagged his finger at me. "If you should have the bad judgment to make a play for this remote, just be aware. Dr.

Avery has a duplicate in his pocket, and he's been told to make sure that Regina dies instantly if you misbehave. Do we understand each other?"

I nodded.

"Okay, then. Off you go." His voice hardened, the false jollity gone.

We walked out into the corridor, which was full of people, none of whom I could ask for help. His arm was slung over my shoulders. It felt heavy, flesh-creeping, repellent, like a poisonous tentacle of some monster draped across my body.

"Smile, Cassandra. Or I turn the dial up." He smirked at me.

I smiled back at him, big and wide and empty. "Will this do?"

"None of your sass, girl. I hold the cards, and you have nothing. Look up at the camera right now, and smile."

I did as I was told, smiling up at the video camera like a painted doll. Then we spun and marched toward the garage. Left foot, right foot. In lockstep with Halliwell.

The big black Porsche SUV idled outside the garage entrance, next to the curb. It was the same deadpan, asshole driver who had taken me to all those hellish restaurant meals. I slid into the seat and stared ahead as Halliwell went around the car and got in.

Thud, the door closed. *Ka-thunk*, the door locks snapped to. I was trapped.

He held out his hand. "Give me your phone, Cassandra."

"Turn down Reggie's dial," I said. "You said you would."

"First, the phone." He made an impatient sound. "You have nothing to bargain with, so don't be annoying. The phone. Now."

I handed it to him.

Halliwell slid it into his pocket, pulled out the remote, and held it out with a theatrical gesture so that I could see it. He turned the dial from 25 to 15. "See? I keep my promises. Little Regina should start feeling better any minute."

"Turn it down to zero," I said.

"Oh, no, no, no," he said, wagging his finger. "Not yet. The monkey has to do her tricks before she gets her treats."

"How are you doing this?" I demanded. "How does it work?"

"All will be made clear in time," he said.

"Make it clear now. What else do we have to do?"

"Don't test my patience," he said crisply. "Regina depends on it." He put the remote in his pocket. "Back to us. You have surpassed my wildest hopes on this operation, Cassandra."

"Operation? What are you talking about? I thought you'd kill me for breaking Masters out of jail."

"Oh, God, no," he said. "That was my idea all along. I set you up. I gave you keys, clues, deadlines, motivations. I nudged you in the right direction, and you performed like a dream. The bold and daring escape! The rescued little sister! Going to the Masters enclave, where you mounted a SmokeScreen attack on the Coatesworth to save her... ah. Beautiful. I never thought it would go so smoothly. Or so quickly."

I gaped at him, bewildered. "Your plan? What do you mean, your plan?"

"I admit that when I recruited you to work for me—"

"Took me hostage, you mean?"

He looked amused. "Don't be melodramatic, Cassandra. Hostages aren't paid top dollar and pampered like lap dogs."

"Bullshit," I said. "You worked me to the bone. You stole my IP. You abused my sister. And I am no one's lapdog."

"Hmmph. So fiery. But I suppose I shouldn't complain. That quality was exactly what made the plan work so incredibly well."

"You planned this from the start?" I said. "I don't get it. I don't see how that works. I didn't know Shane Masters even existed before I got here."

"The idea came to me after you arrived," he said. "Originally, it was just a matter of wanting access to your brilliant malware, for the purposes of acquiring SmokeScreen, of course. And yes, I wanted to recruit your prodigious skills for Halliwell Enterprises. But the only way to get my hands on SmokeScreen was to use Glow-worm to counter a direct attack from the Masters themselves. And when it came to that, you performed as if you'd been coached. Glow-worm slid into their system... and completely swallowed it." He kissed his fingertips. "Superb."

"So you have SmokeScreen right now," I said faintly. "Because they fished for Reggie's cure. To help me." My heart squeezed painfully. Shane must feel so betrayed.

He looked pleased with himself. "Yes, yes. It was very stupid, but I know how sentimental you all are. I got the original idea when Haley tattled on you. She said you'd gotten a crush on our handsome prisoner. But of course you did. What girl would not be intrigued with a dangerous, beautiful, tormented captive? And then, voila! Like magic, you genuinely fell in love with him. It was almost comical."

"But... but..." *What about Jana?* I wanted to yell it, but I didn't want to implicate her, if she had somehow avoided getting caught.

"You're wondering about Jana, I presume," he said.

My heart sank even deeper. "So she was just saying what you told her to say?"

"No, actually, Jana's rebellion was quite real," he said. "I just used it for my own purposes. I believe in using everything. I waste nothing, Cassandra. Not even hatred. It's energy, after all. And hatred can be such a powerful force, don't you agree?"

I didn't want to touch that one with a ten-foot pole. I shook my head.

He went on. "I used Jana's misery to heighten the tension. It was a real shame, years ago, when Jana came across that file at the Coatesworth about Tamiko's Disease. Learning the truth about what happened to her mother broke poor Jana's nerve. She was never the same after. She just couldn't break that sentimental maternal tie, even years after her mother was dead. Such a tragic waste of potential. It ruined her."

"You ruined her." I couldn't help but say it, even though I really, really needed to shut the fuck up and not make things worse for myself. Or for Reggie.

"Don't interrupt," he snapped. "So, I used Jana to get you all the tools you needed for the escape. I set the time for Shane Masters' execution, and then I let you and Jana do all the rest. Getting him out. Saving the sister. Sending you into the belly of the beast. The histamine pill you took was really quite brilliant, my dear. A dramatic touch. Much appreciated for the entertainment value."

"But how did you find us? I took the GPS tracker off the van."

"Oh, that was easy," he said. "Both you and Shane Masters had tracking nanoparticles in your bodies when you left, him from his water bottles, yours from your morning coffee. I could have tracked you anywhere on earth for days on end before they cleared from your system."

"Ah," I muttered. "Tracking nanoparticles. Of course."

"I'm very pleased," he said. "My gamble paid off. I got everything I wanted. An algorithm that will give me vast power, and infinite wealth, which is essentially the same thing, if you know how to administer it. And you. I have you, Cassandra. And I will keep you."

That made me extremely nervous, but I pushed it aside for now. "Hold on," I said. "If you wanted me to get away, why did you send those guys after us when I ran? That makes no sense. They could have killed us!"

"Nonsense," he said briskly. "It made sense for the narrative. It was a risk, yes, but I know what Shane Masters is capable of. And the struggle made it all the more convincing, don't you agree? The Masters family were on high alert. They would never have trusted you if your escape had gone too smoothly. And the fact that Masters killed nine of my men really cemented your emotional bond, didn't it? He's a formidable opponent, compromised as he was. Those poor fellows that came after him were doomed." He shook his head. "Pity."

I didn't want it to be true, but I had to swallow it down. I'd been used to hurt people I cared about. I'd been turned into a witless tool for this monstrous man.

"But... what about Jana?" I asked carefully. "Did you... did she—"

"Did I punish her?" He laughed. "Well, I have been doing some housecleaning, I admit. It's a new era at Halliwell Enterprises, and I want only the best at my side going forward. And of course, that means you."

"Me?" My voice rose to a squeak. "After what you did to me?"

"Oh, come on. Once you've cooled down, you'll see the advantages. Have you even considered what it means to be my heir? To run a corporation like Halliwell Enterprises, and manage a fortune of this size, which is sure to double in five years? You will be the richest human being on the planet, Cassandra. By a very large margin."

"Heir?" I laughed. "Really. With a bomb in one of my back teeth that explodes when you die? Is that the legacy that you're talking about?"

"Not at all," he scoffed. "I would never give you the tooth. Those are only for the duds that need to be kept in line for my own safety, not for a shining star like yourself, who delivered the moon and stars to me on a silver platter. You're a true

Halliwell, Cassandra. The only true Halliwell of this generation."

The guy looked almost sentimental. It made my stomach lurch.

"Did you kill Jana?" I asked baldly.

He waved an impatient hand. "You are so annoying some-times. Be grateful that I snatched you away from the hospital when I did. That was the very moment that they discovered that your worm had taken over their system. The Red Queen logo is cycling on Ethan Masters' computer screen as we speak. They're cursing your name, but who cares? You'll soon be floating up high in the sky, in the safety of my helicopter." He beamed. "You're going home, where I will use SmokeScreen to execute all my big plans for the world. Great improvements are in store. And you are going to help me."

"How do you intend to make me?" It came out of my mouth before I could stop myself, even though I already knew the answer to that question.

"Same way as before," he said lightly. "Until you come to your senses and realize that ruling with me could be a rewarding challenge. That will happen eventually. I'm quite sure of it. This is the scope you always needed for your talents and skills."

"And you actually expect me to do this after you poisoned my sister?"

"Oh, for God's sake, stop harping on that," he snapped. "I'll have her brought here, if you insist! As soon as they take the guards off her at the hospital. No more public gun battles. It's inconvenient, and off-brand."

"They won't take the guards off her," I said.

"No? After you disappeared, along with Shane Masters' heart and their precious algorithm? Why should they guard her? From what? They'll lose interest in her quickly. I suppose the state would step in eventually, to deal with an abandoned ten-year-old, all alone in her hospital bed. No one to wipe her brow or pay her bills. So sad."

"You are such a dick," I told him.

The SUV stopped at the airfield. The locks disengaged. We got out of the car, and he put his heavy arm around me again, herding me toward the helicopter, its rotors already spinning.

"Come along, Cassandra," he said. "It's time to go home."

CHAPTER 23

Shane

I was transfixed by the video on the screen. The hospital security camera showed Cass, embraced by Halliwell, their heads almost touching. He was smiling as he squeezed her close. Her lips were moving. Then came that part I hated. When they both stared up at the camera with the same tight, fake smile that said, *fuck you all. Chumps.*

"No," Kat said. "It's impossible. I saw the way she was with Reggie. I had a little sister myself. I can't be fooled. There's no way Cass would ever hurt that girl. Or abandon her. That's what you're implying, right? That Cass would deliberately poison Reggie to manipulate us, and dump her as soon as she got what she wanted? No way! Her love for that girl is genuine. I felt it on my skin. She was for real!"

"So's the worm that ate SmokeScreen," Ethan said grimly. "Maybe we all just saw and felt what we wanted to see and feel." He shook his head. "Shane has an excuse for being tricked, after what he went through—"

"Do not treat me like a goddamn invalid," I snarled.

"The woman was pretty fucking convincing," Remy said.

"The backstory was as tight as a drum. The mom really did die of Varen's. We checked, and found death records for Laurel Clark, deceased two years and four months ago, survived by two daughters, Cassandra and Regina, yada yada. That's all real, or else an unbelievably well-constructed scam. It's too many random details that check out in perfect order for it not to be real. All of them put in place long before our story even began."

"But why work for that prick at all?" Amos said. "She was doing fine on her own with Red Queen. Landing multimillion dollar contracts left and right. There were fifteen people on her payroll, all of whom loved her. At least until she laid off the whole staff three months ago to put Reggie into that clinic and go work for Halliwell."

"You think that Reggie and the clinic was a fabrication? That she knowingly let him make Reggie sick, just to make us sympathetic to her? That makes no sense." Kat shuddered. "Halliwell is a gaslighting prick. Don't fall for his bullshit!"

"Too late," Ethan said quietly. "We already did. The game has already been played, and he won, babe. By a lot."

But Kat kept stubbornly shaking her head. "No. Not in a million years."

"I want to talk to that doctor who interrupted our phone call," I said.

"I overheard him talking to Cass," Amos said. "He knew about us finding the file before Demiguel did. No one had even called Demiguel when that guy came to collect Cass. He knew about the formula Rose was looking into, and all the details, but Demiguel had never seen this guy. No one has. He isn't employed here."

"Which means that one of Halliwell's men got within inches of Holly and Kat," Ethan said. "While everyone was celebrating and kissing and high-fiving."

Amos looked guilty and pained. "I'm really sorry about that, man."

"We were all excited," Jed said grimly. "I would have done the same."

"It's my responsibility to deal with him now," I said. "I let this cat out of the bag in the first place a year ago, and I let him get his hands on SmokeScreen now. I'm the one who has to fix it. I'll take him out and wipe that place off the map. You guys keep your noses clean, for Holly's sake. Plausible deniability."

Ethan gave him a look. "Right. Like I'd let you go after him on your own."

"But I'm the one who—"

"Shut up, Shane. Don't waste our time. Halliwell won't be able to use SmokeScreen right way. It's heavy and complex, and even he will have a learning curve when he gets into it. Plus, he'll have to beef up even his own huge server capacity by orders of magnitude. But we have a short window. We have to end him fast."

"I'm the one who did this," I said. "I'm the one who got snared by a honeypot, not any of you guys."

"Cass is no honeypot, damn it!" Kat hissed. "Get it through your heads!"

"Whatever Cass is or isn't, we're not leaving your ass out in the wind again," Jed said. "So fucking forget it, buddy. The helicopter's waiting. Six minutes, ten at the max, and we're airborne. We can go and take care of business."

I turned back to the screen. I felt blank. Locked behind a six-inch wall of glass again. Like Kat, I couldn't believe it. The data just would not go into my head.

"Play it again," I said to the nervous-looking young security guy at the desk, who looked like he was trying desperately not to overhear our conversation.

Ethan sighed. "We've seen it twelve times, Shane. It's not going to—"

"Play it again," I said again.

The guy's trembling fingers clattered over the keyboard. He scooted his chair back, making himself small as we all shifted closer to the screen to watch.

First, the smiling, excited Cass, bright-eyed and chatting energetically with the balding doctor that Darius, Amos, Kat and Holly had all seen, but who Demiguel and the rest of the hospital staff could not identify. The doctor opened the door for her with a courtly gesture, closed the door smartly behind her, and walked away.

"Demiguel said that examining room was out of use because of an electrical problem," Remy said. "Halliwell must have known that. God knows how."

The video played on. The door opened. Halliwell came out, smiling, pulling Cass behind him, throwing his arm over her shoulder, squeezing her to himself as he said something. And then, that smile, from both of them. It looked weirdly similar, and it did not reach their eyes. They strode out of range.

"He told her to smile."

We jumped at the sound of Holly's voice. She'd slipped into the room unnoticed and had been watching us from behind. "What the hell are you doing here?" Shane said sharply. "You're supposed to be upstairs with Darius and Reggie!"

"I needed to see it," Holly said haughtily. "Because I don't believe it. Cass is good. And that Halliwell guy is fooling all of you."

"Holly, you need to do as we tell you," Ethan said grimly.

"Play it again," Holly commanded the rabbit-like guy cowering in the corner.

The man recognized the whip-crack of authority in Holly's voice, young though she was, and scooted forward, promptly setting the clip to play again. It was a torture to watch, every time. Torture I deserved.

There it was, the moment when the doctor ushered Cass

into the room. A long pause followed... and then came the moment that she came out with Halliwell. The arm. The squeeze. The hideous fake smiles.

"Stop," Holly said.

The security guy stopped the video, freezing the video right on the creepy-eyed stare up at the camera, their eerily similar grimaces.

"What do you see, baby?" Kat asked.

"Halliwell's mouth," Holly said. "Look at the shape. He's saying, 'smile.' He's telling her to smile. He's making her do it. It's not her fault. She's pretending."

"Run that back," I said. "I want to see it again."

We watched it, again, and another three more times, for good measure. Sure enough, now that Holly had said it, we all saw Halliwell's lips form the word. *Smile.*

Ethan let out a sigh. "Babe," he said gently. "You have a good eye, and it was right to call that out. But what you saw in itself does not prove that she's not in on it. He could be reminding her to smile even if she's willingly working with him."

"What I want to know is why we're talking about this stuff with you to begin with," Amos bitched. "You're ten, kid."

"I won't let you cut me out. I care about Reggie. And Cass."

The door opened, and Darius leaned into the room, very relieved to see Holly. "Oh, thank God." He frowned fiercely at Holly. "Really, Holls? You think this is the time to run off alone in a public building, where Halliwell and his goons running around loose? You practically gave me a heart attack!"

"I'm sorry about that," she said. "I just had to see this video, and I knew you wouldn't let me go. And besides, you should still be up there guarding Reggie."

Darius's eyebrows rose. "We still think that Reggie needs guarding? Why?"

"Lots of reasons." Holly's voice rang with conviction. "She definitely needs it!"

"At least until we know more," I conceded, hedging my bets.

Darius let out a huff of air. "Back I go, then. Oh, it looks like she's conscious again, by the way. She was talking to the nurse when I was leaving. Asking about her sister." He shot a tight-lipped glance at me. "Think I might just sit that one out."

Everyone's eyes slid away from mine, as I realized that it was my job to inflict heartbreak on an innocent little kid. That's what I got, for unleashing this hell on my family. I'd brought this poor little girl here, and I'd let her into our inner sanctum. If someone was going to crush her hopes, it had to be me.

"I'll, ah… go talk to her," I said heavily.

Surprise, surprise. Nobody followed me on my way back to Reggie's room.

I'd been such a boneheaded idiot. Thinking with my dick. Dazzled with Cass's beauty and nerve and brilliance. And breaking Reggie's heart was my punishment.

I'd rather have someone break both my legs.

CHAPTER 24

Cass

S amuel parked the big SUV in his usual spot in Halliwell's private garage. Halliwell looked over at me, his eyes keen and appraising.

"You're not going to do anything stupid," he said. "Not with both myself and my operative holding exact copies of this remote. Am I right?"

"I won't do anything stupid," I said stiffly.

"Excellent. Samuel, leave us. We have a great deal to discuss. Come with me."

Discuss, my ass. I had nothing to discuss with this man. He was going to talk at me, and I would pretend to listen while I thought faster than I'd ever thought before. Trying to figure out which answers might keep me and Reggie alive a little longer. It was like having someone throw knives at you and calling it a friendly game.

We walked down the corridor of the top level, toward the Bridge. This place was usually bustling with activity, people desperately trying to be the best of the best in hopes that Halliwell would notice them. Maybe even offer a glimmer of approval.

Today, there was no one. The place was deserted. The computers were dark.

It was eerie. The place had always been unnerving, but now it seemed under a spell, like Sleeping Beauty's castle. Everyone locked in a deep, enchanted sleep.

"Where is everyone?" I asked. "Did you give people a day off?"

"I suppose you could say that," he murmured.

His tone made me nervous. "Wait... what? Meaning what?"

Halliwell made an impatient sound as he opened the door to his palatial office and beckoned for me to follow him in. Lights flicked on, a subtle glow to augment the muted light from the gray, cloudy day that came in from the floor-to-ceiling picture windows. "I told you I was doing some house-cleaning, remember? It was time to trim away the deadwood."

I reluctantly followed him in. "Wait. You mean, your own children? You kicked them all out?" I was appalled at the idea. That crew was so psychologically unstable after years spent under Halliwell's thumb, there was no way they could function normally in the outside world. It would be a disaster for everyone concerned.

He looked irritated. "It was time. I was so tired of all their fits and freaks and fatal flaws. After everything that I invested in them. I even tried some bold surgical and pharmacological interventions over the years. To liberate them, to boost their natural abilities, make them bolder, more fearless. But instead of taking off like eagles, they collapsed as if I had removed all of their spines. It's so ironic that the only one of my offspring even remotely like me is you. The only one that I couldn't alter or mold, thanks to Laurel's small-minded fears. Oh, and Jana, too. I admit, she had more spunk than I thought. Did I tell you that she tried to snoop around in the Coatesworth databanks? I caught her, of course. She was digging for info on Regina's implant, and she was actually trying to contact you when I put a stop to it. Just in time." He shook his head. "Bold of her, yes. Too bad that courage couldn't have been in my service. But no. The answer is always... no." He huffed out an irritated breath.

"Where is Jana?" I demanded shrilly. "What did you do to her? An implant? Reggie has an implant? In her body? Where? What kind?"

"Never mind that," he snapped. "You're missing the point. Forget the implant. Forget Jana. She's the past, and you are the future of Halliwell Enterprises. Which is yours to manage now, by the way. With any staff you choose. Bring your Red Queen Consulting staff onboard, if you think you can control them. They were an eccentric bunch, from what I remember. But it's your call."

It chilled me that he had observed my Red Queen staff so closely. Attention from him was not healthy for them. "I, ah... don't see them doing well in this environment," I hedged.

"But that's the thing, my dear," he said. "It's your environment now. *Tabula rasa.* Entirely new, from the ground up. You will run Halliwell Enterprises for me, leaving me free for the next part of my life plans. Which I can now begin in earnest, now that SmokeScreen is at my disposal. Thanks to Glowworm. And to you."

I tried not to flinch. "What plans do you mean? Like, world domination?"

My question had been pure mouthy snark, but to my horror, his smile widened.

"Right on the money, Cassandra," he said softly.

I felt my blood pressure drop as I stared into his wide, tilted green eyes, just like my own. Halliwell's toxic influence, that maimed or killed or poisoned everything it touched, magnified, spread out over the whole world?

He would turn it into a blasted hellscape.

"You're kidding, right?" I pressed him. "Just fucking with my head. Right?"

"Language, Cassandra. You sound like a rebellious child when you talk like that. You're in the bigtime now, so please, grow up. I am not kidding. It's time to put my plans into motion. I'll be like a god with SmokeScreen. And I want you by my side. My heir."

"I don't want to be your heir," I blurted out.

"You haven't tasted absolute power yet," he said, with a gloating smile. "Trust me. You'll like it. Once you get a taste, you don't look back. You'll see."

I let out a slow breath, reminding myself that this guy did not get to dictate what I thought, what I wanted, who I was, what I cared about. He never would.

But I had to be careful. Rein in my big mouth. Keep myself alive. For Reggie.

I stared down at the Paleolithic goddess figure that adorned his desk, and focused on it, to keep my mind steady. How typical, for that prick to use a priceless prehistoric representation of the divine feminine, painstakingly carved by some caveman or cavewoman untold tens of thousands of years ago, as a fucking paperweight. The guy didn't even use paper.

"Is that an original?" I asked, gesturing at the goddess.

He looked amused. "What do you think, Cassandra?"

He pulled a phone from his pocket which I recognized as my own. "What the hell are you doing with that?" I demanded.

"Moderate your tone." He tapped into it swiftly. "I'm sending a message to your ex-boyfriend. So that he understands the new order of things. It features you demonstrating your intention of working with me."

"But I never—"

"I took the liberty of anticipating that you would change your mind when you saw the possibilities. You're not a stupid woman. There. Sent. Haley did the deepfake work for me. She took the technology miles beyond where anyone else has. Not even a forensic video expert would be able to tell that it wasn't you in that video. And I have plenty of video and audio of you, with all my eyes and ears in this place. Haley did a beautiful job. She's the best. Or... well. Was the best, I should say."

"Was?" I demanded. "What do you mean? What did you do to her?"

He slid the phone back into his pocket. "There," he said, with satisfaction. "Now everyone knows the score, and we can all move on."

He looked at me expectantly. For a moment, I wished that I'd used my misspent youth studying abnormal psych instead of computer science. This guy was not just a psychopathic asshole. He was utterly deranged. He scared the shit out of me.

What had he done to Haley? Jana? And everyone else here?

"Listen," I said, keeping my voice even and reasonable. "I'll work for you. I like power, I admit. But I can't function with this threat to Reggie hanging over my head. That just won't work for me. You've got to cut her loose if you want me in top form."

He looked irritated. "I thought from the very start that this might work better if I removed Regina from the picture before we even began. Sad and unpleasant, but it would be so much simpler for you and for me. You wouldn't have your emotional energy divided. And it would be a kindness to the poor girl, after all the suffering she's gone through. Besides, if she lives, she'll be tormented by being compared to you, which isn't fair to anyone. I should've done this long before." He pulled out the remote.

"No!" I yelled. "Don't you dare! If you kill my sister, I will never, ever, ever work with you. Ever. I swear to God. I'd die first."

He studied me, eyes narrowed. "And you will work with me if I spare her? Is that the corollary?"

I swallowed. "Yes," I ground out, through my teeth.

"You do know that you won't be able to see her again, right?" he warned. "I require one hundred percent commitment. Nothing left over for frivolous pursuits."

"Fine. You want me, you got me. One hundred percent. So what's the mechanism of this implant? How have you been making her get sick? Let me just make some calls so I can dismantle that, and then we can get right to work, okay?"

He laughed at me. "Do you think I got to this point in life being stupid and trusting? Leverage, Cassandra. Nothing ever happens without leverage."

"But I can't," I wailed. "I can't do this. Not with this thing hanging over my head like a guillotine!"

"Sorry," he said. "You must. You will learn to live with the discomfort, the uncertainty. And it'll make you stronger. You'll see."

He gave me an encouraging smile. As if my desire for my sister to stay alive was a regrettable personality trait, but possibly correctable. As if he would actually be doing me a favor by pushing that button. Hurting me in order to help me. It made me furious.

He came closer, bending to open a desk drawer. Without stopping to think, I lunged for the stone goddess. I grabbed her by the head, and spun the heavy, bulbous stone body around—*thunk.*

It whacked the side of his head.

He let out a startled grunt, stumbling down against the desk, and I swiftly hit him again on the back of the head. And again. I let out a feral, grunting cry with each blow.

Halliwell slid heavily to the ground. I backed away, panting heavily. I was on the verge of screaming. He just lay there, his white hair a bloody mess.

Now, Cass. Now. Move your ass. Do what you have to do.

What was that? What did I have to do? Fuck me. I couldn't think. Couldn't plan.

Killing him was the smartest, most practical thing to do, I supposed, but I couldn't cold-bloodedly bash in the head of an unconscious man. Not even a monstrously evil man. I should, but I couldn't. That would make me like him.

Besides, there was the explosive tooth thing. Who knew how many people who would die the same moment he did? All their deaths would be on my head.

I knelt beside Halliwell, searching through his pockets. I found the passcard, Reggie's remote control, my phone, his phone. I swiftly turned Reggie's dial down to zero, hoping desperately that Halliwell hadn't been lying about that.

How was I going to find out more about Reggie's implant? With that doctor up there, right near Reggie, with instructions to kill her if... if what? What was the catalyst? What was the signal? How could I know? How would the evil doctor know? I wanted to scream, with fear, frustration, desperation.

It was like being stuck in a maze, and every option ran me into an electrified wall.

But he'd said that Jana had been trying to figure out what he'd done to Reggie. She had probably paid the ultimate price for trying to help me. But Halliwell had been so coy about it. He had never said that he had killed her. Not in so many words.

If Jana was still alive, she was the only one who could tell me about this implant. Maybe she was alive, and still had that phone I'd left under her pillow, with Invisibility Cloak loaded on it. I had tagged all my secret phones, so I pulled up the app on my phone, and scanned for them.

There they were. Seven phones, all clustered in my old apartment, still hidden in the secret compartment of my suitcase, in my closet. And the eighth was... oh *fuck*.

The eighth one was down on Level Eight.

CHAPTER 25

Shane

"She went away with him? Cass? With Halliwell?" Reggie's voice rose in a horrified squeak. She sat straight up in bed, eyes wide. Still pale, but much better than she'd been even just an hour before. "Then why are you here? Aren't you going to go after her? Save her? Why are you wasting time here talking to me?"

I rubbed my face, trying and discarding several different ways of saying it, then realizing that there was no good way. "It didn't look like she was abducted," I said reluctantly. "It happened right after the worm took over our computer system. Seconds after that, she walked out of the hospital with him, apparently unforced, making not a peep to anybody she saw or walked past. She got in a car with him and drove away. No one hit her over the head or stuffed her into a trunk."

"Of course not! He forced her! Because he told her that if she didn't, he'd make me sick again!" Reggie said sharply. "It's so obvious! Can't you see it?"

"But how could he do that?" I asked. "There isn't anything

in your body that can explain your symptoms. No one has touched you since we got you from the clinic."

"If we knew how it worked, none of this would be happening!" Reggie wailed.

I shook my head. "Honey, I'm so sorry. I don't know what to think—"

"I know exactly what you should think, and what you should do! Right now! You should save her! She saved you, right? She was really brave! She put herself way out there for you! It's only fair! So go do it, quick!"

"I'm not sure it's that simple anymore," I said.

The energy faded from Reggie's face. It went stiff and deathly pale. "Ah. I see. So you think that Cass was playing a horrible trick on you guys," she said. "And me getting sick is all part of this trick? So she played it on me, too? That's actually what you think about her?"

Holy shit, the kid was as sharp as a new razor blade. "Reggie, I don't know—"

"She didn't." Reggie's voice was haughty. "I know you won't believe me, because I'm her sister, and because I'm just a kid, but it's true. I know her. You don't, not really. You think she's doing this for money. But Cass doesn't care about money. She has plenty, because she's so good at what she does, but she doesn't care about it. She doesn't care about fancy clothes or cars or yachts, or any of that stuff."

"I know that," I tried again. "But I—"

"You actually think that she let him make me sick, and then dumped me."

"Reggie, I didn't mean—"

"So I guess I'm, what, like, homeless, now? Once the hospital discharges me, I'll be out on the street, sleeping under a bridge, right?"

I recoiled at that. "Hell, no!" I said. "You will not be homeless!"

"But I'll probably go into the system, then, right? I saw this TV show about foster kids. They carried their stuff around from foster home to foster home in a garbage bag. I guess that'll be me. Except I don't have anything to put into my garbage bag."

Holly burst in. "No, you will not!" she announced. "You'll stay with us!"

Reggie gave her a sad smile. "You're just a kid, Holly. You keep forgetting. It's not up to you. I'm not his responsibility. Definitely not if he thinks that Cass is bad."

"I didn't say that," I objected.

"Well, I know that she's not," Holly said forcefully. "I know it, and you know it." She turned to me. "So? Is she going to be a foster kid? It's up to you, right?"

Fuck. I was not up to a parenting challenge this emotionally fraught right now.

"Holly, now is not the time to discuss this," I said. "Reggie is staying right where she is until she is better. And we are not having this conversation."

"That's no kind of answer," she told me.

"It's the only one you'll get right now. Unless you want to be driven home."

Holly's tightly pressed mouth quivered. Her eyes were filled with angry tears. "You turned mean while you were gone," she said. "You didn't used to be mean."

"Home it is," I said, pulling out my phone. "Remy will drive you back to the—"

And the phone rang, right in my hand. It startled me so much it leaped up off my hand like a wild thing. I grabbed it out of mid-air, fumbling, almost dropping it. Holly was right next to me, close enough to see what was on the display.

Red. We exchanged shocked glances. Holly turned to Reggie, before I could stop her, or signal her, or muzzle her. "It's Cass." Holly's voice was hushed.

The ringing stopped. A text message notice appeared. I clicked on it. No text, just an attachment. A video attachment.

This could not be good. In fact, this was almost certainly very, very bad.

"Well?" Holly said. "Aren't you going to look at it?"

We stared each other down. "Not with you breathing down my neck," I said.

Reggie made a shooing gesture. "Go look at it. Then come back and show us."

Like hell I would, I thought as I strode out of the room.

It occurred to me that I kept on expecting Holly and also Reggie to be the ten-year-olds that they would have been if their lives had not exploded. Both girls had suffered traumatic loss, terror, violence. They were enmeshed in this whole terrible business, all the way up to their necks.

They weren't normal ten-year-olds anymore. The rules about what was appropriate for children didn't apply to them. I would have protected them if I could, but it was too late for that. I couldn't be anything but brutally real with those two.

They'd see right through anything less.

I went into the corridor, staring at the phone in my hand as if it might blow up in my face. Ethan, Frey and Jed saw my face. They were on me in a hot second.

That was the downside of having a family who cared about your business. They were all up in your face and all over your shit. All of the fucking time.

"What's going on?" Ethan said. "What's with the phone?"

"Text message," I said. "From Cass. A video."

Freya gripped my shoulder. "Well?" she said. "Halliwell has already done his worst. He just wants to taunt us now. Let's see it."

I nodded. My voice wasn't working, but who cared. There was nothing more to be said. I pulled up the video and set it to play.

There he was, that smirking son of a bitch. He was perched on the edge of a huge desk in a luxury office. Floor-to-ceiling windows overlooking the Pacific. Next to him was Red. She wore a tight, high-necked, clinging black sweater dress with flouncy lace sleeves, and her hair flowed down around her, smooth and glossy and perfect. She, too, was smiling. That same cold, empty smile that I'd seen on the security camera.

"Hello, Shane." Halliwell nudged Red. "Go on, my dear. Aren't you going to greet your former flame? Where are your manners, Cassandra?"

She waved, flirtatiously. "Hello," she said archly. "It's been real."

"So by now, you've figured out my plan, right?" His voice was jovial. "Let me introduce you to the woman of many faces... my beautiful and gifted daughter, who is now my sole heir, Cassandra Halliwell. The new CEO of Halliwell Enterprises."

"Fuck me," Jed muttered.

"Holy shit," Ethan said.

Frey's fingers tightened on my shoulders as she shushed them.

"... sorry to have inconvenienced poor little Regina in the process, very stressful for poor Cassandra. But it was a necessary evil, to inflame all your tender sentiments. Since you have such a pretty little one of your own. You really were primed to be manipulated. All of you."

"Fuck you," I burst out. "Asshole."

"Shhh." Frey's nails now dug into my shoulder hard enough to break the skin.

"... see the family resemblance now, right? I bet you're kicking yourself that you didn't see it sooner, hmm? But one sees what one expects to see. I just wanted to thank you formally for your spectacular collaboration, both in the past, and going forward." He lifted a bottle of champagne. Red held up two cups, which he filled.

He took one, they lifted the glasses, clinked them as the video ended.

I stared at the still video image of the champagne glasses touching, as the ground fell away beneath my feet into a yawning black maw.

CHAPTER 26

Cass

J ana. Oh please, please. Be alive.

Hurry, hurry, hurry. If Halliwell woke up, vicious as he was, he'd kill Reggie on the spot, just for spite. But I couldn't immobilize him, not without wasting precious time. The Bridge was an office environment, with nothing one could use to bind a man. No duct tape, twine, rope, electrical cord or plastic ratchet cuffs.

I just had to leave him as he was, unconscious and bleeding, and run down into the dungeons, praying to that benevolent mother goddess to do me one more good turn.

Just one. Please. For Reggie, not for me.

I pounded through the place, buzzing through doors with Halliwell's stolen passcard. The place was so echoingly quiet. Also weirdly cold, like a meat locker. Or maybe that was just my own perception of Halliwell's cold, dead heart.

Please, Jana. Hang on. Be there. Be alive.

Dread swelled in my belly as I held up the card to Level Eight. The light flashed green. I walked inside, slowing down as I walked past the glass-walled cells.

I stopped short at the sixth one with a gasp of horror. The floor of the cell was strewn with bodies.

Halliwell's children. My hell-siblings. Six of them on the ground, twisted and contorted, eyes bulging, faces dark. It did not look like they had been there very long.

Jana was not there, but of the faces turned my way, I saw Haley's body. I glanced up at the gas canister loaded into the mechanism. It was red.

I forced myself to keep moving, but I knew what I would find when I looked into the next cell. My hand was clamped over my mouth. I was making a sound, high pitched, barely human. I recognized Dean, Sybil, Jared and George, because their faces were turned toward me, but once again, I didn't see Jana's pale blond hair.

Tears were running from my eyes. It surprised me. I had barely known these people, and I had not bonded with them, or liked them at all. They were cold, emotionally dead, unreachable. Like zombies. Whatever Halliwell had done had destroyed them inside.

But it hadn't been their fault. They were victims, like Reggie. Even Nicole and Vincent had been victims, from what I understood. It was sad and cruel. And it could so easily have been me. Used and discarded like garbage.

The last cell was the one Shane had occupied, and it had only one body sprawled on the floor. Blond hair. She lay right next to the glass. Face down. Jana. Her canister was red, too, like the other two cells. Oh no, no, no. That ... fucking... *bastard*.

I pounded on the glass. Sprang up and hit the button to open the microphone. "Jana?" My voice wobbled, high and desperate. "Jana? Are you still there?"

I waited, not breathing, but I was sure that she was dead.

And amazingly... she moved.

Slowly, at first. Her hand clenched, then opened, pushing against the glass to roll herself over.

She was wearing a gas mask, like the one I'd seen on the day of Shane's execution. It covered her nose and mouth. She had an oxygen tank on the ground, hidden inside her coat. I heard it rattle and clank against the tile floor as she forced herself to sit up.

She looked at me with bleared, confused eyes. "Girl. What the fuck are you doing here?" she said thickly. "Didn't I go to a lot of trouble to get rid of you? And here you are again, like a bad penny. This is not a healthy place for you. Don't you get that?"

"Jana!" I yelled. "How do I open this door?"

She shook her head and pushed herself up onto her knees. "Only Halliwell has the codes, Cass," she said. "There's no way out of here unless he inputs the code himself, using his own unique biometrics. No way at all. He was careful about that."

"But... but how did you get a gas mask and oxygen?"

She shook with silent, feeble laughter. "I put it in there myself, just in case," she said. "He ordered me to switch out the canisters. To make cells six, seven and eight death cells. It felt like an end game move to me, so I hid a gas mask and an oxygen tank inside all of the meal drawers. In every single cell. He didn't bother to watch our death throes, so he probably didn't even notice that I'm still alive. He wouldn't care if he did."

"Jana, I have to get you out of there!"

"You can't," she repeated. "Face it, and let it go. Funny, how the others never knew the oxygen was there. Just as well, since there was only one mask. Can you imagine the carnage? Those buttheads, fighting over it? That would have been some true Halliwellian entertainment. He lured the others down here on false pretenses, but he had his thugs drag me down by force. I guess he figured I was onto him, after telling me to load the poison gas. He knows I'm broken, but he also knows that I'm not stupid."

"You are not broken! Far from it! There has to be a way to

reprogram this damn thing. I have to get you out, Jana! You need to live!"

Jana shook her head. "My oxygen is almost out. I'm not sure how many minutes I have. Not many. But if suffocating is too uncomfortable, I can always just take off the mask. Nasty, but quicker."

"No! Don't! I'm good at jerry-rigging code. Maybe I can find a way. But please. Could you tell me what he did to make Reggie sick? Halliwell said you found the file."

She waved her hand. "Yeah," she said, her voice vague and faraway. "Um, let me think. My brain's not working too well. It's the oxygen. It's almost gone. Makes you stupid."

"Please, try," I pleaded. "Before he tells his man to kill her."

Jana blinked rapidly. "It's... an implant," she said slowly.

"That can't be!" I wailed. "She was scanned up the wazoo for implants! There are none!"

"They would never find this one," she said. "It's cutting edge. Made of a new kind of biological material. An extremely thin membrane. It wouldn't show up on any scan. It has nano-bots on it that attack her cell metabolism and her immune system whenever a certain range of frequencies activate them."

"Where?" I begged. "Where did they put it?"

"It's, ah..." She frowned, tapping her forehead as if to stimulate the memory. "Under her scalp. Yeah. I saw the diagram. They put it in a week or so before she got sick. In the park. They knocked her down some steps, stuck a needle in her, and in the implant went, and any pain and swelling was chalked up to a bump on the head from the fall. Back right quadrant, ear level. A vertical slit about a centimeter long. The membrane under her scalp is a flat square. Six by six millimeters. I tried to contact you to let you know. I got busted, though. Then he had me dragged down here. Sorry."

"No. I'm the one who's sorry." Tears were running down my

face again. "I'm so sorry, Jana. I'll tell them about the implant right away."

"Yeah. Better hurry with that. And then get out of here. Quick."

"But I can't just leave you here to die!"

"It's okay. I'm ready. Plus, I did a thing. With your Invisibility Cloak app."

"What thing?"

"I set bombs." A smile flashed briefly across her face. "I used your awesome app, in the night. I hid them all over. This whole place is going to blow up to the stratosphere. So you need to get out."

"When will it go off? Is there a timer?"

Jana pulled down the patch on her chest, and the little wire dangling from it.

"I'm the timer," she said, with a whispery laugh. "It's set to go off when my heart stops. I got the idea from him. From that fucking tooth. Poetic justice, right? As long as he's here when it happens, of course. That bit is key."

"Oh, he's here, all right," I said.

"Good. But so are you, which I did not intend. So leave, Cass. Please. I want you to live." She pried a phone out from where it was tucked into her sock. "I brought the phone down here. I was going to call him right before the big moment. When it was too late for him to run." She let out a weak giggle. "Run, now. Tell them to get that implant out of your sister and run like hell."

"But you're—"

"Run, goddamn it!" She hit the glass. I only heard the dull thump through the microphone.

I ran, scrambling out of Level Eight and up the stairs, to the nearest computer station, on Level Seven. The one where Halliwell had lurked to watch me and Shane on the monitors that night, that now seemed like a hundred years ago.

I dialed Shane's number as I buzzed the door open. First, I would deal with Reggie's implant, with Shane's help, as usual. Then, I had to strong-arm myself into Halliwell's system and find a way to change that code that opened the cell doors.

I had to be fresh, creative and innovative... under deadly pressure.

So what else was new.

CHAPTER 27

Shane

Freya was gripping my shoulder, but I couldn't feel it. "Holy shit," I muttered.

"It's more or less what we guessed, right?" Ethan said. "I'm just sorry that it had to be rubbed in your face like that."

Holly pushed between me and her aunt, her arms crossed. "Well?" she said, in ringing tones. "Let's have a look!"

"No!" the four of us all said in unison.

Holly's lower lip stuck out as she scowled at me. "Why not?"

"You do not need to see this," I said savagely. "You are a kid, Holly."

Holly tilted up her chin. "I saw a video Nicole sent of you chained to a ceiling with that collar with the chain pulling you up, so the wire almost cut your throat."

"You what?" I looked at Frey, aghast. "What the hell? How did she see that?"

"Not by our choice," Frey said grimly. "Nicole sent the video directly to her phone. She saw it before any of us even knew it existed."

"Well, anyhow," Holly said briskly. "My point is, it can't be any worse than that, right? Does anybody get killed or cut up into pieces in it?"

"No," I admitted. "But it shows Cass being all chummy and friendly with Halliwell. Which appears to confirm that she doesn't give a damn what happens to her sister. I don't think Reggie needs to see that."

"I think you're wrong," Holly said. "I think it's a fake. And if it is, Reggie's probably the only one who might be able to tell us why. She'll see things we don't see."

"Of course she will. She's emotionally biased," I said.

"Like you're not?" Holly shot back.

I gave her a narrow look, but she stared straight back without blinking. My innocent little girl had developed a steel spine and a smart mouth while I was gone.

"Actually, she's not wrong," Jed offered cautiously. "We can't afford to tiptoe around anybody's feelings. We need all the info we can get."

"Besides, it'll kill her if you don't let her see it," Holly announced. "Cass is the only family she has left. It would drive her nuts if she couldn't see it."

"I think it's you who'll be driven nuts by curiosity, am I right?" I asked.

Her lips tightened. "I'm thinking about Reggie, not me," she said primly.

"Let me watch it. Right now."

We spun around to see Reggie swaying in the doorway of her room, in her hospital gown. She hung onto her IV rack like a crutch. Her eyes burned with determination.

"Reggie! You shouldn't be out of bed!" Freya and Kat sprinted over, grabbing her by the arms and hustling her back into her room.

"I'm just getting back up again and coming out again if you

don't show me that video," Reggie called from inside. "Until I fall down dead! And then it'll be your fault!"

"Just what I need," I muttered. "More pressure."

Holly tilted her head and gave me a 'what-did-I-tell-you' look. Jed and Ethan just shrugged. I shook my head. Un-fuck-ing-believable.

"Okay," I said. "Really? You think she should see it? So today is all about heartbreak and disillusionment for everybody, then? Nobody should be spared."

"There's no way to spare anybody. Don't even try," Holly said, more gently. "Come on, Daddy. Let's not waste more time."

The phone rang. The display said 'Red,' once again, and oh God, how I hated being jerked around by that self-important prick.

I hit "talk." "Who the hell is this?" I snarled.

"Who do you think?" It was Red's voice. She sounded like herself again, not like she had in the video, just stressed and breathless. "Listen up. I think I found out how to help Reggie—"

"You think we'll believe anything you say after that fucking video?"

She paused for a second, puzzled. "Huh?" she said, blankly. "Oh, wait. You mean that video that Halliwell sent you? It's a deepfake. Never mind it. Listen, you have to tell Reggie's doctors to look for a—"

"Don't try to make me think you care about her," I said. "You shouldn't be allowed anywhere near that poor kid. Cassandra Halliwell, huh? Favored, long-lost daughter? Heir to two hundred billion dollars?"

She huffed out an impatient breath. "Is it my fault that I'm related to that psychopath? Like I care about his goddamn money!"

"It's your fault for lying about it!"

"It's not a connection I'm proud of, okay? I didn't want to acknowledge it, not in dire straits, with Reggie on the line. Listen up, Shane. Be pissed if you want. Don't believe me if you want. But if you don't get that implant out of Reggie, he'll kill her to spite me, and you'll have that on your head forever. Just do this one small thing for me. Check for the scar. It's on her scalp, ear level, right side, back of her head. If it's there, have the surgeons remove the implant. It should be very small. A flat little piece of some kind of membrane, a half centimeter square. It has nano-bots on it. They're making her sick, whenever a certain frequency is—"

"I don't believe a word you say," I told her.

"Fine, whatever. Hate me if you want. But cover your ass, and check Reggie's scalp for that scar. It costs you nothing, but it's life or death for her. Just do it. Tell me you'll do it, Shane. Please."

"I don't follow your orders," I told her.

"I am not Halliwell's stooge. But as it happens, I'm probably going to die today. Will you take care of Reggie if that happens? She doesn't have any other people."

"Goddamn it, Red. You just never stop, do you?"

"No, never. Gotta go. Check for the scar. Please, Shane." She hung up on me.

They were all staring expectantly when I looked at them.

"She told me where to look for the implant that's making Reggie sick," I said.

The others followed me into Reggie's room. I sat down on the chair by her bed, my phone still clutched in my hand. "A couple of things, before I give you this," I said. "Is it true that Cass is Halliwell's daughter?"

Reggie looked back defiantly. "Yes," she said. "But she's not happy about it."

My heart sank. "And... you?"

"Not me, thank God. I was an 'oops' baby. My mom was

experimenting with having a boyfriend. The boyfriend didn't work out, but she kept me."

"Why didn't Cass tell me?" I asked.

Reggie lifted her eyebrows. "Come on. How would you have reacted?"

"Not as badly as I'm reacting right now," I said. "All things considered."

"He's not family," Reggie said heatedly. "He's a monster. A nightmare. My mom ran away from him when she figured out how dangerous he was. He scared her to death. He wanted to do, like, some kind of brain surgery on Cass, when she was really little, to make her more like him. He did it to his other kids, too. A couple of them died in surgery, Mom said."

I exchanged glances with the other adults. "That would explain the state that Victor and Nicole were in," Freya said. "If they were surgically altered by a megalomaniac hack."

"Are Victor and Nicole the ones who kidnapped Holly?" Reggie asked.

"Yes," Ethan admitted. "Very bad people. We had some trouble with them."

"Well, Halliwell's bad people, too," Reggie said. "She only worked for him because he said he could save me from Varen's Disease, but she hates his guts, and she couldn't wait to leave." Reggie gestured impatiently at my phone. "Can I see? Please?"

"One more question," I said. "Do you have a sore spot on your scalp?"

Her eyes widened. "How did you know? I never told anyone about it."

"Where is it?"

"It's here." She reached back and touched her scalp. On the back, on the right, at ear level. "It's from when I passed out on the school grounds that time. Then I got so sick, I forgot. I told the doctors at the clinic, but they didn't care."

"Can I look at it?"

"Sure," she said. "But hurry, please. I want to see that video."

I parted the thick, glossy locks of curly red hair, shining, the flashlight from my cell phone onto her scalp.

Frey and I saw it at the same moment, and I felt rather than heard her soundless gasp. She touched it gently with her fingertip. It was a small, straight, recently healed scar on her scalp, vertical, a little inflamed.

"Wow," Jed said, peering over Freya's shoulder. "Well, I'll be damned. Look at that."

"Shane?" Reggie urged. "The phone? Can I see the video? Please?"

"Wait." I looked up at Kat. "Call Demiguel and the surgeons right now. Let's get this checked out immediately."

Kat's ear was already to her phone. "On it."

"So that's taken care of, right?" Reggie said impatiently. "So can I have the phone, please?"

I handed her the phone. Holly scrambled right up on to the bed next to her, putting her arm around Reggie's shoulder and giving her a reassuring squeeze.

Reggie set it to play. We all stood there, jaws clenched. Staring at the two little girls faces as they watched raptly. The phone's blue illumination reflected in their eyes.

We followed the tinny audio. Reggie frowned in fierce concentration through the whole thing, holding it close to her eyes. It finished, and she set it to play again, stopping it to enlarge the image, replaying individual moments.

Holly waited quietly. I was proud that she knew when to keep her mouth shut without being told.

After a few minutes, Reggie handed the phone back to me. "It's not her," she said. "It's a deepfake."

I let out a sharp breath. I'd been holding my breath. Well, duh. Nice fantasy, but of course Reggie would come to that conclusion. No one could blame a lonely, scared, sick little girl for going straight there, and holding her ground. To the death.

"How do you figure?" I asked. All of us were clustered around the bed now. Frey and Kat sat down at the foot of the bed, on either side.

"Well, her hands, to start with," Reggie said. She ran the video back. "Look how she waves. Cass doesn't wave like that. That twinky-wink finger thing, that's totally not her. Plus, those arms have no freckles. Cass has freckles everywhere, like me. Whoever's hands they used for that video doesn't. See my arms?" She held up her freckly forearm, with the dangling IV line. "Look at my freckles. Cass has even more."

"It could just be the light, washing them out," Ethan warned.

Reggie just gave him a look. "And then there's the hair," she said. "Her hair was straight in the video. Cass's hair was in a really tight braid yesterday. It takes time to get to that place, and she braided it wet yesterday. So if she brushed out her braid, there would be crimped braid-waves. Unless she got there, took a shower, and blew out her hair, which take forever. There wasn't enough time to change into the dress, put on that makeup and blow out her hair. Cass is slow with girly stuff."

Kat and Frey stared at each other. "I didn't think of that," Kat said. "I have straight hair, and never longer than my shoulders. Didn't even occur to me."

"But the biggest clue is that there's no tattoo," Reggie went on.

"Cass has a tattoo?" Frey said. "I didn't see one."

"She was always wearing big sweatshirts with long sleeves since she's been here," Reggie said. She pointed to her left wrist. "She has 'Regina,' in cursive, right up her arm. Her tattoo artist knows about ancient Chinese medicine, and she put it right on the heart meridian. When I'm big enough, I'm going to have one on my heart meridian that says 'Cassandra.' This girl didn't have it. She's definitely not my sister. Cass made me some temporary tattoos with her name, but they took them away from me at the bad clinic. And washed off the one I had. The bastards."

I digested that, all my nerves buzzing with... no. Goddamn it, I couldn't afford anything as stupid as hope. I just didn't dare. It was too damned tempting.

But the scar on Reggie's scalp, the blown-out hair, the missing tattoo... that was huge. I'd seen Red's tattoo, the morning we woke up together, but I'd forgotten it. We'd never had time for the kind of lazy bed talk where tattoo histories were discussed.

It made bombing Halliwell's place into dust much more complicated, if Red was there. And if she was still the Red that I had always believed her to be.

The Red I'd fallen hopelessly in love with.

The doctors were filing in, talking excitedly. Demiguel was shooing us all away from the bed and out of the room. Stuff was happening in here. Thank God.

It was time to make it happen out there, too.

I looked at Ethan. "I'm ready," I said. "Let's extract Cass and grind that motherfucker into the ground. We'll sort the mess out later."

"Amen," Ethan said.

We raced toward the parking lot, boots thundering on the pavement.

CHAPTER 28

Cass

I couldn't get into his system. Damn him. I was an excellent hacker, but Halliwell was always ten steps ahead of me. You could say what you wanted about him being a blood-sucking, power-mad, narcissistic monster, but he was freaking smart and very detail oriented.

Ten minutes. Twenty. Twenty-five. Somehow, Jana was still alive down there on Level Eight, or the place would be floating in the stratosphere by now, and me with it. I couldn't even activate the vents to blow the poisonous gas out.

Halliwell had me blocked at every turn.

But I couldn't just leave her. Jana had risked everything for me and Reggie. She'd given me the key to free my little sister. She'd paid for it with everything she had.

Jana was my sister too, whether she knew it or not, and I wanted her to live. To come back from this and be who she always should have been, if she hadn't gotten sucked into the lethal vortex that was our father.

He'd killed enough of us. It had to stop.

My phone buzzed, and I almost screamed. I grabbed it and saw Jana's number.

I picked up. "Hey! I'm still upstairs trying to find a fucking override, but I can't—"

"Stop. Stop trying." Jana's voice was even weaker now, a thin thread of sound. "Too late. Get out now, or you'll die in here with me. Run, Cass."

My eyes were streaming. "Fuck, Jana! I can't!"

"Sucks, right? Thanks for caring. Thanks for giving me something real to do before the end. It almost feels worth it. And I'll see Mom soon. So it's okay. Really."

"Jana." I snorked up tear snot desperately, wiping my face on my sleeve. "Please. Don't give up hope."

"Never had any to begin with. Goodbye, Cass. Get lost." The call cut off, and I let out a shriek of pure frustration.

But she was not wrong. Halliwell's security had defeated me. The only way to get those codes was to force Halliwell to give them to me. And even if I had the stomach for that, Jana would be gone before I achieved it.

And, by definition, so would I.

I got up and headed for the stairs, pulling out the passcard for the garage level. Maybe I could find a car in there. But there would be no key, and hot-wiring a car was not in my current skillset. And no ice-sculpture van was coming to save me this time.

Maybe I could just run out on foot, sprint up the driveway toward the gate. It was a half a mile of road. That should be far enough to survive any bomb blast. I hoped.

I held up the passcard to the garage exit... and it flashed red. *Shit.*

My throat clutched, along with my gut. I tried again. Again. And again.

"Cassandra." The voice sounded over the PA system, grotesquely amplified. Halliwell's voice. Harsh, slurred... and fucking furious. "I see you're trying to escape from the garage level. Don't bother. There's no way out. I've changed the access codes. All doors are locked to you now. I have also called my man at the hospital, the one who brought you to me. I told him to turn Regina's dial all the way up. She's dead by now. But it hardly matters, since you will be too, soon enough."

My heart clutched. I hoped that Shane had come through for her. His curiosity alone would have impelled him to look for the scar. Once he saw it, he wouldn't have wanted to risk being wrong about something so huge. I had to believe that about him.

Please. Let that be true.

"Such a waste," Halliwell complained. "To think of what I offered you. All that you could have been, with my help, my mentoring."

I ran down the corridor toward the closest camera and gave him the finger.

He chuckled. "Charming. If you'd grown up with more of my influence, you would have had more graceful manners. A more elegant vocabulary, too. You swear like a stevedore. It's exhausting, you know?"

"Up yours, dickhead," I yelled, as I ran past the next camera trying door after door, though I knew it was useless.

"Case in point. Look at you. Poor Cassandra. Just a rat in a trap now."

I tried the door to the stairwell. Locked. The door that led the central courtyards, the lawn, the tennis courts. All flashed red, but I couldn't stop trying. The nervous energy impelled me. It needed somewhere to go.

His disembodied voice chuckled. "You never know when to stop, do you?"

"You're not the first person to tell me that today," I said.

"I'm not surprised," he growled. "Oh, by the way. Invisibility

Cloak. I found it in the system, you know. Lovely bit of work. Inspired."

I rattled the door to the library, the archives, the computer lab. "Up yours," I yelled.

"When you're dead, I'll take it for my own, and make a pile of money with it," he said. "I need some recompense for all my trouble. The Russian mob would love it. Or maybe some humorless, bloodthirsty jihadists. Someone you'd disapprove of, you snotty, moralistic little bitch. I'll make a special point of selling it to someone like that."

I turned, looked around at which ways remained open. There was only one. The bonkers, wrong, counter-intuitive one. The last thing on earth that I wanted to do.

If I couldn't run away from him, I had to run straight toward him. Claws out.

But it was an exercise in frustration. Every door to a place that might have objects that could be repurposed as weapons, i.e., a kitchen, with knives and shears, or a gym with weights, was locked. I had nothing in my pockets except what I had taken from him. I wish that I'd brought the friendly stone goddess, at least.

If I could get my hands on any kind of a weapon, I could at least try to bully him into giving me those codes. I pulled out my phone and texted Jana as I ran.

> hey

She replied.

> you're not gone yet?

> doors locked now. missed my chance

The letters appeared slowly now.

sux. thx anyway for trying to help

anytime sister

I entered.

don't get sentimental on me. you're supposed
to be smart. outwit that motherfucker. Go
crush him.

On it

I typed.

Smart, hah. On it, was I? Here it was again, that fucking bar set so high it made my eyes water and my stomach flip. I was running toward my doom unarmed, poised between Jana's ticking bomb and empty oxygen tank, Reggie's killer nano-bots, and that cackling goblin out there, hungry for my blood. I was supposed to outwit him, crush him, in this state? God, I wished that Shane were here. Shane was brilliant in situations like this. He'd just snap right into action, do some improbable, mind-blowing thing right off the cuff, like catapulting an ice sculpture into a car full of goons, or jumping out of a plane without a — oh... holy... *shit.*

My startled thought made me stumble. I recovered, picking up frantic speed.

"I see you, Cassandra," Halliwell taunted me. "I see everything."

"See this, dickwad." I flipped him off once again and sped straight toward the French doors that opened out onto the huge terrace.

The open air was cold and damp. Wind rushed in my ears, the surf, the screeching of wheeling seabirds. I closed the door, got myself behind one of the potted trees, pushed like hell. It didn't move. Then I saw Halliwell, emerging from his office, which gave me that panicked burst of energy I needed... and I moved it, howling with the effort.

It slid, slowly, blocking the French doors from the outside.

I scrambled for the base-jumping single parachute back-pack that I had stowed in that gardening cupboard. I struggled to put it on. It was ice-cold, damp, and my hands were clumsy and shaking. I'd watched the jumpers in horrified fascination during that depraved party, always with the thought in my mind that base-jumping was the very last fucking thing that I would ever do, in this life or the next.

Hah-hah. Just another of life's amusing little pranks.

I snapped the clasps of my harness, tightening them and hoping it had been packed properly. I was trusting my life to some rando I never met. Then again, the alternative, i.e., being vaporized, really put that kind of risk into perspective.

A huge crash made me stagger back with a cry, losing my balance. I was showered with shards of glass. The French doors had shattered, and the bloodied stone goddess that I'd used to clobber Halliwell flew out, hit the ground, spinning and sliding in the glittering shards.

Halliwell swung the barrel of a gun at the sides of the big hole in the glass, smashing on either side to widen the hole, and then stepped through it, his feet crunching on the broken glass, teeth shining in a maniacal grin. Blood streaked his face. He looked terrifying, his eyes bright, glittering, and utterly mad. He advanced, pointing his gun right at me. Driving me back.

"Don't move," he said. "Or I'll shoot you."

"You'll shoot me anyway," I said. "You just want to run off your mouth first and I don't want to hear it. Do your worst, asshole."

"Language, Cassandra." *Bam.*

I staggered back, hitting the stone balustrade with a gasp,

sagging down. It felt like a punch to the shoulder, but when I touched it, it came away red, sticky.

I was shot. So this was the end of the line. I thought about Reggie's sweet smile. Shane's kisses. The hunger in his eyes. The wild, wonderful possibilities that I had to let go of now. The beautiful future that was now no longer an option. I hoped that Reggie would have a future, at least. My sweet baby. I wouldn't be there to see it, but she would have to live for both of us.

I had to pitch myself over that cliff. I didn't want to die up here. Better to fall into the sea, or onto the rocks. Anything was better than dying here with Halliwell.

I struggled up onto my feet. My blood pressure was dropping. The world going dark. Not yet. Not yet. *Stay strong, Cass. Almost done. Almost there.*

I dragged myself up with the balustrade. My ears were roaring. So loudly. The sound was overwhelming and getting louder. Halliwell wasn't looking at me anymore. He was looking past me, mouth open. Shocked confusion on his bloodied face.

A huge crack of gunfire sounded over the roar. Halliwell clapped his hand against his belly and staggered, eyes wide with disbelief. Blood ran over his hands.

I spun around, and saw a helicopter, hovering about thirty yards away. Shane lay inside the open door behind a rifle stand. Poised to shoot again.

Oh God. If he killed Halliwell, Jana's bomb would go off, and take the helicopter right along with it. Oh, no, no, no. I lurched over and put myself between Shane and Halliwell, who had fallen to his knees. Shane gestured fiercely at me to get out of the way. I shook my head, mouthing the word with as much exaggeration as I could. Waving my arms, a go-away gesture. Repeating the word, over and over.

Bomb. Bomb. Bomb.

CHAPTER 29

Shane

W hat the fuck? Why was she shooing me away? Blocking my fucking shot? Was she was actually protecting that son-of-a-bitch? I looked through the rifle sight at Red's face, which was chalky white, her pale lips repeating that word, shaking her head, violently. If the helicopter moved, she shifted too, always blocking my shot. What the hell was she saying? It looked like 'mom.' The hell?

Then she crawled up onto the wide balustrade and stood there, teetering, wobbling. That splotch of red from Halliwell's bullet was dark on her shoulder and spreading. She looked up at me, still desperately waving her hands, shooing me away. I focused on her lips, her desperate eyes, her go-away gestures. Her hands were bloody. She was forming the same word, over and over. What the hell? Mom, mom, mom?

It hit me like a brick. *Bomb.*

Then she pitched herself off the balustrade and fell. *Fuck!*

"Bomb! Bomb! Get away from here, quick!" I bellowed into the mic.

Amos instantly did as I asked, swerving the chopper away

as my eyes followed her down, down, down... three seconds...
four... and a white parachute flowered open.

Oh, Jesus. My heart had almost stopped in my chest.

"Follow her!" I bellowed into the mic. "She's landing in the
water!"

The wind had caught the chute and filled it, carrying her
out over the heaving waves.

Boom.

The blast wave was huge, buffeting us. We looked up. The
entire fucking complex was expanding out into a huge fireball.
Red had warned us away just in time.

Amos swept us away from it, following that white parachute
as it floated out over the water. Jesus, that was a tight jump. I'd
done plenty of parachuting in my day, but never from a fucking
cliff. Base jumping was not my jam. I didn't crave adrenaline
that much. On the contrary, I was sick to death of it. That
woman had a set of brass gonads on her. Or else she was out of
her fucking gourd. Or maybe both.

Remy and Ethan both helped me secure the rope in the
helicopter as we descended closer to the water, knotting it
around me. We had no safety harnesses, so we'd just have to
wing it. Red had hit the water. The chute was billowing out like
an enormous jellyfish, parts of it sinking fast. Red's head was
nowhere to be seen.

They let the rope out and lowered me down. I fought panic.
Had to stay cool, methodical, as I swayed over the soggy fabric
billowing in the water, searching... searching... and then her
dark head popped up, hair over her eyes, gasping for air. *Yes.*

The helicopter shifted. They let my rope down further.

My feet hit the water. I seized her under the arms, pulled
her up. Undid the snap buckles, pulled the harness off her
shoulders. I wrapped myself around her and hung on for dear
life as my people pulled us back up into the sky.

I was never letting go of her again.

CHAPTER 30

Cass

Thoughts fought for space in my head. *Don't look down, don't look down. He came for me, he came for me, he came for me.*

I was alive. Halliwell was gone. Shane was here.

Jana. The thought of her clutched my heart, but it was too much to process right now. I would have to mourn Jana later.

I would be grateful to her forever. I owed her everything.

Many hands pulled us into the helicopter. There was a confusion of pain and cold and noise, being shoved around, strapped in. My scream as someone applied pressure to the bullet wound was lost in the roar of the machine.

I looked over at Shane. Placed my hand on his chest. My bluish hand. He was still covered with knotted, sodden ropes. *Reggie?* I mouthed.

He smiled, and gave me a thumbs up.

So it was over. Shane had swept me up out of that bloody mess like an eagle, and any wonderful thing was free to happen now.

No more limits.

CHAPTER 31

Cass

I wandered for while in a strange, foggy no-time of dreams and nightmares. Finally, I felt the constant, beckoning pressure of light against my eyelids.

The feeling got stronger and stronger. At some point, I heard muffled giggling, and slowly opened my eyes. Holly and Reggie were on either side of my bed.

Reggie leaned to kiss my cheek. Joy expanded in my heart.

"You're finally awake," Reggie said. "It's been, like, days."

"Really? Wow." It felt more like years to me. I stared at her. She looked great.

She stroked my wrist, the one where her name was tattooed. "I told them about your tattoo," she told me proudly. "That's how they knew the video was a deepfake."

"Of course you did." I swatted feebly at Reggie's arm. "Shouldn't you still be in bed? You're recovering too, right?"

"Nah, I'm way better now that they took that thing out of my head," she said cheerfully. "Better than before, even. It's awesome. All my dreams came true all at one time. Now Angela is planning this huge party to celebrate, as soon as they send you home. Like Christmas, except with prime rib and leg of lamb. She says she's going to celebrate our own family's Independence Day for the rest of her life, and me and Holly are supposed to help! It'll be a tradition!"

"Wow. Sounds... celebratory." Overwhelming was more like it.

"It'll be awesome, and you're the big heroine!" Holly told me excitedly. "You blew that bastard up like a boss!"

"Holly." It was Kat's reproving voice, from the door. "You're not supposed to say that word."

"But I have to call him something bad," Holly complained. "I could use way worse words for him. I've heard 'em all. Want to hear?"

"No, please don't," Kat said swiftly. "Not necessary. I'm familiar with them."

"It wasn't me," I kept repeating, but I didn't have enough breath to be heard.

Kat sat on the chair near the bed, trying not to smile. "What did you say, Cass?"

"I wasn't the one who did it," I said. "Jana set the charges. Shane was the one who shot Halliwell and fished me out of the ocean. All I did was run around like a chicken with its head cut off and jump off a cliff."

"With a bullet wound in your shoulder," Kat said. "Fleeing a massive bomb, and a homicidal maniac. Right. No biggie."

"That's not the point," I said impatiently.

"Yeah, yeah. Point taken." She smiled at me. "You're a woman after my own heart. I'm developing quite a collection of them. Who knew there were so many."

"Hey," Shane said, appearing in the doorway. "You're awake." He came in and stood at the foot of the bed, holding a bunch of sunflowers in his hand.

My eyes drank him in. He looked good. More color. Already less thin.

"Don't wear her out," he said to the girls. "Amos is heading back up to the Mountain House, so catch a ride home with him, okay? I heard from Angela that you two have cookies to bake and decorate."

Reggie looked down at me, a shadow of doubt in her eyes. "Will you be okay? If I go away?" she asked anxiously. "Are you sure?"

"I'll be fine, and so will you, with our new friends," I whispered. "We have nothing to worry about anymore. He's gone forever, baby. We're free. For real."

"It's just hard to believe," she said. "I still have nightmares."

"They'll get better," Shane offered. "Mine are better already."

Holly grabbed Reggie by the hand and pulled her out the door, chattering all the way. Kat gave us a misty smile and backed toward the door. "I guess I'll leave you two alone, then. And Cass? Thank you."

"For what?" I said, exasperated.

"For ending it. It's been hanging over us for so long. None of us really know what to do with ourselves now. How to behave. All the rules are suspended, all the parameters have flipped. It's... mayhem. In a good way. If that makes sense."

"Yeah," I told her. "Perfect sense. But don't thank me. It was a group effort."

"Right, right. That's your song, so you just go on and sing it. Later, babes."

She shot us a conspiratorial smile and walked out, shutting the door behind her.

Shane approached the bed, looking helplessly at the bouquet that he held.

I glanced around the room and gestured toward the table by the wall. "Looks like there's a vase over on the table. Thanks. They're really pretty."

Shane deposited the flowers into the vase and came over to

sit next to me. We looked at each other, smiling. I felt bizarrely awkward and shy. Intensely excited.

"Have I thanked you yet?" I asked.

"For what? I can't believe that rude shit I said to you on that phone call."

I laughed. "Oh, please. I would never hold that against you. That was just Halliwell mind-fucking you. Besides, you listened to me. You saved Reggie, you saved me, you shot down Halliwell, you fished me out of the ocean. And you managed somehow not to die in the process. Yay, you. You get the gold star."

"Do I?" He reached out to take my hand. "Can I choose my prize?"

My heart thumped. "And what prize might that be?"

He shrugged. "I thought maybe we could reopen that conversation we were having right before everything went to shit."

"Um…" I racked my tired brains. "My life is sort of out of sequence at the moment. Remind me. What conversation was that?"

"The one about tempting the gods. The one where we were starting to talk about the future. Right before the worm ate SmokeScreen and Halliwell snatched you. It was a great conversation. Lots of great possibilities were alluded to. I didn't want it to end."

"Oh. That one." I felt my face start to heat. My lungs squeezed joyfully.

"Just so you know, I'm ready to tempt the gods now," he said. "I'm so crazy about you, I can't see straight. I'll rub the gods' noses in it. Whatever they do to us, it can't be worse than what we've already been through. I'm ready to accept on faith that you exist. You're too good to be true, light years too good, but you're true all the same. You break the rules of nature. You are fucking spectacular, Red. And I love you."

I was flustered speechless. My face was even hotter, and now I couldn't breathe at all. Particularly not when he pulled a small black velvet box out of his pocket.

"So," he said, not meeting my eyes. "Here. Can't blame a guy for hoping."

I stared at the box, tear-blinded, as usual. I was so weepy now. It was a brand-new personality trait. Maybe that kind of sentimental goopiness just came right with being in love. Certainly I'd never experienced it before Shane came into my life.

"What's this?" I asked. "Isn't this a little premature? Are you sure? I can be really annoying, you know. I have all kinds of character defects you haven't had a chance to get pissed off about yet."

"So do I," he admitted. "And absolutely, I'm sure. I am nailing this down at my earliest opportunity. Which is to say, the second that you're conscious. And if you're in a weakened and confused state, so much the better. I'll take any advantages that luck and fate offer me. Open it."

I opened the box, and stared down, astonished. A wide band of yellow and white gold formed a pattern of a crown, the points of which were decorated with rubies, the white gold studded with a milky sparkle of tiny diamonds. It was lavish, stunning. Utterly unique.

"Holly suggested it," he said. "A crown, for the Red Queen. Frey is friends with a great goldsmith. He worked fast. While you were all drugged up."

I couldn't speak for several moments, but my choice had been made a long time ago, and it had been brilliantly clear to me the moment I leaped off Halliwell's terrace.

Shane was my man. I wasn't letting him slip away.

I slid the ring onto my finger. It fit perfectly. It felt wonderful. Heavy, smooth, almost alive. "Wow. I sure do wish I wasn't all bashed up in a hospital bed full of bullet holes. I'd rather hop right into your arms and be swept away to be ravished."

"Ahhh…" His voice trailed off. "I'm going to assume that's a positive response to my formal declaration of marriage. If I'm wrong, tell me now."

"Nope, you're not wrong," I said. "It doesn't get any more positive than this."

His grin transformed his face. "I'll make up for lost time as soon as possible, with the ravishing, as soon as you're back in form. Demiguel said you can go home in a couple of days and finish recuperating there. When you're home, we'll celebrate."

"So much to celebrate," I said. "I can't even pick a thing. There are too many."

"Yeah, and Holly will be celebrating having a sister. She's always wanted one," Shane said. "She'll be over the moon that this is happening."

I laughed at that, wiping my eyes. "Reggie, too. I've never seen her so happy."

"The girls have been helping me open up my apartment, down below Ethan's and Frey's. We're going to need our privacy, when you get home. For all that ravishing, you know. It can get noisy."

"Can't wait to see it," I said.

"I think you'll like it," he said. "I have a town house in Seattle, too, but Holly and I always liked this place best. There's a nice bedroom for Reggie. The room I was thinking for your home office has a great view of Mt. Rainier. Very inspiring."

I reached up, grabbing a piece of his shirt and tugging him toward myself. "I'm feeling inspired right now," I said. "Get over here, you."

"Careful! Your shoulder is still—"

"Don't worry about my shoulder," I assured him. "I'm medicated. I'm feeling no pain. You're all compliments and gorgeous jewelry and declarations of love and ravishment, but guess what, buddy? You're all talk and no action. Get your fine ass down here right now and kiss me, already."

He obliged me, and the intoxicating taste of him was a divine elixir. I could have leaped up and danced a passionate tango, though that might have been the morphine talking. Still. Every sweet detail of soft, warm lips, and tongue, and tenderness. Trust.

So good. So delicious. It just rolled over me like a wave of shining glory.

He leaned back for air, stroking my cheek reverently and gazing intently into my wet eyes. "I love you, Red," he said roughly. "I can't believe my luck."

"That makes two of us," I admitted. "I guess we'll have to learn how to believe it. We can teach each other, and remind each other whenever we forget. The kissing helps."

"Sounds like a great plan," he muttered, as our lips met again.

EPILOGUE

Shane

The waiter left out drinks on the little tables on each side of the beach recliners, and we snuggled up, inhaling the scent of salt and sand. The sweet coconut scent of slathered sunblock. The zingy lime of the cold margaritas.

I readjusted the beach wrap so that her bullet scar was properly covered. "The plastic surgeon said not to let any sun get on it while it's healing," I scolded her gently. "You have to be careful."

She twitched the wrap open, and touched the puckered, shiny red scar. "I'm thinking I might dress it up with another tattoo, once it's completely healed," she mused. "Some big, fun flower. A huge poppy, a Bird of Paradise, something like that."

I leaned down to kiss it. "If you want. But I think it's beautiful just like it is. It says to me, I survived the impossible. I conquered all. That makes me happy."

"Awww. That's sweet," she murmured, grabbing her drink for a sip through the paper cocktail straw. She glanced over to Holly, who had just leaped headfirst into a warm, green-blue wave of seawater. "The girls are having fun," she murmured, as Reggie followed suit, shrieking in delight. "I love to see that. It heals my heart."

"Yeah, but the whole household seemed pretty shocked that we opted for a honeymoon with two ten-year-olds in tow," I said. "But after all that time in that cell, I don't want to take my eyes off Holly. Or Reggie, either. She's a great kid."

"So glad we're in agreement about that. And about staying stuck to them like glue. Besides, any minute now they're going to turn into adolescents and tell us to piss off, so we should enjoy these moments while we can." She took another sip, and her eyes flashed over to my untouched cocktail. "Don't you like your margarita?"

"I'm sure it's fine," I said. "It's just hard to let go."

"Of what?"

I shrugged. "I can't let down my guard," I admitted. "Alcohol makes me relax, and relaxing feels dangerous. I can drink a beer up at the Mountain House, with a gate and a wall and a security staff and sensors and cameras always running. But a beach resort? Any random asshole off the street could come walking down the beach with bad intentions."

"They could," she agreed. "But statistically speaking, they won't."

"Once the press gets wind of that Halliwell inheritance, those statistics might change," I warned her.

She winced. "Ay-yi-yi. As if that guy hadn't screwed with my life enough. He had to unload that particular truckload of bricks onto my head, too."

I laughed at her. "I bet you're the only person in the world who has ever looked at two hundred billion dollars in that particular way. Load of bricks, huh?"

"When you've been staring death in the face for yourself, your sisters and the man you love? Yes, actually. That's the moment that you understand what two hundred billion dollars of ill-gotten gains is actually worth. Which is to say, not worth shit. And it's a full-time job for a whole army of number-crunching, bean-counting accountants who need to be managed and monitored. Which is not how I ever wanted to spend my days."

"So delegate," I suggested. "You want that money spread where it's most needed, right?"

"Yeah, sure," she said, her voice doubtful. "Delegate how?"

"Ethan knows this woman, Raine Lazar, in Seattle. She runs a top-rate philanthropic organization, the Grace Foundation. She already has the army of bean-counters ready to go. They'll help you. You can unburden yourself of Halliwell's legacy with no trouble at all. They'll know just what to do with it. And they are totally on the level. They do great projects, all over the world. You can pick and choose."

She relaxed slightly. "You think? And then we can relax?"

I looked over to where Reggie and Holly played at the water's edge in their bathing suits, giggling and squealing as they outran the foaming surf. "I don't know," I said. "Just because Halliwell is dead and SmokeScreen is wiped out of existence, that doesn't mean that the world is suddenly a bed of roses. It's still full of danger. All the time. Particularly if you have kids. Relaxing still scares me to death. Sorry."

Cass took a sip through her straw, smiling. Then she draped her lithe body over mine, reached for my margarita, and put it in my hand. "Take a sip," she urged me.

I did as she said. It was nice. Ice-cold, tangy and sharp, with the slight burn from the salted edge. She rattled her ice cubes, set down her glass, and cuddled closer.

"It scares me, too," she said. "But the trick is, we might be scared, but we just don't stop. We just keep at it, scared or not. We've had practice, right?"

I thought about it and took another drink. "True thing."

"I happen to know first-hand that you function spectacularly well when you're scared. Catapulting ice sculptures, flinging knives, sniping from helicopters. You rock."

"You're pretty damn impressive yourself when it comes to that, babe."

She shrugged that off. "So let's just go up to the room while the girls go to their dance thing. We can passionately congratulate each other on how incredibly brave we are."

"Yum." I was smiling like a fool. "Sounds like fun."

"Remember this one thing," she said. "Write this down. On the bathroom mirror in lipstick. Every good thing that comes your way? You deserve that thing. Got that?"

"Got it," I said dutifully.

"And every bad thing that comes your way?" she went on.

I waited. "Yeah? What about every bad thing?"

"Fuck that thing," she said crisply.

I let out a crack of startled laughter and pulled her close. "God, I love you."

Want another fun epilogue? Join Shane and Cass at Kat and Ethan's blow-out wedding! Get it by joining my newsletter list right here and get two more scorching Unredeemables novellas along with it! One features Freya and Jed, the other is about Kat and Ethan, and there are other treats as well, destined only for my super-readers! So join... and enjoy!

ALSO BY SHANNON MCKENNA

The Unredeemables

Master of Lies

Master Of Secrets

Master Of Chaos

The Hellbound Brotherhood Series

Hellion

Headlong

Hellbent

Heedless

Havoc

The Obsidian Files Series

Right Through Me

My Next Breath

In My Skin

Light Me Up

The McClouds & Friends Series

Behind Closed Doors

Standing In The Shadows

Out Of Control

Edge Of Midnight

Extreme Danger

Ultimate Weapon

MEET SHANNON MCKENNA

Shannon McKenna is the NYT and USA TODAY bestselling author of over thirty novels, ranging from sexy contemporary romance to action packed, turbocharged romantic thrillers. She loves tough and heroic alpha males, heroines with the brains and guts to match them, terrifying villains who challenge them to their utmost, adventure, blazing sensuality, and most of all, the redemptive power of true love.

Since she was small she has loved abandoning herself to the magic of a good book, and her fond childhood fantasy was that writing would be just like that but with the added benefit of being able to take credit for the story at the end. The alchemy of writing turned out to be messier than she'd ever dreamed, but whatever, she loves it anyway and hopes that readers enjoy the results of her experiments. She loves to hear from her readers. Contact her by email at her website, shannon mckenna.com, or find her on Facebook to keep up with all her news! Follow her on Bookbub to get new release and discount alerts!

If you'd like to know when new books will come out, and hear about discounts, giveaways and promos, join Shannon's newsletter. She has special goodies waiting for you there... exclusive bonus stories that are just for her subscribers, and a free Obsidian Files novella! She hopes to see you there!

www.ingramcontent.com/pod-product-compliance
Lightning Source LLC
Chambersburg PA
CBHW050009120726
47903CB00006B/1698